Praise for *True Believers*

"The arc of the book . . . is beautifully drawn. This is Andersen's best book to date, which makes it a great American novel."
—*Vanity Fair*

"Andersen spins out a diverting political thriller, which also serves as a vehicle for keen cultural criticism."
—*The New Yorker*

"Intelligent and insightful . . . Think *The Heart Is a Lonely Hunter* and *Atonement*, a '60s-era female Holden Caulfield hearing the beat-beat of The Tell-Tale Heart. . . . Andersen is an agile storyteller, alternating convincingly between . . . then and . . . now."
—*USA Today*

"Fascinating and wisely observant."
—*O: The Oprah Magazine*

"So epic: Part thriller, part coming-of-age tale, the novel alternates between the present and the 1960s, capturing some of America's most pivotal moments in history like a time capsule."
—*Marie Claire*

"Andersen has written a historical romance about the 1960s. . . . [He] is doing something harder than the novel's amiable, energized surface might suggest."
—*The New York Times Book Review*

"A big, swinging novel . . . full of witty . . . insights . . . This could be the most rambunctious meeting your book club has for a long time."
—*The Washington Post*

"Andersen has given us an absorbing, well-told tale. It's also the best reverie on the 1960s and their legacy—scrupulously neither glorified nor demonized—that I've seen." —*Fortune*

"This book is full of twists and turns, popular culture references, spook-talk, black ops, deception, and duplicity. And *True Believers* is ambitious, seeking to take the measure of the 1960s—and their impact on our own times." —*The Philadelphia Inquirer*

"[A] fiendishly smart, insightful and joyously loopy novel." —*San Francisco Chronicle*

"[A] persuasively detailed re-creation of the 1960s and equally sharp portrait of contemporary realities . . . *True Believers* proves smart and accessible, a book as entertaining as it is illuminating." —*St. Louis Post-Dispatch*

"[*True Believers* is] a literate suspense story set in the present married to thoughtful historical fiction. And this grafting of two genres is an unmitigated success. . . . Andersen's realizations of time, place and politics are convincing as he spins a story that pulls you along with intelligent old-fashioned readability. . . . All the players in this story are richly drawn, and the settings are niftily rendered. And the plot is nigh-on perfect—nicely hinting and teasing about not just where it's going, but how it's going to get there." —*Winnipeg Free Press*

"Andersen takes us back to the 1960s to weave a timely story about counterculture and intellectual rebellion . . . at once brilliant and irreverent, brimming with equal parts intelligence and humor. A master of simple yet tremendously evocative narrative, [Andersen] moves swiftly between well-timed wit, without a hint of smugness, and . . . keen cultural observation." —*Brain Pickings*

BY KURT ANDERSEN

True Believers

Reset

Heyday

Turn of the Century

The Real Thing

TRUE
BELIEVERS

TRUE
BELIEVERS

A NOVEL

Kurt Andersen

RANDOM HOUSE TRADE PAPERBACKS

New York

2013 Random House Trade Paperback Edition

Copyright © 2012 by Kurt Andersen
Reading group guide copyright © 2013 by Random House, Inc.

Published in the United States by Random House Trade Paperbacks, an imprint of
The Random House Publishing Group, a division of Random House, Inc., New York.

RANDOM HOUSE and the HOUSE colophon are registered trademarks of Random House, Inc.
RANDOM HOUSE READER'S CIRCLE and design are registered trademarks of Random House, Inc.

Originally published in hardcover in the United States by Random House, an imprint of
The Random House Publishing Group, a division of Random House, Inc., New York, in 2012.

Grateful acknowledgment is made to the following for permission
to reprint previously published material:

Alfred Music Publishing Co. Inc. and Hal Leonard Corporation: Excerpt from "I Don't Want to Set
the World on Fire," words by Eddie Seiler and Sol Marcus and music by Bennie Benjamin and
Eddie Durham, copyright © 1940 (renewed) Bennie Benjamin Music, Inc., Ocherie Publishing Corp.,
and Eddie Durham Swing Music Publishing, copyright © 1940, 1941 by Cherio Corp., copyright
renewed © 1968, 1969 by Ocherie Publishing Corp., Bennie Benjamin Music, Chappell & Co.,
and Eddie Durham Swing Music Publishing. All rights for Bennie Benjamin Music, Inc.,
administered by Chappell & Co., Inc. All rights for Eddie Durham Swing Music Publishing
administered by BMG Chrysalis. All rights reserved. Reprinted by permission of
Alfred Music Publishing Co. Inc. and Hal Leonard Corporation.

Hal Leonard Corporation: Excerpt from "Be My Baby," words and music by Phil Spector,
Ellie Greenwich, and Jeff Barry, copyright © 1963 (renewed 1991) by Bug Music–Trio Music
Company (BMI), Universal–Songs of Polygram International, Inc., and Mother Bertha Music, Inc.
All rights for Mother Bertha Music, Inc., controlled and administered by EMI April Music, Inc.
All rights reserved. Reprinted by permission of Hal Leonard Corporation.

Andersen, Kurt
True believers: a novel / Kurt Andersen.
p. cm.
ISBN 978-0-8129-7889-6
eBook ISBN 978-1-58836-686-3
I. Title.
PS3551.N34554T78 2012
813'.54—dc23   2011049326

Printed in the United States of America on acid-free paper

www.randomhousereaderscircle.com

Book design by Jo Anne Metsch

For Kristi, David, and Erika

Bliss was it in that dawn to be alive,
But to be young was very heaven!—Oh! times,
In which the meagre, stale, forbidding ways
Of custom, law, and statute, took at once
The attraction of a country in romance!

—WILLIAM WORDSWORTH,
  "The French Revolution as It Appeared to
  Enthusiasts at Its Commencement"

I dreamed I was born, and grew up . . . and
this dream goes on and on and on, and
sometimes seems so real that I almost believe
it is real. I wonder if it is?

—MARK TWAIN, a letter to his sister-in-law

I shouted out, "Who killed the Kennedys?"
When after all, it was you and me.

—MICK JAGGER, "Sympathy for the Devil"

TRUE
BELIEVERS

I

MY PUBLISHERS SIGNED me up a year ago to write a book, but not *this* book. "A candid and inspirational memoir by one of the most accomplished leaders and thinkers of our times," their press release promised. They think they're getting a slightly irreverent fleshing out of my shiny curriculum vitae, a plainspoken, self-congratulatory chronicle of A Worthy Life in the Law and the Modern Triumph of American Women, which they're publishing, ho-hum premise notwithstanding, because I've written a couple of best sellers and appear on TV a lot.

By far the most interesting thing about my life, however, is nowhere in my résumé or official bio or Wikipedia entry. I'm not exactly who the world believes I am. Let me cut to the chase: I once set out to commit a spectacular murder, and people died.

But it's not a simple story. It needs to be unpacked very carefully. Like a bomb.

Trust me, okay?

I am reliable. I am an oldest child. Highly imperfect, by no stretch a goody-goody. But I was a reliable U.S. Supreme Court clerk and then a reliable Legal Aid lawyer, representing with all the verve

and cunning I could muster some of the most pathetically, tragically unreliable people on earth. I have been a reliable partner in America's nineteenth largest law firm, a reliable author of four books, a reliable law professor, a reliable U.S. Justice Department official, a reliable law school dean. I've been a reliable parent—as trustworthy a servant, teacher, patron, defender, and worshipper of my children as anyone could reasonably demand, and I think on any given day at least one of the two of them would agree.

I was not an entirely reliable wife for the last decade of my marriage, although my late ex, during our final public fight, called me "reliable to a goddamned *fault*," which is probably true. And which may be why the surprising things I did immediately afterward—grabbing his BlackBerry out of his hand and hurling it into a busy New York street, filing for divorce, giving up my law firm partnership, accepting a job that paid a fifth as much, moving three thousand miles away—made him more besotted by me than he'd ever seemed before. As my friend Alex said at the time, "That's funny—telling Jack Wu 'Fuck *you*' finally made him really want to *fuck* you."

I am reliable, but I'm not making the case that reliability is the great human virtue. Nor am I even making the case that reliability is *my* great virtue. In fact, after four decades in the law, I've lost my animal drive for making cases for the sake of making cases, for strictly arguing one of two incompatible versions of the truth, for telling persuasive stories by omitting or twisting certain facts.

So I am not arguing a case here. I'm not setting out to defend myself any more than I am to indict myself. I'm determined to tell something like the whole truth—which, by the way, I don't believe has ever been done in any American court of law. To tell the whole truth in a legal case would require a discovery process and trial that lasted years, hundreds of witnesses each testifying for many weeks apiece, and rules of evidence rewritten to permit not just hearsay and improperly obtained information but iffy memories of certain noises and aromas and hallucinatory hunches, what a certain half-smile or drag on a cigarette decades ago did or didn't signify during some breathless three A.M. conversation.

In any event, for the purposes of this book, I am extremely reliable. I have files. Since long before I went to law school, for half a century now—*half a century!*—I've saved every diary and journal, every letter I ever received, catechism worksheets, term papers, restaurant receipts, train schedules, ticket stubs, snapshots, *Playbills*. At the beginning, my pack-ratting impulse was curatorial, as if I were director of the Karen Hollaender Museum and Archive. I know that sounds narcissistic, but when I was a kid, it seemed like a way to give the future me a means of knowing what the past and perpetually present me was actually like. Prophylactic forensics, you could say.

My memory has always been excellent, but the reason I'm telling my story now is also about maximizing reliability: I'm old enough to forgo the self-protective fibs and lies but still young enough to get the memoir nailed down before the memories begin disintegrating.

Only one in a hundred people my age suffer dementia, and the Googled Internet is like a prosthetic cerebral cortex and hippocampus, letting us subcontract sharpness and outsource memory. But after sixty-five? *Atrocious:* the incidence of neurodegenerative disease increases tenfold during that decade, and it's worse for women. I turn sixty-five next May.

So, anyhow, here's my point: I am a reliable narrator. Unusually reliable. Trust me.

2

Starting in fifth grade, I thought of myself as a beatnik. I first heard about beatniks from my father in the spring of 1959. He was a social psychologist who earned his living doing market research. He'd just come home from a convention in San Francisco and was telling us about a study that a psychiatrist had presented—well, telling my mother, really, since my brother and sister were only three and seven. But I was almost ten, fascinated by what Dad was saying and eager to distinguish myself from the little kids. This psychiatrist had spent a hundred nights studying beatniks in the beatnik neighborhoods of San Francisco, attending all-night parties in their "pads," and administering personality tests, my father said, "to a full quarter of the tribe."

A *tribe*? In a big city in modern America? "Like the Lost Boys in *Peter Pan*?" I asked.

"Yes, *exactly*," my father replied with a smile.

Notwithstanding my antiestablishment precocity, I became a member of pep club, the same as every girl at Locust Junior High School in Wilmette, Illinois, in the early 1960s. My cheering was always just this side of pointedly unenthusiastic. Our uniforms—

black tights, black skirts, black gloves outdoors in cold weather—
made the whole business easier for me to rationalize, as did the fact
that we were the Locust *Wolves*. Wolves seemed like a beatnik animal.

Near the end of eighth grade, for the entire week before the last
baseball game of the school year, Chuck Levy had been going on
and on about how I was going to go *bananas* when I heard the band
play at the game. He and Alex Macallister had written the arrange-
ment with the music teacher. But neither Chuck (sax) nor Alex (percussion) would tell me what their surprise song was, which finally
irritated me so much that on the morning of the game I lied and
told them I might skip it and go to a ban-the-bomb rally in Chicago
with my mother and father.

My parents thought it was important to keep an eye on what Dad
called "even the reasonable war machine." He'd grown up in Denmark and had been involved with the Danish Resistance as a young
man, then spent a year as a political prisoner in a Nazi camp at the
end of the war, which made our Republican neighbors cut the
peacenik foreigner some slack.

"You'll regret it forever if you're not there, Viv," Chuck told me.
His big smile made the nickname even more annoying.

"I'll regret it more if World War III starts and I didn't do everything I could to prevent it."

Alex had a big grin, too. He was dying to spill the beans. "It'll be
a cooler experience if it's a surprise, trust me."

" '*Cooler*'? We're talking about the *band*." I tried guessing while
simultaneously pretending I didn't care.

"You have got to come, Hollaender," Chuck said, sounding a little
desperate. "Seriously. It's going to be amazing. For *you*."

For me? Maybe "Where Have All the Flowers Gone?" The band
had already played that at the Thanksgiving concert after the Cuban
Missile Crisis. "Blowin' in the Wind"? They shook their heads. I
couldn't keep guessing unsuccessfully and maintain an air of omniscient ennui. "Well, enjoy yourselves. I'm late for study hall. Bye."

I don't remember the opposing team that afternoon, or who

won, but I remember with absolute clarity the first song the band played during the seventh inning. As the musicians lined up and readied themselves, I noticed Chuck wasn't among the other saxophones and clarinets, which worried me. Then I caught Alex's eye, and he was grinning and excited, drumsticks at the ready.

I didn't recognize the tune when they played the first four long, low notes, the tuba squeezing off a quick blast between each one, nor when the same sequence repeated—a kind of dohhh, *wah,* rayyy, *wah,* meee, *wah,* rayyy, *wah.* But when the electric guitar broke in with the loud, twangy eighth notes, however, I shrieked and jerked my hands and knees up as if I'd gotten a shock. Tears formed, and I started giggling. All of which would've been a major embarrassment if the song hadn't also startled all the other pep club girls, who were smiling and murmuring and glancing around.

It was the theme music from *Dr. No.* Not many of the other kids knew the song, since the movie had come out only a couple of weeks earlier, and it was the first James Bond film. But an electric guitar played fast and loud at an official school event in the daytime in 1963 was unprecedented, subversive, thrilling. And the big amplifier was right beneath us, under the bleachers, with the volume turned all the way up. We felt the sound hitting our thighs. There had never been a more glamorous moment at Locust Junior High.

I was in the top row, as always, and a girl nudged me to turn around and look down. Standing on the grass behind the bleachers was Chuck Levy, in his band uniform, long legs slightly apart, staring down at his right hand, willing his fingers to pick out the correct notes at super-speed, he and his silver Stratocaster awash in the pink light of the late-afternoon sun. He was the soloist, but he was off-stage, an anonymous star; how cool. Near the end of the song, as the trombones and trumpets blared their final, rising notes, and Chuck prepared to strum the big final chord, he looked up and saw me and smiled.

By the time he unplugged and trotted out onto the field to take a bow with the rest of the band, my fond, sisterly, quasi-adversarial regard for Chuck Levy had changed.

I had a history of going a little nuts for certain adventure novels. The first was *Through the Looking-Glass,* back in fourth grade. When I got to page six, I felt as if some new section of my brain had been activated. I shivered with a pleasure I hadn't known. " 'Let's pretend there's a way of getting through into it, somehow,' Alice said to her cat as she stared at herself in the mirror. 'Let's pretend the glass has got all soft like gauze, so that we can get through.' And the glass *was* beginning to melt away, just like a bright silvery mist. In another moment Alice was through the glass." Then I read *The Once and Future King,* and for most of a year I *was* young Arthur, Dad was Merlyn, and it was my destiny to create the perfect kingdom of Camelot somewhere beyond northeastern Illinois.

Chuck and Alex and I were not just James Bond "fans." We were in thrall to Bond. It started the summer after sixth grade. On one of those summer-vacation days that waver between luxuriously open-ended and achingly dull, I happened to pick up my mom's pink hardcover copy of *From Russia with Love,* which I figured was some kind of soft-on-communism Soviet-American romance. Around the same time Alex read his father's brand-new hardback *Thunderball.* When we discovered, one afternoon at Centennial Park swimming pool, that we had independently discovered and fallen in love with the world of James Bond, we (as my mother enjoyed saying for the rest of her life) bonded. Up until then I hadn't known Chuck Levy well, even though the three of us and two girls and Jimmy Graham had been the Smart Kids in our class. But Alex and Chuck were already best friends, and Chuck took Alex's lead in many things cultural—abandoning Ricky Nelson in favor of Duane Eddy, skipping the second half hour of *Route 66* on Friday nights in order to watch *77 Sunset Strip.* And then James Bond.

At the beginning it was just a book discussion group, like the Hobbit Fellowship my little brother Peter and his friends started a few years later. But when the Wall went up in Berlin at the end of that summer, our interest in Bond spiked—the books seemed more

legitimate, like extra-credit reading for social studies. Alex and I had a head start on Chuck, but in the fall he caught up quickly and then passed us, since every member of the Levy family was a certified Reading Dynamics speed reader. By Christmas vacation we had acquired all nine Bond books, and each of us had read every one—although just to make sure, I created, typed, and carbon-copied a hundred-question exam covering the minutiae of the eight novels and five short stories.

We didn't have formal meetings, but that first year, all through seventh grade, when we were alone at lunch or walking together to and from school, we'd fall into discussions of characters and scenes and plot points. Even basic facts were open to debate: we once spent days arguing over what year Bond had been born and whether he aged. Alex loved the wordplay titles (*Live and Let Die* and, later, *You Only Live Twice*), but the books he liked best were *Doctor No* and *Thunderball* because the villains had nuclear ambitions, whereas stealing gold or smuggling diamonds struck him as ordinary uninteresting criminality. Chuck's favorite was *From Russia with Love* because he thought it was the most realistic—the way, for instance, it says professional assassins start feeling guilty about killing people. What I loved about *Moonraker* was the fact that Sir Hugo Drax, a British industrialist, is actually a secret Nazi madman, and that the Special Branch operative who figures out Drax's nuclear missile plan is a young woman, Gala Brand.

We all loved Bond's line in *Casino Royale* after Vesper Lynd's suicide, "The bitch is dead now," which became a jokey private catchphrase, employed whenever we were angry at one of our sisters or mothers or the crone who served as Locust Junior High's Rosa Klebbian assistant principal.

It wasn't exactly a secret club. I didn't hide the books or my extreme interest from my parents. They were entertained, I learned later, by the contradiction between the softhearted politics I'd inherited from them and the ruthless Cold Warrior fantasy life I acquired from Ian Fleming. The Macallisters wholly approved of Alex's Bond hobby, his mother because *Life* magazine had reported that *From*

Russia with Love was President Kennedy's favorite novel, his father because it seemed like hopeful evidence for his son's fundamental manliness. One of Chuck's mother's Hadassah friends had told her that *Goldfinger* was anti-Semitic, which gave Chuck a new opportunity to remind her that she drove a Volkswagen.

But for various unspoken reasons, we conducted ourselves discreetly. We were discreet because we were twelve-year-olds—two boys and *a girl*—devoted to books that depicted sadism and boozing and nakedness and unmarried amoral strangers (including women with strippers' names—Pussy Galore, Honeychile Rider) having sex. And, of course, committing cold-blooded murder. As junior high began, we were already considered geeky—especially Alex and I—so why advertise this peculiar new strain of oddness to classmates already primed to be suspicious?

But our secrecy wasn't mainly about avoiding ostracization, either.

It pleased us, in those days before we had many important secrets to keep, that our devotion to this fictional world of conspiracies and ciphers and agents and weapons remained unseen and shadowy.

We had reached a new level of obsessiveness the summer before eighth grade, right after *The Spy Who Loved Me* was published. I loved it because the narrator/heroine is an ordinary twenty-three-year-old American girl who happens to meet Bond (and then has screaming orgasmic sex with him). Alex hated it because its narrator is an ordinary American girl, not a foreign spy or killer; Bond doesn't appear until halfway through, then disappears; the villains are run-of-the-mill thugs; and the whole thing takes place at some crummy American motel. Chuck was torn: he approved of the realism (ordinary girl, ordinary crooks, chance encounter, motel), but the romantic stuff seemed to him so entirely un-Bond, he argued for weeks that maybe Ian Fleming had paid someone else to write the book for him.

"Hollaender, I mean *seriously,* come *on,*" he said the first afternoon after we'd all read it. We were at Bob's, our burgers-and-ice-

cream place on Wilmette Avenue. Chuck put his palms on his chest
and tried to coo girlishly. "'Every smallest detail would be written
on my heart forever.' Don't tell me you take that kind of crap seriously. I thought the *tough* chicks were your heroes, like Gala Brand."
Chuck's use of "chick" was one result of Bond immersion.

"I just think the first-person point of view is really interesting.
Like in *On the Road*."

"Oh, I *see*, Miss Maynard G. English Teacher," Chuck said, "let
me take some notes on that." He went to get his french fries.

Alex was smiling. "I figured one of the things you liked about
Gala," he said softly, "is that she, you know, isn't a slut."

Alex was right, which I hadn't realized until that moment. Gala
Brand and Solitaire (in *Live and Let Die*) were the only major female
characters who didn't have sex with Bond. I liked Gala Brand for her
seriousness and professionalism, and now I liked Vivienne Michel
because of her shameless capacity for both lust and love. Which,
needless to say, I couldn't say.

"Do you think," Alex asked, now in a whisper, no longer smiling,
"that women really do like to imagine they're being raped when
they're having intercourse?"

He was referring to Vivienne's theory of female sexuality. "All
women," she says in the book, "love semi-rape. They love to be
taken. It was his sweet brutality against my bruised body that had
made his act of love so piercingly wonderful." Until that moment at
Bob's, our group discussions of the books' sex had been vague and
glancing.

"How would I know?" I said.

"But what do you *think*? Seriously, like imagine if you and Rob
Norquist were taking a shower together—"

"*Stop*, Alex." Smiling giant tanned blond Rob Norquist was the
smartest and nicest of the jocks, and Alex had delighted in telling
me that his pubic hair was the most luxuriant of any boy's in gym
class. In *The Spy Who Loved Me*, Vivienne's first sexual encounter
with Bond takes place after he surprises her in her shower. "James
saved Viv from being raped by the bad guys, okay?"

"James?"

We always called Bond "Bond."

"What Viv likes about Bond," I said, hoping I wouldn't blush, "the 'sweet brutality' or whatever, is because he isn't *really* raping her. It's a make-believe thing, only in her mind. And I guess maybe his mind, too."

"But which is it, the feeling, make-believe or real? That's what I don't get."

"It's both. I guess it's both. I mean, soldiers in war probably have all kinds of make-believe ideas in their heads while they're fighting, imagining they're John Wayne or something. Okay, so with Viv, when she's, you know . . . with Bond, she's herself, doing what she's doing, but in her *mind,* she *also* turns it into a make-believe scene."

Chuck returned with a steaming cardboard basket and scooted back into the booth next to Alex, as always. In junior high, any other public seating configuration for the three of us—me with either of the boys across from the other one—might have implied a coupling. We were best friends, but just friends.

"Hey," Chuck asked as he dribbled ketchup over his fries, "you know who that new grill guy looks exactly like? Scott Carpenter! I mean *exactly.*"

Carpenter was the astronaut who'd orbited Earth three times the previous week. In order to let us watch his splashdown, the assistant principal wheeled TVs into the cafeteria and made us whisper while we ate lunch, which was sort of exciting, as was the fact that Carpenter had landed hundreds of miles off-target. But John Glenn's orbital flight three months earlier had been the big deal, so this latest flight struck me as an anticlimax. The space program was the first time I ever experienced sequel boredom.

"The astronauts all seem the same to me," I said. "Like gym teachers."

"*What?*" Chuck replied, aghast. "They're real-life James Bonds!"

We all badly wanted to be cool, but at thirteen, Chuck was finding it difficult to grow out of his space-program excitement. His main nonmusical hobby, apart from reading the Bond books and

swimming, was making and flying giant radio-controlled model airplanes with his dad, what he called "RC aerobatics."

Alex was ignoring us. Chuck waved a french fry in front of his face. "Alex Macallister, this is Cape Cap Com on emergency voice, do you read me, over?"

Alex sighed and finally reengaged. "I have an idea for us to do this summer. A cool idea, I think."

"Is this the smuggling-explosives idea?" I asked. The previous summer, Chuck got some serious firecrackers from his cousin in Milwaukee, and ever since he had talked about pooling our money and taking the bus to Wisconsin to buy a gross of cherry bombs or M-80s that we'd import to Wilmette and sell for five times what we paid. "Because if so," I went on, "*no—I hate* selling things." When I was in Camp Fire Girls, I'd made my mother buy my entire case of candy, and we still had unopened boxes of Almond Caramel Clusters and P-Nutties in the pantry.

"Uh-uh," Alex said. "Remember last fall, Hollaender, when you thought we should make up and then act out our own scenes playing characters from the books"—by which he meant, naturally, the Bond books—"and film them with my parents' movie camera?"

"And you said, 'That's *retarded,* Hollaender, who wants to make *silent* James Bond movies?' Yeah, I remember."

"Well, so I was thinking," Alex explained, "that we could do, you know, *theater.*"

Chuck grimaced and made an elaborate choking sound.

3

OW, GRAMS, FOR real?" Waverly, my only grandchild, age seventeen, is visiting me for Christmas and New Year's and lying prone in front of the fireplace as I write. It's late. She's in her nightgown playing My Little Pony: The Runaway Rainbow on my antique Game Boy as she sips her glass of tonic water. I just told her that when I was about her age, I'd once gone rainbow hunting with two boys. "That is *so gay*," she says.

"It wasn't 'gay' at all. We flew in our own little airplane, bouncing around on the edge of a thunderstorm for an hour. It was completely terrifying."

Waverly continues poking at the tiny Game Boy buttons with her fast-motion thumbs and fingers. "Was it a hippie thing? Were you, like, high?"

"No! We weren't hippies. Although it was the summer of 1967."

"Whenever you talk about the past, it's funny how you make such a big deal out of the exact year. 'It was 1967—the *summer* of 1967.' I mean, 1964, 1967, 1973, whatever. Like when we went to see *X-Men: First Class*? And you were all, 'There were *not* miniskirts in 1962!'"

I smiled. "I know, but—I bet you'll be the same way when you're older."

"*Uh*-uh," she says, "because how is right now any different than 2007 or 2002? I'm seventeen instead of eleven or six, but in terms of the way people act and talk and dress and style their hair, and music and movies and *everything*? Everything's been the same forever. It's like everything's *stuck*."

"Politics are different," I say. "Crazier."

"Nine-eleven is my earliest memory—"

"Really?"

"—so America's been at war but not *really* at war my whole life. At least when Mom was growing up, personal computers and video and the Internet got invented."

"A couple of days ago you told me you thought life was better before VCRs and DVRs and Hulu—when people had to make choices about what TV shows and movies they were going to watch at a certain time and commit to their choices."

"I'm just saying the Internet was something *new* and *big* that happened."

"I know what you mean. When I was a kid, it was as if the whole country—the whole world, everything—slipped into a wormhole and shot out the other end in some alien sector of the space-time continuum."

"Awesome."

There's been nothing like it since. It's hard for her and for my children to appreciate how different 1962 was from 1969. I think of each year of the 1960s as distinctly as they think of whole decades. My brother, Peter, born seven years after me, has never considered himself a baby boomer. Our experiences were so different, he thinks, because I'd been old enough to know the world as it was in the 1950s and early '60s, before everything changed, whereas he was still a child when the late '60s arrived. By the time he got to high school and college in the '70s, he says, the youth revolution had already cowed the grown-ups into doing away with all the old-fashioned codes of behavior.

"All the digital stuff is all new," I say to Waverly. "That's what people your age have."

"No, that's what people *Mom's* age had. The new computer stuff today is just . . . a little faster than when I was a kid, and more unavoidable. I mean, *this*," she says, nodding down at the Game Boy, "is really old and kinda clunky but not really that different than things now."

"I should buy some new games for it."

"No, no, I'm not saying that. The less stuff we buy, the better."

She loves the simple black rubber Armani raincoat I gave her for Christmas. I bought it on sale, but even so, she'd be grossed out if I told her how much I paid. At IKEA you could buy a sofa for the same price.

"I mean," Waverly continues, "I've paid for *nothing* except Christmas presents and food, locally grown food, for the last two months almost."

"Not including your airplane ticket here."

"We didn't actually pay money for it. Mom and Dad used miles."

"Also: nice iPad Four."

"It was a birthday present from Mom and Dad, and I didn't even *ask* for it. Anyhow, I actually like playing these *old* games, and— Oh, *fuck!*" She had made some Game Boy error. "Buying new games for this would be kinda gay. To *me*." She turns off the device and sits up in a lotus position. "I mean, I'll be *eighteen* in less than a year! How weird is that?"

"Super-weird," says Grandma. "To me." I put down my legal pad. "Wavy, I've got a question for you."

"I'm sorry I said 'fuck.'"

I make a "Phhhht!" noise and roll my eyes. "No, I mean 'so gay'— I just wonder exactly what you mean, someone like you, when you say something is 'so gay.'"

"My LGBTQI friends don't mind when I use it that way, if that's what you're asking."

"Bingo." I wonder when that *I* got appended to LGBTQI and what it stands for. As a university dean in 2013, I ought to know.

"When I said it last fall in English when we were discussing Keats or Byron or one of those guys, the teacher reprimanded me, like, whoa, this truly mad beef. I mean, he stopped the class and everything. It was crazy. But the two *gay* kids in my class *laughed* at *him.*"

I pick up Waverly's empty glass on my way to make myself another gin and tonic—or maybe, since the tonic's almost gone, a martini. (Stirred, not shaken, and I don't buy Gordon's or Beefeater, Bond's brands.)

Late-night cocktails at Christmastime with the one and only child of my children, high on a hill overlooking Los Angeles in an odd and perfectly cozy wooden house built in 1946: *perfection,* or close to it.

When Greta, Waverly's mother, was seventeen, her brother, Seth, was eight, and we were living in Brooklyn Heights. I was a litigation partner at a big New York law firm working twenty-four hundred billable hours a year, plus another several hundred pro bono that involved trips to Eastern Europe, as well as devoting Lord knows how many hundreds more, nonbillable, trying to jolly up the successful triathlete and increasingly unhappy composer whom I'd married for better and for worse. And also teaching at Yale. Which is to say, my life didn't allow for much meandering, apparently purposeless conversation between teenage daughter and forty-two-year-old mother. We were not *The Gilmore Girls.*

Back then I used to say that I despised the new coinage "quality time," that it was yuppie parents' smiley-face equivalent to lawyers' "billable hours." Which is true enough. But I've come to understand that my noisy aversion to the phrase was meant to hide (from me) my guilt about failing to give my eldest child enough quality time. My plan as a young woman had been to have my first kid around thirty-three. I had not intended to raise a one-year-old as a twenty-six-year-old clerk for the 7th Circuit in Chicago, or to raise a two-year-old while clerking eighty hours a week for the Supreme Court in Washington. To my friends at the time, going through with an unplanned pregnancy at age twenty-five had been the one unfathomable, shocking thing about me.

Anyway, unlike my friends my age now, whose children's children are mostly infants and toddlers, I've already got a granddaughter who takes birth control pills and calls herself "freeganish" and "a culture-jammer." In other words, for a couple of weeks every year I am the guardian of a teenager with whom I enjoy hanging out the way I should've enjoyed hanging out with Greta when she was young. So my relationship with Waverly is kind of a do-over.

"That's the last of your brew," I say, handing her a glass of tonic.

"I can make some more." She's looking at her screen, which is a patchwork of five or six instant-messaging windows, several containing live video images of young faces. It looks like a wanted poster from the future.

"Good," I say, "because otherwise all that stuff will rot before you're back."

Waverly has boiled up a batch of homemade tonic water. I think I've shown heroic restraint by not mentioning that the ingredients she made me buy (cinchona bark, allspice berries, citric acid) cost as much as a case of Schweppes, and also by not wondering aloud about the carbon-footprint cost of shipping cinchona from Peru to Southern California. Our only two arguments during the last ten days were over my refusal to replace the low-water-use toilets, purchased three years ago at her insistence, with locally built dry-composting ones, and her discovery that I have a stash of incandescent lightbulbs in my pantry, which she thought were illegal to own as well as to sell. ("Oh," she said after I explained, "so it's sort of like weed.")

She turns away from her computer to face me. "My friend Hunter? He got diagnosed with diabetes in the fall, Type 1, and his doctor told him he shouldn't drink alcohol."

"That's probably good advice."

"How come you do?"

"Because I never get drunk, and over the last forty years, I've learned how to manage my blood sugar around it." And because it would be wrong—aesthetically, if not morally—for a sixty-four-year-old to smoke weed in front of her seventeen-year-old grand-

daughter. I live in Los Angeles, but I have not gone completely native.

"Hunter and I are thinking of going down to Miami in March for Occupy the G-20."

The global economy is so screwed up that the overlords have decided to hold two G-20 summits this year, one in Australia and an extra in South Florida, as if more meetings and sunny photo ops will fix everything. Two falls ago Waverly attended the Occupy Wall Street demonstration in lower Manhattan for five weekends running, each visit chaperoned by her mother. I told Greta that instead of being a hockey mom, she'd become a protest mom.

"Exactly why," I ask, "do you want to go protest the G-20 summit?"

"Are you *kidding* me? Because even though we live in a post-scarcity time, the World Bank and the IMF and all those smiling assholes are all about the rich white people and the giant corporations trying to stay as rich and powerful as possible at the expense of the poor dark people."

My friend Sarah Caputo, who went to Malawi for three years after college to work for the Peace Corps, runs the clean-water programs for the International Development Association, the arm of the World Bank that lends money to the poorest countries. During the G-20 summit in Canada a few years ago, some protesters dumped a tub of manure on her, then took smartphone videos of her, which they posted on the Web.

"There are good, decent people who work for the World Bank, really trying to improve the lives of poor people."

"I'm sure," Waverly says. "There were nice Nazis, too, right, who wanted to ship the Jews from Europe to Africa to start their own country. But the Nazi system was still the Nazi system."

My peevishness with her is so intense that I wonder if I'm on a hypoglycemic downward slide. I keep glucose meters all over the place—bedroom, bathroom, kitchen, right here on the coffee table—so I prick my finger and squeeze out a drop: 117. Good: I'm just angry, not too low, for my meter tells me so.

"You okay?" Waverly asks.

"All good." In the fifteen seconds it's taken me to find out how many milligrams of sugar are floating in each deciliter of my blood, my love has dissolved my anger. But not my disapproval. "You know," I say, "it's a dangerous slippery slope to start comparing anybody you disagree with to a Nazi."

"It's an *analogy*. I'm not saying everyone who runs the whole, you know, global *machine* of disaster capitalism is a Nazi, literally. But they're so sure they know best and so sure people like me are idiots. They're just so fucking . . . what's the word? Dis-*ingenue*-us. And smug."

"It's 'disingenuous,' honey." God, I love her. Last year when she pronounced "epitome" incorrectly—declaring her father's new enthusiasm for Senegalese drum music "the absolute EP-ih-tome of self-satisfied pseudo-progressive NPR bullshit"—I laughed so hard, I almost cried. "And yes," I say, "smugness is a good thing to avoid."

"Grams," she says as she types a flurry of characters into two of her text-messaging windows, then shoves the machine away, "I have a question."

"No, I don't think it's a terrible idea for you to think about becoming an actor, and yes, you could live with me here for free after you graduate from college and you're starting out. If you wanted."

"Ha. No, do you think I could maybe get a grant from somewhere to expand my Virtual Home project?" Growing up in New York City, Waverly was always fascinated by the tons of stuff that homeless people drag around in shopping bags and supermarket carts. This past summer, she started introducing herself to street people and offering to scan and digitize all their documents for free, then provide a simple, password-protected, visually indexed online archive that they could access from public libraries or anywhere else. So far she's signed up eight men and five women and digitized a thousand pieces of their ephemera—medical records, birth certificates, marriage licenses, military discharge documents, photos, newspaper and magazine clippings, old bills, bits of Scripture, box tops, addresses, weird drawings, random scraps, anything they want.

"What I'm thinking," she explains, "is that kids in other cities could do it, too, and maybe even not just kids, and I could make the user interface much better? My digital arts teacher said he thinks it's 'scalable.'"

Yes! Which multibillion-dollar pot of money provided by which contemptible global capitalist would you prefer to tap? Rockefeller, Ford, Carnegie, Mellon? Hewlett, Packard, Gates? Steady, Grandma. "What a *great* idea, Waverly! You know, I'll bet that is a project somebody might fund."

"How would I go about doing it?"

I'm wired in to half of them, and we can set up meetings with the correct program officers right after the New Year. And if that doesn't get you into fucking Harvard or Brown, the world's gone mad. I'm really no better than her father, with whom I got into a fight a couple of years ago when he was pressuring her to join the fencing team and learn to play Grandpa Jack's old theremin as college admission ploys. "I know a couple of people who work at foundations," I say. "Let me check it out for you."

"Cool." She grabs her computer with her right hand, props it up on the rug, and stands, moving her torso and left leg perpendicular to the floor and shooting her left arm straight toward the ceiling. She holds the yoga pose—a Half-Moon—and takes four slow, deep breaths before standing up straight, holding the iPad tight to her chest beneath crossed arms, in exactly the nice-girl way I refused to carry my schoolbooks when I was a teenager. She pats it with both hands. "I'm gonna go watch the new *Hobbit*."

"My God, there's a *second* one already?" I stop myself from asking if she's stolen the movie off the Internet.

"Uh-huh. It's supposed to suck. You staying up?"

"Nope," I say, standing. "It's bedtime for this Bonzo. Have to get up early and work, work, work!" Meaning: in the morning I've got to email Alex Macallister and finally tell him I'm writing this book and that he features in it, um, er, uh, somewhat prominently. "Sweet dreams, baby duck."

I search for "LGBTQI" and discover (thank you, Google) the "I"

stands for "intersex." I take my blood one last time (107), load up a syringe with five bedtime units of insulin (thank you, electrical and genetic engineers and Big Pharma), and find a fresh, unbruised spot on my thigh to plunge the needle and shoot. I turn on the little bedroom TV and scan through Movies on Demand—huh; the newest James Bond film, set in India; Judi Dench does look amazing for seventy-seven—and then turn it off.

I get the lighter-sized electronic vaporizer from my bedside drawer, put the merest pinch on the tiny platter, close it, push the button, and deeply inhale once. Yes, a former Justice Department official and former candidate for appointment to the Supreme Court of the United States admits she very occasionally smokes legal, physician-prescribed marijuana. So? I'm no longer *angling* for anything. Besides, what's the point of a memoir that isn't candid?

Seven years ago, around the time I moved to L.A., Greta told me about some new research into memory loss. Marijuana, she told me, reduces inflammation in a certain brain receptor in older people that's associated with Alzheimer's. It also acts on other brain receptors to generate new memory neurons. Losing my memory terrifies me. Thus, after a forty-year hiatus, I started smoking pot again.

Also, I find I enjoy getting a little high. One night in Washington when I was working for the government, I was with my friend Sarah at the bar in the Hay-Adams. In the middle of our second martini, she called me "Hillary on the outside and Bill on the inside."

I knew what she meant—I dressed Ann Taylorishly, and I do have a strong taste for physical pleasure. But I have never been a liar, not in any routine Clintonian sense.

My editor's suggestion that I write a memoir came the day after I delivered my "be careful what you pretend to be" and "honesty in the defense of liberty" speech at a Harvard commencement. It was in the course of that speech that I announced I was withdrawing myself from consideration for appointment to the Supreme Court. For a year afterward I made a few notes for the book we imagined I was writing.

But I decided to write the present book a little over a month ago, during the . . . commemoration? celebration? wall-to-wall media opportunity? . . . surrounding the fiftieth anniversary of John F. Kennedy's death. I recall the very moment: I'd just seen the new IMAX documentary, and, shaken by its digitally reconstructed 3-D 360-degree version of the Zapruder assassination film, I'd taken a sip of gin, then sobbed for several minutes in my banquette at a Mexican restaurant in West Hollywood, allowing my date to misunderstand why the ninety-eight-foot-high snuff film had shattered me.

Those weeks last fall of national Kennedy hoo-ha amounted, I think, to the baby boomers' dress rehearsal for their generational funeral. For me, at any rate, it was a two-minute warning. Time's running out. After fifty years of elaborate JFK conspiracy theories and conspiracy-theory refutations, the unending re-investigations of the investigations into ballistics and cover-ups and murky connections among Cubans and CIA agents and the FBI and mafiosi, and the endlessly regurgitated disingenuousness about America's lost innocence, I knew I was obliged to figure out and come clean about my own secret episode of 1960s berserkery and lost innocence.

My lawyer, the one person to whom I've described in detail what I'm doing with this book, calls it "suicidal," says it will "besmirch" my "legacy" and ruin my life, blah blah blah blah blah. Even though I am doing it to myself, my motives are the very opposite of a suicide's: instead of chickening out, allowing the shock and scandal to bloom posthumously, I decided I want to be alive when the truth comes out. It's not masochism. It's closer to honor. Plus, I suppose, an old litigator's obsession with having the last word and wanting to see the case all the way through to a verdict.

And by the way? For the record? America didn't "lose its innocence" all at once on November 22, 1963. That was the midpoint, the end of the beginning, the moment when a wild new strain of crazy could no longer be denied or ignored. I started reading the newspaper every morning when I was eight, in 1957, and my scrapbooks, full of crinkly Elmer's-glued press clips, seem like the libretto of a dark

modern opera, all the darker now for my schoolgirl conscientious-
ness.

On the scrapbook page opposite my pale green report card from
the first semester of third grade is a *Chicago Sun-Times* article about
Charles Starkweather's murder spree across Nebraska with his
fourteen-year-old girlfriend. The Starkweather story is followed immediately by a tiny article from *New World*, the local Catholic
weekly, about St. Clare of Assisi being named the patron saint of
television. At the end of fourth grade, the *Action Comics* cover introducing Kara Zor-El ("Look again, Superman—it's me, Supergirl!
And I have *all* your powers!") is pasted next to a photo of the actor
George Reeves in his Superman costume, illustrating the news story
about his suicide, and then a motif emerges, Grown-ups on TV
Misbehaving—articles about Charles Van Doren admitting his quiz
show championship was fixed, Jack Paar walking off *The Tonight
Show* in a huff, the divorce of Lucille Ball and Desi Arnaz.

From sixth grade is my census of the ravages of Dutch elm disease in our neighborhood, with my color snapshots of eleven dead
trees, as well as articles about the Bay of Pigs invasion, Ernest
Hemingway's suicide by shotgun, and a protest (3,000 BEATNIKS
RIOT IN NEW YORK'S GREENWICH VILLAGE) that I fantasized about
having attended. Starting in seventh grade are some James Bond
bits and pieces ("BOND" AUTHOR FLEMING SPIES ON CHICAGO), and a
Sun-Times article about the Supreme Court's decision outlawing
prayer in public schools, but I was still archiving the terrors of the
day: a government pamphlet about the new community fallout
shelter program, a wordless *Newsweek* cover illustration of a skull
and mushroom cloud hovering above the earth, Marilyn Monroe's
suicide by Nembutal, a plane crash near O'Hare that had been
watched by a man whose wife and four children were on board,
Sylvia Plath's suicide by coal gas, a U.S. Air Force pilot parachuting
live pigs in wicker baskets into besieged South Vietnamese army
outposts so they could be slaughtered and eaten.

My last scrapbook, only half filled, is from ninth grade. Slipped
into it is the entire *Tribune* front page about Kennedy's assassina-

tion. We got only the Sunday *Tribune,* so my father must have bought it in Chicago for me as a souvenir. The news had shocked me, of course, but so did the size and baldness of the headline— KENNEDY SHOT—DIES—and the fact that the page-one photos of JFK and Lyndon Johnson were printed in color.

"So back then were you, like, more emo or more nerdy Goth or more punk?" Waverly asked a few years ago when she was looking through my scrapbooked chronicle of America Spinning Out of Control. I explained to her that, mainly, I'd been a cheerful, ambitious, good-humored child and young adult—self-obsessed, sure, and slightly morbid, but not sullen. "Your scrapbooks are death death death, Grams."

Because I was very young, I told her, and living in peaceful, prosperous America, death was totally theoretical to me. Plus, because my father had survived the Nazis and contributed in his small way to the Allied victory, I grew up believing in happy endings. And even though things were beginning to fall apart in the early '60s, I said, thinking out loud, the world—my comfortable bit of the world— was also becoming fizzier and shinier and more *fun* than ever.

In other words, those old scrapbooks provide a skewed history of my tween years, because I neglected to document our nonstop and virtually sexual excitement over all the *newness.* The sudden arrival, all at once, of stereo records and the Beatles, Bic pens and Instamatic cameras and live transatlantic TV broadcasts and in-flight movies and printed circuit boards and TouchTone phones, area codes and zip codes, Frisbees and Slip 'N Slide and Silly Putty, instant tanning lotion and stretch fabrics and bikinis, McDonald's and Tang and SweeTarts and Sweet'N Low and zip-top cans of Tab. There's no mention of my dad's business trip to Rio de Janeiro in 1961 on the same 707 as Rock Hudson or the new supersonic jets announced in 1963, or of Alex's brother Flip driving his brand-new green Mustang to New York City for the World's Fair. All in all, back then, I told Waverly, I was a lot more manic than depressed.

Take our James Bond shenanigans, for instance: total mania.

4

FROM THE SUMMER after seventh through the winter of eighth grade, from just before the publication of *The Spy Who Loved Me* until the release of the *Dr. No* film, we went whole-hog. My home-movie fan-fiction idea turned into Alex's real-world-theater idea, and our little Bond discussion group had become something vastly more elaborate.

In the profile of Alex published in *Vanity Fair* last year after he announced he was donating his entire art collection to L.A.'s contemporary museum, he claimed that during "one weekend the winter of 1963," right after he turned fourteen, he experienced his "seminal aha moment as an art person" when he attended a Happening put on by the artist Claes Oldenburg at the University of Chicago. Alex told the *Vanity Fair* writer that he remembered watching "a man in a scuba suit reciting poetry, a woman kneading dough and telling the scuba guy to put a sock in it, and someone else playing 'America the Beautiful' on a trombone."

Maybe that's true. It certainly makes for a good Alex Macallister backstory. However, I have no memory of the event or its allegedly transformative effect on Alex, and thanks to Google, I know that

Oldenburg's 1963 Happening happened at the U of C on Saturday, February 8, the same date my journals tell me that Alex and Chuck and I performed a Bond mission all day in Wilmette.

Alex also told *Vanity Fair* the following: "The funny bit is, before I'd even *heard* of Happenings, I'd sort of invented Happenings on my own. I'd staged a whole series of them—these absurdist, surreal, Living Theatre–type pieces, at the age of *thirteen,* if you can imagine! I was a little Outsider Performance Artist! They were all done around a theme, sort of the dark side of JFK and Camelot and globe-trotty glamour. With props and costumes, all performed in public spaces, unannounced, site-specific. And intertextual. It was bonkers. It was *fabulous.* So when I saw the Oldenburg, I thought, *Crikey, maybe* I'm *an artist!*"

Alex insists he told the writer that Chuck and I were his coequal collaborators but that she'd left it all out. "You know *journalists,*" he emailed me. Yes, I do: would a *Vanity Fair* journalist in the fall of 2012 really omit best-selling author and former Supreme Court candidate Karen Hollander from such a cute backstory? Also, for the record, our Bond theatricals weren't a bit "absurdist" or "surreal," except for the fact that we were children playing the parts of spies and saboteurs and assassins and criminal masterminds.

For our first mission, I wore my sleeveless purple knit (Orlon? Dacron? rayon?) party dress covered in big black dots. I'd told my parents the boys were taking me out for a belated birthday celebration—a movie, maybe ice cream at Peacock's, maybe a game of pool at the Macallisters' country club. Spies give cover stories. It was more exciting to lie a little, more real.

"Oh, 'at the club,' huh?" my mother said. "Lah-de-*dah!*"

"I disapprove," said my father, smiling.

"The eye shadow looks pretty, honey. You used my good perfume?"

"Just a tiny bit." Balmain's Vent Vert, which the Bond girl Solitaire wears.

As Dad kissed my forehead, he said, "You smell fantastic."

My father often used the phrase "in the cold light of day," which he said was the first cliché he'd learned in English, "before it became a cliché," from reading Orwell as a boy. He told us he never got drunk because "afterward, in the cold light of day, I always feel like a fool and a weakling." He hadn't stayed in Denmark to start a jazz radio station with his brother because "after the war, in the cold light of day, it seemed preposterous." He moved to the Midwest because it seemed the most Danish part of America, "a place where it's *always* the cold light of day."

As I stepped out into the soft, buttery summer Saturday dusk in June 1962, I wondered how I'd feel about our adventure tomorrow in the cold light of day.

During the two-mile ride to the lake, we coasted as much as possible, because that allowed us to imagine that our Schwinns were actually motorcycles, that we were riding from, say, NATO central command in Versailles into Paris. My dress also made pedaling tricky. The boys wore neckties and sport jackets, and Alex and I had on sunglasses. The mission equipment was in Chuck's bike basket.

"People must think we're weird," I said after exchanging a glance with a fascinated little boy in the back of a passing car.

"Maybe they think we're going to Shabbat services," Chuck said, "or Mass, or whatever."

A Corvair packed with laughing, shouting high schoolers zoomed past, and a kid in the backseat aimed an "L for losers" hand sign at us.

When we'd plotted that inaugural mission, choosing which characters to play had been easy, except when Alex said that Chuck should be Sol Horowitz, one of the hoods who tries to rape Vivienne in *The Spy Who Loved Me.* Since we were inventing our own narratives, we were free to pick characters from different novels and stories who never appeared together. But choosing the venue had required a long debate.

No Man's Land, a few blocks at the north tip of town along Lake Michigan, seemed to me the perfectly obvious place. When my

mom was young, No Man's Land actually had been a lawless no man's land, part of neither Wilmette to the south nor Kenilworth to the north.

"It's just like Monte Carlo," I'd said to Alex and Chuck. "The lake is the Mediterranean Sea, like in *Casino Royale*. And Spanish Court"— an old (that is, thirty-five-year-old) shopping mall with red tile roofs and a bell tower—"is sort of Monaco-an."

"The word is 'Monegasque,'" Alex corrected.

Chuck smiled and shook his head and suggested Los Angeles instead. Bond goes there in *Diamonds Are Forever.* "I think Spanish Court is really more Californian."

Given the lakefront, I proposed, we could also imagine we were in Geneva, where Goldfinger captures Bond. "But Monaco or Los Angeles or Switzerland," I said, "come on, what's it really matter? It can be any of them. I mean, it's not *real.*"

"No, no, *no,*" Alex insisted, "it's got to be *specific.* Mr. Hendricks says good acting is all about *specificity.*" Jerome Hendricks, the head of the drama department at New Trier High School, also ran a theater program for "gifted" younger children, and Alex had been one of his star pupils since fifth grade. Alex regarded him as a mentor not just in theatrical matters but also in fashion (turtlenecks), music (Bob Dylan), and general demeanor (supercilious). "It's especially important," Alex added, undoubtedly quoting him again, "since we're doing an *improvisation.*"

Alex had his heart set on the mock-Tudor Michigan Shores Club, where his parents were members and which, he said, "might as well *be* Blades," the fictional Mayfair club to which several Bond characters belong.

I proposed we could be *serially* specific, that our first mission could have two different settings on two different continents. So on that Saturday in June at the golden hour, we were heading to both, one after the other.

I adored No Man's Land, the twenty-two acres as well as its name and peculiar history. By suburban standards, it was disheveled and disorderly. It had no nice big houses or nice neat yards and very few

trees. Instead, there were a few dumpy three-story apartment buildings; no one we knew lived in an apartment. There was a barbecue
restaurant where we'd once watched a drunk man stumble out the
door and pass out on the sidewalk. And yet it wasn't a slum. The
Spanish Court had a movie theater, the Teatro del Lago. Altogether,
No Man's Land was the most urban, foreign-seeming place we could
reach easily by bike, both raffish (a word I'd learned in English class)
and louche (a word I'd learned from my father).

Alex handed Chuck the cooler of the two toy cap guns—the machine pistol that fired five times with each trigger squeeze and spat
out plastic shell casings. Chuck stuck it in his leather shoulder holster. Alex put one of the two Blinker Code-Lites and the smaller
pistol, a Luger, into the metal tackle box. On the lid of the box was
a monogram, raised white letters on a shiny little red plastic strip—
ESB, short for Ernst Stavro Blofeld, the head of SMERSH in
Thunderball—that he had made with a Dymo LabelWriter.

"Check this out," Alex said, pointing to a russet-colored splotch
the size of a silver dollar inside Chuck's tackle box. *"Blood."* Perch or
smallmouth bass blood, but a nice touch nonetheless.

I stuck the other Blinker Code-Lite into my pink vinyl handbag,
from which I pulled an unopened pack of cigarettes I'd bought a
week earlier from a machine—Chesterfields, Bond's brand whenever he visited America. As I dug around for matches, Alex pulled a
Zippo from his pants pocket. No one had ever lit me before. I
grinned as I exhaled, but Alex remained absolutely straight-faced.

He lowered his eyelids a millimeter and his voice a half-octave.
"Miss Lynd?" For a thirteen-year-old, he did come across as pretty
steely.

"Yes, Number One?" I was Vesper Lynd, the Soviet double agent
who works for MI6 in *Casino Royale.*

"Double-oh-seven and his CIA friend are nearby. I'll remain to
your southwest at all times." The Blinker Code-Lites had little com-
passes built in to their pistol grips.

Nodding, I took another drag on the cigarette, then tossed it to
the ground with as much world-weary élan as I could muster. Ches-

terfields were unfiltered, unlike the Winstons I occasionally swiped from my parents, so I was feeling a little dizzy.

And we were off, headed in separate directions, the idea being to spread out but to make sure Alex could see me and Chuck could see Alex. After I found James Bond and the CIA agent Felix Leiter, we would keep them under surveillance and then, in an hour, meet up near the bike rack—that is, as Chuck said, we would "rendezvous at the drop point at nineteen hundred hours." Then we'd kill them.

I walked away at half-speed, swinging my handbag, toward the Teatro box office. I was modeling myself on the character Tuesday Weld played on *Dobie Gillis.*

"When does *Hatari!* let out?" I asked the lady in the glass box.

She pushed her button to speak. "Quarter past. Price goes up to a dollar at six-thirty, y'know."

"Yup, thanks." I shouldn't have said "yup."

"Real cute dress, honey." She smiled and raised her eyebrows in that annoying grown-up way. "Expecting somebody?"

"In a way, I suppose, yes." Now I was attempting British locution—Hayley Mills?—without the accent. "But I'm afraid I don't know for certain where he is."

The smiling ticket lady pursed her lips and shook her head. "*Boys,*" she said through the tinny speaker.

I sat down on a bench facing the lake. I took out my compact and started applying lipstick. Rather, I gingerly touched the pink tip to my lips and pretended to apply it, using the compact's little mirror to look behind me. And it *worked:* I found Alex, thirty yards away, leaning against the opposite corner of the theater. I put away the mirror and lipstick, checked my watch, and took out the newspaper—a month-old copy of the London *Guardian.* Another compromise: Bond reads the *Times,* but through her Hadassah chapter, Chuck's mom had just bought a special commemorative pack of international front pages with articles on Adolf Eichmann's execution in Israel, and the London *Times* hadn't covered it.

I read the Eichmann story and thought of my father. Despite his Danish accent, it was always hard for me to believe, really believe,

that my own dad—this chuckling suburban man who could juggle tangerines and wore colorful neckties and took the train every day to an office in Chicago—had watched Nazi soldiers shoot people he knew and threaten to shoot him. The war had ended only seventeen years earlier, but it seemed like an event from another epoch.

I put away the newspaper and stared up at the freestanding five-foot-high cursive neon letters that spelled out Teatro del Lago, resisting the urge to trace them in the air the way I did when I was little.

As people started pouring out of the theater, I turned to pay attention, making a clandestine examination of dozens of young and middle-aged men in order to find a suitably single, rugged, handsome one—Bond. I was frustrated in the attempt, since every one of them who looked to be in his late thirties (except for Benny, the Locust Junior High janitor, who didn't see me, thank God) was accompanied by children or a wife.

Giving up, I crossed Sheridan Road and entered a different existential zone. Partly, it was a function of proximity to the lake itself, which you could suddenly hear and smell, and the sandy lakefront soil. But the lake side of Sheridan was also much sketchier than anywhere else on the North Shore.

On the beach were the foundations of a couple of failed private clubs and casinos from the Depression and the charred remains of a Jazz Age roadhouse that we called the Ruins, one-off fast-food places with hand-painted signs, and a penny arcade to which I was explicitly forbidden by my parents to go alone. As I entered the arcade, I found myself smiling and had to force myself to stop. The atmosphere—the racket of shouts and flippers and springs and bells and steel pinballs and wooden skeeballs, the smells of burning popcorn and molten sugar and cigarettes—was sensational. I thought of the first sentence of *Casino Royale:* "The scent and smoke and sweat of a casino are nauseating at three in the morning." I pushed my dark glasses up to the top of my head, as I'd seen women do.

Although I wanted to play a horse-racing machine, in the spirit of the mission I headed for a gun game that involved shooting a bolt-

action rifle at a hopping kangaroo. After each game, as I took another dime from my rubber coin purse, I looked around. I was the
only single female in the place. I saw a couple of ninth-grade boys I
recognized, which wasn't good, and a lot of greasers.

The man at the next machine was as old as my dad, but he was
too fat and poorly groomed to be Bond or Leiter. And every time he
swung his right arm to pound the side of his machine, I got a gust
of BO.

"You're a good shot," the smelly man said to me as I finished
what I decided at that instant was my last game.

"Fair to middling," I replied. It was a phrase of my mother's that
I'd never spoken. It seemed British-ish.

As I approached the door, I saw Alex, outside, abruptly turn and
run back across Sheridan, just barely ahead of a car that sped past,
its long fading honk Dopplered into an after-the-fact reprimand. Almost like a European siren! And a moment of actual physical jeop-
ardy!

I kept walking up the road and glanced over at the construction
site on the lake where the town's first high-rise apartment building
was going up. I noticed the light in a construction trailer go off, and
two men stepped out. The older one, dark-haired and maybe thirty-
five, was wearing a tie, and the other, a little older with a crew cut,
had on a denim jacket. The one in the necktie carried a briefcase,
and the other held a thick tube several feet long under his arm. An
attaché, like the ones all oo agents carry. And the tube? A rifle case,
obviously.

I'd found James Bond and Felix Leiter.

They were headed in my direction. I grabbed the Blinker Code-
Lite from my purse and aimed it away from Lake Michigan, vaguely
southwest, then pulled the trigger fifteen times to flash the signal
into the dusk: five long, pause, five long again, pause, two long and
three short—*007*. Chuck knew Morse code, and for the mission,
he'd taught us a few letters and numbers. I was a little surprised and
totally thrilled when Alex signaled back and I understood—dash-
dash-dash, dash-dot-dash, *OK*.

Leiter opened the trunk of a car—a *convertible!* (not a Bentley, just a Ford, but *still*)—and they put the Q Branch attaché and rifle inside. Bond took a pint bottle from his jacket pocket and offered a swig to Leiter, who laughed loudly before taking a drink. *So perfect.*

Alex was supposed to signal Chuck, and then they would get close enough to fire kill shots, but not so close that the men would be aware of two boys with toy guns pretending to murder them.

Bond and Leiter started walking up toward the road, toward Alex and, presumably, Chuck. I was still holding my Blinker Code-Lite, so I pointed and signaled again—dash-dot, dash-dash-dash, for *NO*—then put it away and began walking after the men. They passed Peacock's and went into Luigi's, the hot dog stand everybody called Red Hots.

I stood right behind them in line and saw that Leiter had an ear-piece connected by a wire to a device in his jacket pocket. He announced to Bond, "New York is *done.*"

This verisimilitude almost scared me. Then he continued his report.

"Cubbies six, Mets three, bottom of the eighth."

Alex and Chuck arrived at Red Hots together, both panting. They stood in the doorway, looking at me, then at each other, then back at me. I nodded toward the men, who were ordering. Alex touched the tackle box, and Chuck put his hand over his heart—over his pistol. I shook my head. I had a new plan.

"Small onion rings and a small cherry Coke," I said to the girl behind the counter. I didn't really want the rings, but I needed my order to take a little time and come out after Bond and Leiter got theirs. At the condiment station, I slipped the cellophane wrapper off my cigarettes and poured one gram of a white chemical into the wrapper.

I sat down on the stool next to Bond's. Alex and Chuck had gone back outside but stood only a few feet away on the other side of the wooden half-wall, looking in through the screen and eavesdropping as they pretended to ignore us. Alex was smoking, but I could see the Luger gripped in his other hand.

Bond, speaking with an American accent in order to remain incognito, was talking to Leiter about ductwork construction schedules and air change rates—clearly a discussion of some secret poison gas system.

I ate an onion ring and took the first sip of my drink. Then I turned away—the boys could see what I was doing, but not the two men—and poured the powder from the cellophane packet into my drink, stirring it with the straw. I took another sip and affected a look of quizzical surprise, smacked my lips, shook my head.

"Excuse me? Sir?" I said to Bond, holding my cup toward him. He turned to me. "I ordered a cherry Coke, but I think they maybe gave me a vanilla one instead. Would you mind tasting it?"

He took a gulp and cringed. "No, that's cherry, all right, but gosh, it does taste funny. Way too sweet."

"Yeah, I thought so, too," I said as I stood up. "Thanks." I carried my purse and the drink in one hand, the onion rings in the other, and headed for the door. Perhaps the men found it strange that I didn't ask for a replacement Coke. But before they saw through my ruse, Commander Bond would be on the floor of Red Hots, trembling, paralyzed, suffering respiratory failure, seconds from death—thanks to the dose of a poison a hundred times more lethal than cyanide that I had just tricked him into swallowing.

"Double-oh-seven," I said to Alex and Chuck as we waited to cross Sheridan Road, "has been terminated. We'll deal with Agent Leiter some other time."

Alex was so excited about what I'd done that he stepped out of character, huffing and puffing and jumping around like a marionette.

"Holy *crap*, Karen, you *talked* to the guy! What was it you put in the Coke?" His voice was cracking.

"Tetrodotoxin. From the Japanese pufferfish. In *Doctor No*."

"No, *actually*."

"Sweet'N Low?"

"That took guts," Chuck said.

In their eyes, I had, in one stroke, turned into a different person—

no longer just the slightly argumentative girl who read the same books they did and got good grades, but unpredictable, cunning, brave, perverse, *exciting*. For the first time, I felt like a woman—a modern woman.

We sped down Michigan Avenue, our hair and clothes flapping in the wind, looking at the vastness of the darkening lake and sky to our left, feeling masterful and free, filled with the joy of living dangerously. Of course, the actual deadly risks we were taking—the cigarettes, biking at night without lights or helmets—did not even register as dangerous.

We followed Alex as he swung right into the circular driveway of the Michigan Shores Club, and left our bikes near a tree by the tennis courts. Alex put the Luger back in the tackle box. Chuck borrowed my compact mirror to fix his tie and asked if he could use my brush to neaten his hair.

"Jesus," Alex said, "don't be such a homo. You look fine."

I'd been to Michigan Shores once before, to drink mulled cider and watch a performance of *A Christmas Carol* in which Alex played Tiny Tim. "I know it's a *club* and everything, and seems all stuck up," I said to Chuck, "but it's really not that big of a deal."

Alex took some offense. "It's the best private club on the North Shore." Then he patted Chuck on the back. "Tiny Tov is just worried they'll be mean to him because he never believed in Santa." Tiny Tov of Torahville was the star of a Sunday-morning kids' show produced by the Chicago Board of Rabbis.

"Well," Chuck said, "they don't let Jews join the club, do they?"

"Is that true?" I asked, whispering as we approached the door.

"It used to be," Alex said, "but not anymore, I don't think."

"Yeah," Chuck said, "*right.*"

"Eat me, Levy. They wanted Hollaender's dad to join, didn't they?" This was a clever, complicating argument on Alex's part: Chuck's mother suspected that my Danish father, having survived a Nazi camp unscathed, must be Jewish passing as gentile. "And my parents aren't anti-Jewish—why do you think they decided not to buy that house in Kenilworth?"

"Because it cost eighty-nine thousand dollars," Chuck said.

Jews did not live in Kenilworth, the next village up. My father referred to Kenilworth as "our adjacent Republican ghetto" and never pronounced the town's name without ridicule, *Kane-ul-verth,* as if he were saying "Berchtesgaden."

Despite my reassurances to Chuck, the Michigan Shores Club was a daunting place, all gray stone and leaded windows, wood paneling and dim sconces, the furniture upholstered in brass-studded leather. The fact that three unaccompanied teenagers were nicely dressed made people smile at us. We went to a small dining room where Alex ordered authentic Bond meals—for himself, soft-boiled eggs, he instructed the waitress, "cooked for three and two-thirds minutes," and scrambled eggs for Chuck and me, asking if they could make them with "fine herbs," which he believed to be the English pronunciation of *fines herbes.* The waitress said they came with parsley. "And Gala?" Alex said, turning to me. "Anything else for you?"

"No, thank you . . ."

I waited for the waitress to leave.

". . . James."

We had shifted identities. Alex was now Bond, Chuck was Felix Leiter, and I was Gala Brand of MI5. After supper we took a tour of the club and wound up sitting in a small parlor with a fireplace. Nearby, two men were rolling dice from a leather cup, and at the table closest to us, two couples were playing cards.

The three of us smiled and shared a glance: *bridge* and *backgammon,* just like in *Moonraker.* I doubt if a group of middle-aged suburbanites playing bridge had ever before struck teenagers as sexy.

For this part of the mission, we were to kill whichever villain, Goldfinger or Drax, we spotted first. Both had red hair, so the practical challenge was to find a short man (Goldfinger) or one with a scarred face (Drax). A few minutes later, the older of the two backgammon players rose and shuffled toward the door. He was stubby, but he had gray hair slicked straight back.

Alex stood. "It used to be red," he declared, and followed Auric Goldfinger out of the room.

A moment later, Alex returned. Goldfinger had not.

"I followed him to the W.C.," he told us.

"And then what?" Chuck was smirking. "You left the Luger outside with the bikes."

Now Alex smirked back. "I certainly did," he said, and pulled from his jacket pocket—surprise—a two-foot length of piano wire to which he had attached short Lincoln Logs at either end. "Garotte. *Silence* is golden. For Mr. Goldfinger."

Before we went home, Alex wanted to show Chuck the indoor swimming pool. It was deserted except for a woman doing laps and a muscular man lying prone on a chaise, with a towel wrapped around his bottom and a newspaper open on the floor beneath his face. We stood on an unlit mezzanine walkway, looking down.

"It's Red Grant," Chuck whispered. "At his villa in the Crimea." That's the SMERSH executioner in *From Russia with Love*'s opening scene. The antique tiling and old-fashioned light fixtures, the echoes of splashing water in the empty room as big as our school gym, the humidity and chlorine stench, the absence of chatter: it did seem foreign and somber, maybe even Russian. Alex and I smiled and nodded.

Alex led us to a spiral staircase, and we tiptoed down to the pool level. We were still in the shadows but now just ten yards from our Red Grant, aka Krassno Granitsky.

Chuck looked around, both furtively and mock-furtively, to see if anyone was watching, then drew the machine pistol from his shoulder holster. Back then kids held toy pistols like gunslingers in Westerns, one-handed, elbow bent—not like the movies subsequently taught children to shoot, in a two-handed combat stance or else with the arm fully extended and the gun sideways, gangsta-style.

He aimed the gun at the man and then, as he pretended to fire, very softly vocalized the standard gunshot sound—"*Pkew!*"—and then another—"*Pkew!*"

Then Chuck fired the gun.

The boys had forgotten to remove the ring of plastic caps from the machine pistol, so when Chuck pulled the trigger, he automatically fired five shots, five distinct explosions of gunpowder over the course of a second or two. No typographic rendering, not *bang-bang-bang-bang-bang* or *pop-pop-pop-pop-pop,* does it justice. The cavernous room, all flat surfaces of ceramic and concrete and glass, amplified the explosions and echoes, and our absolute surprise turned it into an experience of shock and terror beyond decibel measurement. (In 1968, when I fired a real handgun for the first time, I learned that the powder in toy caps is designed to maximize the bang—in other words, toy guns can be louder than the real things.)

Immediately, the frenzy of incoherent noise got even worse. I screamed. Alex screamed. The man shouted. His wife, still in the middle of the pool, began splashing and yelling.

Chuck had dropped the cap gun when it fired, and as he scrambled to retrieve it, he accidentally kicked it toward the man, who had leaped to his feet and now screamed as the pistol and Chuck hurtled across the tiles in his direction. When the man made a move to run—toward us? away from us?—he slipped on the newspaper and his towel fell off and, as he stumbled into the pool, I saw that he was, like the SMERSH killer in the novel, naked. His was the first penis I'd ever seen other than my father's and little brother's.

I've wondered ever since if the couple were more or less frightened than we were. Or maybe their fear and our fear were apples and oranges. But it was the most terrifying instant of my life up to that point.

Five minutes after the shooting, however, after we'd walked at a strenuously normal pace out the front door, and as we pedaled west and north as fast as we could, our shock and terror cooled into mere anxiety—maybe the man had sprained a wrist or broken an arm when he fell, maybe he or his wife had recognized Alex, even though we'd stayed in the shadows. Chuck thought the guy looked familiar.

"You definitely got the gun?" Alex asked Chuck for the second

time. He worried that if the club had the toy pistol, they might show it to all the members and his parents might recognize it—or, less plausibly, dust it for fingerprints. But yes, Chuck had the pistol in his pocket.

Five minutes after that, as we arrived at Alex's house, out of breath, sweaty, we already considered the episode hilarious and wonderful.

"I realize who that guy was," Chuck said. "I've seen him at the RC field." RC was what he called his radio-controlled airplanes. "He's got this really beautiful, really big biplane."

"We can't tell *anyone* about this," Alex said.

"No shit, Sherlock," Chuck said.

The Macallisters were out to dinner in Chicago, so we went to Alex's basement and mixed several celebratory cocktails of vodka and 7-Up in plastic Flintstones cups, and recounted the highlights of the mission. I had never gotten drunk before. The third or fourth time Alex played the 45 of "Twistin' the Night Away," we all got up and danced the Twist together, which, each of us confessed, we had secretly learned and practiced at home, watching *American Bandstand*.

But what I most clearly remember about the night of our first mission is the clatter and chaos and terror of the swimming-pool shooting and the sulfurous smell of the caps. I find that memory heartbreaking because at the time it didn't contain even a whiff of tragedy.

That fall, once we started eighth grade, our last year at Locust, doing algebra homework and attending student council meetings, fulfilling our goody-goody gifted-children destinies as reliably as ever, our secret missions gratified me deeply. Because then it no longer felt as if we were just putting on little shows, filling up another endless summer with do-it-ourselves entertainment. During the school year, the cold light of day made our secret missions all the more glorious: I was actually leading a double life.

5

LAST NIGHT I went to Alex's Facebook page and saw, on the tiny map next to his photo, that he's south of Turkey, at sea, a dark blue blinking dot on the pale blue expanse of the Mediterranean. I clicked on the dark blue dot: he's at latitude 35.37, longitude 33.38. He must be going ashore in Cyprus.

Such a miraculous immensity of useless and fascinating data! When will we stop getting a kick out of having instant access to so much information we don't need? My freshman year in college, I read two Borges stories, "The Library of Babel" and "On Exactitude in Science," fantasies of the ultimate repository of text and of an actual-size national map, and then forgot about them for decades. But these days the Internet often makes me think of Borges. He saw it all coming seventy years ago.

Electronically spying on Alex halfway around the world has also made me think, naturally, yet again, of James Bond. Staging Bond games like ours would be so much easier now, with GPS and Internet search and digital databases and cellphones and texting and Skype and live webcams and real-time freeway traffic monitoring and laser pointers and the forty-dollar SpyNet stealth recording

video glasses I was instructed to buy for my ten-year-old nephew this past Christmas. *Too* easy, I suppose, and therefore not so interesting as a fevered adolescent fantasy. On the other hand, back when we were pretending to be ruthless foreign killers and saboteurs, no one in Chicago was very worried about ruthless foreign killers and saboteurs.

Although both of us live in Los Angeles now, Alex and I have seen each other only twice in the last seven years and exchange very occasional hi-how's-tricks emails in which we reaffirm our mutual intention to get together sometime soon. The last time we spoke was when he called me during the media speculation about my possible nomination to the Supreme Court.

Despite the fortune he's amassed, despite the fact that he's at least as honorable a member of his (artsy, techy, show-businessy, gay) sectors of the Establishment as I am of mine, Alex still likes to think of himself as some kind of outlaw. He made a big stink in the art world some years ago when he declared that collecting was his "art practice." His best-known piece is an assemblage consisting of four works for which he reportedly paid $100 million and then assembled into a kind of collage: in front of the head of an oversize ancient Roman statue of Venus, he's suspended one of Andy Warhol's portraits of Marilyn Monroe and, in front of the sculpture's breasts, two of Jasper Johns's smaller target paintings.

I fired off an email last night, telling Alex, "I'm in the middle of writing a (God we are f-ing *old*) memoir" and asking if he had any "letters or notes or whatever from our Wonder Years" that he could scan and send me when he got home from his "completely jealous-making vacation. And happy 2014!"

His reply arrives this morning, right after I log on. "so, hollaender, u trying to cadge my aide-mémoires for yr memoir, huh? ;)"

Still calling me Hollaender, like when we were kids, still spelling my name the way I did then, now using the abbreviations and emoticons of an all-lower-case twenty-first-century youth—but also a French phrase, complete with an *accent aigu; OMG, so* Alex Macallister.

"mega-kudos on the new book! but it's the chronicle of yr brilliant career, no? practicing law, teaching law, reinventing the law, improving the usa, hear me roar? silly me surely won't figure into all that important fate of the republic business."

By which he means: *How flattering that I am so fabulous that you intend to name-drop me to spice up the otherwise dull story of your drone's life!*

"btw this is just a *brief* sailing r&r after weeks in kabul—exec producing remake of the 3rd man, afghanistan now instead of ww2 vienna, phil hoffman & daniel craig in the welles & joe cotten roles. also hopped over to qatar. new museum there wants the cars. fun never stops."

I guess he tries to sound British only when he's speaking. I begin composing a reply to his reply. "Oh, Alex," I write, "*The Third Man* in Kabul! That is just brilliant, truly." We had seen *The Third Man* together our freshman year of college, Alex for the second time and Chuck and Buzzy Freeman and I for the first, on a double bill with *The Battle of Algiers.* "This book of mine, for better or worse, is turning out to be a lot broader than the Career. A real memoir, including childhood, including family and friends, a true life, not just the good but the bad and the ugly. Yes, a little about practicing law—but even more"

And there I stop. I was intending to write *but even more about breaking the law.* I decide that's too glib, too sudden a revelation, too closing-argument dramatic, and delete everything after *the bad and the ugly.* "In other words, my dear," I finish, "over the next few months I'll just want to fact-check some things with you, Wilmette & college & etc., OK? To help with my memory gaps & blind spots."

Especially on all the "etc." stuff we haven't talked about in almost forty-three years. Ordinarily, I don't use ampersands, but here I figured they'd strike the right tone, blithe rather than solemn and terrifying like a subpoena.

"I saw my little coyote," I say to Waverly as I come into the backyard and put down the reusable bamboo water canister she forced me to buy. "He seems to be limping less than he was last week."

"Cool. How far'd you go?"

I look at the tiny device strapped to my leg that measures my heart rate (102 beats per minute) and distance traveled. "Three-point-sixty-three miles," I tell her.

I was not sporty or outdoorsy growing up. I sort of am now. I'm still astounded by the huge wild parks and mountain views and 68-degree midwinter afternoons, all the sweet, easy availability of vegetation and sea, of bright sun and blue sky—the unembarrassed *sluttiness* of nature in Los Angeles. Living here makes me feel as if I'm always getting away with something. Which I now clearly see— *note to book clubs*—is a major theme of my life. When I was in my twenties, before I'd ever been to L.A., my notion of the place was a Joan Didion construct, all entropy and zombie smiles and luminous dread, hell passing for heaven. Now that I'm in my sixties and living here, I think that having denied myself its delights for so long makes me appreciate them more now. I've earned the pleasure. "It's dessert," I tell people who ask, seven years after I moved to Los Angeles—to Wonderland Park Avenue, if you can believe it—how I'm enjoying the place. "Wilmette, Illinois, was a hearty breakfast, New York and Washington were lunch and dinner, and I saved L.A. for dessert." Angelenos don't seem to mind their city being compared to a crisp, warm, golden churro sprinkled with fresh raspberries and powdered sugar.

Waverly, wearing a bikini, lies on a chaise in my backyard. More than once a day I find myself astonished by her beauty. This is an objective truth, not automatic grandmotherly pride. Her grandfather and I were sevens at best when we were young, although he moved up to an eight as he got older because he ran 43.75 miles every week (ten kilometers every day) and therefore didn't fatten up in his thirties and forties and fifties. Her mother, Greta, has always been an eight, in part because her father was named Jack Wu—that is, because she's half Chinese. So in addition to Waverly's particular good fortune, I think she's a nine (arguably a ten) because her half-Chinese mother married a man whose grandparents grew up in Osaka and Port of Spain: Waverly is half white, a quarter Japanese,

an eighth black, a sixteenth Punjabi, another sixteenth whatever—thus, to my loving postcolonialist eyes, approaching Earth's aesthetically ideal racial mix.

"Clarence Two's inside, yeah?" I ask. Clarence Darrow the Second is my cat. A coyote killed the first Clarence.

"Yup," Waverly says as she stands to angle the chaise a few degrees so that she continues facing the sun. Even a dark-skinned freegan culture-jammer, when she visits L.A., uses every opportunity to improve her tan. She lies down again, her thin, sleek computer resting on her thin, sleek body, propped between knees and sternum, her black flash-drive necklace dangling above her décolletage. "Oh," she tells me, "Mom called."

Sometimes when she says "Mom," I think for a split second that she's referring to my mother rather than my daughter. I think of my mother, who died a few years ago, at age ninety-one, still giving her age as "sixty-plus."

"Grams? I said Mom called."

"Sorry. Did she want me to call back?"

"No? Yes? I don't know. She probably just wants to make sure I make my flight tomorrow."

I sit on the grass next to Waverly and unstrap my bionic instrumentation. "I'll get you to the airport in plenty of time." I extend both legs and start to stretch, lunging toward my feet.

"I know. She just . . . you know."

"I know," I say between grunts.

My daughter treats almost everyone like children, amusing but unwise wanderers who need to be managed in order to stay out of trouble. I wonder if it's because I didn't treat Greta enough like a child when she was one. Or maybe it's just sensible, given that adults these days act like children, and children act like little adults.

Waverly touches her computer, commanding it to become black, and lays it on the chaise. She stretches out her legs and closes her eyes, letting the California sunlight have its way with her.

"Did you put on sunscreen?" I ask.

"Grams," she replies, moving only her mouth, "don't try to be

like Mom just because she doesn't trust you to get me to the airport two hours early. Yes, I did."

I smile and snort. My husband, Jack, always hated my smiling snorts, although this one is a totally loving nonverbal guilty plea, which the thousands I did with Jack, I'll admit, seldom were.

"So when I tell Mom and Dad I'm going to Miami? And they say I can't?"

"Honey, it really won't help your cause if I chime in. Probably the opposite."

She opens her eyes and turns her whole body toward me. "I'm thinking if you remind them that when you were my age, you did all that crazy Vietnam antiwar shit and you turned out fine, you know, became this big important person—and also make them, Mom especially, feel guilty for never doing anything political when she was young—that's the tact I think could work. You know?"

"'Tack,' not 'tact.'" My correction provides a convenient pause to let me process her suggestive key phrase. "And what did I supposedly *do*, according to your mother?"

"What do you mean?"

"My 'crazy antiwar shit.'"

"Oh, you know, screaming at Pentagon guys and getting clubbed and doing sit-ins and trashing offices and all that civil disobedience stuff."

"I never trashed an office." But my instant emphatic denial of Waverly's inaccurate lesser charge reminds me of the indignant denials of criminals I defended in New York in my twenties, such as the robber who told me, *No, he's a fuckin' liar, I just shot a little* Glock *at that cop, not no motherfuckin' AR-15.*

"You've been arrested, though, right? Mom said."

"Yes, once." At the moment of my apprehension, I was nineteen and thought my luck had run out, that I was falling into the black hole of 1968, lost forever.

"In any case, I'm going to Miami in March. The only moral choice is to *act*, right?"

This conversation is making me a little anxious, so I borrow Wa-

verly's computer to check my email. There's no reply from Alex, which makes me more anxious.

I wonder if he'll sue me. On the one hand, at our twenty-fifth college reunion, around the time a pop star was suing him in Britain over a passing mention in an interview that Alex had once given the guy a Vespa in return for sex, he'd ranted to me for an hour about the stupidity and injustice of libel laws. On the other hand, I could definitely see him letting his thousand-dollar-an-hour litigators file a suit against me for defamation, intentional infliction of emotional distress, misappropriation of his name, invasion of privacy, and God knows what other torts they might dream up. If so, *bring it,* gentlemen. Every sentence I'm writing here is true, and Alex is unquestionably a public figure, but my ace in the hole would be what they call *Ex turpi causa non oritur actio*—"from a dishonorable cause an action does not arise." When I get to the details of our dishonorable cause, this will make sense, I promise. As I said, I'm a reliable narrator. Trust me.

But a reliable person of character? Here I am, endeavoring once and for all to come clean, to keep no more secrets—yet, in the process, dissembling about the nature of this project to my oldest friend and one of the very few people who already knows the truth. I will have to explain to Alex exactly what I'm doing. When the time is right. And what about Buzzy? Do I have an ethical (or tactical) obligation to give Buzzy Freeman a heads-up, too? Maybe. Probably. Maybe. But will he then try ratting me out to his friends at FOX News?

"Grams? You look kind of pale."

By which Waverly means: *Is your blood sugar low?* The form of diabetes I have is Type 1, the rarer type, the type that used to be called juvenile diabetes, the one that Caucasians of Northern European descent get disproportionately, the no-fault kind where your own immune system mysteriously and suddenly destroys crucial bits of your pancreas—*not* the diabetes caused by a crappy diet and being fat.

The tricky part of the whole Type 1 diabetes game, and the down-

side that most people have no clue about, are the minutes of mental weirdness you experience every so often as a result of overdosing just a little on insulin. That's because the precise amount of insulin you inject each time is always a rough guess. Responsible diabetics play doctor with themselves all day, every day. The goal is to keep your blood glucose level as close to normal as possible, neither too high (which eventually wrecks your organs) nor so low that you feel unpleasantly or dangerously befuddled. "It's as if you're Goldilocks in the Three Bears' house, always trying to get it *just right,*" my mother said when I was young and newly stricken, to which I replied snottily, "More like Odysseus holding on to his raft between Scylla and Charybdis." If I inject half a drop of insulin too much, a fiftieth of a teaspoon extra, within minutes my glands are pumping adrenaline and cortisol into my blood and brain, I become silent, sometimes pale, and on rare occasions a little panicky and confused. My UCLA endocrinologist, a funny Scot, calls it "slipping into the slough of despond." My daughter, Greta, who's a neurobiologist specializing in the brain mechanics of love and hate, calls it "abnormal mentation" and "nonspecific dysphoria." The same thing can happen if I eat too little. Or if I exercise too much. And I did just walk several miles up and down Coldwater Canyon.

"You want me to get a meter for you?" Waverly asks, already up off the chaise and headed toward the kitchen door.

"Thanks, Wavy." I do feel unsettled.

A silver lining of eight-times-a-day blood tests: usually, you discover that a snappish mood or vague fear is some meaningless neurochemical squall, the result of low blood glucose, nothing that chewing a few fruit-flavored sugar tablets won't cure right away.

And a silver lining of experiencing low blood sugars for twenty-five years before my dad got Alzheimer's, I think, was that I had an inkling of what he felt. Early on, before he started speaking Danish to dogs on the street, he could give lucid descriptions of his symptoms—of the sudden mood swings, the confusion, the anger, the frightening and infuriating inability to form sentences. It sounded very much like extreme hypoglycemia.

Anyhow, when Waverly brings me the meter, I prick the tip of my index finger and squeeze a smidgen of blood onto the test strip, as I've done a hundred thousand times. And five seconds later—88 milligrams of glucose per deciliter of blood; fine—I have the proof that, in fact, my anxiety is real, the result of thinking about 1968 and how my old friends will react when I tell them I'm breaking the oath of silence we took forty-six years ago.

An old Ink Spots tune is suddenly coming out of Waverly's computer. It seemed ancient when I was a kid and my dad played it every week on our hi-fi. Back then, the only part of the song to which I ever really paid attention was what I considered the dirty bit, when a very deep, very black voice speaks the words "way down inside of me, darling . . . nobody else ain't gonna do." When I was thirty, driven by ambition for worldly acclaim and wanting only to be the one my daughter loved, I rediscovered the song and bought an Ink Spots' greatest-hits album and started playing it all the time.

> *I don't want to set the world on fire,*
> *I just want to start a flame in your heart.*
> *In my heart I have but one desire,*
> *And that one is you, no other will do.*
>
> *I've lost all ambition for worldly acclaim;*
> *I just want to be the one you love.*
> *And with your admission that you feel the same,*
> *I'll have reached the goal I'm dreaming of, believe me.*
> *I don't want to set the world on fire,*
> *I just want to start a flame in your heart.*

Unlike nearly all the pop lyrics I osmotically learned as a kid, which seemed trivial once I got older, these still strike me as meaningful, especially the line *I don't want to set the world on fire*. I hadn't heard it for a decade until one night in 1979, when Jack and I were watching TV. An ad came on for Chanel No. 5. The music was "I Don't Want to Set the World on Fire."

"Oh my God," I said to my husband, "I *love* that!"

"You're joking, right?" said Jack, the modernist composer.

The man in the ad was called Charles, and the tagline was *Share the Fantasy.*

I ask Waverly why she has that song on her iTunes.

"It's the soundtrack to this game, Fallout 3."

The sun dips beneath the top of the eucalyptus tree between us and the little mountain that's between us and the ocean.

"Fallout 3 is what I imagine it is?"

"Life after nuclear war, yeah." She looks up. "I wish I didn't have to go home, Grams."

The jolt of intense love—oxytocin gushing from thyroid a few inches heavenward to amygdala, according to my daughter—is instantly tainted by guilt about Waverly preferring my company to her mother's, the oxytocin expert Greta Wu. And then cut short entirely when I look again at the Apple device.

Alex has answered me. The subject line of his email is "WTF."

And I think: *If eighteen-year-old Chuck Levy were here, he would urge me to tell the truth and hold back nothing.*

6

I DO VIVIDLY REMEMBER things about my childhood that had nothing to do with Alex or Chuck or James Bond or the official Day-Glo red dawn of the 1960s.

I remember my mother in her nightgown sitting on the edge of her unmade bed for several minutes every morning, brushing her long hair as my sister, Sabrina, and I counted to a hundred; then she would pick the strands out of the brush and, no matter the season, stand up and toss the brushings out the open window.

And I remember the fall afternoon in sixth grade, sitting all by myself in the crook of the oak tree in our backyard, staring up at jet contrails, which were a new phenomenon, when a bird flew past within inches of my face. It landed just a few feet above me, then walked along a limb upside down and disappeared into a hole. A minute later, when the bird popped out and flew off, I stood and looked into its hole.

There was a nest. It consisted of grass and twigs and dirt plus a few cigarette butts and bits of cellophane, but the main material was my mother's red hair, and in the bottom, arranged as neatly as an Easter basket, were seven tiny pink eggs with gray and lavender

speckles. I remember staring at those eggs on the thatch of my mother's hair in the shadows inside the oak tree, worried that my breath might contaminate them but unable to turn away. I knew I was at a perfect privileged age to find and behold this wonder, to have an adventure, still a wide-eyed child but *capable.* I was young Arthur in the Forest Sauvage, Alice down the rabbit hole, Lucy Pevensie peeping through a knot into Narnia. I was agog.

"I see London, I see France!" By the time I registered what had startled me—my little brother, shouting up from six feet below—I had already slipped and fallen. Before Peter had a chance to say *"I see Karen's underpants,"* I was on top of a crumpled, crying four-year-old whose arm had fractured when it came between plummeting me and a large rock at the base of the tree. Later, after I identified the bird, Peter started calling me White-breasted Nuthatch. I got my mother to make him quit the "White-breasted" part, but he called me Nuthatch until we were adults.

I remember our vacations, and my mother always bringing along an aerosol can of Lysol and a box of Dixie cups. Before we were allowed to enter any Minnesota motel room or North Carolina gas station bathroom, she'd go in first and fill it with an antibacterial fog. (My father called the enormous Lysol can her *flammekaster,* or flamethrower.) In order to keep our bottoms from touching unfamiliar public toilet seats, Sabrina and I had to pee into cups my mother held under us.

I remember my family going to the circus for the first time one Friday night when I was twelve. In retrospect, it's odd that we hadn't been to a circus before, because one of my father's own fondest childhood memories was seeing a circus every summer near the Tivoli Gardens in Copenhagen in the 1920s and '30s. Dad and I were alone on our back porch after dinner before we drove down to Chicago, and I told him that a lot of my friends were frightened of clowns. "Americans," he said, lowering his voice a little, "don't like clowns very much, I think, because so many Americans are dopes who believe they are very clever. While clowns, of course, are very clever people pretending to be dopes." I laughed really hard, which

pleased him a lot. My mother didn't like it when he made broad generalizations about "Americans," because it reminded her that he wasn't one, even though in reply he always reminded her that he earned a living—in marketing—by making broad generalizations about Americans.

I remember going out to dinner at Walker Bros. Original Pancake House in Wilmette just after it opened. It was a special treat, and I complained that Sabrina got to come, since she'd stayed home sick from school that day with an upset stomach—an illness that I, in my egregious junior-litigator fashion, wasn't buying. I remember my father ordering the "Danish apple pancake" and then laughing so loudly when it arrived that people turned and looked at us. He'd expected the delicate little sliced-apple popovers of his youth, *æbleskiver,* not this steaming two-pound LP-sized thousand-calorie hillock of apple and cake drenched in melted butter and brown sugar and cinnamon. "God, I love this country," he said, more sincerely than not, staring at the giant pancake as he cackled and shook his head. Although a ten-year-old, at least in 1960, couldn't precisely parse his reaction—disgusted *and* delighted?—I thought I more or less understood. My eager little brother wanted to guffaw along with his dad. "It looks," Peter shouted, "like a pile of *barf."* Mom said, *"Peter!* It does *not,* it looks scrumptious. And the polite word, young man, is 'upchuck.'" At which point Sabrina vomited all over the table.

I remember almost every weekend, usually Saturday night around seven-thirty but sometimes Friday, my dad mixing two big Tom Collinses and putting his precious old Ink Spots 78 on the hi-fi. It was the last record he'd bought in Denmark, in 1942, during the Nazi occupation. The opening guitar riff of "I Don't Want to Set the World on Fire" was the weekly cue that my mother and he were hereby ignoring us for the rest of the night, that we were meant to scram—go to our bedrooms to read, or to the basement to play Monopoly or watch television (our family's single most un-American oddity: no TV in the living room), or, once we were older, get out of the house and wander off.

I also remember things like watching *American Bandstand* and *Kukla, Fran and Ollie* a thousand times. But so what? In that way, my life was the same as your life or your parents' lives. Everyone my age has more or less the same checklist of the same moments, the package of entertainment-and-TV-news highlights that the entertainment-and-TV-news industry has cherry-picked and recycled continuously since people my age took over. Whereas each of my parents and grandparents and great-grandparents all the way back filled their mental attics with memories derived from their own idiosyncratic real lives. Almost all of our ancestors' meaningful memories were *theirs,* custom-made, no more than occasionally supplemented by a dazzling scene from a movie, or a memorable bar of music, or a line from a sermon, or a famous old poem about a barbarian invasion. Nowadays our authentic memories, except for vague recollections of mood and aroma and shimmer, and a few extreme moments—finding a hidden bird's nest made from your mother's hair, breaking your brother's arm, your sister puking in a restaurant—have been squeezed into a second-rate mental ghetto, supplanted by the canon of slick universal media memories.

I'd barely finished living my childhood when show business started replacing my private and odd and fragmentary memories with its special, shiny reconstituted versions. It started suddenly, the moment I became an adult, with the movies *Woodstock* (1970) and *American Graffiti* (1973) and the musical *Grease* (1971). Artists and audiences have always done this, I suppose. But Homer and Shakespeare wrote their stories a century or five centuries after the events, not so quickly that the people who lived through the events were tricked into believing they had *experienced* the fictions and docudramas. A man I dated in 2007 loved *Mad Men,* for instance, so I watched half the first season, and now I can't help but think of my dad as Don Draper with a foreign accent and a sense of humor, which pisses me off.

It was at the beginning of eighth grade that I became acutely aware of something large and strange under way in the world, a sudden global unraveling way beyond what my dad called "this

wonderful picnic-y informality" of America. It wasn't just from knowing about beatniks or discovering Dylan, but because my English teacher was so angry about a new dictionary and my mother was so euphoric about Pope John and his special conclave of bishops at the Vatican. Of course, the fact that puberty and the 1960s were kicking in at precisely the same moment was synergistic: each made the other seem more remarkable and important—to me, to the millions of mes, and to millions of confounded adults. As I morphed into a shocking new version of myself, the whole world was morphing the same way.

Locust Junior High opened that fall, all spick-and-span, its dramatically sloped roof and beige brick and low long wings and grids of big windows so modern, so aggressively, blandly new. The blackboards had no patina of chalk dust. The maps on the walls were unwrinkled and unstained and showed Ghana and Nigeria and both Congos as independent nations. The black paraffin covering the bottom of every dissection tray was virginal, unblemished by pinpricks and frog juice. The tumbling mats in the gym—the "multipurpose room," because it was also where we ate lunch and watched concerts—smelled of chemicals, factory-fresh. Even the waterfountain water came out stronger and colder than it had in grade school. Almost every book was uncracked, from *A Wrinkle in Time* to *Modern Elementary Algebra* to the unabridged thirteen-pound dictionaries that sat on their own special metal pedestals in the library and each classroom.

Our English teacher made it clear on the first day of school that the *Webster's Third New International* was a loathsome thing enabling and celebrating the decline of civilization but which he was required by the school district to abide. Mr. Fortini was young, maybe thirty, so his hardcore fogeyism was fascinating.

He didn't mind the inclusion of smut—"damn" and "shit" and "piss" and "tit" and every bad word we knew except "fuck." Rather, he disapproved of the new dictionary's abandonment of disapproval, its replacement of all the old *Webster's Second* labels—"incorrect,"

"improper," "erroneous," "ludicrous"—with the weenie word "non-standard."

When we were in high school, we heard that Mr. Fortini had left teaching to attend seminary and become a Roman Catholic priest. I wonder now what he thought about the Second Ecumenical Council of the Vatican, the first sessions of which took place that same fall. My mother was a rabid fan of Vatican II, as it came to be known, and of Pope John XXIII. On the day of the Vatican Council's opening ceremonies in Rome, she kept us home from school for an hour so we could sit in the basement and watch the live Telstar broadcast on NBC.

Over the next few years this Vatican Council, after long debates in Latin, decided to let priests say Mass in languages other than Latin. In that great earnest moment of the new and improved, my mother believed—sweetly, incorrectly, sadly—that the Vatican II reforms would keep all her children in the Church's embrace as we became teenagers.

As a little girl, I liked being a Catholic. St. Joseph's Church seemed both gigantic and cozy, and the costumes and incense and Latin made for a great show. I managed to impress everyone by memorizing the Nicene Creed at age six—"We believe in one God, the Father, the Almighty, maker of heaven and earth, of all that is, seen and unseen"—and I *loved* the phrase "all that is, seen and unseen."

However, my relationship with the Church was traumatically put asunder at age seven when I made my first confession.

"Forgive me, Father, for I have sinned." I tried to be succinct and get quickly to my one big mortal sin. "I broke the First Commandment. At Christmastime, we were at Marshall Field's watching them make Frango mints, and then my mom said it was too late to go talk to Santa because we had to leave to make it to Saturday Advent Mass. But I said Santa Claus is just as important as Jesus, like the Holy Ghost. My mom said I was putting strange gods before God, like it says not to do in the First Commandment. But I cried, and so we stayed in line and talked to Santa and missed Mass."

"Aha."

Then, before Father Linehan spoke, he *chuckled*. Confession was serious business, the most serious business to which I'd ever been party, and he was *laughing*? He assigned me only one Our Father and one Hail Mary.

In retrospect, I can see that Father Linehan's reaction to this eager, penance-craving little Catholic seems charming and correct. But I was shocked. From that afternoon on I harbored a skepticism—not yet about the existence of God or the body and blood of Jesus Christ or any of the other magical mysteries, but about the *Church*. If they didn't take my troubled conscience seriously, if it was all a big joke, *Dominus noster Jesus Christus te absolvat ha ha ha,* then why should I trust them to guide me along my path toward redemption? I started thinking that when it came to behaving correctly, I was probably on my own. I started thinking that my unchurched dad—every Sunday while we were at Mass, he watched *Meet the Press* and prepared our weekly Danish lunch of sweet cured salmon on dark rye—must consider confession and Holy Communion a ridiculous charade but didn't have the heart to come right out and say so. Sort of the way I spent the next several years pretending, for Peter's and Sabrina's sakes, that Santa Claus existed.

I continued making confession and attending Mass and receiving Holy Communion and enduring the daylong annual embarrassment of Ash Wednesday, and I kept my growing disbelief to myself. Because I saw how this was eventually going to end—several against one, a bunch of serially wised-up kids and irreverent Dad versus eternally faithful, hopeful Mom—it seemed preferable to postpone the uncomfortable moment of truth as long as I could.

Which came when I was thirteen. Not long after my mother performed her (successful) novena for peace during and after the Cuban Missile Crisis, I decided that I had to take my stand. It was a Saturday afternoon. My friend Mary Ann's mom had just driven me home from the ninth of my twenty-two weekly confirmation classes. My parents were in the living room, reading. I sat down on the floor next to Curiosity, our cairn terrier. (As a puppy called Jake,

he had played to death with one of the neighbors' kittens, and my father renamed him Curiosity.)

After rubbing the dog's tummy for a minute, I announced that I wasn't going through with my confirmation. My mother closed and put down the Christmas issue of *Vogue* very carefully and slowly. Her attempts to appear calm always had the opposite effect.

"Don't be silly. Of course you are, Karen. You are a fine Catholic. A 'spectacular young Catholic,' the archbishop himself said."

She was referring to the social studies paper I'd written about American poverty, in which I'd quoted from the Book of James— "Well now, you rich! Lament, weep for the miseries that are coming to you." My mother sent a copy of my paper to Archbishop Meyer, who gave it an award.

"I'm not like Saint Gertrude," I said. I had been planning to take Gertrude as my confirmation name because as a young woman, seven hundred years earlier, before she saw the light and returned to the Church, Saint Gertrude had been a young intellectual and writer who rejected Christianity.

"You don't have to be a saint to be Catholic."

"But you have to believe in Catholicism to be one. It would be fake. It'd be a lie."

"Is this about your problem with the virgin birth and miraculous apparitions? Listen, sweetheart—"

"And the Holy Ghost. Whatever *that* is."

"I've told you what Saint Augustine said about not taking Bible completely literally—and 'doubt is but another element of faith.'"

"And transubstantiation. I don't believe that Jesus Christ was God's son. I don't believe he was resurrected."

"You can't do this."

"I can't be confirmed. I won't defend the faith. I don't want to be a soldier of Christ, Mommy." I had long since phased out "Mommy" in favor of "Mom" and "Mother," and she despised the phrase "soldier of Christ," so now I was being shrewd.

She looked at my father, who smiled wanly and shrugged, which made her angry.

She closed her eyes and shook her head. At last my father spoke. "Karen," he asked, undoubtedly knowing what my answer would be, "do you believe in God?"

"I'm not sure. Probably not. But I know for *sure* I don't believe that Helen is burning and suffering in *hell*."

My coup de grâce. Except there was no grace or mercy involved, just blood-tingling adolescent cruelty. Five years earlier, my sister Helen, the fourth Hollaender child, was stillborn. I'd assumed that her little soul flew from the Evanston Hospital delivery room directly up to heaven. But when I asked Father Linehan to explain how babies such as Helen, who die before they learn to speak, are able to communicate in heaven, he set me straight on Catholic doctrine. I never quite got over the shock. Babies suffering eternal damnation if they die unbaptized—or *maybe,* if such a place exists, Father Linehan wasn't certain, spending eternity in limbo—seemed like the most ghastly injustice imaginable. Between Father Linehan's laughter at my first confession and this information about God's mercilessness, I felt that I'd glimpsed a deep satanic streak in the Church.

Anyhow, when I played the baby-Helen card that afternoon in 1963, my mother said nothing but instantly crossed herself, stood up, put on her coat, grabbed her gloves and purse, walked out of the house, and drove away. I assume she went to St. Joseph's and prayed for me.

The next morning at Mass, as we stood up to recite the Lord's Prayer, a little boy in the pew just behind me said in a loud whisper, "Mommy, that girl got *hurt.*" Somewhere around *lead us not into temptation but deliver us from evil,* I felt a rivulet dribble between my underpants and the top of one of my stockings. I'd gotten my first period, and blood had stained through the back of my dress. As the priest prepared the Eucharist and I knelt in the pew, imagining myself about to eat the body and sip the blood of Christ at the altar with my stained bloody backside exposed to the entire congregation, I decided I couldn't endure the nightmare.

As mother and Peter and Sabrina filed out of the pew and turned

right, without a word, I turned left and walked down the aisle and then down the stairs to the ladies' room. I waited forever outside in the cold by our car in the lot. As my mother approached, glaring at me, the December wind whipping hair around her face, I thought she looked like the witch in *Sleeping Beauty*. Sabrina was trying not to smile. After I explained what had happened and lifted my coat and turned around to prove it, my mother hugged me, and we both started crying. That was the last time I attended Mass, apart from Sabrina's confirmation, and funerals.

7

WHENEVER I DROP off someone I really care about at an airport, I choke up the moment I drive away. (I sometimes think that if I'd driven Jack to JFK and La Guardia for his weeks-long composing residencies in New Mexico and Norway and India during the '80s, I'd have realized sooner how much my love for him had shriveled. But he always took a taxi.) And my new electric car is so eerily quiet as it accelerates that the extra sonic space gives my emotions more room to roil. So I'm crying, a tear or two running down each cheek, as I wave back at Waverly on the sidewalk and start to concentrate on escaping LAX.

The woman reading the news on *Morning Edition* is black, I learned not long ago from a friend who works at NPR. I'd had no idea, because there's nothing identifiably African-American about her voice. NPR has a bunch of black on-air talent, but because they all sound white, my friend told me in an embarrassed whisper, and because it's radio, "nobody *realizes* it. We get no credit. What we'd *kill* for are some first-rate journalists with, you know, African-American *names*. Kadisha, Jameel."

The NPR newsreader introduces a report from Denmark, where

four Jews have been killed and twelve more sickened in a poisoning plot carried out by Islamic terrorists. The terrorists coated the mezuzahs affixed to the front door of at least fifty Jewish households in Copenhagen with botulinum toxin. The Danish prime minister promised that "the full resources of the nation are focused on apprehending the perpetrators of this fiendish plot."

In Danish, I happen to know, "fiendish" is *djævelsk*. As children, when we did amusingly naughty things, snapping Polaroid pictures of my parents as they stepped from the shower or eating entire sticks of butter coated in brown sugar, my father, who rarely resorted to Danish, would call us *lille djævel*, little devils, little fiends. Otherwise, "fiends" and "fiendish plots," like "dastardly deeds," existed only in comic books and Looney Tunes, as antiquated and self-parodying hyperbole.

These murders in Copenhagen are, of course, like something from James Bond, a scheme devised by a grinning Blofeld or Drax for his henchmen to carry out.

The one time I met George W. Bush, at a dinner in New York before he was governor, when we were both in our forties, I immediately thought of him as Felix Leiter, Bond's Texan CIA helpmate. Life was surrealized for everybody on September 11, but a week after the attacks, as I sat alone in our new apartment on Desbrosses Street in lower Manhattan, burning dogwood-scented votive candles to cover the stench of smoldering rubble and flesh wafting up from Ground Zero, I was talking on the phone to my Washington friend in the intelligence community. He was angrier than I'd ever heard him, talking about all the squandered opportunities to kill bin Laden—"six months ago we had the prick literally in our sights, from a drone I was *watching* him on a *monitor*." When I hung up and turned on my TV and saw live coverage of Tony Blair's visit to Washington, I felt like I was tripping: Felix Leiter was president of the United States, talking about "Wanted: Dead or Alive" posters, with a somewhat fey British prime minister James Bond committing himself to join in the free world's war against crazed foreign evildoers.

In September 2001, real life abruptly and completely flipped into full Bond mode. A wealthy freelancing supervillain in a secret underground lair, four hijacked American jetliners, the Pentagon struck, iconic 110-story Manhattan skyscrapers vaporized—this was precisely the kind of absurd, baroque scheme that Commander Bond trotted the globe trying to prevent. Since then, half our politics and news have concerned fiendish, nihilistic masterminds in their hideouts, charismatic and stateless psychopaths who dream of committing spectacular mass murder for its own spectacular sake, with the battle against them fought by daring, steadfast agents of MI6 and CIA and special ops equipped with fantastic gadgets and licenses to kill. Afghan guerrillas in the heroin business and Colombian guerrillas in the cocaine business, a world-famous Pakistani physicist selling nuclear secrets to rogue states, an American-born Colorado State grad in a beard and turban brainwashing killers by remote control from Yemen, Mexico commandeered by psychopathically depraved drug lords, entranced suicide bombers, proud videos of beheadings? A global confederacy of disparate madmen and terrorists? In the Bond novels, it was called SPECTRE. The director of the National Counterterrorism Center under Presidents Bush and Obama was a young former naval officer named—yes—Leiter. Truth is not stranger than fiction, it's *exactly like* the pulpy fiction I loved in junior high.

As I turn off Wilshire onto Westwood toward campus, I'm thinking about the Danish mezuzot botulin murders. I remember the first mezuzah I noticed in L.A., right after I moved. Waverly, visiting me at age ten, spotted it. It was pewter, affixed to the doorjamb of Dr. Benjamin Silverstein, a make-believe Jewish physician with a make-believe old-timey office on Main Street in Disneyland.

"Morning, Professor," the UCLA parking garage guy says as I pause to let the little latticework of red laser beams read my card. "Fantastic day, huh?" He means the weather. It's the greeting he gives me almost every day.

"Beautiful," I reply.

The life of a tenured university professor is rather grand in a way

that barely exists elsewhere anymore. Every job exists along a spectrum according to how frequently one is required to lie and to act like a jerk, from many times a day at one end of the chart to maybe once a year at the other end, and my current job is way toward the pleasant side. Unlike at a law firm, at a university almost nobody seems perpetually on the verge of panic or keeps track of your hours, and unlike when you're a litigator or a prosecutor or a judge, you don't really have the opportunity to wreck people's lives.

I didn't hate corporate litigation, but I rarely reveled in it, as most of my colleagues did. I worked hard and became a partner on schedule. People talk about how relentless and stressful it is working in a big New York firm, especially for women, especially for mothers, and that's true. But I'd manned up at age nineteen, reconciled myself to a life unnaturally twisted by stress.

So I was not overwhelmed by the exhausting hours and travel; the breathtaking wastefulness and meaningless triumphs; or the clients whose arrogance and mediocrity—guys suffering from a kind of MBA Tourette's, unable to speak for two minutes without saying "mezzanine financing" or "basis points" or "reps and warranties," and who actually display the little Lucite monuments to each of their deals—more than justified the five and ten and finally almost twenty dollars a minute I was charging them. But without the teaching—first at NYU, then at Yale—and the book writing, I think I would've been bored out of my mind.

Life at a university, on the other hand, I find nearly qualmless. We think and talk and write without heart-attack-inducing schedules, and we try to sharpen fine young minds. We're paid well but not lavishly. We are the Establishment flaunting its kindly and humane side, The Man doing penance for being The Man—our Institute on Sexual Orientation Law & Public Policy, our Native Nations Law & Policy Center, our Center on Climate Change & the Environment.

I like it here, and most people seem to like me. Last spring, when my name started to appear on the lists of possible nominees to the United States Supreme Court, my star rose dramatically. People smiled at me more and paid closer attention to anything I said. After

I removed my name from consideration for the seat, people seemed even more delighted to be in my presence. Maybe because envy had been removed from the mix.

This afternoon I have a department chair meeting where I'll announce higher cost-of-living pay increases than they're expecting and listen to a proposal for a new course on the law of transgenderedness. Then I have a meeting with a Hollywood attorney whom I think I've convinced to donate $2 million to the school. Then I teach my constitutional law seminar. And then I'll be home on Wonderland Park Avenue before six-thirty. A day's work, done. Like I said: sweet.

That's one big reason I've managed these last seven years to finish my biography of Chief Justice John Jay (*The 7th Founder*), which the *Times* said "proves Americans' appetite for thick workmanlike books about Founding Fathers is insatiable"; to write my first novel (*Objection, Your Honor*), which the *Times* called "an arch but surprisingly tough-minded aging-chick-lit confection, *Rumpole* meets Scott Turow"; and to publish a cover story in *The Atlantic* ("The Trouble with the Constitution"), which the *Times* said "seems to be upsetting Ms. Hollander's friends at least as much as her enemies."

Anther boon to my productivity was becoming single. A gradually failing marriage is a whole lot more time-consuming than either a happy one or a viciously rotten one. It was like living on a leaky old boat I spent half my waking hours bailing out. And then at around sixty, I got a second wind. Maybe it's the equivalent of the endorphinated final burst of speed that Jack talked (and talked and talked) about feeling in the last few miles of his best marathon runs. For my previous nonfiction books, *Hating Lawyers* and *Shouting Fire in a Crowded Theater*, as well as the Jay biography, I methodically gathered all the facts before I wrote a sentence. That's what lawyers do. But with this one, it felt as if a fuse had been lit, and I had no choice but to *go*, get it done before I lost my nerve.

I have most of the information I need. It's in my head, or else in the scrapbooks and journals and papers crammed into the soft, dusty old corrugated Kellogg's Corn Pops boxes next to my desk at

home. But not all of it. There are large gaps in my knowledge, a few important things I don't know.

I'm not certain where those missing pieces are. I suppose that's true of most people. Who knows what secrets other people—family, friends, enemies, lovers, husbands, bosses, colleagues, acquaintances, strangers—have kept from us? We don't know what we don't know.

Unfortunately, I have no subpoena authority or rights of discovery, only my archive and memory and powers of persuasion and inference. And the Freedom of Information Act, which lets you ask the government for copies of any records they may have about you. I mailed my Freedom of Information requests to five different federal agencies a month ago. So far I've heard nothing back.

Maybe my FOIA letters are drifting among bored and clueless GS-5s and GS-9s, clerks who've never heard of me and don't regard my requests as more or less remarkable than any of the dozens that come in every day. Or have I risen, possibly, to the attention of some GS-14 who takes her mission or her civil service career seriously? Has she passed a photocopy and covering memo to a member of her agency's senior executive service, maybe an SES Level 4, a general counsel, a serious keeper of secrets? Maybe there's a meeting scheduled to discuss my case with a Level 3 or Level 2, a deputy director, an undersecretary. And will someone with a well-known name, a cabinet secretary, a Level 1, finally be asked to decide what, if anything, his underlings will be permitted to tell me about my past? In other words, how steaming hot are any of my potentially hot potatoes?

When I worked for the federal government in the late '90s, it once took me a month to dredge up a file about an historical incident on an Indian reservation. The record keeping is *very* twentieth-century, a lot more *Brazil* than *Bourne*. The information I want may be classified. Or it may have been evanescent, contained in a few sentences uttered by some official several decades ago and never written down. Each of the other agencies to which I've sent my inquiries—the Department of Homeland Security; the Army Intel-

ligence and Security Command; the Central Intelligence Agency; and the Federal Bureau of Investigation—keeps its own special troves as well. Depending on whether someone decided sometime that the information I seek might cause "exceptionally grave damage" or "serious damage" to the national security, it could be categorized, respectively, as Top Secret or Secret.

In the '90s, my baby-boomer president signed an executive order to declassify classified information more than twenty-five years old, and to forbid officials from declaring a document Confidential or Secret or Top Secret in order "to prevent embarrassment." There's a famous song from *Hair* that has a relevant lyric: *A dying nation of moving paper fantasy / Listening for the new told lies / . . . Let the sunshine in!* It did occur to me when Clinton signed his executive order that the new sunshine might one day result in damage, serious or even exceptionally grave, to my life and career.

By then I didn't exactly live in fear of inquisitive phone calls, but it was one of those unpleasant possibilities lurking in the background, like the awful diagnosis you fret about when you visit the doctor. It turns out, however, that ever since Clinton's Executive Order 12958 took effect, employees of the darkness-craving agencies, the bureaucratic vampires and wolves and tarantulas and moles, have been quietly crawling through every inch of those declassified files, *reclassifying* thousands of them, dragging them page by page out of the light and back into their federal caskets and nooks and burrows.

So I'm not counting on the government to shrug and hand over the missing pieces of the puzzle it may have. I'll pursue other tracks. I'm about to spend a long weekend in Washington, flying out to celebrate Sarah Caputo's twenty-fifth wedding anniversary. I've also scheduled drinks with another well-placed pal—a man I shouldn't name, a former beau, the closest friend I made during my three and a half years in D.C.—who might be able to pull a string or two to help with my research.

"Dean Hollander?" I look over to see my assistant, Concepción

Perez. "Mr. Alex Macallister of Wheel Life Pictures is on the line. He's calling from *Beirut.*"

I smile. "Of course he is." Another Bond moment. Although weirdly, in the books, Bond never went to an Arab country. With a fingernail, I slice a Nicorette out of its foil-and-plastic bubble. "Close the door, Connie?"

"Hal*lo,* Hollander! It's been such a bloody long time!"

Again I smile. I never quite remember until he opens his mouth just how British Alex sounds. The enduring impact of his four years in London during the 1970s is incredible. "Your ears must have tingled last winter," he goes on. "I was in Prague for the renaming of the airport after Havel, and raving with your old pal Přemek about how much we adore you. Why on earth do you and I never see each other in the City of Angels?"

Why? Because you've invited me to your place exactly once, almost two years ago, during my Supreme Court fame bubble, and whenever I asked you to dinner during the previous five years, you had your assistant cancel at the last minute, once with a text message.

"Hiya, Alex! Great to hear your voice. Vacationing in Beirut, huh?"

"It's over forty here, maybe forty-five!" On Planet Alex, temperatures are in Celsius. "Although not as dodgy as you'd think. But I'm hardly on holiday. An acquisition mission, actually. I'm trying to cobble together *Cars Two.*" An exhibit that Alex assembled, which he considers art and calls *The Cars,* has been traveling around the world for a couple of years, drawing large crowds. It consists of automobiles in which famous people died—General George Patton's Cadillac, James Dean's Porsche Spyder, Jackson Pollock's Olds 88, Albert Camus's French coupe, Jayne Mansfield's Buick Electra. The only one not a wreck is the 1961 Lincoln Continental convertible in which John F. Kennedy was shot. I remember reading that The Cars, the band, reunited to play at the opening of the show at the Armory in New York, and that the only vehicles Alex wanted

but couldn't acquire were Grace Kelly's Rover and Princess Diana's Mercedes.

"Can I trust you?" he asks.

"Sure," I answer immediately. "Yeah."

"But really. This is hush-hush. Completely confidential. I demand lawyer-client privilege."

"I'm not your attorney. What is it?"

"Celebrated people don't much die in road accidents anymore. The Princess of Wales was the last. For a new piece, a piece about *this* century, I'm trying to buy up the important car-bomb cars."

I am speechless for a moment. Is he joking? Of course not.

"Day before yesterday we acquired the remains of the pickup truck that killed Rafic Hariri. Remember?" Hariri was the former Lebanese prime minister assassinated by a suicide car bomber— truck bomber—nine years ago in Beirut. "Karen, this is *so* much more difficult for me than *The Cars.*"

"Yeah, I would imagine."

I wonder for an instant if he means difficult psychologically, emotionally. Of course not.

"Luckily, we've got some significant friends over here. Americans. We're still working on getting a loan of Rafic's Mercedes, which I really must have—the piece only works as a diptych, the truck and the Mercedes together. The family are softening. An important fellow in Pakistan *really* wants to sell me bin Laden's last Land Cruiser, and I was tempted, but it's off-message for the show. And in Afghanistan, Iraq, oh my God, you can imagine the provenance issues. People try to diddle you with fakes constantly. Or else they're offended and call me sick."

"Really? Huh. Fancy that."

"Yeah, well, that's what the Nazis said about modern art, too. So, Hollander: this autobiography of yours, cleaning off and tarting up this old picture of yourself to put on display. I guess with me in the background. You doing restoration or conservation?"

"I don't know what you mean. I'm a lawyer, Alex."

"No, you're a *writer*, Hollander, like you always dreamed of being,

and now you're a writer of *fiction* as well, an artist, a fabricator of tales. Although the gal in your novel, the heroine? Seemed *highly* Karen Hollanderesque to me."

His flattery throws me off track. "You read *Objection, Your Honor?*"

"I considered optioning it. Anyhow, my point is that you *know* now that nonfiction is never the entire truth, and fiction is almost never pure fabrication. In painting, in the art world, restoration, some wise people, the Russians, the Italians, think that old pictures are what they've become—and *don't* uncover the repainted sections, *don't* fill in the scratched-away patches, accept and respect what the years have done to alter the image. Whereas American restorers go for what they call 'deceptive retouching.'"

"Whatever I'm writing, it's not deceptive. The opposite."

"No, no, you're misunderstanding. Deceptive retouching tries to make an old picture look *exactly* as it did *originally.* Like people who color their hair."

"Are you suggesting my hair color isn't naturally St. Petersburg Champagne Blonde?" Trying to keep things light!

"Which is impossible, of course. Deceptive retouching is fiction-alizing that pretends it's the real truth. Like Colonial Williamsburg."

"You're losing me here. I've never even understood what 'post-modern' means."

"Just a straight-shootin' plainspoken old-fashioned midwestern lady lawyer. *Please.*"

"I'm trying," I say, "to write an honest and accurate account of certain parts of my life. Our lives. Our dreams and fantasies. There's so much I'd forgotten."

"So you're writing some kind of 1960s *Our Town* set in Wilmette? The upper-middlebrows should go for that big-time." He's audibly relieved. "'One sweltering summer afternoon, as the cicadas chirped and heat lightning flashed over Lake Michigan, Chuck Levy and I stopped at Smithfield's grocery to buy some lemon drops for a nickel, and the moment I spotted that poster for Dr. King's speech on the village green, my life was changed forever.'"

I force a laugh. "Not exactly."

He's pissing me off, which feels good, because it makes me want to stop beating around the bush and tell him the truth about the truths I intend to tell. Or maybe he's baiting me, trying to provoke me into doing exactly that. I was a litigator. However, Alex's own knack for negotiation has helped him make several fortunes—not just producing movies but, earlier, in technology (video-editing software) and retail (two clothing store chains he cofounded and sold, One-Dimensional Man and, for women, S&O, which secretly stood for "stylish and overpriced"). Steady, girl.

This isn't the first time in a stressful, delicate human encounter when I've found myself thinking of the two flying lessons Chuck Levy gave me over Lake County when we were eighteen. *As you start your descent, think of the glide path and maintain a consistent approach to the runway.*

"It's about growing up, yes, being kids. Wilmette but also college, freshman year, all the craziness. *All* the craziness."

Too much speed is what messes up landings—you're going too fast, bring up the nose.

"And my life afterward." *Control your rate of descent.* "You know, the roads taken and not taken, there but for the grace of God, etcetera." *Keep lowering the flaps, but increase your power.* "Mistakes were made. And I'm writing about those. We don't need to keep the old secrets secret anymore." *You've touched down.*

The pause lasts so long that I start to think the call dropped or he's hung up. But now I hear him breathe, so I go on.

"I am not trying to lay off the blame on you or Chuck or Buzzy. We each did what we did. What happened, happened. It was 1968, for God's sake. We were eighteen, nineteen. I mean, it's not as if, you know . . ."

"Hollander? I'm afraid I'm losing the plot here."

"I'm not recording this call, Alex." Although I ought to be.

"I've no idea at all what you're talking about," he says. "None. Zero."

"You know *precisely* what I'm talking about."

"Easy-peasy, darling, don't get all . . . shirty. I haven't a *clue*, hon-

estly. I do sometimes have some *short*-term memory issues from the Topamax, which I take for the bipolar, but nothing long-term." I learned only recently, from *Vanity Fair*, that he was diagnosed ten years ago with bipolar disorder, which led to his investments in biotech. "'Dreams and fantasies,' you said, Hollander. I think maybe you're mixing up the real and the fantastical, sweetheart."

"Alex, stop it. Don't do this."

"Are you feeling all right? I think you could be a tad low. Maybe you need a fizzy drink or something? Test your blood?"

"*Don't.*"

"What? Of all people, *I* know how strange you can get. I've seen it. I'm just worried about you, Hollander."

"You're really going to play it this way, huh? Deny, stonewall, deny? Christ, Alex, I figured you might be freaked out by what I'm doing, but I never thought you'd do *this.*"

"You really are sounding a little barmy. If I didn't know your assistant was there with you, I'd be arranging to get you to hospital right now, calling Cedars-Sinai to send over the EMTs. You'll realize later I'm right. I love you. Go get some sweets. See a doctor."

"*Fuck you*, Alex."

I hang up the phone, open my top desk drawer, stick a test strip in the meter, prick a finger, squeeze out blood, watch the five-second countdown—98, absolutely normal—and slam the drawer shut.

8

During the year before the first Bond movie appeared, the world had come to seem even more like an Ian Fleming concoction—the resumption of nuclear weapons testing by the U.S. and USSR, the Soviet missiles in Cuba, the new hotline between the Kremlin and the White House, the defection to Moscow of the British intelligence agent Kim Philby, the British war minister caught having an affair with a nineteen-year-old who was also a Soviet spy's mistress.

Our Bond devotion had become even more elaborate. We performed half a dozen more missions. For one, Chuck mounted a little camera on his radio-controlled airplane—I hadn't realized how gigantic the thing was—and we flew it near the navy base by Highland Park, taking spy pictures.

And then came the movie *Dr. No*. Starting that summer, 1963, all the other kids suddenly knew about James Bond. Wendy Reichman owned the 45 of the *Dr. No* theme song before I did. At the Crawford twins' pool party, everyone said Susie Crawford's white two-piece suit made her look just like Ursula Andress as Honey Ryder, and

Jimmy Graham pretended his glass of 7-Up was a cocktail and introduced himself repeatedly as "Graham . . . *James* Graham."

Chuck and Alex and I didn't say so, but our private world of fictional violence and glamour paled pathetically in comparison to Hollywood's official version. The movie explosions in particular made Chuck yearn to blow up stuff. We had been a secret cell of cognoscenti performing a secret homage, taking actual risks out in the real world, inventing everything on the fly, scaring and surprising ourselves. Now all at once Bond was like a Barbie doll or a Disney-branded Davy Crockett coonskin hat, everywhere and available to everyone for a dollar. We no longer felt so knowing and subversive. We had been demoted to . . . fans.

Also, we knew we were getting too old to be doing this. When we'd discovered Bond, we were barely twelve, but in the summer of 1963 we were fourteen, headed for New Trier in the fall. Twelve-year-olds pretending to be spies and make-out artists was clearly a fictional conceit, but now that we were going to be in high school, racy behavior was supposed to be on the menu for real.

One night that summer, the three of us went bowling at the alley near my house. Alex and I were drinking Fresca—new, like everything that year. Including my romantic interest in Chuck, unleashed when he played the *Dr. No* theme song on his Stratocaster.

When I sat next to him on the bowling alley bench and our thighs touched, I wanted to believe he was excited, too.

I pretended not to know how to fill in the scorecard so that he would lean over me from behind, his chest against my shoulder, his warm right arm rubbing against my left as he wrote. Did he feel my goose bumps rising?

For no reason in particular, I suggested that on the next mission, I might be a man.

"No, no, no," Chuck said. "I mean, without a girl character, we might as well just play *army*." No self-respecting boy older than eleven, twelve max, would ever play army.

"We could invite another girl," I suggested.

"It's too late."

By which he meant that our club and its rules were too well established to assimilate an outsider, and that anyone our age was either too old to buy in to it or too uncool if they would.

Chuck's ball guttered. As he walked back toward me, I watched him rub his hands together, then rub them on his hips and his rear.

"Also?" he said to me. "*You've* got *blue eyes*. Almost all the female characters do."

Chuck Levy knew my eyes were blue!

"One of you guys could play a woman," I said. Maybe I was serious. Mostly, I was messing with them. "That's what actors did in Shakespeare's time."

This prospect amused Chuck. "Yeah, Mr. Fresca," Chuck said to Alex, "you could be Rosa Klebb." Uh-oh. "*Some Like It Bond.*" Alex had made the mistake of telling Chuck that *Some Like It Hot* was one of his favorite movies.

Chuck rolled again and got a spare. Even before he punched a fist in the air, the sight and violent sound of him knocking down all the pins made bowling more thrilling than it had ever been.

"Hey, *you're* the one who thinks the *Crawfords* are *gross*," Alex finally retorted. "You're the one who likes 'em *flat*."

Chuck scowled at Alex as he walked back, sat down, and penciled in his score. He was pissed. I was thrilled. (I was flat.)

The carnal tang of our Bond hobby was undoubtedly part of why we found reasons to put off the next mission for most of the summer. We were all busy. I had summer school in the mornings—touch typing and, as a sop to my mother for leaving the Church, advanced Esperanto—plus, I worked afternoons at my uncle's law firm in Evanston. Alex had youth theater and took two family vacations, to Toronto and Acapulco. Chuck mowed lawns almost every day.

One Saturday morning when Alex was in Canada, Chuck phoned.

"I'm going down to Evanston to see the first showing of *The Great Escape*. Want to come with?"

Finally. Not lunch in the cafeteria or an after-school snack at Bob's

with Chuck and Alex, or a study session at the library with Chuck and Alex, or watching TV with Chuck and Alex, or a mission. A *movie*. With *Chuck*. I grinned. I tingled.

"Sure!" I said, already imagining us making out, as I had imagined many, many times during the previous three months.

"Great."

Yes: *great*.

After the movie, Chuck and I wandered toward Northwestern. Being by myself with him—really by ourselves, outside school, outside Wilmette—made me nervous, which I attributed to his sudden, shocking maleness. I opened my purse and took out Dad's transistor radio, which I'd borrowed for the day to deal with exactly this one-on-one contingency. Music could fill the dead air.

But Chuck was talkative. The movie had made him jitter with boy-man excitement, the way he got after missions. "God," he said, "that was so *unbelievably* great, wasn't it? I think it's the best movie I've ever seen." The last best movie he'd ever seen, a year earlier on TV, was *Rebel Without a Cause*. He was grinning and breathing heavily. "And Steve McQueen *not* getting away at the end, back in the camp, back in the cooler with his baseball and glove! Man oh man. Can I have a cigarette?"

Chuck, who swam competitively, had been conscientious about smoking only on missions. A few months earlier, I would've teased him about this transgression. He leaned in toward me and I lit him, his hands cupped around mine to keep the flame from blowing out, his fingers touching my skin for three, four splendid, breathless seconds.

"Thanks," he said, smiling, then stepping back and taking a deep drag.

It was as if we had just made love. Ian Fleming had taught me that people smoke after having sex.

"I liked it a lot better than *Dr. No*," I said, "because it was actually funny and actually serious. Instead of never quite funny and never quite serious."

"Yes, right, that's exactly right, Karen."

Exactly right. And not Hollaender—*Karen*.

"That's a problem with Bond, you know?" he said. "Not just the movie but the books get so unbelievable. I mean, *this* was so cool because that actual story, *The Great Escape,* it really happened."

"Yeah. But SMERSH was real. MI6 and the KGB are real. Ian Fleming did intelligence and espionage."

"Yeah, twenty *years* ago, during the war. Everything about the Russians, he probably makes up. And SPECTRE? Come on. It's such phony baloney. Also? Every single mission Bond goes on, he gets caught by the villain."

That afternoon, two years into our worship of Bond, I found his heresy exciting. "Alex'd be going nuts if he were here," I said. "His 'Fiction can be truer than facts, you retards,' and all that."

"Yeah, well, he's not here, is he? And I'm not saying the missions haven't been fun."

Secrets from one another within our secret cabal, doctrinal fissures, Chuck entrusting me alone with his doubts. Thrilling. Almost too exquisitely thrilling. "I never really liked *Maverick,*" I said, "but he was great, James Garner." He'd played one of the POWs in the movie.

"He kind of reminds me of your dad. He's funny like that, and he knows German." Chuck took a last drag on his cigarette, and as he flexed his arm to flick it into the gutter, I noticed his biceps, lightly draped by his T-shirt sleeve, bulging. Had he always had such muscles? Could six weeks of pushing lawn mowers account for it? Chuck Levy had turned into Steve McQueen. "I wonder if his Nazi prison camp, your dad's, was like the one in the movie."

"With secret tunnels and guys sewing disguises? I don't think so. But he never talks about the specifics. The only thing he says is that it could've gone so much worse for him, that he was just unbelievably lucky."

After a pause, Chuck said, "You know, I don't care if your dad's Jewish or not—"

"He's not."

"—and you know that even if he was, *you* wouldn't be Jewish."

"What?" I snapped, realizing immediately I was upset that this new information somehow may have reduced my chances of living happily ever after with Chuck Levy.

"It goes through mothers, Jewishness. God, I would *love* to have a motorcycle." He held his fists out on the invisible handlebars. He was imagining himself as McQueen, racing across the Bavarian fields, jumping a barbed-wire fence ahead of Nazi pursuers. I watched his muscles again as he throttled and swerved.

I swooned.

Just as quickly, he deflated and turned back into a fourteen-year-old boy in the suburbs, loping into the university where his father was an engineering professor. "My goddamn parents would kill me if I even *rode* one."

After a little while, I asked, "Do you think you could kill people?"

"What, you mean like in the movie, Nazis, in the war? Sure. Yeah, absolutely. Couldn't you?"

"Maybe. If I was convinced it was good versus evil. But even then, jeez, you don't necessarily have the big picture."

"What, you're worried about your whole 'unintended consequences' thing?" I'd written a short story in which the teenage American heroine travels back in time to 1929 to seduce and assassinate Hitler, but when she returns to 1963, she finds her family imprisoned in a Soviet gulag in Montana—because she had killed Hitler and prevented World War II, she had also enabled the Soviet Union to develop more quickly, create the first atomic bomb, and then defeat the U.S. in a war in the 1950s and take over the world.

"You can't overthink everything," Chuck said, "'on the one hand, it might turn out this way, and on the other hand, it could turn out that way.' Sometimes you have to take a stand and act, do the thing that feels right."

"Yeah. Like the monk in Saigon." I'd been galvanized by the newspaper picture of a Buddhist monk sitting on a street in flames. He had doused himself in gasoline and lit a match to protest the treatment of Buddhists by the Catholic regime in South Vietnam.

"No, not like the monk, like the Jews in Warsaw in World War II.

Like your dad. *Fight* the bad guys. Damn the consequences. You know?"

"Yeah . . ."

Do the thing that feels right. I was no longer thinking of political morality and armed resistance.

Damn the consequences. Hold my hand. Touch me. Be my boyfriend, Chuck Levy.

". . . I guess."

"So you want to go to the library and hang out? It's pretty cool, and it's open until six, I've got my dad's pass."

Back then, "hang out" and "cool" were real signifiers, fresh and meaningful, not yet unremarkable Americanisms used by squares and adults. So was a middle-class teenage boy wearing blue jeans and a T-shirt in public. So was carrying my transistor radio tuned to WLS, listening to its tiny speaker play Little Stevie Wonder as we walked, just the two of us, toward an old ivy-covered stone building across a hot, fragrant, freshly mowed campus green.

The library was almost empty. It was like a dream cathedral, with arches and leaded glass windows and a black-and-white checker-board floor but books instead of figures of Jesus and Mary and the saints, a card catalog with hundreds of drawers in place of an altar. We wandered without any plan, sometimes together—was this *his* plan? to kiss me in the dim deserted stacks?—but mostly alone, our heads cocked as we examined spines on shelves, squatting as we looked at journals and obscure magazines, sitting in carrels, leaning in doorways, skimming this and that, ricocheting from room to room, returning to the card catalog every so often before venturing off on some new search that caught our fancies, one accidental discovery leading to another.

I'd always liked libraries, but *this*—my God, this treasure house wasn't nice and handy like the (new, nice, beige, bland) Wilmette Public Library. It was old and vast and dark and a little scary, like Lake Michigan the first time I swam away from shore. Here was *everything*, all information and knowledge, an infinitude of print, things I'd heard about but never seen, things whose existence I'd

only inferred or suspected, things of which I'd been entirely ignorant. I'd moved over to the adults' table, and I was not so much
feasting as nibbling from every dish and platter, and no one was telling me to stop or go away. I was in paradise.

I lost track of time, but I also knew time was short. Because I
couldn't check anything out, and I didn't know when, if ever, I'd
return, I became more frenzied as the afternoon passed. It felt like a
quest.

The Miracle Worker had been one of my favorite movies last year,
so I found a biography of Helen Keller in which I learned that she'd
been a pacifist and a socialist (no wonder my mother named baby
Helen Helen). Then on to discovering the *Readers' Guide to Periodical
Literature* and *Current Biography*, which I loved, because unlike regular reference books, these combined the important, like U Thant,
with the frivolous, like Patty Duke, from *The Miracle Worker*. I discovered she was not even three years older than I was, that she was
about to star in her own TV show, and that she'd recently met Bri-
gitte Bardot in Paris.

I found an article about Bardot and read about her new movie,
Contempt, directed by Jean-Luc Godard. I looked up Godard—my
first time reading microfilm, which felt very grown-up and modern.
Breathless sounded wonderful, especially its documentary footage
of Parisian crowds cheering the actual President Charles de Gaulle.

From there I found a recent issue of the French magazine *Paris
Match* and made out the gist of a two-page spread about all the attempts on de Gaulle's life. I'd heard on the news about the machine-
gun ambush of his limousine outside Paris, but I had no idea that
assassins had also planted four kilos of plastique near his Citroën,
dispatched a sniper to shoot him in Athens with a gun rigged as a
camera, and plotted to sprinkle poison on the hosts at the church
near his country house where he took Holy Communion. *So* James
Bond!

As soon as I spotted an issue of *Evergreen Review*—with its hand-
lettered cover lines, its antiwar poem by Allen Ginsberg, its anti-
heroin essay by William Burroughs, its Jack Kerouac short story—

I knew I'd found a portal directly into the bohemian world I'd been reading about second- and thirdhand in *Newsweek* and *MAD*. Another issue had a cover photograph of a torn, dirty campaign poster of President Kennedy's face; another had an article about the legal case over the American publication of *Tropic of Cancer*. I'd heard of the novel from Alex, whose older brother said it was the dirtiest book ever published.

"Dear?" A librarian had crept up and startled me. "It's after five-thirty," she whispered. "The library will be closing soon."

I put back the magazines, rushed to the card catalog, found *Miller, Henry,* and made my way into the stacks on the third floor. The book was on a special shelf, inside a locked steel mesh cage. Back at the card catalog, I found a listing for an academic book (*Miller's* Tropic of Cancer: *A Critical Appraisal*), returned to the stacks and, *yes,* there it was, out in the open. And filled, conveniently, with excerpts of some of the most outrageous passages. " 'I am fucking you, Tania, so that you'll stay fucked. And if you're afraid of being fucked publicly I will fuck you privately.' " And " 'There's my Danish cunt,' he grunts. 'See that ass? Danish. How that woman loves it. She just begs me for it.' " And from a *female* character: " 'He kept begging me always to fuck him.' " And my favorite, maybe because of its recapitulation of what Chuck had said to me a few hours earlier about killing Nazis: " 'Fuck your two ways of looking at things! Fuck your pluralistic universe . . .' " My life was imitating art! Anticipating art!

I took a deep breath and stuck the book in the elastic waistband of my skirt, pulled my blouse over it, and walked past the guard out of the building. And then stopped.

A few paces in front of me, Chuck was lying on the grass, staring up at the sky, his hands behind his head. Why do boys and men do that but not women?

Between his jeans and T-shirt, two inches of flesh was exposed. I stopped and beheld. I stared at his navel, let my eyes examine certain denim creases and seams and shadows as I never had before.

What if he happened to glance back and see me ogling? I crammed the stolen book into my purse and ran to him. "Sorry."

"That's okay. I figured you'd come eventually." He stood, brushing bits of grass out of his beautiful dark hair and off his gorgeous, tanned arms. "I was looking at college catalogs and stuff." We were still days away from being high school freshmen, but it was *New Trier;* college was already on our minds. "Stanford? Is an hour from the ocean." Chuck was desperate to become a surfer. "And did you know that at the Air Force Academy, they *pay you* to go to college?"

I wasn't sure I knew there was an Air Force Academy. "Really?"

"Completely free college in the Rocky Mountains, plus a *thousand bucks* a year! And when you get out, you're a lieutenant. You think Alex could get his old man to ask Senator Douglas to nominate me? That's how you get in."

"Because of *The Great Escape*"—Steve McQueen and most of the other POWs were fliers—"you want to join the air force?" I was surprised, but I worried that I sounded snippy. My old comrades-in-arms manner hadn't been fully updated to jibe with my new feelings for Chuck. Rushing to seem interested in this air force idea, I made things worse. "I thought you said the military is full of homosexuals."

He looked at me. "The navy, I said, and I was just quoting my dad. Imagine being a *jet fighter pilot* for real."

"It'd be nerve-racking. It's incredibly sweaty in the hot little cockpits." Desperate to seem engaged and knowledgeable, I was drawing on my combat aviation research from half an hour before, the Ginsberg poem in *Evergreen Review: The bombers jet through the sky in unison of twelve / the pilots are sweating and nervous at the controls in the hot / cabins.* I very much wished I hadn't said "hot little cockpits." "I found this interesting article about all these different assassination attempts on Charles de Gaulle. By this secret group of French soldiers against Algerian independence. They had a kamikaze who was supposed to crash his plane into de Gaulle's helicopter as it took off. But because the French security had all these decoy helicopters, the guy didn't know which one to go for."

"Sounds like *From Russia with Love*."

We had arrived at the bus stop and sat on the bench, just us. Service was infrequent.

This would be the moment for him to take my hand.

He didn't. I took out the radio and turned it on. "Puff (The Magic Dragon)" was playing.

"So what else did you find?" I asked Chuck. "In the library?"

"There's no statute of limitations for murder."

"I think I knew that."

"All the new elements that have been discovered since we've been alive, like a dozen? Every single one because of the atom bomb."

"Huh."

"In New Jersey you can marry your first cousin—and it's legal to have sex there at thirteen."

"Huh," I said again. A random fact or a deliberate conversational turn? Should I chuckle? It seemed like an opportunity, but I was too stunned to take advantage.

And then the opening closed, because Chuck shot up off the bench and out to the curb to peer down Green Bay Road, as if for the bus. If we'd biked, we'd be home by now, but this was the summer that riding a bicycle had come to seem to me both unfeminine and uncool.

"Something else I discovered," he said when he sat back down, "you know how the Pledge of Allegiance says 'one nation *under God*'? The Catholics convinced the president and Congress to stick that in when we were in kindergarten. I assumed it was *always* there."

"Wow, that's like what Mr. Fortini says about the dictionary— the people in charge change things, and then before you know it, everyone forgets and assumes that's normal, the way it's been forever."

Chuck pulled his damp T-shirt from his chest with two fingers and pumped it like a bellows to cool off. It was the sexiest thing I had ever seen in real life.

"Can I have another smoke?" he asked, and I was so nervous that

I bobbled the cigarette. This time I handed him the matches to light himself.

I recognized the next song on WLS as soon as I heard the opening drum line—*bass, bass-bass, snare . . .*

> *Oh, since the day I saw you*
> *I have been waiting for you*

"I'm really not a homo, you know," Chuck said.

I know, I know. "I didn't think so."

> *You know I will adore you*
> *Till eternity so won't you please*

"Good. Thanks."

"Me, neither," I said, trying to keep things light as I engaged in the most intimate conversation I'd ever had with any boy, let alone— Jesus God—*Chuck.* "A lesbian, I mean."

He chuckled and nodded. I took that as a good sign. Then he turned to look right at me. "Alex says because I think some of the girls who aren't as developed are the prettiest ones that I could be. A homo."

"That's stupid," I said as I thought of one of Henry Miller's lines: *"He kept begging me always to fuck him."*

> *So come on and be*
> *Be my, be my, be my little baby*
> *My one and only*
> *say you'll be my darling*
> *Be my, be my, be my baby now.*

"Plus," I continued, "I wouldn't take Alex's word. For that."

He nodded again and, fortunately, didn't ask, *What do you mean?* "You know, at the Air Force Academy?" He was changing the subject.

I could breathe again. I nodded, and he continued.

"They have this really simple, really serious honor code that the cadets all swear to: 'We will not lie, steal, or cheat, nor tolerate among us anyone who does.' I was thinking we should make that *our* honor code."

Oh, God, God, *God.* My face flushed. Since I hadn't yet sworn the oath, maybe the stolen copy of *Miller's* Tropic of Cancer: *A Critical Appraisal* in my bag didn't count as a violation. "An oath . . . between . . . you and me?"

"All three of us, I mean."

Crap, crap, *crap.* I'd overreached. "Oh. Sure."

"We should start planning a new mission. A great big one. To do before school starts. Because once we're at New Trier . . ."

"We'll be busy. Homework, activities, everything."

That wasn't what he meant. He meant performing Bond missions would be conduct unbecoming a high school freshman. "Yeah," he said, "that, too."

I know I've insisted I don't like how memory and history are automatically sugarcoated and shrink-wrapped in generic pop nostalgia, but the following moment was what it was: as the Wilmette bus finally arrived and stopped, its air brakes making that mechanical-dinosaur sigh, Ronnie Spector sang her last *Be my little baby* and segued to her final, fading *oh-oh-oh-oh, whoa-whoa-whoa-whoa* ululation.

When we got to my house, our parting was a little more awkward than usual, which I interpreted, hopefully, as a good sign.

After dinner, Peter retreated to his room to work on his mail-order model rockets. Sabrina and her friend with cystic fibrosis, who was sleeping over, went out to the backyard to whack croquet balls and catch fireflies. I sat down on the rug in the TV room to watch *Saturday Night at the Movies* with my parents. It was *The Sun Also Rises.*

During the first commercial, after I said I'd thought this was the one about the Spanish Civil War and my dad said that was *For Whom the Bell Tolls,* he told me about his friend Einar who, the day after

they'd finished their high school exit exams in Copenhagen, enlisted to go fight in Spain and had been shot dead by the fascists before the end of the summer, at eighteen.

"There but for the grace of God," my mother said.

"There but for my lack of balls," my father replied.

"*Nils,*" my mother scolded.

I didn't ask exactly how his war experience made Jake Barnes unable to have sex, even though I knew the question would've made Dad chuckle. I also silently noted that Ava Gardner was sort of flat-chested.

"I think I'm gonna go to bed and read," I announced at the next commercial. Curiosity followed me out of the basement and up to my room and jumped up on the bed. He snuggled in next to me, as usual, laying his head on my leg. I started the book at the beginning, the preface first, then the introduction, then chapter one. I really was interested in the novel, in Miller's intentions, in its fraught publishing history, in its influence on postwar writers, the full scholarly and critical appraisal.

But soon I was skipping pages, searching for the good parts. And then I was reading certain quoted sentences again and again. "He bent down and kissed her breasts, and after he had kissed them fervidly, he stuffed them back into her corsage." I'd never encountered that meaning of "corsage." "She commenced rubbing her pussy affectionately, stroking it with her two hands, caressing it, patting it, patting it." I'd never read the word "pussy" in the anatomical sense.

Before long I was rubbing myself affectionately, stroking with just one hand, caressing, caressing, thinking of Chuck Levy's muscular arms and tanned belly and sweaty chest.

Curiosity stood up on the end of the bed and looked at me with his head tilted to the side. *What?* he seemed to be saying. *You okay? What?*

I'd not had a lot of orgasms before that night—even by myself, I played slightly hard to get—and I had never had one so violent or transporting. I felt like smoking a cigarette.

9

I'VE GOT CHANNELS on my cable TV that show pornographic movies. I've watched a couple and both times felt an odd emotional alloy, bemusement plus sadness, a cousin to what I felt when I visited Disneyland with Waverly and attended a Sunday service with my assistant at her megachurch in Garden Grove, a sense that Americans are adorable and ridiculous, both overliteral and desperate to immerse in fantasy.

One of my UCLA colleagues, a woman, has a client in Estonia who wants to distribute child pornography that he's produced without using any child actors—the videos are entirely computer-generated. Digital animation is apparently moving beyond what they call the "uncanny valley," where animated human characters look more real than regular cartoons but not quite fully human, either—eerie, unsettling, uncanny.

As junior high schoolers, I've come to think, Alex and Chuck and I were living through something like our own uncanny-valley phenomenon. No longer children, not yet young adults but enacting travesties of adulthood—adults who lie and betray and kill and make love lovelessly—I think we became a little eerie and unsettling

to ourselves. This is part of what most adolescents feel, I suppose, being neither one thing nor the other, pretending to be a butterfly and feeling like a caterpillar, chrysalids alternating between narcissism and self-loathing, stuck for a few years in a beautiful and monstrous pupal stage.

Yet when children *finally* become adults, they don't feel as if they've achieved paradise. I think it's a problem with all utopias. For instance, my searches and discoveries these days online are never as delightful as they were that blissful afternoon ranging through Northwestern's library. And not just because I'm no longer fourteen years old. Except in fairy tales and religious visions, perfect and permanent bliss never arrives all at once. Plus, awesomeness has a half-life. You grow accustomed to every new marvel and miracle. You forget that a visit to a great library was once precious and astounding. You forget that you didn't see color TV until you were fifteen or a cellphone until you were forty, that the murder rate in New York City was four times as high when you arrived than when you moved away. And you forget that it was once cool to say "cool" and wear blue jeans, that "under God" wasn't always part of the Pledge of Allegiance.

We forget.

Could Alex really and truly have forgotten what happened, what we did way back when? It's possible. Certainly a defense lawyer could claim post-traumatic stress disorder.

Ladies and gentlemen of the jury, you have heard uncontradicted testimony that the events of 1968 were traumatically stressful for Mr. Macallister.

No objection, Your Honor.

According to the psychiatric profession's authoritative guide to mental disorders, the Diagnostic and Statistical Manual, *a person suffering from PTSD, quote, "commonly makes deliberate efforts to avoid certain thoughts, feelings, or conversations about the traumatic*

event and to avoid activities, situations, or people who arouse recol-
lections of it." And indeed, you have heard testimony from Ms. Hol-
lander that Mr. Macallister has compulsively avoided her, his former
best friend, even though they now live nearby one another.

In 1981 he phoned me to discuss a movie he wanted to make
about a former Black Panther, and at our college reunion in 1996,
we chatted at length about a panel discussion of the mob-bullying
that passed for campus protest in the late '60s. And collecting celebrated car-bomb cars? That sounds to me like a deliberate effort to
arouse and commemorate certain traumatic thoughts and feelings,
not avoid them.

Ladies and gentlemen of the jury, I call your attention to Criterion C3
for PTSD in the Diagnostic and Statistical Manual: *"This avoid-*
ance of reminders may include amnesia for an important aspect of
the traumatic event." And indeed, there has been no testimony and
no evidence that at any moment during the last four decades has Mr.
Macallister recalled any of the alleged actions or events in question.

Yes, we did weirdly steer clear of the subject for the last three
years of college, all of us more or less pretending it hadn't happened, ignoring the elephant in the room, the monster in the box.
But I do remember a conversation about it with Alex, one night just
before we graduated, when he started sobbing.

Spontaneous crying: evidence of acute traumatic stress. But that was
forty-three long years ago—and since then, nothing, no mention, not
even a glancing reference. Once again, members of the jury, I quote from
the Diagnostic and Statistical Manual: *"There may be a delay of*
years, before symptoms appear." And those symptoms, I remind you,
"may include amnesia for an important aspect of the traumatic event."

Maybe. But I don't think so. Alex Macallister, I believe, is pulling
a Hugo Drax on me—Drax the *Moonraker* villain who pretends to

suffer from amnesia about the political crimes of his youth. I know
PTSD is real, and I know amnesia exists outside fiction. However, I
also know a bogus psychiatric defense argument when I hear one,
because I made them myself a few times in court.

Maybe Alex's forgetting is more recent. Maybe he has moved beyond NARF (normal age-related forgetfulness) to severe AAMI
(age-associated memory impairment) or SDAT (senile dementia of
the Alzheimer type). He's going on sixty-six. But even after my dad
had wandered off into the Alzheimer's wilderness, imagining my
mother was his mother and calling the car "the rhino," his recollections of the distant past remained crackerjack. I was visiting them in
Wilmette in 1994 when a Danish TV crew came to interview him
about the Nazi occupation and resistance for a fiftieth-anniversary-
of-the-end-of-the-war documentary. The filmmaker told me that
my seventy-four-year-old dad's Danish was impeccable, as was his
ability to recall names and dates from the 1940s.

I don't think dementia has wiped away Alex's memories of the
demented thing we did in 1968.

When I ran into him at a political fund-raiser in Pacific Palisades,
right after I'd arrived in L.A., he went on and on about his biotech
investments. He talked about "the incredible breakthroughs my
boffins are making" in cosmetic neurology, such as a drug called
"ZIP," zeta inhibitory peptides, that Alex said could be used to "edit"
and "optimize" memory. "From now on, Hollander," he said as we
stood with our goblets of wine watching the sun dip into the Pacific, "it's all about SENS." He waited for me to ask what SENS
means, and when I did, he smiled and answered with the combination of excitement and irony that has been his default affect forever:
"Strategies for engineered negligible senescence." A pause. "It's the
end of aging." I smiled but said nothing. I think he probably knew
what I was thinking: *Bond villain.*

Is it possible that Alex has somehow ZIP'd away his inconvenient
memories of the 1960s? Could an insistent billionaire financial
backer convince his eager biotechnologists to go for broke and test
zeta inhibitory peptides on *him,* to edit and optimize *his* memory?

At this end of this century, outside of the movies—*Eternal Sunshine of the Spotless Bourne Quantum of Solace?*—I'm betting not.

I think Alex isn't suffering from PTSD or dementia and hasn't rewired his hippocampus with an experimental miracle drug. I think he's simply engaging in a regular old-fashioned human habit. I think he's lying.

Thus my desire for corroborating evidence has intensified. During the last month, since I spoke to Alex, I've received form-letter acknowledgments of my Freedom of Information requests from all the relevant federal agencies, but not yet any actual answers. The agencies may eventually tell me they can find no records, and that may be true. Or they could give me what's called a "Glomar response," a phrase coined in the 1970s after the CIA refused to say whether the agency did or didn't have certain records about a secret ship called the *Glomar Explorer.* Or they could admit they've got files but decline to give me copies. I could appeal such a denial. And then they could leave me in limbo, trying to wait me out. A UCLA colleague who knows all about the Freedom of Information labyrinth tells me there are national security appeals that have been pending for nineteen years.

Yesterday I realized that the problem, if there's a problem, might just be bureaucratic confusion, stupid but not malign. So this morning I resubmitted all the requests for my files using the original spelling of my last name, the way I spelled it when I was a kid—not Hollander but Hollænder, with the smushed-together *a* and *e,* how they did it in Old English and still do it in Scandinavian languages. My father's one unbudging point of ethnic pride was insisting on the Danish spelling. "Tell them," he instructed us as kids, "it's our *brand* name, as in *Encyclopædia,* like that sign on Wilmette." Encyclopædia Britannica Films had its headquarters on Wilmette Avenue. Sophomore year in college, when I started doing my best to seem as standard as possible, I became Hollander, simplified and Americanized and unproblematic.

I'm not sure I'd have gotten to the point of doing what I'm doing now—reassembling the skeleton in my closet, then putting it on

display—if I hadn't been living alone the last seven years. I spent the first fifty-seven years of my life sharing houses and apartments with other people. It turns out that parents and brothers and sisters and roommates and spouses and children in close proximity occupy a giant swath of consciousness. Mine, anyhow. Living with other people, especially people I love or wish I could love, is like having music on in the background, several different songs at once, all the time. It's not that I entirely blocked out thoughts of my youth. No, I've revisited certain unforgettable moments obsessively. But "obsessive" is the key word, the way some people with OCD touch a particular object or spot on their bodies in the same special way, over and over for years, to no constructive end. I've spent all these decades touching, touching, touching, touching, touching my memories of a few vivid moments, each time with the same quick ritualized private gesture of regret and (if such a thing is possible) retroactive dread. Until I lived by myself in this very comfortable solitary confinement of Wonderland Park Avenue, I didn't stop and open those memories and try to think about each of them deeply. They were like computer-screen icons for old files that I repeatedly, ruefully glanced at with a sigh and never dared click open.

Living alone has also made me much, much more conscious of inconsequential things, the sweet banalities of a day in a life. I feel now as if I spent most of my previous time on earth in a state of perpetually frenzied obliviousness, intent on executing all the Important Tasks at Hand. The test to take. The application to finish. The man to marry. The job to get, the brief to write, the motion to file, the verdict to appeal, the meeting to schedule, the PowerPoint to prepare. The apartment to buy, the meals to organize, the two miles to run, the sex to have, the kids to get to school and playdates and doctors and volleyball games and SAT tutors and colleges. The marriage to end. The books to write. I was always good at screening out the noise and focusing exclusively on the signal, which made me successful in school and at work and (more or less) as a parent. Until I lived alone, I was not so good at understanding—really understanding, beyond the obligatory modern lip service to smelling the

roses and living in the moment—that the extraneous noise can be lovely. The Buddhists call it mindfulness, a word I sort of hate but an MO I've come to believe in.

Such as right now, when I put the half-full quart of grapefruit juice back on the refrigerator shelf hastily, and watch the sloshing make the carton swivel and teeter before it rights itself, like a wobbly drunk almost falling and then too firmly planting his feet to stand *perfectly* still. We deprive ourselves if we ignore all the tiny, inconsequential bits and pieces, the flotsam and jetsam of life. Quarks and neutrinos and atoms and molecules, the earth, asteroids, stars, the shaft of light angling through the kitchen window right this second, illuminating the slow-motion Dance of Ten Thousand Dust Motes: isn't it *all* flotsam and jetsam?

The phone's ringing.

"Why—why are you there?"

"Greta?" My daughter, Waverly's mother.

"*Why* are you still at *home*?"

"Because it's seven-twenty A.M. and the drive to campus is only twenty-five minutes even with the construction on Laurel Canyon Boulevard."

"Right."

She does this regularly, forgets the three-hour time difference. I think it's partly because she's felt abandoned since I moved across the country, and partly because she's got a lot of things to juggle and lives her New York life in a state of somewhat frenzied obliviousness.

"What's up?"

"Just calling."

Ordinarily, she "just calls" at bedtime.

"I saw your ice storm on TV over the weekend," I say. "I cannot tell you how happy I am to be in my post-blizzard stage of life. And I won't tell you what the temperature is here."

"Thanks."

"Seventy-two. How's Wavy?"

"Did you tell her that Jungo's NGO is 'total crap'? That's what she told him you said."

"I didn't say that." My son-in-law, Jungo Dixit, an MBA and management consultant who earns his living as a coach for business executives—using what he told me is "a proprietary cross-disciplinary approach to positioning and strategic communications for C-level executives seeking to optimize performance and visibility"—has started an organization called Life Coaches Without Borders. Life Coaches Without Borders sends people like him to places like Haiti and Libya and Myanmar to advise people, pro bono, how to get their lives on track. "I just told her I was surprised Axl Rose was one of his big funders. I may have rolled my eyes."

"She also says you told her it's cool to say 'fuck' whenever she wants."

"No, I said she didn't have to worry about watching her language around me. That's all." Jesus fucking Christ. "Is this why you called?"

"No, I called to see how you are. What's new? How do you *feel*?"

"I'm fine. I'm great, in fact."

The pause that follows goes on a beat too long.

"You know," Greta says, "you're almost sixty-five, and Morfar wasn't that much older when he started becoming impaired." Morfar, Danish for "grandpa," is what all his grandchildren called my dad. Greta and her brother, Seth, loved it because it made him seem like a character from *The Lord of the Rings*. "And *he* didn't have to remember to test his blood and administer injections."

"Thanks for the reminder, but don't worry. My memory is *superb*—in fact, writing this book, I find I'm remembering more and more stuff all the time. I'm fine. Really."

There is a long silence, followed by what I take for grudging capitulation: "Okay. I love you."

When the phone rings again fifteen minutes later, I'm in the garage, plugging in my car, which I seem to have forgotten to do last night.

The caller ID tells me it's from DIXIT-WU: Greta again. "What?" I answer.

"Are you okay? Why are you out of breath?"

"Because I just ran like hell up here to answer the phone."

"Do you have a minute?"

I sit down. I've got no appointments this morning. "Sure." I won-der if this is going to be another anxious discussion about Waverly's interest in a career as an actress and her general bohemianism. Last week she and Hunter were caught Dumpster-diving at a Whole Foods on Houston Street, having filled three shopping bags with overripe tomatillos, two-day-old sushi rolls, stale focaccia, and cacao-dusted chocolate-covered goji berries that had melted to-gether. The cops let them go, and the kids took the food to a home-less shelter.

"I just wanted to make sure you feel okay. Because now that I'm not drinking, I feel so much clearer. About everything. And so much more willing to look at the truth squarely. Even when it's painful."

Greta gave up booze two years ago, right after her father died. I was on her Twelve Step list of people who had been "harmed" by her alcoholism (Step 8). She flew from New York out to Los Angeles to "make amends" to me (Step 9) in person. Until then I had been unaware that she'd considered her nightly cocktail and two glasses of wine problematic. I always figured our telephone bickering and her long silences and occasional dudgeons were just one of those irremediable mother-daughter things.

"Then we're in complete sync, honey. What I'm writing, the memoir, is exactly that. Lots of painful truth."

"Okay."

"You don't sound convinced. I'm fine, totally fine. Tip-top, handy-dandy. Why did you call back?" Maybe she wants to tell me she's realized in her crystal-clear sobriety that she finds Jungo insuffer-able.

"We'll talk more when you're here."

"In *March*?" I ask. Spring break is a month away.

"I was just wondering if . . . maybe you'll let me read some of it. The book."

Aha, now I get it: this kid is worried that I'm spilling unlovely se-crets about my marriage to her father and our family's private life. "Sure, maybe, some of it, if you'd like. But now I'm late, I haven't

packed, really gotta get going, flying to D.C. this afternoon. Sarah's big anniversary shindig."

Among other important engagements in Washington. My friend the senior national security and intelligence-community apparatchik has agreed to meet with me.

10

I RECENTLY FOUND THE numbered list of Reasons for Loving Summer that I made the summer after I turned ten. I can date it precisely because it's crayoned on a mimeographed church hymn sheet in copper, a color that didn't exist until Crayola inaugurated the sixty-four-crayon box with the built-in sharpener, which I got for my tenth birthday. That gift is my earliest memory of intense ambivalence, because I was just barely too old for crayons. When I abandoned them at the end of that summer, ceremoniously presenting the box to the little kids as "a permanent lend," I delivered a speech about how lucky they were, how much more austere my childhood had been than theirs—no TV in the house until I was eight, a bedroom shared with Sabrina until we moved to Schiller Avenue, no record player of my own and no Barbie or Hula-Hoop at all.

When I became an actual adult, and Greta at age thirteen accused me of being "some kind of Amish yuppie" because I refused to buy her aerosol Silly String or let her dress like Madonna, I laughed and congratulated her on the turn of phrase, which naturally made her all the angrier. Like Danish father, like American daughter.

Among all my Reasons for Loving Summer at age ten—School Out, Longer Nights, Fireflies, Insect Sounds, Playing Frisbee, Going Barefoot, Swimming at Centennial Park, Eating Dinner Outside, Driving to Get Ice Cream—only two were not generic: More Luck Happens and Being with Violet. I rarely saw Violet, our cleaning lady, during the school year because she arrived at our house in the mornings after I went to school and left before I came home. Her presence during the summer—rather, my presence as she cleaned our floors and dusted our furniture—made the summers distinct, more fun and interesting, and somehow *summerier.*

Until I became a beatnik, I wore pigtail braids, and first thing every Monday and Thursday morning in the summers, I sat on a red stool in the kitchen so Violet could braid my hair. She did them tighter than my mother, so tight they hurt a little the first hour or so, but I felt improved by the rigor, and loved the feeling of her rough fingers on my neck and head, and never complained.

On summer Mondays, I'd sit on the big lint-covered cushion in the corner of the laundry room and draw or read as she washed and dried and folded our clothes and answered my occasional questions about her sons, and her husband who disappeared after the war. ("Disappeared like—like a *ghost?*" I asked at age six, embarrassing myself.) Down there in the basement on one of my parents' ancient radios, she listened to horse races from Arlington Park and to what she called her "hillbilly songs." My mother disapproved of both horse racing and country-and-western music, which made those times with Violet all the more delicious.

For lunch she'd make us waffles covered in bacon and Cheez Whiz, and lemonade. She always let me stir the mayonnaise into her potato salad ("the Hellmann's," she called it, as if it were beurre blanc, to distinguish it from the Miracle Whip in her own kitchen), which she always made on Thursday afternoons for our Friday picnic-table dinners in the backyard.

When I was ten, she told me the reason her hours were nine A.M. to three P.M. was because it took her almost two hours to travel to and from Chicago each way. I thought she was joshing, and when

she assured me she wasn't, I felt terrible. I'd never known about her long commute, and I blurted that she should quit and get a job closer to where she lived. "And never see my Kay-Ray again?" she said, kissing me on my forehead the way she always did. "Uh-*uh*." I believe the one day she ever missed work was after her daughter-in-law was murdered.

The only complaints I heard from her were about her inability to afford bets on the Arlington Park horses she picked every day, and how "they always take away my music"—by which she meant WLS changing from country to rock and roll. She never complained about her asthma, either, and when she got a modern inhaler that replaced her old-fashioned squeeze-bulb gizmo, she told me that it made her believe in progress.

Violet was the only black person with whom I'd ever spoken until I was almost in high school.

The week before I started at New Trier, early on the last Thursday of the summer of 1963, I was lying in the hammock on the back porch reading *On Her Majesty's Secret Service*. I shook my head and harrumphed when I read M praising the Swiss because they "cope with the beatnik problem." No wonder the book begins with Bond wanting to resign from MI6.

"For a girl all done with her summer school, Kay-Ray is up bright and early."

"Hi, Violet! It was too hot to sleep. I was sweating like a pig up there."

"*Perspiring* like a pig. Where your mom and the kids at?"

"Choir practice and the allergist."

"Which dress you plan on wearing at work this afternoon? I'll be putting a load in the machine after I finish these." She gripped a paper sack of potatoes in one hand and a big yellow Pyrex bowl full of water in the other.

"Yesterday was my last day. They closed Scattergood O'Donnell and went up to Uncle—my uncle . . . He and his law partner and their families went up to Tom's place in Wisconsin for the long weekend, to their, you know, the lake house there." My mother's

brother, for whose law firm I'd worked part-time, was named Thomas Scattergood, and I'd suddenly realized I did not want to say "Uncle Tom's cabin" to Violet.

She sat down on the bench, emptied the potatoes into her lap, and started to peel them into the empty sack.

I kept reading, although I wanted to discuss civil rights with Violet. My earliest memory is my mother standing and crying as she listened to a live radio report about thousands of white people down in Cicero rioting outside an apartment building into which one Negro family had moved. And for the last few years I'd read news articles and watched the TV reports about Negroes fighting white Southerners to end segregation. Back in fifth grade, after the Negro college students' sit-ins at a segregated Woolworth's lunch counter in Uncle Ralph and Aunt Gaby's town in North Carolina, I'd suggested to my mother and Violet that *we* all go to *our* Woolworth's lunch counter in Wilmette, at the Edens Plaza shopping center. Mom thought it was a grand notion, but Violet quietly, firmly refused to play along, which mystified and mortified me.

So as the civil rights movement burgeoned, I didn't talk about it much, because the one colored person I knew had swatted me away when I'd butted in. Nor did it help that my mother and dad were such total bleeding-heart liberals, so proud to be members of the NAACP and sign open-housing petitions and attend vigils for racial justice. With Pope John's death that summer, Martin Luther King, Jr., had ascended to first place in my mother's pantheon of living saints. At fourteen, I wasn't looking for new ways to *agree* with my parents.

But during that summer of 1963, the "civil rights movement" turned into the "Negro revolution," and I was devouring the coverage. I now felt connected to great events, no longer a child reading stories—I was working in a law firm, and the Negro murdered in Mississippi had been an NAACP lawyer. The first Negro to attend the University of Alabama appeared on *Newsweek*'s cover, a girl not much older than I was. On the news one night, as my family watched the Birmingham police set snarling German shepherds on protest-

ers and then blast the Negroes with fire hoses, my father shook his head, and I saw that my mother was crying when she went to get dinner ready. I found myself performing a charade of sadness that night, feeling not depressed or disturbed, not like I'd witnessed a tragedy, not a bit, but awestruck to be seeing history firsthand, as it happened, absolutely thrilled to watch kids my age—kids Sabrina's and Peter's ages!—jumping over the walls of the schools where they'd been locked down, actually *rebelling*. And getting hosed and beaten, paying the price for their rebellion on national TV. I had never seen anything so dramatic in real life.

And now, in late August, there was the large event of the day before. I decided it would be rude not to broach the subject. I would have my first real conversation about the Negro question with a Negro. I closed my Bond book.

"Violet? What'd you think of the march on Washington?"

"Haven't read my paper yet today."

"But it was on TV! Live! Mom and I and the little kids all watched."

"Didn't see it. The Stuarts"—the family in Highland Park for whom she worked two days a week—"won't have no TV or radio on in the house during the day. And by the time I got home, *Huntley-Brinkley* already talked about it, I guess." She was peeling, not looking at me. "They're about to make the news thirty minutes long starting next week. So maybe I can get to see it sometimes."

Perhaps Violet complained more—more slyly—than I'd realized as a child. "Well, there's a lot more news to cover these days."

"Uh-huh," she said, "that's true." She plonked her peeled potato into the water. "My neighbor says movie stars were there, the *Ben-Hur* man—"

"Charlton Heston."

"—and that cute colored boy, Sidney Portoo . . ."

"Sidney Poitier. He was. And Bob Dylan sang."

"Who's that?" Violet asked.

"That singer you say looks like Chuck who you think can't sing worth a darn?"

She smiled. "So it was a whole *show*, huh?"

"Yeah, and the biggest demonstration ever in Washington. *Ever*, in history. Martin Luther King's speech came at the end. It was on all three channels at once, the whole speech, live, for like fifteen minutes. I don't think that's ever happened before, either, in history."

She stopped peeling and looked at me. "What'd Dr. King say?"

"Well, you know. He said he has a dream of everybody being equal and everybody treating everybody else fairly."

"Huh. That's what he said for a quarter of an hour?"

"No. He said that—" I stopped. "Is it okay—do you mind if I say 'Negro'?" Violet referred to Negroes exclusively as "colored people."

"It's okay, honey."

"He said that Negroes aren't free in America, even in the North, because of segregation and discrimination. That it's shameful for America to be this rich, rich country where Negroes are forced to live on a poor island. That America gave the Negroes a bad check and now we won't cash it."

She chuckled. "Dr. King called it that? 'A bad check'?"

"Yeah, and that we can't have freedom happen *gradually*, that we have to do it right now, immediately. That he's leading a revolt that won't stop."

I could see she was a little shocked. "A *revolt*? He used that word?"

"Yup."

"Well," she said, shaking her head, just barely smiling again. "I'll be."

"And you could hear people in the audience shouting back at him, 'Yes,' 'Uh-*huh*,' '*Say* it.' It gave me goose pimples."

"Did it upset you, Kay-Ray?"

"*No!* It made me excited. And he said that Negroes shouldn't hate white people, and they need to let the *good* white people, who want to help them, help them."

"Mm-hm," she said, and started peeling another potato.

"Have you ever seen police brutality, Violet? He talked about the 'horrors of police brutality.'"

"I seen a horror all right. A great big horror with the police right there. That's why I live in Chicago and not in Arkansas no more."

"What happened?" In the hundreds of hours I'd talked with Violet over the previous decade, I'd learned that she'd been born in Arkansas, had arrived in Chicago as a girl, and had lived in the same neighborhood ever since, somewhere between Hyde Park and the Loop, although she'd recently moved to a smaller apartment, since her three boys were grown. Her ex-husband had worked at a meat-packing plant. Her eldest son's wife had been murdered in 1957. Violet's friends were always "pushing on" her to attend church, which she called "the A.M.E." Lady's slipper orchids were her favorite flower, fried chicken livers her favorite food, and *The Real McCoys* her favorite TV show. Her left hip hurt lately. She loved country music and horse racing. She had asthma. Those were the facts I knew about Violet Woods. "What was the big horror that made you move here?" I asked.

She used her asthma inhaler and took a deep breath and looked at me, and in the moment I saw her deciding that I was old enough to hear the truth, I felt the enormous pleasure of being taken seriously. She stood up with her potatoes and bowl and asked me to "skooch the bench a little, would you, out of the sun," then sat down again and proceeded to tell me her story. Violet was not ordinarily chatty.

Violet said she'd lived outside the town of Moscow, Arkansas. Her parents were tenant farmers growing cotton—"renters, not croppers," she made a point of saying. The winter and spring she was eleven, in 1927, it rained and rained, and the levees on the Mississippi and all the other rivers broke, and on Easter Sunday the land flooded "just like it says in the Bible. Everything washed away, our little place, all the equipment, the mules, everything. I saw the Arkansas River run *backwards*. The land was an ocean, with a few islands where we gathered up. At the Red Cross camp, my little brother Joe caught sick and died right away."

"My gosh, it sounds like a nightmare."

"Uh-huh, that's right, exactly what it was, like a terrible dream. It didn't seem like it could be real. It was like a *story*."

"That was the horror that made your parents decide to move to Chicago?"

She shook her head. She said they weren't allowed to leave the Red Cross camp until the man—she did not say "the white man"—who owned the land they farmed came and signed them out. This made her father angry—"since Daddy wasn't no *cropper*, he was a *renter*"—which in turn made a policeman hit him with a club. Then the National Guard soldiers arrived and forced her father to work rebuilding a levy, standing in the cold floodwater heaving sandbags all day long. After another week, the family escaped the camp in the middle of the night.

"*Escaped?*" I said, astonished. *Slaves* escaped, not people thirty years ago, not someone I *knew*. "Oh my God!"

"Uh-huh."

She started peeling the last potato. I reminded myself that my parents paid Violet twelve dollars a day for six hours of work—way above the minimum wage, Dad said.

"Then you came to Chicago?" I asked.

She shook her head again. "To Little Rock, where my mama's people lived at. We got to Little Rock on a cool, bright Sunday, the first of May. First city I ever saw. *That* was like a story, too, so big and busy and fine." She plopped the last naked white potato into the bowl of water, rolled up the paper sack full of peels, and gripped it with both hands as she continued.

"Right away we found out Little Rock was all terrified. The day before, they found a girl murdered in a church, a white girl, and they'd caught the one who did it, the janitor at the church, a colored man. So the white people in Little Rock was angry and upset. And then, after we been in the city just a couple days, some white woman said *another* colored man attacked *her* and her daughter. The man they said did *that* turned out to be a cousin of ours—he was simple, Mama said. You know, retarded? Anyhow, at dusk, this whole pa-

rade of cars come driving slow down the big main street where we was staying at, honking horns. Cars and cars full of white men, and in the colored neighborhood there. We all looking out the front windows, watching, and then one of my aunties shouts, 'Holy Jesus, it's *Johnny,* they *killed* Johnny!'

"This colored man, his body, was tied onto the bumper of a car, just dragging and bouncing along the road half-naked. And he *already* been hung. *And* shot. First time I ever saw Cousin John, he was all bloody and ragged like some dirty side of hog meat. Then they stopped, and pretty soon there was *so* many white people, hundreds, all excited, and they lit a great big fire right in the street and burned him up."

"Oh my God, Violet!" Tears were dribbling from my eyes. Once again, as when I'd watched the Birmingham police with their fire hoses and German shepherds, along with shock and disgust, I felt excited to be getting the plain and ugly truth firsthand. "You must have been so scared. Didn't the police come?"

"They came. But didn't do nothing to stop it. Even when people was tearing apart that boy's burned-up body."

"Oh, God, no! *No!*"

"My daddy saw a man carrying and waving John's burned arm like it was a prize he won at a fair."

"People are evil. People are *monsters.*"

"Mm-hm, some people."

I wiped away my tears and took a deep quivering breath. "I don't know why all colored people don't hate all white people. *Seriously.*"

She leaned over and hugged me. "No, no, I'm sorry, Kay-Ray, honey, I didn't mean to make you cry."

"You know what? I wish I could travel back in time, and take a gun, and go to that street in Little Rock, and shoot all those people." I made fists and vibrated them close together, firing a big machine gun like in a war movie, mowing down that lynch mob around the bonfire in Little Rock.

I could see that I'd upset her a little. Suddenly, Peter ran out onto the porch—"Hi, Violet!"—and past us, down the wooden stairs

straight out to the backyard. My mother caught the screen door before it sprang shut. She looked at Violet and me. She sensed the unusual emotional weather.

Violet stood and picked up the bowl of potatoes—not wanting to seem like a shirker or troublemaker, I understood. "Morning, Mrs. Hollaender."

"What's going on here?" Mom asked with a big smile, her voice in a high register. Strenuous good cheer with a strong undercurrent of anxiety became her default affect for dealing with my adolescence and the 1960s.

"Karen was telling me all about Dr. King and the march on TV yesterday."

"Oh, you didn't get to see it, Violet? It was *so moving*. The Lincoln Memorial looked beautiful. It was just wonderful. It made us proud."

"*Proud?*" I said. "Really? I don't know how any white people in America can *ever* feel proud, Mom. Even people like us."

In *Newsweek* a few days later, I would read every word about the March on Washington and the Negro revolution, and I'd fill five pages of my final scrapbook with the articles. I would circle certain paragraphs. I would underline the quote by Roy Wilkins, the nice, moderate Negro who ran the NAACP: "The Negro citizen has come to the point where he is not afraid of violence. He no longer shrinks back. He will assert himself, and if violence comes, so be it."

11

BECAUSE I'M CONSCIENTIOUS to a fault, I phone my hotel in Washington. Despite our on-time takeoff from LAX, I tell the clerk, it turns out I will arrive two hours late, due to an unscheduled stop in Omaha, Nebraska.

Just after we crossed the Rockies, a large, middle-aged Hispanic woman in a fringed leather jacket who was reading Ron Paul's book *The Revolution: A Manifesto* became convinced that a Sikh man in the seat next to her was "a Tibetan terrorist." She stood declaiming—"We are in *danger*! Dear *God*, somebody tell the damn pilot to take this aircraft down *right away!*" People got nervous. A woman across the aisle started crying. The guy sitting next to me seemed less terrified than resigned. "If it's your time, it's your time," he kept repeating until I asked him to stop.

By the time we landed in Omaha, a lot of the passengers were under the impression that the loud woman was the alleged terrorist—the shouting, the "God," the "damn pilot," the "take this aircraft down," maybe her brown skin, maybe the title of her book—but in any event, FBI agents hustled both her and the Sikh off the plane. Somewhere over Iowa, the captain came on the

speaker and calmly explained: the woman had misunderstood her neighbor when he'd mentioned that he was a breeder of Tibetan *terriers,* that he had "three good boys" in the cargo hold who weren't a bit scared but whose tranquilizers fortunately would wear off before the plane reached the nation's capital. "The gentleman and his three puppies," the chuckling pilot said, "will be put on the first flight east in the morning, with our sincere apologies." We all applauded and laughed and shook our heads and have been guzzling free wine and cocktails ever since.

The terror caused by the 9/11 attacks had a half-life, it seems to me, of eighteen months. By the spring of 2003, we were definitely half as scared as we'd been on September 12, 2001. The half-life of the terror following the Boca Raton yacht bomb has been about a year, although we've all learned of a new acronym (RDD, for radiation dispersal device) and a new radioactive element (californium), and we have opinions about dispersal radii and an obscure new Muslim country (Mauritania). Given how ineffectual the attack was by 9/11 standards—eleven deaths, four pleasure boats, and a pier—the fear it whipped up seems remarkable to me. Even now, tourism to Miami and the rest of South Florida is two thirds what it was before the bomb.

For a few years when I was young, we had political bombings in this country, and not just a couple. Believe it or not, during 1969 and 1970 there was an average of eight bombings *every day* in America. Security at office buildings and government facilities did not get noticeably tighter. Travel didn't become more difficult. No squads of soldiers with automatic weapons appeared. Sweeping new law enforcement protocols were not passed by Congress. Those hundreds of bombings caused no wholesale national freakout. Maybe people who had endured the Great Depression and World War II were not so easily spooked by bombings of police stations and recruiting offices and banks. Or maybe that same generation had been so utterly discombobulated already by the spectacle of the previous few years—assassinations and race riots, a bewildering, unstoppable hedonism at home and a bewildering, unstoppable asceticism in

Vietnam—that by 1970 they simply had no more outrage and panic to spare for the small-bore dynamite antics of a few far-left freaks. And most of our homegrown bombers back then did scruple to avoid killing people.

Imagine if bands of militant young American outlaws today were setting off dozens of bombs a week around the country, hitting banks and the Capitol and the Pentagon and getting away with it, as the Weatherpeople did forty years ago. Twenty-first-century America would be crazed, consumed, talking of nothing else.

I think I know what the big difference is. Those bombings back then seldom made the national news, because the national news consisted of twenty-two minutes each evening on the three broadcast TV networks. Which meant that only stories deemed important by the Establishment received attention, and the attention they received was always calm. There was no alarmist electronic drone about the sky perpetually and sensationally falling. The radicals' bombings in the late '60s and early '70s were publicity stunts, and our national publicity gatekeepers refused to rise to the bait. Bill Ayers and Bernardine Dohrn badly *wanted* to be revolutionary celebrities, household names, but they never were, not really, in their prime. Even after their *n*th bombing, the nightly news still had to identify them as "a radical group calling itself the Weather Underground." Bill Ayers finally became famous when he was a harmless sixty-three-year-old professor, because now our proliferating electronic media are free to focus on the irrelevant, obliged to fill air time and keep viewers and listeners riled by any means necessary. We've given the bad guys—a radical group calling itself al Qaeda—an unprecedented opportunity to scare us silly.

As we begin our descent toward Reagan National Airport, I shut down my computer and return my seat and tray table to their upright and locked positions, brush the pretzel crumbs off my skirt, and glance out at the obelisk and dome shining white against the night sky. They always look like splendid toys to me.

12

WHEN ALEX RETURNED at the end of August 1963 from Toronto, he was distinctly Alexier. "It's so *sophisticated*," he said. His sense of Canadian sophistication derived mainly from their television programs, and he wouldn't stop talking about an old movie he'd seen called *The Third Man*.

He had missed seeing the March on Washington two days earlier. "*Rats*," he said when Chuck and I told him about Dylan.

"'He can't be *blamed*,'" Chuck sang, Dylanishly, about the Klansman who'd assassinated the Mississippi civil rights lawyer two months earlier, "'he's only a *pawn* in their *game*.'"

Did tiny little hearts fly out of my crossed eyes and circle around my head for a couple of seconds?

It was the last Saturday of the last summer before high school, and we were preparing to embark on our final Bond mission—spying on a crypto-Nazi U.S. senator, then assassinating his secret fascist compatriot who was a UN diplomat. We'd never been to Chicago by ourselves.

Alex's brother gave us a ride down to the Riverview amusement park.

"So are you nerds *trying* to get beat up?" Flip Macallister asked.

We were overdressed for Riverview, Chuck and Alex in white dress shirts and hound's-tooth jackets, me in an aquamarine shift with a scoop back. Chuck was carrying an old attaché of his father's.

"I mean, for Christ's sake," Flip said, "at least unbutton your top buttons and loosen the ties."

"I'm wearing sandals," I said.

From the backseat, I could see Flip look at me in the rearview and grin. "Yeah, of *course* you are, Brenda Beatnik."

Alex had pushed for Riverview because its giant Ferris wheel was like the one in Vienna that he'd seen in *The Third Man*. We also rode on the new Space Ride, a tram that crossed back and forth over the park, pretending the older man in our car was the Nazi senator.

We took the El down to the Loop, headed for a jazz club called London House. The inspiration for this was a chapter in *Live and Let Die* in which Bond visits Harlem nightclubs looking for the Negro villain Mr. Big. The Chicago River and the brand-new Marina City, whose sixty-story cylinders we called Jetson Towers, looked supersophisticated in the summer twilight.

Alex had phoned a week before, telling London House we were students "arriving on holiday" from Europe. To my astonishment, the lie worked. The young woman with the beehive hairdo at the front desk, and then the guy in charge, treated us like honorary adults. He apologized that they wouldn't be able to serve us alcohol. "Drinking age here in the States," he said, "twenty-one."

"Would you care to check your briefcase?" the girl asked Chuck.

"Thanks awfully, but no," Alex answered in a more extreme Etonian voice than he'd ever used. "All our passports, the visas and so forth, you know."

"Gosh, I love that accent," she said as she led us to a table. "Are you two from England also?"

"I am Sweess," Chuck said. He sounded like a Spanish Count Dracula. "Frome Gee-neva."

"Ukrainian," I said. "Part of USSR."

"Oh, I know—my granddad's from Ukraine. I didn't realize they let you come here. I mean, travel overseas."

Uh-oh: she knew what Ukrainian-accented English was supposed to sound like.

"Tanya is a *fantastic* ballet dancer," Alex said. "One of the best her age in the Soviet Union. And also her father, Comrade Romanova, happens to be a very important commissar, one of the senior men at the Kremlin, a great chum of Mr. Khrushchev's, so she's free to go anywhere. *Wherever* she pleases." He winked.

The London House girl, apparently impressed by this elaborately improvised backstory, didn't ask any more questions.

As soon as she was out of earshot, I said in my Natasha-from-*Rocky-and-Bullwinkle* voice, "And we are to be expecting two friends before music begins—when they arrive, please show moose and squirrel to table."

Chuck laughed and Alex shushed us, but we all grinned at one another, three North Shore kids on our own in downtown Chicago, playing European secret agents playing European students.

Whenever we went to Chuck's house before a mission, he'd put on the Miles Davis album *Kind of Blue* to get in the mood. One of the saxophonists on that record, Cannonball Adderley, was performing that night. Until a middle-aged man appeared at the bar, the only Negroes in the place had been the musicians and two busboys.

Although the music was a perfect soundtrack for the mission, I couldn't imagine loving jazz, easily and naturally, the way I did "Wipe Out" or "Heat Wave," songs that were nervous and a little crazy but also as fun and easy to gobble down as a McDonald's hamburger.

"Zo," I said when the first song ended, "wheech man is secret ringleader of Tyranny League?"

Alex suggested that we go stand at the bar to get a better look at everyone. "Right next to Mr. Big," he said. He meant the bald Negro in a suit and eyeglasses who was writing in a notebook.

Shockingly, as soon as we stationed ourselves at the bar and lit

cigarettes, Mr. Big turned to us and smiled. "You're the kids from overseas?"

It felt wrong to carry on our masquerade with this nice man, but we had no choice now.

"Yes. I am Tatiana, and these are school friends"—I thought fast—*"Hillary,"* Bond's alias in the latest novel, "and, um, *Emilio,"* the main villain in *Thunderball.*

"Very good to meet you all," he said. "I'm John Levy."

I glanced at Chuck, whose mouth opened and eyes bugged as he asked, "You're the *bass* player John Levy?"

"Yes, sir."

Chuck turned to us—"He played with *Erroll Garner* and *Billie Holiday!"*—then turned back to Levy. "Who you with now?"

"Leave the gigs to the great players nowadays. I type up contracts and sign checks. Management."

"Therefore," I said, "in American jazz world, you are . . . *Mr. Big.*"

Levy laughed. "You're a funny girl, Tatiana. So you aficionados liking the show?"

"Completely," Chuck said.

"How long you all visiting?"

"We've been in the States for a fortnight," Alex said, "and jetting back across the Atlantic on Monday. But sir, I have a question—is that a Windsor knot on your necktie?"

"Uh-huh."

"Then I guess you disagree with a man in England I know who says a Windsor knot is the mark of a *cad."*

He was quoting Bond, and I thought of his brother's crack—*Are you nerds* trying *to get beat up?*—but Levy put his arm around Alex's neck and laughed loudly. He was so tickled by this impertinent little English twit that he instructed the bartender to give us all drinks, on him—real drinks, gin and tonics and a Negroni. Mr. Levy mentioned that there was another European visitor in the club, "a West German fella." He pointed out a handsome blond man with gray temples and excused himself.

The German was wearing a turtleneck and a red pocket square.

He was smoking a cigar, and smiling a lot, and accompanied by two younger women, one of them in a low-cut dress. His table was on the edge of the room, near the door. We had found our assassination target.

I went to the bathroom. I couldn't tell if I was feeling the effects of the gin or of the spectacular success of the mission or both. Staring at myself in the mirror as I touched up my lipstick, I imagined it was a one-way mirror, like the one through which Tatiana and Bond were filmed having sex by SPECTRE. I grinned at myself. I was tipsy.

Chuck, as usual, would be the triggerman. In the shadows beneath the bar, Chuck opened his briefcase and took out the Luger, which he'd fitted with a silencer—a thick Tinkertoy dowel wrapped in black electrical tape—and wedged the gun into his inside jacket pocket. His plan was to make his way, just before the set ended, close to the UN Nazi's table, then take his shot during the applause.

None of us noticed the man approaching from the front of the club.

"Hello there."

We turned. He hadn't taken off his hat. He was holding up his open wallet. "I'm Lieutenant Murray, from the Chicago Police Department."

I figured it was because we were underage. The maître d' and the woman at the podium near the front door were staring at us. I felt frightened and embarrassed and . . . underage. The mission was over.

When Chuck spoke, I was startled all over again, afraid in a new way.

"Hello, *signore,* I am Emilio Largo, pleased to meet you. How may we help?" He was still Swiss.

The policeman looked at me. "You are Miss Tatiana Romanova?"

Oh, Christ. I paused, took a breath. Then caved. "My name is Karen Hollaender, actually." I was using my normal voice and trying to smile.

The policeman's face tightened. By telling the truth, I'd made him angry.

"We're from Wilmette. And we didn't order these drinks or lie about our age."

"Didn't you identify yourself earlier tonight as a Soviet citizen by the name of Tatiana Romanova?"

"Yes, but—well, we were just goofing around. Pretending. That's a name from a book, from a James Bond book."

The policeman stared at me. "Nice shade of lipstick, *Karen.* What do you call that?"

Oh, *Jesus.* "Coral."

"That's what you used to write 'Death to Fascists' on the mirror in the ladies' washroom?"

Actually? I'd written DEATH FOR FASCISTS. "I'm sorry."

For a long moment the policeman said nothing and looked each of us over. "Do you have identification on you?"

There was only one form of identification that any fourteen-year-old American might carry in 1963, and we hadn't brought along our Wilmette Public Library cards. We shook our heads.

"And I suppose you're not British?" he said to Alex.

"Uh-uh, no, sir. Born and raised in Wilmette."

"Who's Ernie Banks?"

"What? Who?"

"Ernie. Banks." He was testing us, the way soldiers did in World War II movies, to see if we were actually Americans.

"A baseball player," Alex said. "For Chicago? The pitcher for the White Sox—no, the Cubs?"

Oh, Alex.

The policeman was getting excited, and his lips verged on a smile. "What league are the Cubs in?" the cop asked.

"Um . . . the American?"

"*National* League," I said, "and Ernie Banks plays first base. He doesn't really follow baseball, Lieutenant."

Lieutenant Murray turned back to me. "What place are the Cubs in?"

"Low. Out of the running for the pennant."

Now he smiled. "Good guess."

"Seventh place, I think. And the White Sox are in second, twelve games behind the Yankees."

His smile disappeared. I had finally managed to convince him we were not junior Soviet spies.

"*You* got very quiet all of a sudden, Emilio," he said to Chuck.

Chuck just shrugged. It was an impressively cool move, like James Dean's character in *Rebel Without a Cause* imitating Brando's in *The Wild One*. I found it scary as well as sexy.

Lieutenant Murray had us each write our name and address on a note card. He said that if any of us "ever get on the radar of the Chicago Police Department again," we would regret it, because— and I couldn't believe he said this—"Big Brother's watching." He told me to "go clean up your mess in the little girls' room." And then he left.

Chuck was angry. "I cannot believe the way you wussies just immediately finked out and left me hanging. *Jesus.*"

"I can't believe *you're* not thanking your lucky goddamn *stars*," Alex whispered. "What if he'd found our *guns*? We lucked out. We *completely* lucked out."

"Alex is right. We could've really gotten in big trouble," I said.

"Yeah, and we could've kept going and made it the all-time perfect mission that we'd be proud of forever and always remember. It was *real*! It was everything we've ever imagined coming true! I'm just surprised at the two of you."

I went to wipe my anti-Nazi graffito off the mirror, and on the way out, I avoided the stares of the maître d' and his snitch.

Alex was alone out front on the sidewalk. Had my boyfriend, who wasn't really my boyfriend, gotten so pissed off that he'd already broken up with me? Left in a huff, ditched us?

"He won't quit," Alex said softly.

"What do you mean?"

He nodded up the street. The West German in the turtleneck was standing by the curb. Chuck, smoking a cigarette, was having a jolly-looking conversation with him.

A parking attendant pulled up the car. The two girlfriends got in,

then the German man shook Chuck's hand and patted him on the left shoulder, slipped into the driver's seat, and closed the door.

Chuck whipped his toy Luger out of his jacket, pointed it at the driver's-side window with the tip of the silencer inches from the man's head, and pulled the trigger two, three, four times. The car moved forward, then lurched to a rocking stop. Meanwhile, Chuck had popped open the briefcase and taken out a cherry bomb, which he touched to the tip of the cigarette in his mouth until it started sparking, and tossed it low, like he was skipping a stone. It exploded under the back of the car as they screeched away.

By the time Chuck reached us, we were already running the other way along the river as fast as we could. I wished I hadn't worn sandals.

13

CHUCK LEVY WONDERED for years after that if Lieutenant Murray and the Chicago police had passed our information along to the FBI. As I walk up Pennsylvania Avenue and see the ugly concrete fortress up ahead, I look for the sign. On their website, I noticed they keep the official name of their headquarters on the down-low, buried beneath layers of HTML. But here in the real world, it's right up front, bronze letters over the door, immune to any discreet digital revisionism: J. Edgar Hoover FBI Building.

It's warm for February, and I'm wearing flats, so I decide to walk the mile back to the hotel. I've just been to the National Gallery to see a show called "Deep Surfaces: Masterpieces of American Pop Art." Two of the paintings in the exhibit, I noticed, were on loan from the collection of Alexander G. Macallister III.

The Willard is not my favorite kind of hotel, too big, too marbleized, too fussy. But Sarah's anniversary dinner is here, so it didn't make sense to book a room elsewhere. And when I arrived in the middle of the night via Omaha, the clerk recognized me and upgraded me to a suite, which made me love the place. I'm easy. He claimed my room is the one in which Martin Luther King, Jr., wrote

the "I Have a Dream" speech fifty years ago. I wonder if it's the same room that the FBI bugged a few months later in order to record Dr. King having sex with a white woman while shouting "I'm fucking for God" and "I'm not a Negro tonight."

The beautiful Ethiopian girl now at the front desk tells me my "gentleman friend" phoned to confirm our "engagement" at ten tonight in the hotel bar.

In my room, as I put on makeup and look at my hair, I wonder, as always, if a blowout makes me look better or older, more attractive or simply more ladylike. And I wonder, if the chambermaid were to find DEATH FOR FASCISTS scrawled on the mirror in pink lipstick (Admirable by Chanel), would she just Windex it off or notify her supervisor?

Down in the Crystal Room, I hug Sarah and Victor, hand them my officially unwanted gift.

"Don't worry," I say, "I *also* donated to Water-dot-org."

After a minute of Sarah and me telling each other how fabulous we look and how wonderful it is to see each other, Victor, who just retired from *The Washington Post,* asks how my new book is going.

"You know how it is," I say, "it's going."

Sarah gives me a funny look because she hears the evasiveness in my voice. "We'll talk, Hollander," she says, and with another hug and kiss, I release her to the next arrival.

Half the guests are staring at their devices, bored or mesmerized or some odd new modern combination of the two. Smartphones turn grown-ups into faux-teenagers, annoyingly oblivious, shamelessly self-absorbed—although my son, Seth, says the ubiquity of handheld devices has made him feel less freakish about his Asperger syndrome.

My toast at dinner goes over well, especially the end. I say that Sarah and Victor and I were barely fifty when we all celebrated *my* twenty-fifth anniversary, and that I suspect they're throwing a big shindig for their twenty-fifth because it makes them seem much younger than they are. I finish with the last verse of Dylan's "For-

ever Young," which would cost too much to quote here, but trust me, in the room, the lines kill. Even I choke up a little.

I arrive early at the Round Robin bar and order sparkling water. I'm waiting for my friend, a man I met when I lived in Washington.

He worked for the federal government then and works for the federal government now, has only worked for the federal government or for private firms that do most of their business for the federal government.

His name is almost never in the press, and he's probably never appeared on television. But among those he calls "the function zero-fifty, one-fifty, and seven-fifty people"—the federal budget identifiers for national security, foreign affairs, and law enforcement—he's sort of famous.

When we met in 1997, he was vague describing his occupation and affiliations, but merrily so, with an openhearted smile, acknowledging his bobbing and weaving even as he bobbed and wove. "I get detailed all over the fucking place," he told me during that first encounter, as I was trying to get a fix on his job, "at the assistant director level." I knew by then that ADIC was the relevant acronym, and I knew how it was pronounced. "So you're sort of a big swinging ay-dick," I said, "roving around the nomenklatura," which made him laugh. Such is the nature of flirtation in Washington, D.C. He's six years younger than I am, single then and single now. He's not as skinny as Jack was, but he's not fat, and he's got a great sly smile and an excellent head of hair.

Our affair ended in 2001 when I left government and moved back to New York full-time. I'll call him Stewart Jones.

We hug like we mean it.

"Welcome back to our nation's capital. You smell wonderful. How was it? Sarah's thing?"

"Fine. Lots of people I used to know. Very nice. What you'd expect. I'm really glad I came. Have you ever heard of the Failed States Index? A jerk I met at the dinner was talking about it."

"Useless horseshit. The fake precision. I mean, Sudan is two-point-seven points less 'failed' than Afghanistan? Canada is eight-point-three points more 'failed' than Finland? Please. Pointless think-wanker make-work."

Stewart calls think tanks "think wanks." He orders a double Scotch, neat. I stick to Pellegrino.

He holds up the Round Robin cocktail napkin. "You know what a round robin is? What it was, originally?"

"Some British sports thing? Cricket? Jousting?"

"A way for eighteenth-century subversives to organize protests without really stepping up to the plate. On their petitions to the king, they'd sign the paper in a circle, a round robin, instead of in a regular list from top to bottom. If nobody signed at the top, then nobody could be nailed as the leader."

"I'm not Spartacus . . . *I'm* not Spartacus . . . *I'm* not Spartacus."

He chuckles. "Exactly." He takes a gulp of whiskey. "So I can still be your lifeline?" When we were dating, I told him that if I were ever a contestant on *Who Wants to Be a Millionaire?*, I'd designate him as the friend I would call to help answer questions that stumped me. "That's still about *the* nicest thing anyone has ever said to me."

"That's about *the* saddest thing I've ever heard."

"I'll tell you what's sad—they eliminated Phone-a-Friend a few years ago."

As I tell him my Tibetan terrorist story, he jots something electronically.

"I was surprised," I say, "there wasn't an air marshal on the flight."

"Aww, you cute, trusting girl, you. Even coming into D.C., your odds of having FAMs on board are *maybe* one in ten." He puts his BlackBerry on the table. "I was out in your neck of the woods a couple of months ago."

"In L.A.?"

"Kern County, way out in the middle of nowhere, one day, didn't set foot in Los Angeles, that's how swell my life is. But the whole trip made me think of you."

"Gee, thanks. But not enough to call."

"Because you remember when they renamed National after Reagan, how pissed you were?"

"Don't do that thing where you make me out to be some left-wing nudnik. I was annoyed because he was still alive, and saints don't get canonized until they're dead."

"Yeah, sure. Anyway, I thought of you because I flew from D.C. to Costa Mesa, got bumped over to Burbank—"

"Burbank is only *twenty-five minutes* from my house!"

"—then flew home out of San Diego with stops in Phoenix and Houston."

I wait. "And? So?"

"Ronald Reagan Airport to John Wayne Airport, rerouted to Bob Hope Airport, and then from Charles Lindbergh Field to Barry Goldwater Terminal to George H. W. Bush Airport, quick visit to the Lyndon Johnson Space Center, back to Ronald Reagan Airport. A Republican royal flush plus the liberal the old liberals grew up hating! I've asked a guy at the FAA to find out for me if anybody has ever flown that route before."

Down to business. "So," I say, "I'm working on another book."

"Fiction, nonfiction?"

"Memoir."

"Cool. So, fiction."

"Ha. I won't name you."

"But I'm *in* it? Really? Wow."

He may be the most ostentatiously unsentimental person I know, yet he is touched. Which I find awfully sweet, even stirring. I didn't expect to have those embers fanned tonight.

"So it's one of these huge epic tick-tocks? 'And then on February twenty-fourth, 1992, I flew to Prague and started writing the new constitution with President Havel, blah blah blah'?"

"No, it's mainly about when I was a kid. Remember me telling you about my thing with James Bond, these games we did, with clandestine recordings and foreign accents and toy guns and stuff?"

"Yeah, of course. It explained everything to me."

My brain freezes, then flutters. What does he mean? What does he already know?

"It's why you let me turn you into an adulteress. I was one of your fictional characters come to life."

Ah. I breathe and smile.

"So this new book," he says, "is like *Risky Business* with you as the young Tom Cruise and then twenty years later me as the Rebecca De Mornay hooker character?"

"Not exactly. My whole life will be in there, but with certain parts in much sharper focus. The important parts. The interesting parts."

"No offense, is your life really interesting *enough,* do you think? For a book? I don't mean you're not a significant figure and a beacon to all American women—"

"Fuck you."

"But nice parents, cozy suburban childhood, Ivy League, practicing law, New York bigwig, distinguished pro bono whatnot, working for Fat Boy"—his nickname for President Clinton—"teaching law, *Charlie Rose* appearances, books, distinguishedness. No scandals. It's kind of a standard high-end run, isn't it? Every happy person is the same."

I stare him straight in the eye.

"Aha. It's about you and the Supremes, isn't it? About whatever it was that got you dinked off the list."

"I didn't get dinked. That was one hundred percent my choice. The White House was totally surprised when I withdrew my name." I haven't seen Stewart in three years.

"Interesting. Very, very interesting. I always figured you had to be weirder than you let on." He takes a drink of Scotch. "I didn't expect to want to fuck you tonight."

Stewart has the dirtiest mouth of anyone I've ever known. It's one of the ways in which he manifests his habitual brutal candor, especially since so much of his professional life requires staying mum and revealing nothing to people who don't have at least a Confidential security clearance. On our second date, when we went to

watch Richard Pryor receive a prize at the Kennedy Center and one of the comedians made a penis joke, Stewart told me matter-of-factly, "My dick isn't long, but it is thick."

We spend the next ten minutes talking about sex. I tell him about the last man I dated, a museum director who accompanied me to the 3-D Zapruder movie last fall. How he played Guitar Hero wearing a bathrobe in his bedroom and said "Not a snowball's chance in *heaven*" when I asked if he ever smoked pot. How surprised I was to discover he had an electronic device implanted just above his buttocks called a "sacral neural stimulation device." (Stewart knew it was not a machine to enable or improve erections but prevented incontinence.) How the guy asked, in the middle of sex, if I was "cool with facials" and then, after an awkward exchange during which he made his meaning clear and I demurred, pulled out and ejaculated on one of my breasts.

"I could have the guy killed, if you'd like," Stewart says.

"You're sweet."

"The old-dude demand curve for fucking must be skyrocketing now, with all the sildenafil patents expired and cheap generics flooding the market." He writes himself another note on his BlackBerry, and I lean over to look. It says *ARGUS sildenafil.*

"Argus like in the Argonauts?"

"No, Argus the all-seeing giant with a hundred eyes." He puts down the device. "Advanced remote ground unattended sensor."

"Boys and their toys, bureaucrats and their acronyms. So why would the government care about generic Viagra?"

"Sorry. You don't have the clearance."

"Ha ha."

"Argus is computers scraping foreign media and blogs, all the open-source shit, for 'potentially salient epiphenomena.' Birds and crops dying off more or less than usual, spikes up or down in obituaries, absenteeism, whatever the fuck. I'm thinking maybe it makes sense to tag reports of more old Arab guys knocking up young broads. Creating more suicide-bombing *shahids* for the class of 2034." He orders another Scotch.

"So, my dear," I say, "for this memoir of mine. I could use your help."

"What, my calendar for 1998 and 1999? Like a catalog of our dates or something?"

"Uh-uh. I want to find out what government files exist on me. And like the man says, I don't have the clearance."

"*Ahhhh.* Aha. I'm a back channel."

"Because I don't expect my FOIA-ing to turn up what I'm looking for. Not in this lifetime."

"Who? Which agencies?"

I take a deep breath and exhale. "FBI—"

"From the background check last year?"

"No. I pulled out before they did anything."

"And then shot on their face," he says.

"Ha ha. Anyhow, FBI, CIA—"

"*Oh*, before I forget, I've got to tell you this story. In Pyongyang, we just found out they have a special clinic, a sperm bank for the North Korean muckety-mucks, the elite DPRK dudes, to bank their jizz or donate it to infertile peasants or whatever. And they've got all these young women, 'nurses,' whose *job* it is to *jerk off* the guys into the little cups. Two of them Japanese girls, we're told. Probably abductees. Is that not unbelievably fucking wonderful? Sorry: who'd you write to?"

"FBI, CIA, the army, and Homeland Security."

He grins. "Whoa Nelly! Quadfecta! What are your dates of interest?"

"And the National Archives, just to be thorough; 1967, 1968."

"*Really?*" he says, calculating. "From when you were eighteen, nineteen?"

I nod.

"God, I bet you were a super-hot eighteen-year-old. Miniskirts, man! When miniskirts were new and wild and crazy! And I was twelve, just getting addicted to beating off. I don't need time *travel*, only *communication* across time, so I could tell the twelve-year-old me to take the bus from Buffalo to Chicago to check you out."

"I know this is a huge ask, and it may be impossible, probably is. And I really don't want to get you in trouble."

"In trouble? I live for trouble, Ilsa. Seriously, what the fuck. Early retirement isn't my worst nightmare. If I were an operator, I'd already be aged out. It's KMA time, baby."

"Kill My Associates? Kill the Motherfucking Assholes?"

"Kiss My Ass. It means I'm fifty-eight years old and can do whatever I want. So I'm in."

"Thank you. As far as the details go, I don't know what you need me to tell you about what I—"

"*Nothing.* I don't want to be pre-briefed. Cleaner intel that way. If I want more later, I'll ask. On the FOIAs, have they denied you?"

"Uh-uh."

"Good, that's good, that's better. Homeland Security? Really?"

"Uh-huh."

"Wow. You fucking un-American." I've delighted him. As I figured I might. He sings in a silly falsetto: " 'What a bad little girl I am, I need you to solve it, bad, bad, bad, bad!' "

"Dinah Washington?"

"Ask your granddaughter." He gulps some Scotch. "Rihanna. I'll see what I can do. But tell me: was this the plan, seventeen years ago, why you seduced me?"

"Seduced *you!*"

"In order to turn me into a long-term asset you could cash in when the time was right? Because if so, I am incredibly fucking impressed."

"Sorry. There was no plan. If anything, the opposite. I actually worried, back then, that because of what you do, you, you know, might have found out things about me that would've made it awkward for us. There was no plan. There was just me about to turn fifty, and this slightly insane, very un-boring-Washington, very thick-dicked, very attractive single man."

"You're making me hard. Keep going."

"And a dead marriage." I signal for the check.

"Now I really get it, your mixing and matching of fiction and

nonfiction. I was double-oh-seven come to life—*and* for forty fuck-ing years, you've been this based-on-a-true-story outlaw. A fugitive in your own mind."

I sort of smile and sort of nod. He continues.

"Like I say, I'll do what I can do and find what I can find. In any case. But for right now, your place or my place or none of the above?"

"Mine, but let me use your phone first, okay?" I pick up his Black-Berry and press the browser icon. "I may want to leave later tomor-row and want to check what the last flights home are."

"The phone won't work for you. Ten-twenty, United, Dulles to LAX, gets you there at one in the morning."

His phone *doesn't* work. He takes it from my hand and touches the icon, which blooms normally into a browser window. "It's se-cure," he says. "Configured to respond to the speed and direction and pressure of my touch only. Cool, huh?" He pockets it and stands. *"Vámanos?"*

Buzzy Freeman lives in extreme northwest Washington, D.C., al-most in Maryland. The neighborhood reminds me of where I grew up on the North Shore. Big and biggish houses and perfect yards, lots of old trees, hushed suburban gravitas. People talk about the un-American elitism of life in the District, inside the Beltway, but this is elitism of an absolutely all-American kind. George H. W. Bush lived around here when he was CIA director, as did Richard Nixon in the 1950s. And Lyndon Johnson when he was vice presi-dent.

I haven't had a real conversation with Buzzy since college.

"Wonder Woman! You found us—and my gosh, don't you look *wonderful*," he says at the door. He means, I think, that I'm tan and size-sixish and my hair isn't stiff. Also, maybe he's detecting a bit of post-sex glow twelve hours after the fact. "Life in Tinseltown obvi-ously agrees with you."

Tinseltown. Yeesh. "Thanks, Buzzy—and thanks so much for agreeing to see me on a Sunday."

He's wearing a white dress shirt, crimson V-neck sweater, blue jeans, and Gucci loafers. I wonder if the red, white, and blue is conscious theming. Because I've seen him on television every few years, my mental picture is more or less current. He's not obese, but he's got a big gut; and he's got his hair, but it's thin and wispy. It's hard to believe that I once found him supremely charismatic.

"You've grown the beard back." I remember the day he shaved it in 1968.

"Covers the double chin."

Some residual wit, at least. He leads me to "the den," where there's a fire in the fireplace. "Harleen's so sorry she won't get to see you. Still at church, a confab with our pastor, planning this big community dinner we do every Easter. She's a deaconess." When we were in college, Buzzy and I bonded over being former Catholics. I guess he's moved on to Protestantism.

It's hard to believe that, forty-six years ago, I watched him, for instance, standing outside an army induction center in Boston, chanting "No more war" with breathtaking conviction.

I decline a glass of chardonnay, and while he's gone getting coffee, I listen to the Bach fugue playing on the radio and squint at the photographs on his wall: young Buzzy with Ronald Reagan, middle-aged Buzzy with Ariel Sharon, old Buzzy with Dick and Lynn Cheney and Jon Voight. He made a lot of money in the '80s doing political junk mail, and now he's got one of those vague, expansive Washington portfolios—chairman of a think tank, vice chair of foundations with "freedom" in the name, conference attendee, cable news commentator—that pass for a distinguished career in public service. I see his honorable-discharge certificate from the U.S. Coast Guard and his college diploma. Lame.

He shuffles back in, carrying a tray with two double espressos and a Spode pitcher of steamed milk. I refrain from making a crack about latte-drinking, white-wine-swilling, NPR-listening conservatives.

We say we've enjoyed seeing each other on TV. I tell him I was amused to read that he'd helped organize a screening at the Penta-

gon of *The Battle of Algiers* during the first summer of the Iraq war, since we'd seen it together in 1968 when it came out. He tells me he hasn't spoken to Alex Macallister since their public shouting match about gay rights during a panel at our twenty-fifth reunion. I tell him about my kids, he tells me about his first set of children, as well as the younger kid by Harleen—"premed, but unlike his lazy old man, he'll *make* it to med school." He congratulates me on the success of *Objection, Your Honor* but says he doesn't read fiction anymore, "not even Tom Clancy." However, he loved *The 7th Founder*—John Jay is one of the conservatives' favorites; they think the liberal historian-media elite has demoted him to the junior varsity—and when his right-wing friends accused me of recasting their hero as a "secular civil rights liberal," he asked them, "Whiskey Tango Foxtrot are you folks talking about?" Buzzy served his two years in the Coast Guard before college, and when I met him freshman year, he told me he was "Sierra Alfa Tango seven-niner-zero," by which he meant he'd gotten a 790 on his math SAT.

"I appreciate that, Buzzy, thanks. Some people on the left hate me for portraying Jay as a good guy, you know."

"That's Democrat intellectual honesty for you."

"The reviewer in *The Nation* mentioned that we were college friends, you and I. Guilt by association."

"Give yourself to the Dark Side, Karen. Got a new book going?"

I shrug and nod, but he really just wants to tell me about the book he's finishing up, *Cities upon a Hill: Defending American Values in the Holy Land*. It's a polemic about how we need to cut Israel maximum slack in their fight against the Arabs and Iranians, to "stop worrying about nice neat Miranda distinctions between combatants and noncombatants in kinetic operations when you're struggling to *survive*." I've never heard anyone use the phrase "kinetic operations" in conversation. It means combat.

"But I assume you're against killing innocent civilians?"

He sighs. "Oh, Karen . . . who's 'innocent'? You're the lawyer. People talk about 'guilt' and 'innocence,' but in our legal system, it's 'guilty' or 'not guilty,' right? 'Innocent' isn't a verdict. Anyhow," he

says, pivoting directly from murky moral ambiguity to a celebration of black-and-white moral simplicity, "in *Cities* I'm arguing that Americans need to consider Israel a *spin-off* of America, our national soul mate, *su* Judeo-Christian *casa es mi* Judeo-Christian *casa*. And since I'm not Jewish, I can appear to make the case more . . . dispassionately."

"In the book, do you talk about the Paul Plan?"

Buzzy's eyes narrow and he stiffens, leaning forward, the way he used to do in dorm rooms and coffeehouses and greasy spoons, as we chain-smoked and talked and talked about a culture of total resistance, closing our minds in the name of opening them, hardening our young hearts. His ferocity then set a high standard for us all.

"What Ron and Rand Paul have proposed," Buzzy says, "is soft genocide. It's just a prettied-up version of what Himmler and Göring proposed before they went for the Holocaust—this time, it's ship the six million Jews to Nevada instead of Madagascar."

As you no doubt know, the two Pauls, Republican congressman father and senator son, introduced identical bills that would offer all Israelis virtually automatic U.S. citizenship until 2020. It would also authorize the creation of a new commonwealth on about 1 percent of the American land owned by the federal government, "at least seven million contiguous acres in Nevada, Idaho, Oregon, or other states as appropriate"—in other words, a quasi-nation on the U.S. mainland, self-governed like Puerto Rico, a jurisdiction as large as Israel and richer in natural resources, and safely seven thousand miles west of the Middle East and its several hundred million Muslims. Any Israelis who accepted the citizenship offer could live anywhere they wished in America, but they (and any other American) could also choose to live in what's already being called New Israel, somewhere in the vast boondocks between Salt Lake City, Las Vegas, and eastern Oregon. The U.S. government would create an endowment to build out the commonwealth and resettle as many as six million Israelis in this country.

"It'd cost a lot less than we've spent on the wars in Iraq and Afghanistan and Pakistan," the senior Paul said recently, "and this time

instead of *war* we might get Middle East *peace,* peace forever. Plus
millions of super-smart, hardworking new Americans, exactly the
type of immigrants we *want.*" What they decline to articulate so
bluntly is the endgame. After the E-Z-citizenship offer expired, any
Israelis remaining in Israel would be on their own, citizens of a
country no longer the problematic special ally of the U.S. We wipe
our hands of the endless Middle East tragedy once and for all.

The plan has next to no support among members of the political
Establishment. What worries Buzzy and his friends is that ordinary
Americans seem to like the idea—according to the latest polls, almost 40 percent say it sounds reasonable, and that pool of support
is rather astoundingly broad, coming from left-wingers and right-
wingers and middle-of-the-roaders almost equally. Only 32 percent
say they're opposed. And with Rand Paul planning to run for president in 2016, the idea will remain in the public discourse. "Perot
didn't get *elected* in '92," Buzzy says, "and Ron Paul didn't get elected
last time, but their ideas and their *takes* had a *gigantic* impact. Things
are wild now, Karen. Revolution is in the air. People are ready to
throw all kinds of babies out with the bathwater. The people pushing this are the most dangerous men in America right now. As dangerous as anybody in Yemen or Waziristan."

"You believe that?"

"*Absolutely!* Absolutely." Now he's on a roll. "There are a whole
lot of lazy, cowardly, ahistorical moral idiots in this country who
always want the easy way out. Remember, I *know* those people, I'm
from out there." Because Buzzy grew up in Nevada and served in the
military, he's always cast himself as a more authentic American than
the Ivy Leaguers and cosmopolites he's lived and worked among his
whole adult life. And depending on the particular point he's trying
to make, he can use his rustic roots and firsthand knowledge of
regular folk to revile either the elite-hating People or the People-
hating elite. It's a neat trick.

He stops, leans back, smiles. "Sorry about the rant. You know me."

"I do indeed." In fact, he's weirdly consistent: a radical who passionately despised liberals and other misguided Americans in 1968,

a conservative who passionately despises liberals and other mis-guided Americans in 2014.

I've been here almost half an hour. Because I've kept it friendly, let him rattle on without getting into a real debate, he's relaxed. That was my plan. I'm playing the good cop, and he doesn't even know I'm playing a cop. Finally, he pops the big Washington question.

"Any regrets," he asks, "about taking yourself out of the running for the Supreme Court? Because you'd've been a hell of a lot better Democrat choice than the weasel they picked."

I give an abridged version of my standard answer. "Never served on the federal bench? And sixty-two years old at the time? Wasn't going to happen."

"But you practiced in the real world, private-sector law for profit-making enterprises! And in any case, why short-circuit the process? Frankly? I think you did yourself a disservice." He sips his coffee. "Reputationally."

Can he be serious? *You have no idea the disservice I'm about to do myself. And you. Reputationally.* "Buzzy, I think you can figure out why I couldn't go through with it. The vetting, the White House lawyers' questions. 'Is there anything in your personal history that could be controversial or embarrassing?' We committed *felonies* in 1968. Big felonies, Federal Class C for sure, arguably Class A." The prosecutorial jargon gets people's attention. "People died, Buzzy."

He blanches. He puts down his coffee. He frowns. He sighs.

What if he responds the way Alex did? *I have no idea what you're talking about, Karen, none, not a clue, you're mixing up the real and the make-believe.* Then it'd be two against one. From which I would conclude what? That each of them, independently and spontaneously, when asked to acknowledge the truth after so many years of silence, has chosen to stonewall a person who knows the truth? Seems un-likely. Or that the two of them have hatched some kind of conspir-acy against me? Given their mutual loathing, that seems even less likely. Or that I'm the one who's nuts? "Right," Buzzy says. "Yes." His body loosens. He sighs again. "I understand. Of course."

I must not smile. I have never so completely suppressed joy. I've spent several decades disliking Buzzy Freeman from afar, suspecting him of dirty tricks and double agentry in the 1960s and galled by his hard-core apostate politics since. But now I feel a surge of gratitude.

His eyes are watering. "Kilo Hotel—Bravo Foxtrot, over," he says. Those were our code names in 1968.

"This is the first time I've really discussed it with anybody except my lawyer," I say.

"Me, neither—I mean, me, too. I've never told *anyone.* I once went to a doctor who wanted to hypnotize me to make me quit smoking, but I was afraid of what I might say when I was under. So I quit smoking to avoid being hypnotized."

"I know, I know."

"I'll go for weeks without ever thinking of it specifically," he says. "I have these dreams where I've done something terrible, it's never clear exactly what it is, but I'm terrified of being caught. And then in the mornings I wake up and, well . . . You know. The bad feeling and fear never quite go away. Like an ache."

"I know."

"My ex-wife, when she decided to leave, told me she couldn't get over this nagging sense that I was keeping secrets from her. I offered to take a polygraph test to prove that I'd been absolutely faithful, that I wasn't a bigamist, wasn't gay, wasn't a spy, wasn't any of the things she suspected me of."

He's given me the perfect opening. "Were you a spy, Buzzy? Back then? An agent from Army Intelligence or part of COINTELPRO or one of those programs?"

"*What? No! I* was the one who was always *warning* about that, and you all called me paranoid! I was the one who gave Chuck LSD to test his loyalty!"

"I remember. If you'd been an undercover agent, that would've been a clever way to convince us to trust you. And you had been in the military."

"No. *No. I believed.* Like you say, I'm a true believer now, and I was a true believer then. For better or worse. Believe me."

I do, I think. "After they got Chuck, why were the rest of us allowed to get away with it, walk away? Why did they never arrest us? Or blackmail us? Did anyone ever try to blackmail you?"

He shakes his head.

"If they knew who we were," I say, "and they obviously had to, why did it never come out? We all have people who don't like us." *Especially you, Buzzy.*

"Yeah. That's the sixty-four-thousand-dollar question, isn't it? Maybe because the government had much bigger fish to fry at the time. Or maybe they watched us for a while and then just gave up and sealed the files. I agree, it's mysterious. Luck, I guess. Dumb luck."

For another twenty minutes, Buzzy and I keep talking a mile a minute. It feels so good—so liberating—to speak truthfully. Although I'm lying by omission. I don't mention that I've talked to Alex, and I let Buzzy think I've come to his house for purely private, personal reasons, seeking only (his word) "closure."

If I reveal to Buzzy that I'm publishing our story, he might go wild. He is tort-crazy—he sued an MSNBC commentator and a website for libel; he sponsored some kind of class-action defamation suit on behalf of West Bank settlers; and he won a settlement from Unilever after he scratched his inner ear with a Q-tip that had insufficient cotton. But suing me or the publisher to try to prevent publication won't stop the truth from coming out. He's not stupid.

I can't lie.

"I'm writing about it," I tell him. "In my book, my memoir. All of it."

He stares at me for a long, long time, nods, then gets up and takes away the coffee tray when he hears his wife coming in.

Have I just made a terrible mistake? Buzzy is still a guy for whom the ends justify all kinds of unsavory means.

When my taxi arrives, he embraces me with such fervor and for such a long time that Harleen starts to look a little embarrassed. I make myself smile when I think, *Take your stinking paws off me, you damn dirty ape.*

14

W E NEVER OFFICIALLY suspended the Bond missions, never said out loud that it was time to grow up and move on. However, as soon as we were in high school—not just high school but *New Trier* and its inescapable throb of self-importance—our spy toys and funny accents became childish things to put away, like painted wings and giants' rings.

I've tried hard to recall any specific, telling reactions I had to President Kennedy's assassination. When I heard the news—geometry class, the principal over the PA—I remember thinking how strange it was that Chuck had given a world history presentation that morning about the assassinations of Prime Minister Lumumba in the Congo and President Diem in South Vietnam. I remember thinking: *Lyndon Johnson is the fourth president in my lifetime.* I remember worrying about my brother, Peter, who was in third grade and had an autographed photo of Kennedy tacked to his bedroom wall. I remember my mother fiddling with her rosary and sniffling all weekend.

Two days after the assassination, my dad and I were alone together in the TV room, the way we'd started spending every Sunday

morning. He was reading the *Tribune,* and I was reading *Life*—that is, examining a picture of Yvette Mimieux in an orange bikini standing next to a giant orange surfboard, thinking of Chuck Levy and wondering to what extent I could remake myself as a surfer girl. This weekly time alone with Dad, faintly subversive, had been an unanticipated benefit of my refusal to attend Mass. We usually turned off the TV after *Meet the Press,* but today the set was on because of the assassination coverage. The president's casket was being carried from the White House and loaded onto a horse-drawn wagon.

I asked Dad if anything like this had happened when he was a kid. He told me yes, the Austrian chancellor and the king of Yugoslavia were both shot dead when he was just about my age.

"Who killed them?"

"Nazis killed the Austrian, even though he was a fascist, too. And the king by some kind of revolutionary. There was also an assassination in the States around the same time—the socialist hillbilly running for president from Louisiana, killed by the young doctor . . . Huey Long."

On TV, the funereal hush was replaced by bustle, with a correspondent speaking quickly and urgently. We both looked over at the screen. It was Dallas, a police station, the assassin being paraded in front of reporters.

Dad snorted and shook his head. It was his what-a-crazy-country reaction without any of the humor.

"Did you kill the president?" someone shouted.

"No," Oswald said.

The man accused of killing the president, the actual guy, with a black eye and a cut on his forehead, giving an impromptu press conference, on TV, live, *so* live. I was transfixed.

"I have not been charged with that. In fact, nobody has said that to me yet. The first thing I heard about it was when the newspaper reporters in the hall asked me that question."

I was astonished. He sounded so reasonable. He looked so regular. He was wearing a crew-neck sweater.

"Mr. Oswald, how did you hurt your eye?"

"A policeman hit me."

I started to form a question about whether the police would get in trouble for hitting him, but then someone lunged into the scene, the camera jiggled, and Oswald fell.

"He's been shot! He's been shot! Lee Oswald has been shot!" a man said. And then another man's incredulous voice came out of the TV: "This is unbelievable."

It was as if the TV broadcast had turned into a dream.

I started crying, which upset me more, since I hadn't cried during the previous forty-eight hours. My father the psychologist came over and squatted and hugged me and said that it was probably my grief for the president finally spilling out.

Mom and the little kids got home from St. Joseph's, and we all kept watching. When someone on TV identified Oswald's killer as "a nightclub owner named Jacob Leon Rubenstein," my father sighed and muttered something in Danish and shook his head.

I think my mother never entirely recovered from the shock of Kennedy's murder, especially coming so soon after Pope John's death. The instability and extremism she'd always dreaded, what she called "the cuckoo foreign stuff," had at last infected her America. I was confused by how the death of someone she didn't love, had never met, this remote and essentially unreal figure, could be such a personal blow to her.

I don't recall the days after the assassination being sad so much as weird, weird first because all regular TV programming stopped from Friday afternoon until Monday morning, and then weird again when life snapped completely back to normal on Tuesday. No one had lost their jobs, no one's houses had burned or flooded or collapsed, no war had begun. My favorite new TV shows (*Hootenanny, Patty Duke, East Side/West Side, The Fugitive*) were all on the air as usual the following week, the New Trier Indians played and lost the big annual game against the Evanston Wildkits, we held our first Esperanto Club meeting, I took quizzes and wrote papers and got

A's. In other words, the assassination was this strange new kind of event that was both heavy and weightless, commanding everyone's attention but having no immediate, discernible impact on their lives.

Chuck was joining us late for lunch in the cafeteria. "Hey, Levy," Alex said, "Hollaender agrees that Dylan is better than your goofball English combo."

"That's not what I said. I said I can't imagine the Beatles ever singing a song like 'Only a Pawn in Their Game' and that I wish Bob Dylan would go on *Hootenanny.*"

"I saw them on TV the other morning, the Beatles," Alex said, "on the *CBS News.* My dad thinks they look like Little Lord Fauntleroy."

"I don't know what that means," Chuck said as he set his tray down, "and I don't much care."

Back in the spring Chuck had heard the Beatles' "Please Please Me" on WLS and became an instant fan. One afternoon around Halloween he'd played his new 45 of "She Loves You" for me, just me, picking out George's chords on his unplugged guitar. When his record player automatically started playing it again, Chuck put down the guitar and mouthed the words, smiling.

There we were, alone in his bedroom, sitting on his bed.

Listening to lyrics exhorting a boy to requite a poor misunderstood girl's love. It was him I was thinking of—I loved him, and I thought he should be glad.

I thought the moment had finally come. I hoped my face wasn't as red-hot as it felt. I thought he was going to lean over and kiss me.

Instead, as he stood up and turned over the record to play the B side, he asked me, "Do you think I should ask Wendy Reichman to homecoming?"

That was the day I decided to end my five-month crush on Chuck Levy. And it's why, I think, my fondness for the Beatles was, forever after, a bit grudging.

"I don't know. I hear she likes some sophomore."

As I struggled to keep my anger from precipitating tears, we'd listened to John and Paul sing about thinking of a girl night and day and swearing they'd get her in the end.

Now, in the cafeteria, Chuck said, "My mom showed me this article about Oswald, about his living in New Orleans over the summer. Guess what he was reading? What he checked out from the library there? *Moonraker, Goldfinger, Thunderball . . .*"

"Wow," I said, "really?"

"Yeah, and *From Russia with Love.*" He didn't need to remind us that was JFK's favorite.

"Wow," Alex said.

We sat in silence for a good fifteen seconds, picking at lasagna, sucking milk from two-cent half-pint cartons.

Chuck was the first to speak. "Dr. Kimble's dream was cool, wasn't it, the way they did it so the first time you think it's real?" Now he was talking about *The Fugitive,* which we watched every week. In the previous night's episode, Kimble, the innocent doctor convicted of murder, has a recurring nightmare in which he's cornered and shot by the police detective chasing him across the country.

"My father," I offered, "says that in real life, psychologically, that kind of recurring dream can mean you feel guilty about something real and want to be punished."

Alex said, "What, you think Dr. Kimble did kill his wife?"

"I don't know. Maybe he did and just thinks he didn't. Maybe that's how they'll end the series."

Alex shook his head. "No way. That'd be cool, but on TV? The good guy has to be a good guy."

Finally, Chuck spoke again. "I have a dream like that, where I've murdered somebody and I can't stand that I'm going to have to spend the rest of my life worrying about getting caught. It always seems really real."

15

BACK IN 1963 people thought they were seeing the future when Gordon Cooper spent a day in outer space circling the earth. But when I look back now at the long weekend after John Kennedy's assassination, I realize *that* was the big time-warped glimpse into the twenty-first century. In 1963 it was unprecedented and bizarre to have nothing but news and discussions of news events airing on all three TV channels around the clock for days on end, and to have that clip of Ruby shooting Oswald played again and again. I sit with a plastic pint of sugar-free green-tea gelato and a purring Clarence Darrow on my lap, flipping between MSNBC and CNN and FOX, driven from one to the other and back by ads for pharmaceuticals and gold. On every channel, people are talking about the latest breakdown of talks with Iran. In the last forty-five minutes, I've listened to a dozen different anchors and experts and commentators and have learned absolutely nothing I didn't know from reading the story in the newspaper this morning. For a few months last year, when I stopped watching cable news altogether, I think I felt slightly mellower and happier, like when I gave up ciga-rettes and Diet Coke, or when mosquito season ends. And as with

cigarettes, I've come to believe cable news is slowly killing us, giving us intellectual emphysema, cancer of the mind. After all, people smoked for the better part of a century before they really knew it could be fatal.

On FOX News they're talking about the heavy security planned for the G-20 summit in Miami next month. An unworried man in Opa-Locka wearing dark glasses and a Nirvana T-shirt says that if they'd moved the summit elsewhere because of the Boca dirty bomb, it would mean the terrorists had won.

At the ad for Vizontin, the new serotonin re-uptake inhibitor that's supposed to enable and enhance religious feelings, I switch to CNN International. Their grinning, shouty correspondent who reminds me of Austin Powers is presenting a piece about "controversial political artists." Such as a Canadian who styles himself to look exactly like Adolf Hitler and appears unannounced in public places apologizing in German for the Holocaust. And—oh my God—*Alex Macallister.* Alex has paid $225,000 for a lock of Che Guevara's hair, which he intends to incorporate into a mixed-media self-portrait. I am stunned. Maybe he really has erased his problematic memories of 1968.

The phone ring startles me, which makes the cat jump and run. I see on the TV screen that it's Waverly calling. I feel instantly better, hitched back to reality. She is my anti-anxiety elixir.

"Hello, darling!"

"Hey, Grams, guess what? Your foundation guy's assistant says the grant for Virtual Home's going to get approved at their next board meeting! *Thirty thousand dollars!* I almost can't believe it. Thank you *so* much."

"It wasn't my doing, it's your brilliant project—I just pointed you in the right direction." And also reminded my friend the executive director, in passing, that Waverly is half-nonwhite. "Your mom and dad must be proud."

"Yes and no. Dad thinks it'll help me get into college, make 'a more attractively balanced extracurricular portfolio,' which is his way of saying theater's a waste of time, but he hates that it means I'll be spending even more time with 'the derelicts.' He is such a tool."

Yes, he is. "He loves you."

"You know what else he wanted me to do? Take some genetic test to find out how likely I am to become a junkie."

"*What?*"

"Yeah, it's crazy. They can tell from some certain gene if you're likely to become an addict or not. I told him no way, but then Saturday morning when I was asleep, he snuck into the bathroom and took my toothbrush and strands of my hair to send to the testing lab. He *stole* my fucking *DNA*."

"Wow."

"Hunter says if the test shows I have a high resistance to addiction, I should start doing coke and then tell Dad it's all his fault."

"No."

"I hate coke."

"What?"

"In fact, Hunter and I realized that drugs, drugs you get addicted to, are like some parody of the modern consumer system, right? Shit that brainwashes you into thinking you Must—Buy—More—to—Be—Happy, but then it only makes you temporarily not-*unhappy* and sets you up to want to buy more. Zombieland, Incorporated."

"Very smart. Are you and Hunter, um . . . going steady?"

She laughs. "You're cute, Grams. Yeah, I guess. But he graduates in June, he got in to Wesleyan early. So who knows."

"I'd love to meet him."

"Great! Actually, that's why I called. I looked it up online, and your spring break is the same as our spring break, March fifteenth to March twenty-third . . ."

I am such a lucky grandmother. "Right, that's when I'm coming to New York."

"No, well, what I was *thinking* is that *you* could still come *here* . . . and then—and then go with us down to Miami. If you wanted. We're going down for Occupy the G-20?" She pauses. "I told you, you remember, right?"

Of course I remember. "Uh-huh." She wanted me to convince

her parents to let her go. "What do your mom and dad think of this plan?"

"Dad's worried about me getting busted, but he also thinks it could be a great subject for a college application essay. So Mom's saying I can go if I don't sleep outside and a trustworthy adult comes along. Hunter's brother doesn't count, even though he's twenty-three. So . . ."

"And she considers me sufficiently trustworthy?"

"I haven't— I didn't want to bring up the possibility until I talked to you. We'd be there for four days. I figured you could stay in a nice hotel, I found one for you online not too far from the hostel where we'd be. And the fare's only ninety-three dollars each way."

"You and Hunter and I would fly down together from New York?"

She doesn't answer right away. "We can't *fly*, Grams. You know? To this? It'd be too wrong. And planes are *so* CO_2-intensive, like five times the bus."

"The *bus*?"

"I know, I know, but it only takes twenty-two hours, and you're asleep for like half that."

"I'm flattered you want me to come, I really am, but I haven't been on a Greyhound in, God, forever."

"It's not Greyhound, but it would be fun, right? Like the old days, a road trip, Kerouac, Kesey, the Jolly Pranksters, all that."

"Merry Pranksters," I tell her. "Maybe after it's over, after you're done, I could fly home to L.A. directly from Miami? Which would cut down on my share of CO_2 emissions, not coming back to New York first."

"Absolutely, *yeah*, I think, if Mom agrees to let me and Hunter take the bus home by ourselves, which I think she would. Wow: you'll actually do it?"

Oh, Lord. I guess so. Carpe diem. "Sure."

"*Awesome.*"

"And your friend Hunter is okay with this plan?"

"Completely. He won't believe it, he's a *huge* fan, you're like this big *celebrity* to him. He did a whole thing in history class based on

your article about how the American political system is unconstitutional."

"I appreciate that Hunter's a fan, but that's not what I wrote, honey." She was referring to a minor point I made a few years ago that caused a stink, thanks to FOX News. "One could argue," I wrote in *The Atlantic*, "that we the people are engaged in a systemic de facto abrogation of Article VI—'no religious Test shall ever be required as a Qualification to any Office'—given that only one of our 535 members of Congress can or will admit to being an atheist." Even if I hadn't withdrawn my name from consideration for the Court last year, and I'd been nominated, that sentence alone might have queered my chances for confirmation.

"Whatever," Waverly said, "he'll be super-excited. He's also inspired by your diabetes, that you're so completely *fine* after fifty years of having it."

Forty-six years and nine months. "That's nice."

"You are completely healthy—right?"

"I'm good."

"That's what I thought. No . . . like, mental issues or anything, right?"

"None that I haven't always had. How come? Am I sounding senile?"

"*No,* of course not, Mom and Dad were just talking about, I don't know, scans and new brain studies and whatnot. Mom stuff."

As soon as I hang up, I go online to make a reservation for my ton-of-CO_2-emitting flights to and from the East Coast. And I see that I've received an email from Alex. We've had no communication since we spoke a month ago.

The salutation is "my dearest pal karen." He says that "if I know 1 thing it's that everybody's got his/her own truth," and that he's "felt so SHITTY evr since r misunderstanding," that at the time he was "crazy-frazzled from being in my work/war-zone/rug-merchant head. hope 2 c u f2f IRL soonest. hey! at biotech conference at rockefeller u in nyc i met yr beautiful brainiac greta! SO jealous u have such offspring."

16

I F YOU LIVED in a prosperous American suburb and attended public high school in the 1960s, you know what my life was like. If your era came later, imagine it with a bit less jadedness and drugs and sex, and no hip-hop or computers: those are my teenage years.

I understand now why filmmakers resort to montage to suggest the passage of time.

My family eating Sunday dinner in front of the TV so we can watch the Beatles on *Ed Sullivan,* with Sabrina using her new Instamatic to take a color picture of the black-and-white screen.

Me examining myself in a full-length mirror as I talk to my friend Mary Ann on the new TouchTone phone about how I look in my first miniskirt.

Me on assignment for the *New Trier News,* interviewing the actor Raymond Burr, who plays Perry Mason on TV, just before he addresses the annual dinner of the North Shore Bar Association.

Alex and me in the stands at the state championship swim meet, both of us staring at Chuck's lean, smooth, Speedo'd six-foot-three body as he shakes his arms and flexes his legs in preparation for swimming the 400 freestyle.

The three of us in Alex's basement on a Saturday night with a half gallon of orange juice and a fifth of vodka, Alex belting out "The Name Game" ("Chuck, Chuck bo Buck, banana fanna fo fuck"), me dancing as his go-go-girl sidekick and Chuck applauding.

The sock hop where Chuck debuts his band, me dancing with a short boy wearing a dickey as I watch Wendy Reichman do an impeccable Jerk all by herself as she gazes adoringly at Chuck.

Me in French class carefully writing and underlining *L'existentialisme,* me that night in a Rambler at the Bel-Air drive-in theater (double feature: *That Darn Cat!* and *Die! Die! My Darling!*), with a boy a year older from Loyola Academy, making out for the first time and going to second base for the first time the same night.

Alex and Chuck and me, all three of us in time-lapse close-up, our hair growing longer from freshman to senior year, the boys' extending over their ears and collars, mine inching past my collarbone to my shoulders and then cascading down my arms and back.

Me at home alone on a Friday night, listening to Simon & Garfunkel and looking up from *The Nation* to imagine Chuck (*I was not a rock, I was not an island, I felt pain, I was crying*) at the Beatles concert at Comiskey Park with Wendy Reichman . . . Peter and Sabrina going up to bed at the end of *The Man from U.N.C.L.E.* while I watch *That Was the Week That Was* with Dad . . . me in the backseat of our station wagon reading *Cat's Cradle* by Kurt Vonnegut as we drive to northern Minnesota for a family canoe trip during which I will break my arm.

And so on. Each one of those scenes is absolutely factual, but the portrait as a whole seems half true at best, so much more brisk and fun than the real thing. In a more accurate montage, there would be weirder, less Hollywood-cute moments—me dripping hot wax from a candle onto my little finger to encase it, me using a needle and thread to stitch patterns into the tough skin on the sole of my foot. And all of the five-second glimpses would be effervescent punctuation between long scenes of me reading assigned books and writing key facts on three-by-five cards.

Notwithstanding the arrival of The Sixties like a very noisy circus

parade rolling into town from another dimension, I remained a conscientious student, as did Chuck and Alex. During high school, we never discussed and weren't even quite aware of the straddle we were attempting, studying hard and participating in extracurriculars even while we reimagined ourselves as existential renegades driven by contempt for conventional ambition and hypocrisy. But after several years doing that straddle, one foot on the solid old dock and the other in the new speedboat as it gunned its engines and started pulling away, it eventually became untenable.

At first, as the 1960s turned into The Sixties, nothing political I thought or said amounted to rebellion. I was the daughter of people who thought Mayor Daley was creating a police state in Chicago, who paid dues to the National Committee for a Sane Nuclear Policy, who belonged to a local cell of integrationist parents. I liked knowing Esperanto for the same reason Chuck knew phrases in Tolkien's Middle Earth languages—because we were geeks—but to my mother, Esperantists were virtuous fellow travelers speaking a language that Hitler and Franco had outlawed. When I attended the big memorial in Evanston for the three young voter-registration volunteers murdered by the Klan in Mississippi, my mother was doubly pleased, because I was safely playing my little part in Freedom Summer *and* entering a Catholic church for the first time in a year and a half. When she asked if I'd crossed myself, I lied and said no. Lefty politics were the family religion I had not rejected.

Until Alex and Chuck turned sixteen, somebody's mom usually drove us to and from New Trier, but one day in October 1964, the beginning of sophomore year, we'd all stayed late after school and walked the two miles home together.

It was one of those fall afternoons—great shafts of sunlight beaming between tall trees, startling indigo sky, leaves turning, neither warm nor chilly, every fifth breeze smelling of smoke—when old suburbs are ravishing and suburbanites are most convinced they've made the right choices in life. The three of us were a little hyped up: Chuck from swimming, Alex from acting, me from re-

hearsing my Model UN speech condemning the Gulf of Tonkin Resolution.

On Abbotsford Road in Kenilworth, we came upon a group of kids, two crew-cut boys wearing cardigans and neckties, and two goody-goody-looking girls, one of them wearing a suit and an old-fashioned straw boater. They were carrying clipboards and sheaves of mimeographs and going door-to-door. As we got closer, we saw the girl's hatband was a bumper sticker that said *Au H$_2$O '64*, the smarty-pants campaign slogan for Barry Goldwater, the Republican nominee for president.

The blond girl without the hat, a little older than the rest of us, asked for directions. "Excuse me—which way is Woodstock?"

"That way," Chuck said, nodding in the direction we were headed, "two blocks. Where you from?"

"Maine East," one of the boys said.

Maine Township High School East was somewhere out beyond the expressway, almost to O'Hare. Our ideological disapproval was reinforced by a sense of social superiority.

The head girl offered us flyers and urged us to attend "a really fun Goldwater pep rally" on Saturday. Something in me snapped.

"So," I said, "I guess you're over here because you ran out of war-mongers and racists who wanted your propaganda back in Park Ridge?"

The girl pushed up her thick glasses—I was so glad I'd just gotten contact lenses—planted her black-and-white saddle-shoed feet and folded her arms around her stack of papers. She was fierce. "Senator Goldwater supports civil rights."

"So, what," I said, "he voted against the Civil Rights *Act* by *mistake*?"

"Come on," one of the Goldwater boys said to his pals, "let's go, we've got three more blocks to do." He seemed embarrassed. The other boy and the younger girl in the hat looked scared.

My boys, galvanized by my girl-on-girl bullying, were ready to rumble.

"How many Negro delegates did they have at the Republican convention," Alex asked, "like twenty?"

"Fourteen," I said, "out of thirteen hundred."

"He's going to lose, you know," Chuck said.

The Goldwaterites formed a tight cluster as they turned and walked away from us across Abbotsford toward Woodstock Avenue.

Alex grinned at me, shaking his head.

"Whoa, *Hollaender,"* Chuck said, "I thought the chick in the polio boots was gonna sock you!" He put out a hand for me to slap him five, then slapped mine back.

I thought of the Crystals song "He Hit Me (It Felt Like a Kiss)." A year had passed since my recommitment to being Just Friends, but moments like this always threatened to revive my passions.

I smiled and lit a cigarette. "Like the man says," I said, quoting Goldwater's nomination speech, "extremism in the defense of liberty's no vice, and moderation in the pursuit of justice is no virtue. Come on, let's follow them—they've got three more blocks to do."

At the next house, we paused on the sidewalk as they rang the doorbell and started giving their spiel to the white-haired lady who answered the door. They realized we were behind them on the porch only when the woman looked past them at us.

"Excuse me, ma'am," I said, "we're your *neighbors,* from just over in Wilmette? And I wanted to let you know that the Ku Klux Klan are enthusiastic supporters of Senator Goldwater."

"What?" she said.

"Also," Chuck added, "Senator Goldwater wants to get rid of Social Security. In case you didn't know."

"Oh!" she said. "I—I *didn't* know that."

"No," the head Goldwater girl said, "he thinks it should be *voluntary."*

"Also," I said, "Senator Goldwater wants to bomb North Vietnam with *atomic weapons."*

The woman's confusion had turned to alarm.

"You have such a beautiful home," Alex said, which reassured her.

"Thank you, dear."

As the other boy flipped Chuck the bird, the woman shut her door.

"Come on," the angry Goldwater squad leader commanded. We followed. They stopped briefly for a huddle in front of the next house, and we stopped five paces behind, but they didn't go up to the door, and then they headed into the sunset without stopping. We taunted them some more—Alex called Goldwater "the fascist gun in the West"—until they climbed into a car parked on Green Bay Road and drove away.

The three of us were ecstatic the rest of the way home. As we walked down Green Bay, Alex started singing "The Jet Song" from *West Side Story* and swinging on lampposts. Until that day, politics for us had been a matter of polite pro-and-con discussions, we junior citizens standing up for decency and fairness, all another nice student activity conducted according to the rules. What we'd just done, on the other hand, would horrify our teachers and probably even my parents. We'd been *bad* in service to the good, and it felt great.

Chuck proposed that we go out late some night to tear down Goldwater yard signs. That gave me a different idea.

We mimeographed posters that we spent a weekend taping up all over Wilmette and Winnetka. VOTE GOLDWATER! the signs said. AGAINST SOCIAL SECURITY! AGAINST THE UN! FOR ANOTHER INVASION OF CUBA! FOR NUCLEAR BOMBS IN VIETNAM! I felt as if I had invented irony. Alex took a picture of two freshmen looking at the poster we'd taped to a telephone pole in front of New Trier, and I got the school paper to run the photo on the front page. We had discovered the power of an incestuous self-serving left-wing media elite.

You know how teenagers always think the universe revolves around them, as if they're the only ones who really *get* it, as if they're the first young people to feel the awful ecstasies and sweet agonies of youth? Those years we turned fifteen and sixteen, the universe *did* start revolving around us, affirming our adolescent monomania, making our fantasy of self-importance real. Practically overnight, we and everything we thought and did—our new music, the new ways we dressed and talked, our libertine sensibilities, our real and fake idealisms—became Topic A among the grown-ups. Television,

radio, magazines, books, movies, the whole culture slavishly turned its full attention to us. We were sexy and terrifying, the shock troops of a new age. We were America's cool kids by virtue of simply being kids, even if we weren't cool.

The same month we ambushed the Goldwater volunteers, Alex gave me a copy of *Esquire* in which Norman Mailer had an article about the previous summer's Republican convention in San Francisco. I recall one line in particular: "There's a shit storm coming like nothing you ever knew." I knew that lots of people, older people, my parents, would read that and shudder. But the distant thunder of the coming shit storm was nothing but thrilling to us, a coming attraction, like a trailer for a movie in which we could perform as extras simply because we were fifteen.

The next summer, 1965, my summer of being sixteen, was the blindingly bright dividing line between Before and After. A year earlier, Vietnam had been another one of those obscure, fractious foreign places in the news. A year earlier, it seemed as if the Civil Rights Act had finally taken care of the Negro problem, and the War on Poverty would now take care of the poverty problem. A year earlier, girls were wearing their hair big and poufy, and only the Crawford twins wore miniskirts. A year earlier, rock and roll seemed like a fad. The summer of 1965 was when the term of art changed from "combo" to "band," and when Chuck and three other boys started one. A year earlier, there had been only one New Trier, but now there were so many teenagers that a second campus had to be built on the other side of the expressway, New Trier West. In the summer of 1965, everyone suddenly understood this was only the beginning of something, not the middle or the end.

I started believing I was grown up that summer. I let Channing Payne feel me up at that drive-in movie and attended an antiwar rally unaccompanied by my parents. Tatty No Man's Land disappeared under rows of shiny new lakefront apartment buildings. My dislike of the new rock-and-roll TV show *Shindig* grew into a general contempt for the Establishment repackaging and selling our contempt for the Establishment back to us. I played the Rolling

Stones' album *Out of Our Heads* many dozens of times, and it was "Satisfaction," brutally pro-sex and anti-advertising, with which I convinced Chuck that the Stones were superior to the Beatles.

Although Chuck had given up his dream of becoming an air force pilot, Alex still teased him about it, calling him Lieutenant Levy after he started taking flying lessons. One day in the summer of 1965, Chuck made his first solo flight. "For the first time in my life," he told us that afternoon, "I didn't feel like a kid. I actually felt like— like a man," which to my great surprise Alex did not turn into a smutty joke. In fact, he said, "Yeah, I know what you mean. I feel that way when I'm out shooting." Alex was taking a filmmaking summer school course, for which he shot a short documentary about two boys from Skokie deciding whether to burn their draft cards. He also had his cousin in Canada mail a fan letter to Fidel Castro in Cuba and got a personal reply, and he started dating a large-breasted blonde named Patti who'd joined our chapter of the Student Peace Union.

By the summer of 1965 the single overt vestige of my Bond-enraptured girlhood was the Chesterfields I lit up wherever and whenever I wanted, even at home, and certainly that afternoon after Chuck's first solo flight in the booth at Bob's.

"You should switch to Gitanes," Chuck said to me. "Or Gauloises."

Two years earlier, I would've wondered if he was flirting; now I knew, and regretted, that he was not. I exhaled my stream of smoke just above his head and quoted the Stones—"You can't be a man 'cause you do not smoke the same cigarettes as me."

Chuck bummed a Chesterfield. "Dick, my flight instructor, told me he once dropped a lit Lucky in his lap during a landing and just about flipped the plane."

"Do you ever think about crashing?" I asked.

"All the time. Not, like, scared of the weather or running out of fuel or whatever. But I always think, *I could bring this thing down any time I want. I'm choosing not to.*"

"That's very existentialist," Alex said. He wasn't being sarcastic.

Chuck exhaled and smiled and said, *"Oui."*

Damn you, Chuck Levy, for being so cute.

"At that WMAQ thing last night," Alex said, *"I Spy* was *great."* The Chicago NBC station was one of Mr. Macallister's legal clients, and they'd held a screening of highlights of the network's new shows.

"It's . . . funny?" I asked.

"More *witty.* But realistic. From now on it'll be hard to watch a Bond movie without it looking ridiculous."

"It already is," Chuck said.

There had been two more Bond movies, *From Russia with Love* and *Goldfinger,* each more successful than the last and, to us, more stupid and wrong. I hated that in the movies, unlike the books, the girls were purely sex objects and Bond never showed the slightest regret for anything. When we were watching *Goldfinger,* and he tells the gold-painted girl that drinking warm champagne is "as bad as listening to the Beatles without earmuffs," Chuck turned to me and whispered, "Okay, that's it. I'm done."

Then there were Bond's unfortunate politics. On our missions we'd been agnostic, sometimes playing Bond and Leiter, sometimes playing Communist or criminal masterminds and killers. In high school the scales dropped from my eyes. I understood our Bond-mania had entailed a childish political cluelessness. By the summer of 1965 I'd come to see that the real CIA and MI6 didn't consist of good guys occasionally obliged to do bad things to defeat evil, but bad guys routinely doing bad things to maintain power for the powerful.

"James Bond," I said to Alex and Chuck that afternoon in 1965 at our table at Bob's, "is just an imperialist thug in a sharp suit. He's an evil robot. Period. End of story. I almost couldn't finish the new one." *The Man with the Golden Gun,* Fleming's final novel, had just come out.

Alex screwed up his face. "Oh, I *know.*"

"I've started *The Spy Who Came In from the Cold,*" Chuck told Alex, "and you're right, it's great. *So* realistic. So much better than Flem-

ing. Everybody keeps secrets and lies. Everybody's betraying everybody else."

"Although," Alex said, "you'll see in the end that true love carries the day. Sort of."

It was late. I slid out of the booth. "Maybe I'll see you guys Sunday at the thing on Winnetka Green?"

"Will we get to meet the mysterious Charlie Chan?" Alex asked.

I shrugged. Chan (short for Channing) Payne, my first boyfriend, had told me he'd be working at the thing on Winnetka Green. We were both volunteers for the North Shore Summer Project, which entailed knocking on doors in Wilmette and Winnetka, especially those with for-sale signs, and asking the owners if they were racist or anti-Semitic. Actually, the question we posed—"Would you be willing to sell your house on a nondiscriminatory basis?"—was so polite and anodyne that half the time the women who answered the doors didn't understand what we were asking. When we made ourselves clear—"Would you sell your house to a family of Negroes or Jews?"—they rarely said no, but most of them got embarrassed and nervous, which was the real point of the enterprise, it seemed, more than gathering data.

For me it was a watershed. The girl who couldn't stand selling Camp Fire candy was now selling the idea of integration and practically relishing the awkwardness. After one man shut his door and went back inside, we thought we heard him say something—to his wife? one of his kids?—about "niggers buying our house."

I can't say the North Shore Summer Project experience "radicalized" me, exactly. Instead, my long-standing beatnik-y belief in the timidity and complacency and hypocrisy of grown-ups now had seven sweaty, exhausting weeks of empirical confirmation. I understood that any important change or real progress would be grindingly slow.

I started to feel like the hero in *Invasion of the Body Snatchers,* as if I'd discovered that the people in my hometown were clones. That summer my sister, Sabrina, received the sacrament of confirmation at St. Joseph's. When she and her fellow inductees repeatedly lowed

"I do" on command—"Do you reject Satan? And all his works? And all his empty promises?"—it was one more confirmation of my growing sense that I was surrounded by pod people.

On the last Sunday in July 1965, after my dad and brother and I watched the Cubs lose on TV, the whole family drove up to the Winnetka Village Green and claimed a spot of grass. My mother spread out a Marimekko tablecloth printed with giant pink flowers. We got dinner from a North Shore Summer Project chuck wagon—Chan was serving slices of Wonder bread; we said hi—and drank nonalcoholic sangria from a big plaid thermos that Mom had brought.

I spotted Alex squatting near the podium, holding his 16-millimeter movie camera, panning the crowd. We waved at each other. "And isn't that Chuck," my mother said too loudly, "over there, in line at the picnic wagon, with the Reichman girl?" It was. "Do you want to go invite them to come sit with us? Plenty of sangria left!" I did not.

Sabrina was reading a Laura Ingalls Wilder book, *These Happy Golden Years,* and Peter played with his favorite toy, a black plastic briefcase containing a fake passport and a cap pistol that could be converted into a sniper rifle. Violet was with us, too, more dressed up than I'd ever seen her, holding a handkerchief in one hand and her inhaler in the other, speaking only when spoken to. She and my mother were both self-conscious about her presence, Violet nervous and my mother proud. Every few minutes my mom or dad mentioned how perfect the weather was, sunny, dry, breezy, not too hot—except for a few chiggers, the ideal summer afternoon.

Everyone on the Green must have felt self-conscious. There were hundreds when we arrived and thousands by six o'clock, expectant and antsy, strenuously smiling at strangers and checking their watches as more people streamed in. Dozens of cops stood around the edges.

Suddenly, at the corner of the Green, fifty yards away, there was

a commotion—first shouting, then a parked police car's cherry top flashing. My parents exchanged a worried look, and Violet stared at her hands. People stood on tiptoe and craned their necks. Peter and I wanted to go see what was happening, my mother told us to stay put, I pooh-poohed her—"It's *Winnetka*"—and as we took off, my father came along.

Nazis! I'd never seen Peter so excited. I was excited, too. There were four of them, men who looked to be in their early twenties, dressed in khaki trousers and long-sleeved brown shirts, each wearing a swastika armband just above his left elbow. We got only intermittent glimpses of the Nazis, because half a dozen cops had formed a protective circle around them, and scores of angry bystanders had formed a circle around the police cordon. Shockingly, the librarian from Locust Junior High shouted at the Nazis—"Crawl back under your rocks!" I had never seen more than one or two people at a time so upset, let alone a whole crowd.

"Sick boys," my father muttered. I wondered what it felt like for him seeing Nazis again, twenty years after the end of the war. I'd seen old pictures of fascists wearing swastikas, but it was something else again to see the real things, those black right angles on bright red. After a while my fascinated horror cooled to curiosity—*How do they earn a living? Where did they get the armbands?*—and I realized these four losers were *playing* Nazis, not entirely different than the way we used to play European secret agents and killers.

The Winnetka police chief arrived, made his way through the crowd, and walked to the very center, where he spoke quietly for a minute to the Nazis. Then the Nazis, accompanied by a phalanx of cops, walked out of the park. People applauded, which made it seem even more like a theatrical performance.

It was after seven when the official show began. One of the women in charge of the North Shore Summer Project stepped up on the small unpainted wooden platform. As she delivered her introduction, the buzz of cicadas and crickets got louder and louder and then stopped the instant before she uttered the speaker's name.

As he took the stage and we all clapped, the sun dipped beneath the boughs along Maple Street and bathed him and us in light. My first thought: how *young* he looked.

"He's a *doctor?*" Peter said loudly over the applause. "I thought he was a *priest.*"

"A Ph.D.," I explained to my brother as he snapped shut his James Bond 007 Shooting Attaché Case and started clapping.

We were no more than twenty yards away from the stage. Malcolm X had been assassinated a few months earlier giving a speech in New York. If Peter's gun were real, I thought, he could easily shoot Dr. King from where we sat.

When Dr. King said we all needed to "go all out to end segregation in housing" right here on the North Shore, a few people booed, but immediate cheering and clapping by the multitude, including us, drowned them out. "Every white person," Dr. King told the thousands of white people, "does great injury to his child if he allows that child to grow up in a world that is two-thirds colored and yet live in conditions where that child does not come into person-to-person contact with colored people." When I sneaked a look at Violet, she was wiping tears from her eyes. I knew it wasn't exactly what Dr. King had in mind, but I did wonder if she appreciated the person-to-person contact we had with her.

I was very glad to have been there. When he delivered lines I'd read and heard on TV—"We must learn to live together as brothers or we will perish together as fools"—it was like when I'd finally seen the Beatles at the International Amphitheatre and knew all the lyrics by heart. Martin Luther King was saintly and moving, but what thrilled me that night was the antagonism he stirred up—the Nazis, the spontaneous anti-Nazi counterprotest, the booing, the spontaneous anti-booing. Also the fact that Chuck Levy was served by Chan Payne at the chuck wagon, ate a piece of Wonder bread touched by the fingers that had touched my breasts, and only I was aware of the encounter.

17

A FEW WEEKS AFTER King's speech in Winnetka, thousands of Negroes in Los Angeles burned and looted hundreds of buildings in their neighborhood for days. I still have the *Newsweek* about the Watts Riots in my moldering-cardboard-box archive: on the cover is a picture of four white National Guardsmen holding rifles in an open Jeep at the front of a convoy driving toward the photographer on a wide, empty L.A. boulevard, with the headlines LOS ANGELES: WHY? and, honest to God, THE RIOTS IN COLOR. It was also the week of the twentieth anniversary of the end of World War II, an anniversary that is, astonishingly, mentioned nowhere in the magazine. Can you imagine? We are now so compulsively anniversary-crazy, I think, because people are much more comfortable looking backward than forward. The past, they think, doesn't alter, isn't confusing or frightening, cannot *loom*.

Stewart has been sending me terse text-message bulletins every week or so since I asked for his help. "Working it," one said. Then: "Might have found a new way to retrieve something interesting, but no promises." This morning, when I get off my plane in Newark, I receive another: "Still working it. Stay tuned. P.S.: Your middle

name is Scattergood? LOVE that. And your old man: Hollaender, Nils R., DOB 3/29/20, Danish national naturalized 1946—that him?" As I wait in the taxi line, I answer yes, yes, and yes. My taxi trip from Newark airport to New York City costs more than my bus trip from New York to Miami will cost.

Greta's not home from work yet when I arrive at their apartment, and Waverly's in her bedroom, so it's just Jungo and me. He makes me put on special battery-powered glasses to watch his 3-D TV, and I try to sound enthusiastic. "Those cows do look real," I say. "I've never seen cows like that before."

"Breathtaking, right?"

I won't go quite that far. I take off the glasses. "Cool," I say, and glance at the clock on the TV: 6:03. "How about a martini?"

"Sorry, no gin, but let me see . . ." Jungo crouches down by the cabinet under the kitchen sink, one in which most people keep a garbage can and poisons. He reaches deep into the back, feeling for dusty bottles. "Sambuca? No? Wait, here's a little souvenir bottle of tequila we received at some event. It is what it is."

"I'll pass, don't worry about it." I haven't adjusted to Greta's tee-totaling, Even though I don't eat sugar, I keep plenty on hand for guests. I've never expected the people around me to pay a price for my illness. On the other hand, maybe I'm an insensitive jerk.

Seth shows up, and my motherly pleasure in seeing him has some extra zing because he's brought a cold bottle of sauvignon blanc.

When I left Jack and moved to L.A., Seth was living with us at age twenty-four and told me that even though he knew it was ridiculous, he felt abandoned, like the little boy in *Kramer vs. Kramer.* I still send Seth a few hundred dollars a month, even though when I was his age, I was on my third full-time grown-up job and had a four-year-old.

As a boy, he was a math-and-technology whiz, and we always figured he'd be the scientist, not our artist-philosopher Greta. He was a semifinalist in the Intel Science Talent Search, and even got a patent for his project, a digital camera sensor and software that allow you, as you're taking a picture, to select any section of the

image and replace it with adjacent background bits; in other words, he invented a simple way to make people disappear from photos on the fly. I thought it was a brilliant, perverse work of conceptual art, but eighteen-year-old Seth expected it to make him rich—a cheap VampireCam for kids, since vampires can't be photographed. I guess he was ahead of the curve, vampire-wise, because the camera companies weren't interested.

Seth suspected he'd been screwed by backroom corporate malfeasance. Eventually, he forgave me for refusing to file suit against Intel on his behalf, but when I sold the big family apartment after Jack died two years ago, thus requiring Seth, at age twenty-eight, to move out and find his own place, he told me I didn't have his back, "just like with Intel." He's now an electronic musician of whom certain cognoscenti are very respectful. Like father, like son. Except he's a lot more fun than his father. Seth calls himself Seth Hollander instead of Seth Wu, because he doesn't want avant-garde music people to think he's "some kind of Miley Cyrus or Sean Lennon or something," trying to coast on the reputation of his avant-garde composer father. "I want to be obscure on my *own*," he said when he asked permission to start using my surname professionally.

In addition to the wine, Seth has brought along a medal he recently won in Reykjavík, and the award citation, which calls his music "a sui generis hybrid of extraterrestrial neo-baroque strings and musique concrète interlarded with fat grime beats."

"That's *wonderful*, Seth! Wow. But tell this old lady who hasn't bought new music since Talking Heads what 'fat grime beats' are."

"The turntable sounds I simulate on the computer and use as percussion. What you thought were timpani."

"Here you go, Mom," Jungo says as he hands me a tumbler of wine. Perhaps other mothers-in-law actually enjoy being called "Mom" by their children's spouses.

"Jungo, Greta tells me you're in the running for a new job, at Princeton?"

"Yup—director of institutional effectiveness. Big process-reengineering gig. Setting up an innovation pipeline. Giving back."

I nod, even though I understand what he means about as well as I do fat grime beats. Having glanced at thousands of freshly dealt business cards over the years, I'm accustomed to having no idea what particular job titles mean. When Greta first met him, Jungo was a "coordinator of learning immersion experiences targeting value shoppers."

"That'd be a serious commute," I say.

"It is what it is," Jungo says. "About an hour and a quarter."

"Bullshit," Seth corrects, "two hours door to door if you're lucky." I don't mean to be flip about my son's illness, but his symptoms of mild autism spectrum disorder often strike me as bracing and admirable.

"Well," I say, "there's one key to institutional effectiveness—three hours on the train every day to deal with all the emails in your inbox about institutional effectiveness." I am joking, sort of, but Jungo nods earnestly. This is an established pattern with us. The first night I met him, he told me he was investing in a friend's company that contracted with private schools to pick lice out of children's scalps for $150 per kid, and I'd thought he was joking. A few years ago, when I said the lice-picking firm should expand into "high-margin artisanal bedbug removal," he didn't realize I was joking.

Greta arrives home, laden with plastic bags. I'd offered to spring for dinner out, but she was adamant about eating at home, "to have a real old-fashioned family dinner," so we are eating microwaved Whole Foods sole amandine and broccolini with garlic.

During the meal, Waverly brings up the work in Greta's lab on visual processing, how fascinated she is by the fact that ten billion bits of information reach the eye every second but ninety-nine-point-ninety-nine percent never get to the brain.

Seth comes alive. "Machines kick our asses in so many ways." He saw *The Matrix* seven times the first two weeks it was in theaters. "It's like we're stuck with a permanent dial-up connection in here," he says, tapping his right temple. "It's fucking insane."

Jungo frowns, and I ask Greta if Waverly's statistic is correct.

"It's a lot worse than that," she says. "Our conscious visual per-

ceptions are based on just a few *hundred* bits from those billions of bits of information the retina collects. The brain takes those few specks, this very, very rough sketch, and then . . . *imagines* the rest of the image."

This is why I find Greta's work more interesting than that of almost anyone else I know, including mine. "So everything we think we're seeing," I ask, "everything we're sure looks just *so*—the salt-shaker, the piece of broccolini—it's all just a guess? Really? A *prediction* our brains are making?"

"More or less, probably, yeah," Greta says, standing, taking her plate and mine away, "and consciousness in general probably has a lot of features like that."

"It's not a *bug*," Seth shouts, "it's a *feature!*"

"We think we know why we think something," Greta continues, "or why we feel a certain way, but our minds *hide* the mental processes from us that produced those thoughts and feelings. Some people think that could be a main point of consciousness—hiding the processing states from ourselves."

"I find the point-oh-oh-oh-oh-percent thing sort of beautiful."

"Of course you do, Glinda the Good," Seth says to me. "Every glass half full, even the cracked, empty ones."

Seeing silver linings is one of the family caricatures of me, along with working too hard and being a stickler for accuracy.

"Good old PMA," Jungo says, giving me a thumbs-up. This stands for "positive mental attitude," which he likes to think is the one trait the two of us share.

"Beautiful how, Grams?"

"Because it means that simply in order to *see,* we've got to be like artists all the time, every waking moment, constantly taking those few dabs of information and using them to imagine this whole complex, panoramic picture of reality." We're each the god of our own experience, the maker of all that is, seen and unseen.

Greta and Jungo exchange a quick, weird look. "Who wants apple crisp?" she says. "It's sugar-free, Mom."

"Thanks, sweetie." I'm irritated by well-intentioned people who

make special accommodations for my diabetes, but they are trying to be nice, so I never say it annoys me. "With a tiny scoop of the vanilla, please," I tell Greta.

Over dessert, she resumes the brain conversation. "There's a very senior guy at our lab who's convinced he's figured out the function of this entirely mysterious area of the brain, this area at the very top, V7, that we know is somehow connected to visual processing. He thinks it's semi-vestigial. He thinks it might be the part of the brain that allowed us, eons ago, to see energies and colors we don't see anymore. He thinks it's why people used to believe more easily in magic and angels and things. 'The cerebral seat of enchantment,' he calls it."

"Is he possibly right?" I ask.

"He's got no data. It's more like a hunch." She pauses, takes a deep breath. "We worry he may be going a little loopy."

Jungo shoots her the same look he did before, but this time she avoids his glance.

Sometime after midnight, I'm all alone in their living room working on my laptop, chewing my last Nicorette of the day.

"Hi." Not all alone: Greta has appeared.

"Hi," I whisper back.

The bathrobe suggests she means to join me for a while. She sits at the other end of the couch. "Are you entirely sure you're up to this? The bus trip and chaperoning them down there while they're doing their Occupy thing? You know, you're not obligated to prove you're the coolest grandma on the planet."

"It'll be fun for me."

She tucks her legs under her, her silence signaling skepticism.

"It'll be an adventure," I say.

"You're not seventeen."

"I'm not elderly, either. Anyway, you ought to be happy she's willing to be chaperoned. Another kind of kid would just take off and ignore whatever you said."

"A kid like you at her age?"

"You know, I wasn't as much of a hell-raiser as you seem to think."

"Mom, what did you mean last month when you said you've been discovering new memories that you're putting in the book?"

"What?"

"We were talking on the phone, and you told me you found yourself 'remembering more and more all the time.' And in another call, you said you were 'surprised' by some of the things you were remembering."

"I meant that my memory is surprisingly good, crystal-clear, shockingly better than I suspected now that I'm dredging up stuff from forty and fifty years ago."

"Like *what* stuff?"

I'm tempted to say what she used to say to me when she was a teenager: *Why does everything with you have to be a cross-examination?*

"Little moments from my life, things I thought and said and did when I was eleven and fifteen and eighteen."

"Right. And your book is totally *non*fiction, right? You're not mixing in imaginary things with real things?"

"Greta? Just what the *fuck* are you trying to get at?"

"*Shhh,* don't get upset. Just hear me out, okay? In the literature, there are lots of cases where intense exploration of one's memories—like you're doing now—can produce . . . unreliable results. Especially in older people."

"*I* see. This is why Waverly was so concerned about my mental soundness. You and Jungo have decided I'm senile. Un-*fucking*-believable."

"Mom, people of all ages for all kinds of neurological reasons can 'remember' things that didn't necessarily happen. People generate false memories. There's even a particular aneurysm that can occur, this one tiny artery in the brain can burst and produce . . . confabulation."

"'Confabulation,' huh? You haven't read a word of this," I say, pointing at my laptop with both hands, palms up, "but you're worried preemptively that my mind's gone kaplooey, that I'm fantasiz-

ing, making shit up that I think is real? Christ! For twenty-five years I've put up with you treating me like a fragile freak because of the diabetes, but I *refuse* to be on some kind of dementia watch for the next twenty-five years."

"I met your friend Alex Macallister—"

"Oh, Jesus!"

"—at a conference, and we had dinner. He's extremely well versed in neuroscience on a clinical level, for a layperson, and he told me . . . He says you're threatening to blackmail him, that you've developed some kind of morbid fantasy about, I don't know, about . . . about violence that you and he committed back then, some kind of conspiracy. When you were young."

I feel great relief along with my anger. For the last minute I'd begun to worry—maybe Greta has noticed dementia symptoms of which I'm unaware. But no, her fears aren't her own, they're Alex's doing, disinformation, part of his *Gaslight* plot to make me seem mentally ill. I take a breath. "Alex Macallister is evil, Greta. An evil, lying weasel."

"Mom, *evil*?"

"Lying about me when I'm the one proposing to finally tell the truth about what we did? Christ." Steady, Karen. "Yeah, evil."

"This is exactly what he said you'd say."

"Really—those words? 'Weasel'? 'Evil, lying weasel'?"

"No, how he said you'd react. Anosognosia—the suspiciousness and paranoia when people with a disability are unaware of the disability and deny it."

"How am I trying to blackmail him? What am I trying to force him to do?"

"He didn't say—"

"And exactly what is he claiming I've fabricated? Exactly what is my 'morbid fantasy'?"

"He didn't go into the specifics. He said for possible legal reasons, it was better if I didn't know the details."

"He is such a *pathological* bullshitter."

"Some kind of plot, he said, political violence in the sixties."

Another wave of relief. I'd caught him red-handed. "Really? How interesting. Because in the *only* conversation I've had with him about this during the last forty years, two months ago, in January, I didn't mention *any* of the specifics at all, *nothing*. So whatever he said to you came entirely from his own memory." The defense rests. Or am I the prosecution?

Greta is sitting perfectly still, breathing normally, staring straight at me, as tears start running down her cheeks. I move my computer and put out my arms, and she lets herself fall into my embrace, her head on my lap.

"Honey, it's okay." Now she's shuddering, crying the way she did as a child, almost noiselessly. I stroke her head. "Shhhh . . . Take a breath. Look at me." She looks up. "Have I said or done anything at all that seems off or demented? Tell me if I have."

"*Nooo,*" she says, sounding twelve again, sniffing, wiping the wetness from her face. "So what *did* you *do*? That you're writing about? Blow up a building or something?"

"No."

"*What,* then?"

"It's complicated."

I can't tell her. It was Greta's absolute ignorance that led Alex to overplay his hand and say too much; I worry I'll somehow lose leverage with him if she or anyone else knows the details before the book is finished. She might tell Jungo, who might in turn tell God knows who. Any chatter or rumor that reached Washington could ruin whatever chance Stewart has of finding and quietly plucking confidential files from the government's bowels. For that matter, what if she continues to think I'm confabulating false memories? What if she, a respected Rockefeller University neuroscientist, were to go to my publisher and tell them she's worried that I'm senile and made everything up?

"Darling, I promise you will be the first person to read the whole thing when it's all done," I say, by which I mean edited, locked down, printed, irrevocably headed out into the world for the unseen finally to become the seen. "Until it's done, all the blanks filled in, all

my unanswered questions answered, it's . . . I wouldn't be comfortable. Also?" This is lame and lawyerly but accurate: "My publisher and I signed a very strict mutual nondisclosure agreement."

"Okay." She hugs me tighter. "I was worried. I *am* worried."

"Don't be, sweetie."

As I lie in bed, unable to sleep, I realize that I've never had a serious enemy—indeed, that making no enemies had been an unconscious but defining MO for me. I've gone out of my way to mollify and even befriend rivals. I've mostly steered clear of politics. I've had legal adversaries, but I was always the one who sincerely preferred pleas and settlements to trials. I stayed married to Jack as long as I did so he wouldn't hate me. Since I was nineteen, I've avoided making implacable enemies, tried hard not to give anyone a motive to dig out the truth and ruin me with it. For forty-six years, I've blackmailed myself into being collegial and unthreatening. But now I've become a threat. Alex Macallister, my oldest friend, is now my first true enemy.

Outside Grand Central I see three girls standing on the corner, all in burgundy University of Virginia sweatshirts, each taking cell-phone snapshots of one another, grinning as if they know they're being secretly taped for a reality TV show. They're like a sign of spring, giant red-breasted robins, seasonal urban megafauna. How is it that white tourists in New York seem so much whiter than white New Yorkers?

I miss New York. I miss the hubbub. In particular, I miss the subway. In Los Angeles I'm either entirely alone—in my car, in my house—or among people I know well at my office, in class, in meetings, at meals. But on the New York City subway, I'm a member of a tightly packed group of strangers, alone but not alone, entirely free to read or daydream or snoop, dropped into a random sample of humanity, people of every age and race and circumstance at whom I can stare, at length and close up, examining each one's face and clothing, noting the book she's reading, the music to which the

head right next to mine is bobbing, inferring sensibilities and moods and habits, imagining lives.

I even find the insane people interesting.

"There is *no . . . more . . . witchcraft*," a wild-haired man sitting three seats away on the platform repeats quietly every ten seconds.

In New York, plenty of people actually look and act as I imagined people looked and acted when I was a teenager taking hallucinogens. I get up from the bench, lean out and look to see if a train's coming, then glance down when I notice one of the ties on the track squiggling—it's two rats trying to crawl over the rail. I gasp, disgusted, and turn away. Funny: during the first of my three hallucinogenic experiences I was in New York for the first time and rode the subway. The tracks wriggled then, too, but ratlessly.

"There is *no . . . more . . . witchcraft*," the man says again.

The subway this morning also reminds me of Southern California's apartheid quality. Riding the train between Grand Central and Brooklyn Bridge, I have probably seen more black people than I've seen during the entire twenty-five hundred days I've lived in Los Angeles.

I have one appointment in New York before I'm scheduled to get on the bus for the trip to Miami. I arrive at the restaurant, a diner with café airs west of Foley Square, toward the born-again World Trade Center. In my twenties and early thirties, when I was an habitué of courthouses and prosecutors' offices and the Tombs, we all thought the hokey new name TriBeCa would never take.

"My gosh—Karen Hollander! What on earth are you doing here in New York?"

It's Stewart.

"Expecting someone," he asks, "or may I join you?"

As he gets close, I ask very softly, "You're kidding, right?" He picked the restaurant.

"Uh-uh," he replies, moving his mouth not at all, and as he leans in to kiss me, he whispers, "You never know around here." New York's main federal office building is nearby, and various govern-

ment agencies keep discreet suites all over the neighborhood. He resumes his louder-than-necessary voice of fake surprise and bon-homie. "Oh, I'm just up here for the day from D.C., routine bureau-cratic blah-blah-blah bullshit. But running into you makes it all worthwhile."

He orders oatmeal and blueberries. He's a vegetarian, which is one of the anti-stereotypical quirks that made me like him on our first date. I order an omelet and bacon.

He speaks softly. "Did you know your old man worked with the OSS? In the summer of 1945, in Europe, right after the war?"

"My *father* was in the *CIA*?"

"He wasn't 'in' anything. And the organization to which you refer didn't exist yet. But he was apparently very helpful. It's why he got the instant U.S. citizenship and came here. Meaning, therefore, that Karen Hollander *exists* as a result of the good offices of the intelli-gence community of the United States of America. Yes, we are god-like in our powers."

"Is that—was his connection why—is that the reason I didn't ever get, you know, in trouble? In 1968?"

"No way. You'd have to be Allen fucking Dulles's kid to pull *that* Get Out of Jail Free card, and not even then. Uh-uh. I can say with ninety-five percent confidence that there's no connection. When did you change your name?"

Whoa. "College. I was admitted as Hollænder, with the asch, the æ, but I graduated as H-O-L-L-A-N-D-E-R. Sorry. I should have told you. I sent Freedom of Information requests for both spellings."

"No problem. Anyhow, as a result of your two different sur-names, believe it or not, part of the United States government, the stupid and confused part, the part that can't manage to correctly spell half the fucking Arab names in the database, thinks you're two different people."

"How unintentionally correct of them."

"And in this case, not unhelpful. It's always better when there's a little built-in ambiguity and confusion on the other side of the game board. Have the FOIA cretins sent you anything yet?"

"The army says they have no files on Karen H-O-L-L-A-N-D-E-R. Homeland Security says they've got nothing on me with either spelling."

He nods as if he expected that answer. "You know what? You started your junior year of high school on the very day LBJ signed the Freedom of Information Act."

I often feel as if Stewart is a move or two ahead of me, and even though I know it's an impression he cultivates, I find it both disturbing and attractive. "Why is that significant?"

"It's not. But you were the one who always loved coincidence, your 'synchronicity' bullshit. And speaking of high school, you were in the Model UN *and* SDS *and* the Student Peace Union *and* you started the Esperanto Club? Why didn't you just go ahead and get a fucking hammer-and-sickle tattooed on your forehead? Such an ambitious little commie pinko do-bee."

"Jesus, they have *all that* in my files? What am I saying? Of course they do."

"No, they don't. I bought a copy of your yearbook on eBay. You really were a hottie nerd, by the way. Were you still a virgin junior year? I liked the black hair."

"Dark brown. But thank you."

After our food arrives, he puts his arms on the table and leans in. And talks even more quietly than he did before. "This is an interesting episode. I mean *extremely* interesting. So far I've only got a few bits and pieces. But I can see the outlines of a bigger picture. And there was obviously, I think, some *massive* cock-up, panic about blowback off the fucking charts, epic black-boxing and file-ditching. I mean, this was ass-covering and roll-up the way they did it in the heyday, when it was so much easier to get away with that shit. It looks like the kind of thing that should've come out in 1975, seventy-six."

"After Watergate, you mean, the CIA hearings?"

"The year of the Great Emasculation, when they let the sun shine in and all the dirty deeds of the past were confessed. Supposedly. Yeah. But certainly weren't, in your case, which leads me to think it couldn't have been just one agency. There must have been too many

dirty hands in too many different places. That's my theory. *Everybody* was gonna get fucked if this came out."

"Meaning what, exactly?"

"I don't know yet, exactly." He sips his coffee. "One thing that really piques my interest now is how you passed the background check when you worked for Fat Boy." He whispers so emphatically he nearly growls. "Worked for the fucking *DoJ*."

"I know. I know."

"I mean, that was truly living dangerously, Karen. I'm not your shrink. But did you *want* to get nailed?"

"No. Maybe. But no. After thirty years of getting away with it, I thought I could keep getting away with it. It didn't seem totally real anymore. So I pushed my luck. And then I did. Get away with it. Do you think maybe the FBI covered it up so they wouldn't be blamed for not knowing about it?"

Stewart is shaking his head. "But they had to know, the feebs, you'd think, *somebody* in the fuckin'-F entity should've known about you in fuckin' 1997 when you got the job in their own fuckin' department, and decided to give you a pass for his own reasons. Or if they *didn't* know, then they're more fucked up than even I dreamed."

"I've wondered. I've wondered all those things. That's what I'm trying to figure out."

He takes a deep breath. "You were penetrated, it looks like to me." He takes another sip of coffee. Is he waiting for me to ask what he means so that he can make a dirty joke? "I believe you had a federal asset in your little group."

He knows we were a group. "You mean . . . somebody who—that one of us notified the authorities at the time?" Does he know who it was? Do I detect the slightest possible smile?

"I mean an asset, somebody *working* for the United States government."

"An agent provocateur?"

"That would be the tendentious colloquial term."

"Who? Do you know who?" Buzzy? Or Alex?

He shrugs. "Still working it." He smiles. "You know, I'd figured you for some kind of draft-board vandal, maybe."

"Nope."

He leans in closer and lowers his voice some more. "You must have been a serious fucking enemy of the state."

I nod. "Briefly. Very briefly."

The waiter brings the check. I pull out a credit card, but Stewart insists that we each pay our own share in cash.

"When do you go home?" I ask.

"Detroit tomorrow," he says, "then Ottawa, back to D.C. Tuesday. It's a glamour fucking job. How long are you in town?"

"Just today. And then off to Miami."

"And tonight? It's not a school night." He's smiling his let's-do-it smile.

"I'm staying with my daughter and her family." A couple of hours at his hotel this afternoon I could manage, however. The fact that he's helping me, taking risks and performing his spook-craft on my behalf, I have to admit, I find arousing. Also, as long as I'm being honest—not with him, not entirely, but here, with you—I want to do everything I can to keep him invested. Once a Bond girl, always. "But they're not expecting me until dinnertime. I'm going to MoMA, but I could come to your hotel afterward, at three?"

"Yes. What's in Miami?"

"The special G-20 summit."

He grins at what he thinks is the contradiction at hand—young anti-Establishment militant turned powerbrokering grande dame, from fanatical would-be destroyer of the system to fancy-pants overseer of the system.

"I'm not *attending*. I'm babysitting my granddaughter and her friends. Who are going down to rage against the machine and strike a blow for equality and justice."

"Seriously?"

"And going down with them, if you can believe it," I say, "by *bus*." I think this is what Waverly calls a humblebrag.

"Don't be in the vicinity when they start smashing windows on Collins Avenue. It's an NSSE."

I know "NSSE" means "national special security event," because I was at Justice when they were invented to coordinate FBI and Secret Service and police deployments around State of the Union addresses, inaugurations, political conventions—and, starting a few years ago, the Oscars.

"Don't worry," I say. "I plan on mostly getting massages."

"But seriously—I mean, especially given this book, you've got to watch your step. As of the first of March, there were eleven thousand new CATV cameras installed on every spare square inch of downtown Miami and Miami Beach. Totally swarmed. The undercovers will probably outnumber Waverly and her friends."

"You remember her *name*? You're amazing." I stand.

"The first night you stayed overnight at my shithole was her first birthday. Hey—I think you forgot something." He nods at an unmarked envelope on the table that he's tucked between the salt and pepper shakers. I hadn't noticed it before.

"Oh, right!" I pick it up. "Thanks!" I'm a terrible actor.

18

ONCE I WAS sixteen, I could suddenly see the world and all its machinations clearly. The code had been broken. Everything (with the sole exception of Chuck Levy's tragic lack of romantic interest in me) became obviously and completely understandable. At eight I discovered that Santa Claus didn't exist; at eleven, I learned that companies paid my father to do research to prove whatever they wanted to prove; and at thirteen, I stopped believing in the Roman Catholic God. But at sixteen, I became the truth-telling child in "The Emperor's New Clothes" full-time, seeing naked power and crazed vanity everywhere I looked.

Of course a nation built upon the slaughtered bodies and burned villages and stolen lands of primitive dark-skinned heathens was slaughtering and burning the primitive dark-skinned heathens of Indochina. *Of course* a nation that enslaved Negroes for 350 years still refused to consider them fully human. *Of course* Magnavox and Ford and Mattel brainwashed us to want and buy gewgaws we didn't need, *of course* the weapons companies and the generals wanted Americans to remain in a perpetual state of fear, and itched to *use* the super-weapons in their arsenals. For the first time in years, I

thought of the phrase I'd loved from the Nicene Creed, *all that is, seen and unseen.*

"Karen," my little brother asked one Saturday night in the spring of 1966 while I was doing homework, "how much do you think each Easter Bunny weighs?"

Peter had recently concluded that there must be not just a single Easter Bunny but hundreds or thousands of them. Easter was the following day. At that moment I had another of my teenage *aha* revelations about the System. The supernatural myths of American childhood—Santa, the Tooth Fairy, the Easter Bunny—were ostensibly for the sake of children's enchantment. Their real function was habituating *adults* to perpetuate pretty fantasies, to get them comfortable joining a routine conspiracy of fabrication, to make telling the plain truth seem churlish and wrong. Using cute little Peter as a pawn, Easter was all about trying to turn me into a liar and a cynic.

"How come?" I asked him.

"Well, if ours is my size or even smaller, it'd leave footprints on the grass, especially if there's dew. And if I get out there early enough tomorrow morning, I could track it."

"You're very smart, Peter. But to tell you the truth, I've never seen the Easter Bunny, so I have no idea of his size."

"*An* Easter Bunny. *Their* size."

The next morning, Bach's Mass in B Minor was playing on the kitchen radio as I stepped out on the porch and lit a cigarette and spotted, one by one, each of the dozen eggs scattered around the backyard. So *obvious.* On his way out to join me, my father turned up the volume on WFMT and, for the first time ever, asked me for a cigarette. Finally, Sabrina and my mother appeared at the back door holding Peter back, like a greyhound in his starting gate, then let him go. We watched, the three of them smiling and shouting encouragement, as he crept and scurried from obvious hiding place to slightly less obvious hiding place—the faucet handle, the lowest oak limb, a swing-set seat—holding each egg up in the air before placing it in the special Easter bucket painted (by me, nine years before) with golden crosses and pink bunnies.

Ten minutes later, he was done, Mom and Sabrina were upstairs getting ready to go to church, Dad was watching Dean Rusk or Robert McNamara or somebody on TV defend the war in Vietnam, and Peter was lining up his eggs on the kitchen table according to their colors while I ate Rice Krispies and read the *Tribune*. "I think," he said to me, "that they must either hide their tracks somehow, or else they're weightless. The Easter Bunnies."

"Weightless? Like astronauts in space?"

"Maybe more like the Holy Ghost."

"Do you suppose there are Easter Bunnies in Vietnam?" I asked my ten-year-old brother. "There are lots of Catholics there."

"Then I guess there must be. Easter Bunnies go wherever they have Easter, right?"

"Then that makes me really sad. Because with the war going on, with all the bombs and napalm and everything, the Easter Bunnies in Vietnam must be getting wounded and burned and blown up."

Peter stopped organizing his eggs and stared at me. It was as if I'd punched him, but worse, because I was being so earnest and artificially sweet, like a nun. He didn't shed a tear in front of me, but my sister said later that he cried and cried during Mass that day. "You're really a bad person, Karen," Sabrina told me. "You think you're so smart and sophisticated, and a good person, but you just enjoy upsetting people."

One night watching the news, as they showed some rare Canadian footage shot inside communist China, my mother remarked how chilling it was that the people all dressed exactly the same, in Mao jackets.

"It's probably just the Party members," my father said.

"And in America," I said, "people aren't just as conformist? Short hair, white shirt, necktie, yes, *sir*. Dad looks and dresses exactly like every man in the Loop."

My father chuckled and gave me a salute.

We had just started a chapter of Students for a Democratic Society at New Trier. When I showed Dad my national membership

card and he laughed at its italicized mission statement—*We are people of this generation looking uneasily at the world we inherit*—I got as angry as I'd ever been at him. "Jesus, is *everything* just a big joke to you?"

"No, I'm sorry, my dear. But on something like this, it's usually slogans, exhortations: 'Liberty, fraternity, equality,' you know, 'Victory to the proletariat.' This is so wordy, so self-conscious and cautious and . . . sociological. It's like something someone my age would write *about* people your age."

"People *my age* don't give a shit about the way slogans are *supposed* to sound, the way movements for peace and justice *used* to be in the old days." I had never said "shit" to my parents. "That's why it's the *New* Left."

"Okay. Good."

That, of course, made me even angrier. I turned and stomped up to my room and played "Paint It Black" and smoked a cigarette. My parents were still making it very difficult for me to rebel against them.

Although America at large was capitulating to progressivism, like an anxious dweeb doing whatever the sexy popular kids say to do—the Civil Rights Act, the Voting Rights Act, Medicare, Medicaid, the de facto abolition of capital punishment—my anger was not yet spent. The Vietnam War, growing bigger and uglier every week, was there to satisfy my ongoing need for outrage and bile, daily proof that the system remained hideous. In order to keep the moral high ground—to give *substance* to the natural superiority of our unsullied golden youth—we needed to climb higher and higher. We required enemies, and since Goldwater's defeat had left conservatism in the ash heap of history, the liberals running the country and waging the war became our enemies. In the spring of our junior year in high school, Alex and Chuck and I started calling ourselves radicals.

I'd founded the New Trier Esperantists two years earlier, and now I decided it was my mission to disband it. Esperanto was not really a means to global harmony and peace but one more first-

world missionary charade, this one meant to wipe out indigenous languages. I'd made the club's two least active members—Alex and Chuck, whom I'd forced to join freshman year—attend the crucial meeting. When Jamie Harwood, a freshman boy who was a Bahá'í and the one club member who spoke Esperanto more fluently than I, made an impassioned argument for letting the club continue, and suggested that I resign if membership seemed incompatible with my antiwar feelings, Chuck and then Alex started humming "The Ballad of the Green Berets," which was a patriotic pop hit at the time. People laughed. Jamie turned red. My resolution carried by one vote.

My hidden agenda had been to aggravate my mother. And to the degree that being the founding president of the Esperantists might help me get into college, it had already served its purpose.

"I suppose," my peeved mother said to me, "this means you're *not* going to submit an Esperanto translation of your college application essay?" I'd raised that possibility at the beginning of the school year.

"Yes, I suppose it does," I said, radiating self-satisfaction. "In fact? *Verŝajne mi volo* neniam plu *paroli Esperanton, karega Patrino.*" *I will probably* never again *speak Esperanto, dearest Mother.*

That summer I worked three days a week in an office of a little SDS offshoot called JOIN (Jobs or Income Now) in a poor white Chicago neighborhood called Uptown. I mostly did what I'd done the previous two summers for my uncle's law firm on clean, shiny Sheridan Road in Evanston, mimeographing and filing and making coffee, but instead of getting $1.25 an hour, I worked for free on bleak, crappy Sheridan Road in North Chicago. And instead of feeling like a bored child, I felt like a seventeen-year-old adult, a certified New Left warrior. "Welcome to the Movement, Karen," my young boss said to me when I showed up the first day. The *Movement.* I loved the vague grandeur of that term.

The first week I had the heebie-jeebies as I walked alone from the unfamiliar El station past the groups of pale, unwell-looking teen-age boys and young men loitering, drinking, smoking, staring. But

one morning the second week, one of the boys shouted, "Hey, girl, *smile* sometime at this good-looking Appa-*latch*-in shitbum," I couldn't help but smile, and he kicked one foot on the sidewalk—he was wearing work boots—and said, "*There* you go now." I was very pleased with myself. I was a woman! I was making my way in the city, in the real world! Some weeks after that, when the Chicago police shot and killed one of those neighborhood boys, everybody from the JOIN office attended a protest rally outside the local police station. I was forging bonds of solidarity with the poor! Also, a few months later, I was able to write "Community Organizer, summer 1966" in the Work Experience sections of my college applications.

When Richard Speck raped and murdered eight student nurses in their dorm in Chicago that July, my mother wanted me to quit my job. "He was one of these aimless unemployed Southern boys, too," she said. I'd had the same thought, but I told her she was bigoted against the working class. And in August, when an ex-marine randomly shot and killed sixteen people from a clock tower at the University of Texas, I joked to my mother about those "aimless unemployed white Southern boys" and asked if she'd noticed that the sniper had been an altar boy at his Catholic church.

I took a summer school course at Northwestern called the Literature of Revolution. How wonderful was it? It was a seminar taught by a young visiting professor from the Freie Universität Berlin. There were four students enrolled, of whom I was the only girl, and all four of us and the professor—"Call me Nikolas, please"—drank coffee and smoked cigarettes in class, which met for two hours, twice a week. There were no quizzes or tests, only reading and discussions and a single twenty-page paper.

My paper was on Sartre's play *Dirty Hands,* which I'd read earlier that year for extra credit in French class, and *The Autobiography of Malcolm X,* which had just been published. I argued that Malcolm, like one of the main characters in the Sartre play, was a revolutionary assassinated by comrades who mistrusted him for making alliances with more moderate factions. Just before he was murdered, Malcolm had given the speech in which he said that Negroes had

the right to protect themselves from Klan attacks "by any means necessary." In *Dirty Hands,* Sartre's tough-hearted victim-hero tells his would-be assassin, a middle-class idealist, that "it is not by refusing to lie that we will abolish lies—it is by eradicating class by any means necessary." I wrote that Malcolm was an existentialist hero "in the Sartrean sense: authentic, true to himself as a Negro and a revolutionary, defined by his actions rather than just his thoughts, a man for whom important ends justified radical means and who accepted full responsibility for his actions." I was very proud of connecting those dots, and of using the word "Sartrean."

Instead of having a final class, Nikolas held a half-hour private conference with each of us in his office to discuss our papers. He handed me mine—an A! in a college course! from a European!—and offered me a Gitane.

"It is very fine work, Karen. The original research, the speech you, you . . . what is the English, you shoveled from the earth, dug up, by Malcolm X with *'par tous les moyens nécessaires,'* by any necessary means . . . very impressive." He asked me if I thought—if *I* thought!—that "the American ghettos of this time" were "in a pre-revolutionary condition of turmoil." Based on my extensive conversations with exactly one American ghetto resident, who washed my clothes and made me lunch and preferred to be called "colored," I answered, "Maybe. It's hard to say. In America, there's a lot of false consciousness"—a phrase he'd taught us—"even among the Negroes. I guess, like everything else, revolution is always easier said than done."

He nodded. "Ah, yes, *'leichter gesagt als getan.'* Easier said than done. You are how old, Karen?"

"Seventeen."

He smiled and nodded again, more enthusiastically, as if I'd said something meaningful. "Do you know where you will attend university?"

I shook my head. "I apply this fall."

"If you need a letter, the recommendation, please, it would be my privilege to write for you."

"Thanks!" I dropped my cigarette in my Dixie cup of water. It sizzled. "And thank you for the course. I *really* liked it. More than any other I've ever taken. I learned so much."

He gave a gracious shrug of acknowledgment. "Do you enjoy the cinema?"

My God: the *cinema.* "Uh-huh, sure."

"Well, nearby, at the Wilmette Theater—"

"That's where I live! In Wilmette."

"Ah! They are exhibiting now the film by Jean-Luc Godard. Perhaps some evening you might join me to see it?"

My *God:* he was asking me out on a date. And so, three days later at six o'clock, he met me at the Baskin-Robbins on Central Avenue. I wore bell-bottoms.

Nikolas had shaggy blond hair and wore circular wire-rimmed glasses. He looked like the younger British costar of *The Man from U.N.C.L.E.*

We saw *Alphaville,* whose hero is a secret agent in a dystopia run by a sentient computer which he finally destroys. And he told me about a newer Godard film, *Pierrot le Fou,* in which a rich TV executive played by Jean-Paul Belmondo abandons his family with his children's babysitter, becomes an outlaw, acquires machine guns, kills the lover, wraps his head in dozens of sticks of dynamite and—in the end, unintentionally—blows himself up.

"I was believing all summer you look like this actress who is the Catwoman in *Batman* on TV," Nikolas said as he lit a Gitane and we walked to his car.

"I'm tall, is all."

"But *now* I see you look also like Anna Karina." She was the lead actress in the Godard movie.

"*Elle,*" I said, in the most exquisitely sophisticated riposte I had ever made to anybody, "*est beaucoup plus jolie.*"

"No, not more pretty at all. And did you know she's not French? She's Danish."

"Really? So am I. I mean, my dad's from Denmark."

"Voilà! Before I drive you home, maybe we have just a . . . an *Ab-sacker*, oh, what is the word?"

"Sure, why not?" I answered, no idea what I was agreeing to do.

". . . a *nightcap*!"

His car was a very old blue sedan—a 1949 Hudson, he told me, which he'd got when he arrived in America last winter because it's the car Dean Moriarty drives in *On the Road*.

He bought a six-pack at a little grocery store on Sheridan Road—"To me, the zip-top is a fantastic invention"—and we drove to Gillson Park, where we drank two Schlitzes apiece and talked as we watched the nearly full moon slip into Lake Michigan.

He asked if I had a boyfriend. "No," I said. I'd broken up with Chan Payne over the winter. "Not anymore." Was I blushing because of the beer and the intimacy of the question? Or because my unquenched feelings for Chuck made me feel like I was fibbing? "Not really."

Nikolas was thirty-one and unmarried. I didn't know that seventeen was the age of consent in Illinois, but I think he probably did.

Alex and Chuck were consumed that summer with writing a skit for Lagniappe, the New Trier student revue performed every fall. Alex phoned the day after my date with Nikolas and asked me to come over to his house to hear their work so far.

I was excited to see them. That is, for them to see me, to experience all that is, seen and unseen, now that I was a bona fide woman. *Having had* sex delighted me; *having* sex had not, particularly. But I was happy I hadn't worn stockings, happy that one of us knew what he was doing, and happy to discover that the backseat of a 1949 Hudson was like a couch, with big upholstered arms, so my head wasn't jammed up against the door. And happy, to tell the truth, that it happened with somebody I'd probably never see again.

In Alex's basement, I sat in the beanbag chair across from the two of them on the couch. Alex read all four roles in their skit, and they both sang the three songs, with Chuck playing his Stratocaster and a toy piano.

Watching Chuck's left hand form chords and listening to him sing, free to stare at him since both he and Alex were staring at their scripts, looking at his uncombed curly hair and sleepy eyes, I was a little disappointed that my feelings for him hadn't been evaporated by what had happened the night before.

I applauded when they finished. "That is *great,* you guys."

"It's a pastiche," Alex said. I didn't know what that meant.

"It'll be better with props and costumes," Chuck said.

"And that last song isn't completely finished yet."

"The hell it isn't."

"Well," I said, "it's going to be great. People will freak out. I can't wait."

In their ten-minute play, James Bond is dispatched to Cuba and South America by MI6 and the CIA to track down and terminate Che Guevara. It had an original rock-and-roll score, with each appearance by Bond cued by two bars of a silly toy-piano rendition of the familiar *Dr. No* riff, which had now been featured in four movies. (On principle, we had vowed not to see *Thunderball,* the latest one.)

"A lot of Che's lines," Alex explained, "maybe half of them, are things he's actually said."

"Or written," Chuck added. "Mostly written."

"I figured."

" 'Many will call me an adventurer,' " Alex said, " 'but I am one of a different sort, who risks his skin to prove his platitudes.' And 'The revolution is not an apple that falls when it is ripe—you have to *make* it fall.' Like, those are real."

"And the chorus in the last song, 'I Don't Care,' " Chuck added, "that's a Che quote, too," and he proceeded to sing the line once more: " 'I don't care, I'm not the one, as long as somebody picks up my gun.' We got them from some books about him at the library at Northwestern."

Ah, the Charles Deering Library, where Chuck Levy and I spent our first and final date, on that summer afternoon so long ago, when we were only fourteen . . .

"Any suggestions?" Alex asked me. "You can be our dramaturge."

Speaking of Northwestern and dashing foreign leftists in their thirties, like Che, I had sex with my professor last night in his car! He's thirty-one, and he's German!

"I wonder if a few of the lines won't maybe sound too . . . stiff. They're kind of a mouthful, some of them. Like 'Our enemy is the monopolistic government of the United States of America'? I don't know."

"*Exactly,*" Chuck said. "They'll sound like jokes. People will laugh in the wrong places."

Alex looked up and closed his eyes and shook his head. "That's what Mr. Hendricks says *conventional* people who don't know what they're talking about say about *Brecht*. It's all in the *performance*. And it is still a work in progress."

I heard the Macallisters' automatic garage door opening above us and a car pulling out. "I thought your mom and dad were in Europe?"

"It's Flip. He and his buddies are celebrating before he heads back to Madison." Alex's older brother wasn't doing well at the University of Wisconsin, so that summer he'd had to take the national Selective Service exam in order to keep his student deferment and escape the draft.

"He passed?" I asked, and Alex nodded.

"That is so unfair," Chuck said, "that getting sent to kill people in Vietnam is a punishment for being stupid or poor. The screwed over get more screwed over."

Chuck was picking out a song on his guitar, and nobody said anything for a while. He and Alex were months away from turning eighteen, when they would have to register for the draft, too.

Alex reached into the pocket of his chinos. "Flip gave me a present last night." He grinned and held up and jiggled a crumpled Baggie with two hand-rolled cigarettes inside.

One afternoon that summer I thought I'd spotted two of the guys from the JOIN office sneaking a joint in an alley, but I had never tried pot. None of us had.

We smoked a joint. I felt nothing, and Alex and Chuck admitted they didn't, either. We lit the second one, and Chuck took the first hit.

"When my dad went down to the Amazon to study those Indians for Searle," I said, "the drug company? In seventh grade? He asked the old medicine man, 'Why do you *chant* after you chew your special bark? What's the purpose of your chanting?' And the Indian guy stares at him a long time and finally says, 'Because the bark requires half an hour to take effect, and waiting gets *so boring.*'"

Chuck violently exhaled a cloud of smoke as he began laughing, then kept laughing, then Alex and I joined in. At last we stopped, got our breath, and wiped our eyes.

"We are real hepcats," Alex said, "smoking reefers."

Chuck started laughing again, then Alex, and then, after abandoning a sudden urge to exercise control, me. I'd learned about grass when I was twelve, from Allen Ginsberg's poem *Howl,* but Chuck and Alex didn't know about it until they read *Live and Let Die.* In the novel, at a restaurant in Harlem, Bond smells "marihuana," and Felix Leiter tells Bond that "the real hepcats smoke reefers."

"God, I feel like I just swam a mile," Chuck said, out of breath.

Now that the Macallisters owned two color TVs, their old one was in the basement. Alex turned it on.

"Wow," I said.

"Yeah," Chuck agreed.

It was so . . . *colorful.* We were staring at a new game show we'd never seen.

There was a category, and you had to name something in it that began with the last letter of the last thing named. "Venezuela," said David McCallum, who played Illya Kuryakin on *The Man from U.N.C.L.E.*

"Algeria," his teammate replied.

"Better say Afghanistan, Illya!" Chuck warned. "Only 'A' country that doesn't also end in 'A'! Only escape from the perpetual loop!"

"That's really interesting," I said to Chuck, thinking of perpetual loops.

"Austria," said the actor on TV.

"How old do you think he is?" Alex asked.

"Thirty-one," I answered immediately.

Chuck turned to look at me. "You *know* that Illya Kuryakin is exactly thirty-one?"

"No," I said, "no, but, you know, he—he's probably—I mean, you know, he looks thirty-one. To me. He looks like someone I know who's thirty-one."

"Who?" Alex asked.

"Who?" My face felt sunburned.

"The guy at your community-organizing office, your boss?"

"No. No."

"That guy who taught us the chant?" The previous Saturday we'd gone into Chicago for an antiwar demonstration, where we'd learned to shout "Hey, hey, LBJ, how many kids did you kill today?" as we marched along Hyde Park Boulevard.

"Uh-uh."

"Don't be such a girl, Macallister," Chuck said.

"You are really at sixes and sevens, Hollaender," Alex said. "You've got a *crush* on David McCallum!"

"No, I do not. He looks the same age as my literature professor at Northwestern. Who's thirty-one." The sunburned feeling swept my body.

Chuck got up and turned the channel, first to an *Andy of Mayberry* rerun—

"Not black and white," Alex commanded, and I said, "Goober looks kind of like the star of the new Godard movie."

—and then to a game show in color on channel 7.

"You saw *Alphaville*?" Alex asked.

"Uh-huh, at the Wilmette last night."

Chuck was apparently paying no attention to Alex and me. Was he ignoring our dangerous conversational tangent on purpose? "This is incredible," he said. "I've never seen this. This is really crazy."

Cameras were following a feverish-looking man as he huffed and puffed up and down the aisles of an empty supermarket, grabbing and throwing packages and jars into his grocery cart. He squatted

to sweep off every can of sardines on a shelf. A clock on the screen ticked down. He had forty-eight, forty-seven, forty-six seconds left.

"It's like—it's like he's pretending to be a looter," I said.

"Look, *look*," Alex said, pointing at the TV screen, "one of the TV cameras is *in* the *picture*. I love when that happens."

Supermarket Sweep was a new show, and none of us had known about it until that morning.

Chuck shook his head. "Incredible. I mean, for a second it was hard to believe that was *real*."

"It's *great*," Alex said. "It's hilarious. It's like the best satire of America ever."

I shivered. "This country is grotesque." It was a sincere insight, given emotional oomph by my annoyance at Chuck's obliviousness to the new me. I lit a cigarette.

"You went to see *Alphaville*," Alex asked, his nosiness pleasing me for the first time ever, "with who? Your dad?"

"No. With my professor from the class at Northwestern."

Now Chuck was paying attention. And right after *Supermarket Sweep*, *The Dating Game* came on, with its swingin' Tijuana Brass theme music.

"That's cool," Chuck said. "It was like a class field trip?"

"Uh-uh." It would be too coy to let it hang there. "It was like a date." I forced myself to keep looking at the TV and not at Chuck.

Alex was electrified. "*Hollaender.* What happened? Are you, like, *seeing* the guy?"

I smiled a little and took a drag on my cigarette and shrugged. "He's going home to West Germany." And: "He thinks I look like Julie Newmar."

Chuck put aside his guitar, stood, and brushed against my knee as he headed for the stairs. "Okay if I go make some cinnamon toast?"

Was he surprised, confused? I thought so. I hoped so.

"Make pieces for Catwoman and me, too."

For the long Labor Day weekend, I went with my family up to my aunt and uncle's lake cabin in Wisconsin. On Sunday just before

twilight, when the surface of the lake looked perfectly still, Uncle Tom rowed his motorboat a little ways out, emptied two big cans of gasoline onto the surface, and lit the gas on fire. At which point the kids, my brother and sister and I and our two cousins, all dove off the end of the dock and headed out to the blaze, swimming beneath the aquatic bonfire. The idea was to go as deep as possible and then look up at the fire from underwater. And then surface somewhere beyond the ring of fire.

I went deep and got maybe a ten-second-long glimpse of the spectacle. It was fantastic, otherworldly, a hundred shifting, flickering rods of bright yellow fire-light extending down through the murky water all around me, the silence and beauty and fear making it feel like some kind of religious rite. If I hadn't in the previous two weeks made love with a thirty-one-year-old German and gotten high for the first time, swimming beneath fire on Oconomowoc Lake at dusk would have been the single most awesome moment of my seventeen years on earth.

The next night, back in Wilmette, my summer boss phoned to tell me that the Chicago cops, pissed about JOIN's involvement in the protest over the shooting of the neighborhood boy, had raided the office, roughed people up, and busted some of my former co-workers "on a completely bogus dope charge." The reason I hadn't seen anything about it in the newspaper was "because the Establishment media prefers it that way."

I was lucky to have missed the raid, but instead, I felt entirely unlucky, removed prematurely from the action, snatched by North Shore privilege out of revolutionary harm's way.

19

WHO KNEW BUS travel had gotten so spiffy? I'm going to start evangelizing on behalf of buses, and not just to amuse people at Santa Monica dinner parties. No arriving two hours before departure, no extra charges for bags, no frantic removal of shoes and belts and bracelets and laptops, no child-size tubes and bottles and jars jammed into Baggies, no delays or cancellations. Fourteen hours into our trip, I haven't had that moment when I attempt to reconcile myself to imminent death, the way I do on half the flights I take. I've got as much space as I would in an airline business-class seat, with TV and free Wi-Fi. The air is fresher. I slept, Ambien-free, from Silver Spring, Maryland, to a rest stop near Lynchburg, South Carolina. (Question: why are all the towns with "lynch" in their names in the South?) The pecan-studded French toast at this Stuckey's is far superior to any breakfast I've eaten on a commercial airliner. And there's no such thing as bus lag.

"Ms. Hollander, I have a question."

"I told you to cut that out, Hunter."

"Okay, but I really don't think I can bring myself to call you Karen."

"There, you just did. Anyhow, *Mr.* Phelan, what's your question?"

"Do you use a pump?"

"*Hunter!*" says their friend Sophie, whose parents allowed her to come along because of me. "Are you *high?*"

"I mean an electronic insulin pump," he tells her. "She's a Type 1, too."

"Oh, right," says Sophie. "Sorry."

I wonder what embarrassing pump device she imagined he was asking me about. "I don't use a pump," I tell him. "I never have. Don't like the idea of a thing poking into my body all the time. Do you have one?"

"No. But you didn't go to the bathroom, and I didn't see you inject on the bus, either."

"I did it sitting here, ten minutes ago, in my thigh. Through my pants."

"Really?" he asks, astounded. "Right here? In public?"

"I've had a long time to learn to do it discreetly. I'm sneaky." I pause, waiting for the waitress to finish refilling our water glasses. "I shoot up anywhere."

"You use a pen, huh, dial in the dose?"

"Nope, just a regular syringe."

"But," he says, his voice a half-octave higher, "but what if people, you know, *see* you, see the needle and freak out?"

"First of all, they don't. Second of all, fuck 'em."

"Rad," Sophie says.

Although it wasn't my main intention to impress the seventeen-year-olds, Waverly is smiling proudly. "What do I always say?" she tells Hunter, then turns to me. "I always say he shouldn't be embarrassed about it. That *you're* not, at all."

"In fact," I tell them, "since I ate a lot more of this delicious sugar-coated fried bread than I'd planned, I need to shoot some more." I reach into my bag, take out my little black kit, and, far more brazenly than is my custom, suck precisely four units of insulin into a fresh syringe and then plunge it through my blouse into my belly. "Voilà."

"Awesome," Sophie says.

There are television sets suspended from the restaurant ceiling. The three screens I can see, including one right over our table, are all tuned to FOX News.

"Hey, look," I say, "they're talking about you guys."

One of the FOX morning anchors is wondering why "the mainstream media doesn't want Americans to know that these 'occupiers' in Miami, a lot of them, are connected with groups supportive of terrorist organizations, like Hamas."

"What the mainstream media doesn't want Americans to *know,*" Waverly says, "is that there are millions of Americans who don't think the big banks and the multinational corporations and these governments should get together and rig the system for themselves."

"Word," Sophie says. Until now, I've only heard characters in movies and TV shows say that.

"They're sort of peas in a pod," another of the FOX News people says, "all the G-20 folks *and* these protesters. Right? Young anti-Americans in tie-dyed T-shirts getting ready to scream and yell at middle-aged anti-Americans in suits and ties. And the mainstream media's in love with both sides. It's ironic, is what it is."

It's ironic, all right. *Everybody agrees,* my left-wing traveling companions and the right-wingers on TV: the liberal mainstream media are in a conspiracy with the political elites and international capital to befog and oppress the regular people and squash freedom.

Earlier, Sophie had showed me a tattoo on her lower back, a line of dialogue from *The Matrix,* IF YOU ARE NOT ONE OF US, YOU ARE ONE OF THEM, lettered in perfect Helvetica with the first half in red ink, the second half in black. Now she asks me, since I run a law school, if I think she should include photos of her tattoos as part of her application to college.

"Are you applying to art schools?" I ask.

"Good morning, ma'am."

I swivel. A very tall policeman is standing right by our booth, ad-

dressing me. His partner, standing a couple of yards away, has his right hand on the grip of his automatic pistol.

"I'm Deputy Thigpen from the Sumter County Sheriff's Office? I need to go ahead and take a look in your pocketbook?"

"What?" I'm startled—doubly so, because for some reason, his name sounds familiar.

"Can y'all go ahead and hand that pocketbook to me, ma'am, please, now?"

Even as I ask, "Why, Officer?" I realize why.

"Ma'am, we have a reliable report indicating probable cause to suspect a possible violation of South Carolina narcotics laws."

"Aha," I say, and force a smile as I reach into my bag for the zippered black nylon pouch that holds my diabetes gear.

"No, ma'am, *stop*—I need you to remove your hand right now from inside the pocketbook." His partner takes a step closer to us.

I take out my hand and let it hover just over the open bag, as if he'd screamed *Freeze!* But then I worry that might come across as some kind of disrespectful joke, given that I'm still smiling. But if I stop smiling, I'm afraid I'll look angry or nervous. I am nervous. We are in the rural South. I look like the city slicker I am. Sophie's eyebrow and nose are pierced, and FUCK IT is visible on her left collarbone, each of the tattooed letters—F, C, I in green and U, K, T in red—slightly, alternatingly askew from the vertical. Hunter wears blond dreadlocks. The flap of Waverly's backpack is imprinted with both the anarchist symbol and the peace symbol. One might note, too, that Hunter is wearing a T-shirt that says BAMN!, but I doubt the Sumter County sheriff's deputies know that's shorthand for "by any means necessary." I could also introduce into evidence Waverly's nonwhite racial mix, but—stereotype: denied—Deputy Thigpen is black.

I remember now when I first encountered that name. I wasn't much older than these kids. It's funny how some low-priority memories remain for so many years in cold storage, perfectly preserved.

"Please put both your hands on your lap, ma'am," Deputy Thigpen's white partner says loudly, trying to get in on the action.

Waverly to the rescue. "My grandmother has Type 1 *diabetes,* Officers. She was injecting *insulin.* If she doesn't inject insulin, she dies. Okay?" Dramatically put but true. "By the way? She's a lawyer and a former federal official. Just FYI." Wavy, honey, don't overplay our hand.

Officer Thigpen glances at his partner, who raises his eyebrows in a quick *uh-oh* gesture. Officer Thigpen leans in so close, I can smell that he's a smoker—"Excuse me"—and grabs my purse, which he places on an empty table and starts pawing through. He unzips the diabetes pouch and looks at the syringe and finger pricker and insulin vials, immediately zips it up and sticks it back in my purse.

"If you'd like," I say, "I could have my doctor fax you the prescriptions to your . . . station house."

"Not necessary, and I sincerely apologize for the misunderstanding, ma'am," he says as he hands back my bag. "Y'all have a great Sunday."

I try not to stare as he walks over to our waitress, who is cowering behind the front counter. He gets very close to her and very quietly gives her a very stern talking-to with his index finger jabbing in the direction of her chest.

"That was clutch," Sophie says. She is delighted to have been in such close proximity to unjust hassling by a policeman.

"Well," I say, "it certainly woke me up. I need a drink." The children nod but don't smile. "I'm kidding about the drink."

"Are you all right, Grams? You want to test your blood?"

"Maybe not here, at this very instant."

"You just seemed really . . . scared," Waverly says.

"I was surprised." Other diners are glancing over at us. "And embarrassed, I guess." And scared, panicked, that the cop, as he rifled through my bag, would pull out the queer page of notes that Stewart gave me on Friday, and pass it along to the Sumter County sheriff, who would pass it along to the special agent in charge at the nearest FBI field office, and so on. Which is ridiculous, but that's fear and secret-keeping for you.

Back on the bus, I unfold Stewart's handwritten seven-point progress report once again. It's on a single page in pencil, which might
be an old-school affectation. Or maybe spook stuff—wouldn't
graphite be less traceable than ink or type fonts? Come to think of
it, he was wearing gloves when he arrived at the restaurant. No fingerprints, literally.

*1) Files (except SS/DHS) back-roomed & super-scrubbed, but my
current moderate-high confidence assessment: your infiltrator (as-
suming existence) was not F Entity.*

When I was getting to know him, I noticed that Stewart went out
of his way to avoid saying "the FBI," because it was too straightfor-
ward and respectful. He'd call it the F Entity, the feebs, the G-Men,
oh-dee-envy (ODENVY being a CIA code name for FBI), the First
Bunch (short for First Bunch of Idiots), but never simply the FBI. By
"SS/DHS," he means the Secret Service and Department of Homeland Security.

*2) High-confidence assessment #2: YOU weren't the feeb infiltrator.
(Discredited theory: you, COINTELPRO junior G-chick from 1968,
get special free pass for DoJ in 1997. But no.)*

COINTELPRO is the acronym for the FBI's secret counterintelligence programs, which started infiltrating agents into SDS and
other New Left groups in the 1960s. When I was in law school in the
'70s and the existence of COINTELPRO had just been revealed, my
constitutional law professor one day in class posed a hypothetical
about entrapment. "Miss Hollander," he said, "let's say you work
for the FBI, you're part of COINTELPRO posing as a member of a
radical antiwar group . . ." In my answer, I managed to paraphrase
the due process clause of the Fifth Amendment and make some
quasi-witty reference to the fact that the FBI had only recently started
allowing women to become agents. But I was shaking and breathing

so heavily afterward that a 3L sitting near me, a bearded and extremely cute Southern boy, gallantly asked if I was okay and needed any help. There weren't blood glucose meters back then, so to this day I'm not sure if I was hypoglycemic, or just panicky about the secret I was newly keeping.

And "DoJ" stands for Department of Justice, which vetted me in 1997.

3) No OGA material yet, except indirectly, Out-Damned-Spot-wise—i.e. per my earlier, looks like they scrubbed & purged up the wazoo.

When I was with Stewart, he would also never say "CIA," and he almost cringed whenever I did. I thought it was like an actor who won't say "Macbeth," or a Jew who spells "God" "G-d," or a Skull and Bones member who refuses to hear the club's name uttered. But he said it was because he "just can't stand how civilians get such a boner from hearing it or saying it. Like they're a character in some fucking James Bond movie." This was before I'd told him about my childhood Bond fixation. He sometimes says "the Agency" or "Langley," but usually, he calls it OGA, which is short for Other Government Agency—one of those things that start as a joke but then become normal nomenclature. I was new to federal acronyms the first time I heard him use the phrase, and I guessed that it meant Original Gangsters of America, which he found hysterically funny.

4) SS/DHS files have a 4/1/68 phone call, untraced, from a stray—dorm pal? family member? weapon vendor?—re Levy, Charles A. But no record of you & 2 others.

Stewart had said before that he thought the files kept by Homeland Security—DHS—would be the easiest nut to crack.

Without any help at all from me, he now knows there were four of us, and he knows the names. I find this simultaneously chilling and comforting.

5) Macallister, Alexander G. III's correspondence w/ comandante en jefe in 1965 via Canadian mail drop + 1967 Comecon student junket made him (minor?) OGA subject of interest. Nothing post-1971.

I remember Alex's letter from Fidel Castro—the *comandante en jefe*—that he kept and had framed, and the cultural exchange program to Budapest and Zagreb—COMECON is short for Council for Mutual Economic Assistance, the Soviet bloc countries—that he went on the summer between high school and college.

6) Don't recall if you FOIAd INSCOM. But your infiltrator smells army to me. (Moderate confidence).

I have indeed sent Freedom of Information requests to INSCOM, the army's Intelligence and Security Command.

7) Freeman, Bernard L. "Buzzy", USCG PO3 1965-67, son of AEC lifer w/ right-wing politics & D.C. connections now: sure looks like your fink.

In college we were slightly suspicious of Buzzy at first because he was a Vietnam vet, a U.S. Coast Guard petty officer third class, and also because his father had spent his career working for the U.S. Atomic Energy Commission. But then we came to trust him for the same reasons—because he wasn't a coddled suburban wuss like the rest of us, because he'd seen and done terrible things in Vietnam and was single-mindedly seeking redemption. Although I grew suspicious of Buzzy once again in the '70s, after he became a conservative, surely it can't be personal loyalty to the rest of us that's made him keep our secret all these years.

I'm desperate to email Stewart and discuss all this, add my hunches and caveats here, fill in a gap there. But he's determined to discover as much as he can on his own, and given the precautions he's taking—last time we talked, he said he wished we "had a cut-

out," which turns out to mean an untraceable way of passing information—I maintain Internet silence with him.

I check my email and see that Greta has sent me a second apology, now even sorrier for suggesting the other night that I had dementia, and for believing Alex. But also wondering, perhaps, when I get home, no rush, if I might want to submit to an autobiographical memory interview conducted by a disinterested medical professional, maybe take a confabulation battery test. "Just to reassure *yourself* that your remote memory is totally shipshape," her email says.

"Oh . . . fuck you."

"What, Grams?" Waverly's warm head rests against my shoulder, her eyes closed.

"Nothing, honey. Thinking out loud."

"Where are we?"

"Georgia, almost Florida. Go back to sleep."

She wriggles and readjusts and cuddles back into me. Her right hand rests on the head of the tiny stuffed dog, made of upcycled cashmere, that pokes out of her backpack, its snout pressed against the top of the encircled A.

Another email from Greta, this one much briefer. Waverly has already filed a report to her mother about the incident at Stuckey's. "You almost got ARRESTED?!?" Greta and Jungo had been dubious about my abilities as a chaperone. Now they'll be imagining *Thelma and Louise 2.*

I consider various replies to Greta. *Completely bogus dope charge. Stop. In Sumter County lockup. Stop. Please post bail, ten large, ASAP. Stop.* Or maybe *Almost arrested? Really? Sorry, I have no memory of that happening.* Instead, I write, "It was really nothing. The poor cop was just doing his job. Talk soon! Love from I-95, Mom."

I Google-search "confabulation battery"—it consists of two hundred questions. *Fuck you,* I repeat, this time only in my shipshape mind.

Sunday afternoons make me contemplative even when I'm not staring out the window on a long-distance bus trip. Time's arrow

slows down, and its path is no longer so simple and straight from past to present to future. Sophie, reading the movie tie-in version of *Howl*, asks if a line in the poem is a reference to Absolut vodka ads: "on Madison Avenue . . . run down by the drunken taxicabs of Absolute Reality." Hunter says he doubts it, so I don't point out that Ginsberg's poem preceded Absolut vodka by twenty-five years. Since lunch, we've passed nothing but the green interstate exit signs for off-ramps into the 1960s and '70s—Daytona Beach, Disney World, Cocoa Beach, Cape Canaveral, John F. Kennedy Space Center.

"Chilling?" Waverly asks.

"What?"

"You've been looking out the window a long time," she says, looking down at her pad. "Are you just chilling?"

"You know, I remember when the very first interstate opened." She smiles, thinks that I'm joking the way good-natured elderly people do about having known Abe Lincoln personally. "Our family made a special trip just to drive on it the first time."

"No *way*," she says, reacting not to my interstate origin tale but to a news story on her iPad. "There are a *thousand* undercover cops in Miami, including federal agents, and like a million new surveillance cameras all over Miami Beach. To monitor *us!*" She's excited to be entering the Big Brotherscape.

"So I've heard."

Around Hollywood we start stretching, powering down, gathering up. The kids consent to join me in my taxi, but when we get to South Beach, Waverly asks the driver to drop them a block away from their hostel, as if for convenience's rather than appearances' sake.

Two hours later—they've agreed to let me buy them dinner—we order locally harvested crabs and fried fair-trade bananas. When some older kids they know from New York appear from the restaurant's back room, each of the young people hugs each of the others. This new obligation to hug mere acquaintances reminds me of the new obligation to give standing ovations to mediocre plays—a thought that makes me feel like an old crank.

My granddaughter tells me that even though one of the boys "seems like a total bro, I know" (Dartmouth rugby shirt tucked into khaki shorts, backward "99%" baseball cap surmounted with sunglasses), he has organized something called Occupy Christmas that is awesome. I tell her I once knew a boy like that—Rob Norquist, the nice jock from New Trier, who came to Miami Beach in 1972 as a Yippie protester at both the Democratic and Republican conventions. "And then never left," I say. I do not say that he made a fortune as a redeveloper of real estate in the Art Deco district.

Hunter is immersed in texting, and in the dark restaurant with his phone illuminating his face and neck and front dreads, he looks like a Georges de La Tour painting.

"I wish we'd had texting when I was your age," I say. "Talking to a boy on the phone, I always felt so *nervous*. Texting would've given me time to figure out the next thing to say."

"*Totally,*" Sophie says. "I *hate* phone conversations. It's impossible to do anything else. And *ending* a call? I always feel like such a bitch. I can't do it."

"If you treat it like theater," Waverly tells her, "like a speech in a play, and sort of figure out what the point is ahead of time, it's easier. Beginning, end, *scene.* Goodbye."

Sophie says her parents have "LoJacked" her—installed software on her phone that lets them know her whereabouts within fifty feet. I say I know people my age who track their elderly parents the same way.

Hunter reenters the conversation, smiling, even as he continues thumbing his keypad. "My dad had this car with big-ass control knobs that he bought because he skis all winter, and it's easier to operate with ski gloves? This hot hitchhiker he picked up thought it was some special old person's thing, for arthritis or whatever. So he traded in the car like a month later." He finishes texting and closes the phone. "Dad says hi."

Hunter has been texting with his father for the last five minutes? How sweet. How unlike parent-teenager relations in the old days.

"He's going to be here on a layover on Wednesday," Hunter says, "and wants to get together."

"Your dad's a pilot?"

"Flight attendant."

"That's interesting," I say.

"*Biological* father," Hunter adds, no doubt realizing what I find *interesting* is how on earth a flight attendant could afford New York private school tuition. "My mom's husband works on Wall Street. She hates it when I hang out with my dad. She thinks he's a bad role model."

"How so?" I ask.

"Because he only makes fifty-one thousand a year. And because he has too many girlfriends."

A middle-aged heterosexual male flight attendant: another stereotype refuted.

Sophie says she's "developing a crush" on a boy with whom she's been having sex for two months. The conversation turns briefly to porn, and its effects on female behavior. When I say there's probably more cleavage on display today than at any time since late-eighteenth-century London, Sophie seems a little self-conscious about her spectacular half-naked bosom, so I add that I think late-eighteenth-century London was a swell time and place.

"The thing is," Hunter says, "people always think the way things happen to be right now, the styles, everything, are the way they've always been and will always be."

"My mom," Sophie says, "stopped shaving her legs and armpits in the seventies? She thought it would be that way forever, but like five years later, she started shaving again."

I pray that we are not headed into a discussion of the modern history of female pubic depilatory custom, about which I was clued in by Stewart in 1997 when he pronounced me "old-school."

"That's a great point," I say. "Did you all know that when I started school, 'under God' wasn't in the Pledge of Allegiance at all?"

"What's the Pledge of Allegiance?" Sophie asks.

"Right, right," Hunter continues, on a tear, ignoring Sophie, "one day Social Security and Medicare are socialist plots, and the next day they're these sacred American rights, now they're socialism again. Everything can change, *kaboom*—not just fashion crap but mindsets, everything, like *overnight*. The media and the corporations *want* you to think everything is *locked in*. That we aren't allowed to make real choices."

"Some things need to be locked in," I say.

"But it's like what you talk about in 'The Trouble with the Constitution,'" Hunter says, then recites my words from *The Atlantic*: "'Rethinking precedent and moving beyond the status quo is impossible until, suddenly, it isn't anymore.' Like when *you* were young."

"That's why Occupy was so cool at first," Waverly says, "because it was actually *different* from what'd been done before. But most protests seem like cover versions of old songs. Like we're all in a sixties tribute band."

"We live in the Matrix," Sophie says.

"You think it might happen again now, Grams? Everything melting, all at once? Like in the sixties?"

"Maybe." *But I doubt it.* "Although don't forget, when everything's up for grabs and everything's in flux, people get nuts. And the nuts can wreak havoc."

"What happened back then," Sophie asks, "in the sixties, to make everyone like, 'Whoa, what's going on is totally fucked up'?"

"I don't know. The good guys won World War II and America was unstoppable, and then came this gigantic mob of teenagers shouting that the emperors had no clothes, and their parents didn't have any good answers?"

"But why doesn't that happen now?" Waverly wonders, her hope and disappointment in perfect equipoise.

Because we no longer feel unstoppable? Because as long as they have enough nachos and sex, people prefer order and comfort to liberty and excitement? Because of prescription psychopharmaceuticals and a million TV channels? Because when I was seventeen, we were under the impression

that we'd discovered intoxication and fucking and backbeat and injustice and refusal, whereas you, for better and for worse, are wiser? I don't know.

"I really don't know."

"The world's twice as rich as it was when you were our age," Waverly says. "I mean, I know it's naive to think everybody will agree to share everything equally. But as a way to think about what's fair? If the average income of every person in the world is nine thousand dollars, I mean, that's thirty-six thousand a year for each family on earth. That's enough for anybody anywhere to live okay."

It's less than your annual school tuition. It wouldn't cover even my mortgage, and I live alone. It's what I earned in one week as a partner in a Manhattan law firm. "Well," I say, "that is half again more than the U.S. poverty level."

"*Exactly,*" says Hunter.

The waiter presents the check, equal to several months' income of a Congolese or Malawian, and I hand him my Amex card. At least it's a green one.

The kids walk south to their hostel, and I walk north to the Raleigh Hotel and meet my friend Sarah for a nightcap in the bar. She's here to attend the G-20 summit.

"We really love love *love* the painting," she tells me. My twenty-fifth-anniversary gift was a little Maira Kalman watercolor. "It actually looks like Victor and me! Really, Karen: you were *such* a good egg to come all the way out. Just for that."

"Well, it wasn't *just* for you." I tell her I visited Buzzy Freeman. And got together with Stewart Jones.

"Is he still cute?"

I nod. "We spent the night together."

"*What?*" she screams, and slaps the red leather banquette. "You are fucking incorrigible, Karen Hollander!"

I smile and shrug and tell her I didn't intend for it to happen, that I was talking to him and to Buzzy for book research.

"Oh, right, '*research,*'" she says. "But seriously, you need to interview every old boyfriend you ever had? This is some crazy-detailed memoir."

I explain that Stewart is helping me find certain government files that I need to finish the book.

"What, you can't mail your own Freedom of Information requests?"

I'm tempted to tell all. I resist. "It's more than that," I say, almost whispering. "It goes lots deeper than that. It's—if I'm going to tell the truth, I need his help. That's all. I can't tell you anything more. Trust me."

She looks at me for a long time. "Is this what made you get so weird at the end of freshman year? And then also what was going on that time in 1970-whatever, when I thought you'd decided you made a mistake by marrying Jack?"

What? I'm alarmed. I have no memory of the seventies conversation. "What did I say?"

"You called really late one night from Chicago, crying, but whispering so Jack and the baby wouldn't wake up, and said you didn't trust Buzzy, but then you wouldn't tell me what that meant, but you made me promise to take care of Greta if anything ever happened to you. You said, 'Sarah, she'll need a mom.' I think maybe you were a little drunk."

"Uh-huh. That's it." I take a deep breath and another. "You've never told anyone about this, have you?"

She frowns theatrically. "Have you forgotten I'm Sicilian? Omertà: no joke, sweetheart."

I laugh and wipe the wetness from my eyes. "I love you, Sarah Caputo."

"Likewise, and I cannot *wait* to read this fucking book."

Having lived in Los Angeles for seven years, I am (almost) accustomed to the sound of helicopters hovering a few hundred feet overhead for minutes or hours at a time. But that peculiarly modern noise, always serious, usually sinister, has been vibrating my hotel room windows since late this morning, and now that the choppers' fat grime beats have been joined by an unending wail of emergency-vehicle sirens, I can't stay in bed reading and picking at the remains

of my room-service lunch. So I go out on my little balcony and tiptoe at the edge to look west and south toward the Convention Center and the anti-protester barricades. I see two black smoke plumes.

Oh, *Christ*. During the last decade, I've grown unaccustomed to worrying about teenagers under my care.

I turn on the TV to watch the live coverage. It's on three national and four local channels. Bank windows have been smashed, U.S. mailboxes filled with gasoline and set on fire, tear gas fired, microwave stun weapons deployed, two hundred protesters arrested, more than two dozen injured—one breaking both legs when the fifteen-foot-tall Uncle Sam puppet he was operating collapsed on him, another when a driver, under the influence, pulled a pistol and fired a shot at a group of protesters in white makeup and ripped-up American flags splattered with fake blood, pretending to be zombies, who had surrounded his Mercedes.

I mute the TV. The orchestra of helicopters and sirens is as loud as ever. I call Waverly's cellphone again. She doesn't answer. I text her. Still no reply.

Should I go outside and try to find her among the ten thousand kids playing revolution all over Miami Beach? In order to, what, make myself feel better because I would be pointlessly acting instead of pointlessly fretting? And if by some impossible chance I do spot her, then what—cross the police line and threaten to spank her if she doesn't come with me right this second?

"Guests of the Raleigh," a man's nervous voice suddenly says over the hotel's public address system, "we are in a temporary lockdown situation. For the duration of the disturbances, no one will be allowed to enter the hotel. If you leave the grounds, reentry is not guaranteed. We apologize. These are circumstances beyond our control."

I smell tear gas.

Jesus. I feel responsible. I enabled this.

The zombie girl shot by the drunken Mercedes driver is in critical condition.

Three and a half hours pass, and I have no word from Waverly. I pray she's all right.

"She's here in my room, in bed." Using my laptop and enjoying the free Wi-Fi and the four-hundred-thread-count Egyptian cotton sheets, spending the night at the most luxurious anarchist safe house in history. "She's sort of conked out." Although not asleep: she's mouthing *Thank you.*

"Yes, she threw up," I say into the phone, "and she's got a bit of a rash or something on her neck, and her eyes are watering, but she's perfectly fine . . . Tell Jungo there's no 'permanent record' to worry about, since she wasn't arrested." She's so fine that she's shaking her head and rolling her bloodshot eyes.

"Yes, room service, a big bowl of vichyssoise and a cheese plate and a piece of carrot cake . . . I don't know what RADS is . . . And has this pediatrician ever encountered a case of 'reactive airways disease syndrome' caused by exposure to tear gas? . . . This was tear gas, Greta, *not* the dust and smoke from the World Trade towers collapsing . . . I'm sorry, it's been a very intense day, I know you're concerned, but— I know . . . No, Waverly didn't get pepper-sprayed, only Sophie . . . The emergency room doctor was mistaken, my friend's surgeon said Hunter will definitely keep his thumb." It turns out Scott Norquist, with whom I hadn't had any contact for the last four decades until this afternoon, has a golfing buddy who is also one of Miami's top hand surgeons.

"No, a *stun* grenade, not a hand grenade, and the police didn't 'attack' him . . . Because Sophie didn't tell me she was planning to use the hotel's bike to commit a level-seven felony, that's why, and *I'll* pay for the bike, but honestly, you're acting like I was the master-mind or something . . . What do you mean, Sophie's mother is 'counting on' me? . . . Honey, I am not going to call Janet Reno, and besides, I don't think she's got any pull in Dade County these days . . . The 'finest possible legal representation'? I appreciate that, Sophie's Mother, as I'll tell her when she gets here, but A, I haven't

been in a courtroom since 2004; B, I haven't done a criminal defense since you were in first grade; C, I'm not admitted to practice in Florida; and D, this is not the fucking Chicago Seven, honey. I will be very surprised if the U.S. attorney doesn't file a motion to dismiss the federal charges against Sophie." What the elected state attorney for Miami–Dade County might decide to do to a New York kid with a multicolored FUCK IT tattooed above her left breast, however, I can't pretend to predict. Under Florida law, I learned this afternoon, possessing a "hoax weapon of mass destruction" is a level-7 felony, which, even with no injuries and no priors, could mean a two-year minimum sentence. "Okay. I love you, too, Greta."

Waverly obeyed the police order to leave Dade Boulevard, and she swears she didn't even see the looted Publix supermarket or the FedEx truck that was set on fire.

Hunter admits that he was stupid to pick up the unexploded stun grenade, but he told his father and me in the recovery room that he'd watched so many YouTube videos of so many young protesters around the world picking up smoky canisters off pavements and throwing them back at cops dressed like *Star Wars* storm troopers that it was kind of an automatic response, the stage direction he was supposed to follow in that scene.

And Sophie didn't think of herself as transporting a hoax weapon of mass destruction. She had no idea that after she took a wrong turn on the Raleigh Hotel bike I lent her, and stopped to ask for directions, that she was near a 9/11 memorial. In Sophie's mind, she was heading for her star turn on the protesters' stage at Flamingo Park, where she was going to perform her multimedia performance art piece called "Eve of Destruction." That's why Sophie was wearing a flesh-colored catsuit with two hundred real dollar bills safety-pinned all over it, and why she had a rubber snake, an apple, some kind of electronic hourglass, two hundred black gumballs, and twenty red sticks of realistic-looking fake dynamite in her backpack.

All day I've been thinking of my favorite line from Karl Marx, about how historical events happen twice, the first time as tragedy

and the second time as farce. Now the thought occurs to me that when we were young, playing secret agents with licenses to kill and then playing antiwar radicals, exactly the reverse happened.

"I feel sort of guilty," my granddaughter tells me as I hand her two more Advils. "That Hunter got hurt and Sophie got busted and nothing really happened to me. You know?"

As I settle in for my flight back to L.A., the blonde in the next seat, Becky, thirtyish with a ponytail, recognizes me from television and says she attends Pepperdine's law school in Malibu part-time. Maybe she's sitting in business class because she's an off-duty flight attendant. Ordinarily I'm not a big conversations-with-strangers person, but she reminds me of my sister, who dreamed of becoming a stewardess when they were still called stewardesses. So we talk. I tell Becky that UCLA has indeed accepted transfers from Pepperdine, that "maybe a couple" of our J.D.'s during my tenure have become FBI agents, that assistant U.S. attorneys are seldom hired right out of law school, that practicing in a big firm is doable but tough if you want to have kids.

When I ask how she earns a living now, she says, "Data entry clerk at Glendale Federal Savings & Loan." But after a few seconds she leans in close and whispers, "You were a bigwig in Justice, right, so fuck it, you get the truth—federal air marshal."

She tells me that "every flight in and out of Miami this week and last is crawling with FAMs." I tell her about the Tibetan terrier fiasco scare over Omaha, and ask, now whispering myself, what would happen if she ever had to fire a gun in flight.

Her big "weapon discharge" choice, she says, would be "head shot versus center-mass shot," the downside of the former being the risk of the bullet "overpenetrating" and hitting an innocent passenger. "Although our rounds are frangible for exactly that reason." Meaning, I know, the bullets are designed to break up when they hit something.

"And what if you fire and miss—"

"I wouldn't miss."

"Okay, but if the bullet overpenetrates and shoots through the window, the fuselage . . . ?"

Becky smiles. "What, like in *Goldfinger*? Where he fires at Bond and the cabin depressurizes and Goldfinger gets sucked out? Doesn't work that way."

"I know, although in the *novel*, it's Bond who punctures the hole, deliberately, with a knife, and it's Oddjob who gets sucked out of the plane, not Goldfinger."

"Whoa, dude! James Bond for a thousand, Alex! You're like a Bond super-geek, huh?"

"I was. Once upon a time. One more question for you, if you don't mind."

"Shoot." She smiles.

"When you said at first you're a data clerk—do you tell that same lie every time?"

"A few different ones. The boringer the better, so people don't get interested and start quizzing me. That one's my stepfather's actual job."

Becky starts texting. I can never keep track of which airlines do and don't allow in-flight electronics. When I power up my phone to check in with Waverly, whom I put on the bus for New York this morning, I find I have a text message from Stewart.

Update: Definitely no feebs among yr pals in 68, and no COINTs in end game. And Macallister most def OGA-controlled.

He means that in 1968 the FBI and its COINTELPRO agents were not involved in our scheme at any point.

And Alex *was* hooked up with the CIA. At age nineteen. Mary, Jesus, and Joseph. And maybe still today, I think: when he told me he was relying on influential American friends in the Middle East to help acquire bombed-out cars, I figured he meant business associates. The CIA makes more sense.

Wow, I text back. *Wow. Thx. (But texting?!? Loose lips etc?)*

Yeah. U shld get burners.

He means I should buy disposable cellphones with prepaid minutes, the kind the smart criminals use these days.

And he texts again: *But 2 excited 2 keep quiet. :)*

James Bond, I'm pretty sure, wouldn't use emoticons.

20

I TURNED SIXTEEN HAVING . . . slow-danced. So my sexual evolution was speedy, from never-been-kissed to sex-with-a-grown-man in fourteen months. Senior year we were smoking grass every couple of weeks, then every week, and "we" sometimes included the odd jock (Scott Norquist) and popular girl (both Crawfords), which reinforced our strong unspoken sense that all the old social demarcations were withering by the day. Getting high and going to see *Fantastic Voyage* with well-liked B students today, forging a new world with Negroes and factory workers tomorrow! But I had no wish to become a hippie. Nor did Alex or Chuck. Turn on, sure. Tune in, yes, to the extent that it meant listening to rock and roll, ignoring certain rules, pitying all the human hamsters on their treadmills, and despising the owners of the cages. But drop out? Mmm . . . no. We had places to go. We had things to prove.

"I'm not sure I want to go to an Ivy League school," Chuck said one afternoon in the fall as Alex drove us home from New Trier in his parents' old Cadillac. "Antioch sounds really cool." By which he meant every student and faculty member was a radical, and considered the college an important branch office of the Movement.

Alex and I nodded.

"I could see it as a backup," I said. "Maybe."

"I'm sure it's great," Alex said, "but seriously? All the people in *charge* went to Ivy League schools. The Kennedys, Bundy, every-body in the cabinet, the guys who run corporations. Imagine if *we* were in charge!"

"We"? Women didn't run anything. "Do we want to be in charge?" I asked.

"People *like* us, I mean. That's how things are going to change. That's the only way a revolution can happen. Don't be so literal, Hollaender."

"Don't be so cynical, Macallister," Chuck said.

"Not cynical, *smart*."

"At Antioch," Chuck said, "you go to classes for two months, then work for two months, in a factory or hospital or whatever."

After a long silence, Alex said, "Southern *Ohio*?"

"Yeah, I know," Chuck conceded. And that was that. Although we professed to loathe the very idea of elites, and we constantly ragged on snooty North Shore self-satisfaction, I never had another conversation about the desirability of going anywhere but one of the two dozen most selective colleges in America. Like Ginsberg said in *Howl,* I intended to pass through university with radiant cool eyes hallucinating Blake-light tragedy among the scholars of war, but I wanted it to be a prestigious university.

As the Movement grew, and antiwar protests became regular bi-annual festivals of rage, and we learned from the *Seed,* Chicago's new underground paper, that Negro riots were actually black rebel-lions, the adults grew less indulgent. I saw a poll showing that in the last two years, Americans' support for civil rights demonstrations—civil rights!—had dropped from 42 percent to 17 percent. Which meant push was coming to shove. Alex had mentioned McGeorge Bundy, President Johnson's national security adviser, because I'd just written an editorial for the school paper arguing that New Trier's speaking invitations to him and the White House press secretary should be withdrawn. "These two men," I wrote, "share

responsibility for the deaths of eight thousand American soldiers and the murder of untold thousands of Vietnamese women and children. While freedom of speech is important, refusing to condone needless death can be more important. As Supreme Court Justice Oliver Wendell Holmes once said, if words 'create a clear and present danger [such] that they will bring about . . . substantive evils,' they should be prohibited." My mother called my article "extremely well written." That was also what she'd said about my editorial in the fall approving the assassination of South Africa's apartheidist prime minister. But this time she said that my argument struck her as "nutty as a fruitcake. It'll be your free speech and my free speech that get taken away."

"But Mom, they're murderers."

"Bill Moyers is a murderer?" He was the young White House press secretary who looked like my father.

"What, Goebbels didn't count as a murderer?" And so on.

Around the same time, Chuck had a terrible, terrible fight with his father. Professor Levy ran an electronics research firm with some other Northwestern professors. When Chuck found out that his dad's company had started working on a project for the Defense Department, he accused him of "complicity in war crimes." When his father replied that it was just a scheme for a new communications system, nothing to do with weapons or Vietnam, Chuck had said, using Sergeant Schultz's catchphrase from *Hogan's Heroes,* "Yeah, sure, 'I know *nutting!*'" Even though Professor Levy's aunt and uncle and two cousins had died at Majdanek and Auschwitz, he didn't respond, so Chuck decided to go further. "That's probably the kind of thing the Judenrats in Prague said, too, right? 'Don't worry about it, a little crowded, but trust me—it's just a train trip.'" Professor Levy slapped him and then started sobbing.

"Because he knows you're right?"

"I don't know. Later on I cried, too."

I wanted to hug Chuck. If I hadn't found him more attractive than ever, hadn't still been in love with him, I would have.

I'd started placing bets for Violet on horse races at Arlington

Park. I told her I was using my savings, as gifts to her, but I was stealing money from my parents, five dollars a swipe. And at first Wil-
more Toms placed the bets for me—the good-looking Appalachian
shitbum I met the second week in Uptown going to my volunteer
job. Violet would've been horrified if she'd known the source of my
pari-mutuel stake, but those are the noble lies one must sometimes
tell in the face of self-oppressing false consciousness. My little
scheme was a perfect combination of earnest and noir. I was taking
money from white liberals so well-to-do they didn't even notice the
thefts. I was employing a young white working-class man on behalf
of an old black woman. Violet got all the winnings and suffered
none of the losses. The bets were illegal and the income untaxed.
Expropriation! Reparations! Working in the underground economy! Building interdependence across class and racial and gender
and generational boundaries!

Meanwhile, I was going to high school, working as hard as ever
during the final semester that counted for college admissions, but
also writing screeds for the *New Trier News* and using the bonfire at
homecoming as a backdrop for an SDS puppet show about the U.S.
Air Force napalming South Vietnam (after we were denied permission to burn LBJ in effigy). "License to Shill," Alex and Chuck's Lagniappe sketch, went over surprisingly well—thanks to a line of
dialogue that incorporated the title of Ian Fleming's final book (*Oc-
topussy*), the surprise ending in which Che Guevara killed Bond by
poisoning his martini, and the fact that lovable super-jock Scott
Norquist played Che.

Apart from the evening news, by senior year I'd mostly stopped
watching television. Like all the cool toys that came out right after I
was too old for them, the new TV shows were geared to kids Sabrina's and Peter's age—*The Addams Family, Lost in Space, The Mun-
sters, Star Trek*. My sister was also an *I Dream of Jeannie* fan, and she
started wearing her blond hair in a ponytail updo in eighth grade,
the year she turned from cute to beautiful.

There was one new show I loved. Inevitably and unfortunately,
however, my parents also loved *The Smothers Brothers*. Because my

mother and dad and Peter and Sabrina all smiled and chuckled at the jokes about Vietnam and the Pentagon and President Johnson and segregation, my own enjoyment was diminished. For them it was not just groovy and satirical, proof that progressives had a national platform, but also a heartwarming, generation-gap-bridging ritual. For me, the fact that the show aired on Sunday nights made watching it even more uncomfortably cozy.

My parents thought Tom Smothers's boy-man shtick was cute, but I was fascinated by the serious lunatic rage smoldering beneath his smiling jacket-and-tie cuteness. His catchphrase, "Mom always liked you best," turned the air in our TV room slightly acrid and electric until the next joke came along.

There is no question that Mom liked Sabrina best when we were teenagers. As I was heroically attempting to exceed the bounds of parental likability, my sister rushed in to bask in the maternal sunshine, bringing up *Newsweek* and *Commonweal* articles about the Second Vatican Council, waving away the smoke and pretending to cough whenever I lit a cigarette. As soon as she got to New Trier, Sabrina restarted the Esperantists with her new boyfriend, Jamie, the Esperanto boy I'd crushed the year before. That was the line in the sand for me, after which I started thinking of Sabrina as something more like an enemy than just an annoying, square, too-pretty little sister.

With Mom's help, Sabrina and Jamie organized a screening in the school theater of *Incubus,* a movie filmed entirely in Esperanto— a horror movie in which the hero, played by William Shatner, drags his demon lover to a cathedral to deprogram her with images of Christ and the Apostles. I went only because Alex thought it would be a hoot, and it was: eleven-year-old Peter yelled *"Kie estas* Spock?" (*Where is Mr. Spock?*) at the screen whenever Shatner appeared, and my mother hated the actors' terrible Esperanto pronunciations.

I know I've written earlier that I started feeling like an adult the summer I turned sixteen, and then even more so the summer I turned seventeen. But in the spring of 1967, as I raced toward eighteen, I realized those earlier coming-of-age seasons had been wish-

ful prefaces to the real thing, that *now* my life was finally and dramatically taking shape.

"Karen?" It was a boy's voice on the phone, but not Alex or Chuck, who almost never used my first name. "It's Scott Norquist. Hey—Radcliffe! Way to go."

I'd gotten the acceptance letter only the day before, but at New Trier Township High School, the news of who'd gotten into which college traveled on some mysterious instant-communications network.

"Thanks!" But why was he calling? Scott and I had spoken on the phone exactly twice before, once about an English assignment and once concerning his three-dollar contribution to the twelve-dollar ounce of grass Flip Macallister bought for us. "And you're going to . . . Cornell?"

"My old man's pushing hard for Northwestern."

"He wants you close to home?"

"He wants me to play Big Ten football." He paused. "So Alex and Chuck and you are gonna be all together in Cambridge!" Chuck and Alex had been admitted to Harvard. "You get to stay the three musketeers, huh?" That was the kind of thing people at New Trier sometimes called us, the three musketeers. We were also known as Wendy (me), Peter Pan (Chuck), and Tinker Bell (Alex).

"Yeah. I'm excited." Actually, I had mixed feelings.

There was a long silence, then a throat-clearing. "So, I was wondering . . ." he said. *Scott must want my help buying some marijuana.* "Do you want to go to prom? With me?"

This was the most unexpected and shocking moment of my life since Alex's cap gun went off at the Michigan Shores Club in 1962. Tall, handsome Scott Norquist, the football and pole-vaulting star, the vice president of the senior class, the boy on whom I'd had an almost secret and essentially theoretical crush from age twelve on, was asking me out—asking *me* to *senior prom*. Several supercharged emotions erupted and collided in the instant after his question: surprise, deeply flattered pleasure, lust, embarrassment, a taste of heartbreaking impossibility, then a quick flip-flop of terror and—

when I reminded myself he couldn't know I'd lost my virginity—relief. I was dumbstruck.

"Karen?" Scott said.

"I'll be right there, Mom!" I shouted, half covering the mouthpiece. My mother wasn't at home. "Sorry. Anyhow—that's really, really nice of you. But I can't."

"Oh. Okay. Too bad."

"Yeah, Chuck and I are going out that night. But we're not going to prom." It was true that Chuck and I had made fun of Alex the month before for asking Patti to prom, which had turned into a critique of the prom as a hateful, anachronistic symbol of suburban American backwardness. And which delighted me because it meant Chuck wasn't taking Wendy Reichman or anyone else. However, it was certainly not true that Chuck had asked me out for prom night.

"Right. Okay. Some other time, maybe."

Jesus. I was turning down a prom date with Scott Norquist partly because prom was square but mainly because I didn't have the guts to make my imaginary boyfriend jealous. I was pathetic. And now that Chuck and I were going to attend college together, my pathetic fantasy wouldn't even have the chance to die a normal, graceful natural death after we graduated high school.

A few afternoons later, I drove Chuck home from our SDS chapter meeting. Alex was still at school, rehearsing the spring play.

"You doing anything for *your* birthday?" I asked. Chuck was turning eighteen the following day. I'd bought him a pair of Ray-Ban aviator sunglasses as a combination birthday-graduation gift.

He didn't answer my question. Instead, he said, "So I hear Norquist asked you to prom."

As a swimmer, Chuck was wired in to the jock grapevine. "Yeah. It was sweet, actually." Had Chuck also heard the details of the excuse I'd given? Should I apologize for the fib or lie again? I thought of my mother's annoying line whenever she discovered any of her children engaged in a cover-up: *Oh, what a tangled web we weave when first we practice to deceive.*

"I was surprised you turned him down. Actually, I was impressed. I mean—*Scott Norquist.*"

"Yeah, but—*prom.*" I glanced over at him. Maybe Chuck didn't know about my fabricated prom-night plans. "If I'd gone, it would've given Alex way too much satisfaction."

"Why don't we do something that night?"

That probably meant watching *The Man from U.N.C.L.E.* and eating a frozen pizza in my basement.

"I mean," he said, "go out."

I had learned my lesson well over the last three years. That didn't necessarily mean anything.

"Just you and I," he said. "It's about time, right?"

Being asked to prom by Scott Norquist had shocked me. Being asked out on an actual date by Chuck Levy should have been flabbergasting, too, but it wasn't. I'd spent so much time over so many years pining for and daydreaming about and discounting and dismissing the possibility of romantic involvement, when the moment arrived, it had come to seem equally impossible and inevitable. Does that make sense? It was the way I'd thought about nuclear war since I was little: both unthinkable and thinkable, surprised if it did happen, surprised if it didn't.

But with this, going out on prom night and Chuck as my potential boyfriend, I did feel almost as if I'd acquired the magic power to make my fondest wish—that is, my lies—come true.

"That's *my* birthday," I said, grateful that I was driving, which made it easier to sound nonchalant, "May nineteenth."

"I know."

He knows. "Then sure. That sounds great."

It's about time, he'd said. *No shit,* I thought. I was trembling. I felt like laughing and crying. And did both as soon as I dropped Chuck off.

My GPA wound up being second highest in the class—in part, as the valedictorian, Jimmy Graham, informed me, because I hadn't taken

advanced calculus. In any case, being salutatorian meant that I'd give a speech at commencement. When Chuck suggested that my speech should be a collage of lyrics from our favorite songs of the last four years, I said, loudly and fake-earnestly, "Fellow graduates of the class of sixty-seven, you make my heart sing—you make everything . . . *groovy.*"

I thought I might begin by talking about how sad it was that the birthplace of democracy had been taken over by right-wing colonels in a coup last month—Greece—and argue that the birthplace of *modern* democracy, America, wasn't immune from such a takeover.

"Maybe," Alex said, "although no one gives a shit about Greece." But he offered what I took to be a brilliant piece of advice. He said to write my speech way in advance and with short sentences, then learn to half-read and half-recite it as if I were making it up on the spot.

"You have to learn to perform a slightly fake, more lovable version of yourself," he said. "That's the only way to seem real and get everyone to pay attention. You have to learn to lie."

"Karen doesn't lie," Chuck said.

Oh, Chuck Levy, you think I'm better than I am. I wanted to press myself against him, to kiss him. I wanted him on me. The sexual hunger I experienced during the month between proposed date and date was ferocious, and the secrecy made it all the more intense. It was like five weeks of chaste foreplay, the most joyful pain and painful joy of my life.

"Not about *what* she's saying," Alex explained, "but *how* she's saying it. And you have to fool *yourself* so it doesn't even feel like lying. Be Kennedy, not Johnson."

Alex was a skilled actor by senior year. In May he played the title role in *Henry V* and was billed on the program as codirector with the drama teacher, Mr. Hendricks. I'd never seen a more moving piece of theater. The actors wore contemporary military uniforms and camo, and the score alternated between Sousa marches and Asian lute-and-zither music. Over the two and a half hours Prince Hal and his men changed from prancing imperialists into ragged and noble

guerrillas fighting the arrogant French in Vietnam, the Battle of Ag-
incourt 1415 transformed to Dien Bien Phu 1954. Neither Chuck nor
I had read or seen the play before. In Act 3, when Alex said, "Once
more unto the breach, dear friends," we turned to look at each
other—we knew it as one of James Bond's lines in *From Russia with
Love*. And when Alex, his face covered in fake dirt, delivered the St.
Crispin's Day speech—

> *If we are marked to die, we are enough*
> *To do our country loss; and if to live,*
> *The fewer men, the greater share of honour . . .*
> *We few, we happy few, we band of brothers.*
> *For he today that sheds his blood with me*
> *Shall be my brother . . .*

—I choked up and turned to Chuck. In the dark he touched my
cheeks and wiped away the tears. My insides shook. It was as if we'd
kissed already.

Every morning for the next month, I woke up happy. However,
there was nobody with whom I could revel and squeal. I had girlfriends, but since I'd never revealed to anyone the extent of my
crush, I couldn't reveal the full extent of my delight. After all, it was
just another night out with Chuck Levy, on the surface nothing very
special. My mother understood it was a big deal, however, and I was
secretly grateful for her irritating excitement on my behalf.

Neither Chuck nor I had uttered the D-word, but our first date
was the date-iest of my life, before or since. When he picked me up
around two in the afternoon, he presented me with a corsage—
a parody of a corsage, really, five white daisies, the antiwar flower,
bundled together with a pink ribbon and a peace button to pin it to
my dress, which I did for my mother to take a Polaroid and then
promptly removed.

We could've driven into Chicago in an hour, but instead, we drove
to his flying club's hangar.

Chuck had always been mechanically fluent—he'd used a power saw to build a tree house in sixth grade, he'd made the silencer for his jazz-club Luger, he'd helped his uncle build a duck-hunting blind, he replaced tubes in his guitar amplifier—but as I sat next to him in his rented Piper Cherokee, I was in awe of his competence. He wasn't playing a character on a mission when he said, "Magnetos, check," or that he was flying at "sixty knots." *He was actually piloting an airplane.* As he talked on the radio ("Affirmative, taxi four, Piper seven three niner") and stepped on the rudder pedals and steered and throttled and checked all those dials, he was completely adult, a man.

We flew to Miegs Field, the tiny downtown airport on an island in Lake Michigan, aiming for the planetarium dome as we landed. It was a five-minute walk to Shedd Aquarium, our first stop because, Chuck said, I'd wanted to go there four years ago on the evening of our last, best, scariest Bond mission. As we strolled between the sharks and the otters, Chuck took my hand in his, and I jumped as if I'd gotten an electric shock, which made him smile.

Holding hands with Chuck Levy. Chuck Levy acting like my boyfriend. Chuck Levy was my boyfriend.

We went to a movie, the Bond parody *Casino Royale,* with Peter Sellers and Woody Allen; we went to a comedy show at Second City on North Wells Street; and I had my first dinner ever at a Mexican restaurant, where they didn't card us when we ordered Pabst Blue Ribbons. As we wandered the miles back toward Miegs Field through Old Town, pretending not to stare at the hippies, he put his arm around my waist. I made us stop twice to buy Cokes and go to the bathroom.

Near the end of our walk, Chuck stopped, took a box of stick matches from the pocket of his leather jacket, struck one on the zipper of his jeans, and lit his cigarette, a move I'd never seen. I literally throbbed with desire.

I jacked up my courage. "Why," I asked, "is this finally happening?"

"I've *always* liked you. I mean, definitely since eighth grade. Re-

member the last mission, at Riverview, I wanted to go through Helter Skelter with you but Alex wouldn't let us? I thought the tilting floors and rolling barrels and all that would be my chance to, you know, accidentally get physical."

"But is this also because Scott Norquist asked me out?"

"No. I mean, that got my attention, for sure, but no. I've been planning this a long time. The whole thing." He said that in order to fly at night, he was required to take off and land several times in the dark, which he'd gone out to Palwaukee to do once a month since February.

"But why *now*? Why not last year or sophomore year?"

"Because real life is starting now. Because we're definitely going to college together. I always felt like if we went out in high school, it'd be this *high school* thing. It wouldn't be serious. And after graduation, poof, that'd be it."

"I think I get that." In all the analyses I'd conducted and scenarios I'd run since we were thirteen, that logic had never once occurred to me. Hearing it made me feel superficial. "Like we'd have been doomed? And now we have . . . a future?"

"Right, exactly."

Dreams do come true. And this I hadn't dared dream. But wait.

"What if you hadn't gotten into Harvard or I hadn't gotten into Radcliffe?"

"Why do you think I only applied where you applied?"

"Plus Amherst." Amherst didn't admit girls.

"Amherst only in case *you* went to *Smith*! So I'd be next door! It was all part of my plan. I wanted to tell you so bad. Let's never lie to each other again. Okay? Not even just not lie—hold back nothing."

I put one hand on his leather sleeve, and we kissed on the lips, but only for a couple of seconds. I looked at him. He was beautiful.

I thought of the Wordsworth poem I'd memorized a few months before: *Bliss was it in that dawn to be alive.*

And then we kissed again, our first serious kiss, the kind where you start losing track of whose tongue and whose breath is whose.

I felt radioactive. As we continued walking in blissful silence, I found myself thinking about physics. Last year we'd learned about half-lifes, the time it takes for radioactive material to decay 50 percent. Love must have a half-life, right? But if it's long enough, like uranium-232's, sixty-nine years, who cares? I also thought of the transformations that happen on the molecular level, on the atomic level, at the instant a piece of matter changes from solid to liquid or liquid to gas or gas to plasma—the "phase transition point," they call it. Ever since I'd learned about phase changes, I'd thought something analogous was happening to the whole world. And now, I thought, Chuck and I had unquestionably experienced our own phase change.

I had to find a place to pee yet again, so we didn't get back to the airfield until almost midnight, after which the control tower would close and we wouldn't be able to take off until morning. The deadline added to the perfect Cinderella glamour of the evening, and the chance of missing it, of being stuck in Chicago until morning, added to the sense of reckless bohemian romance. We took off at 11:58 P.M.

Having made our political point by skipping prom, we decided it wouldn't be a dignity violation to attend the Crawford twins' afterparty in Kenilworth. I was also eager to show our classmates that Chuck and I were *together*. However, given that he and Alex and I had been inseparable forever, the new permutation proved difficult to signal.

Except to Alex. For the last month we'd dissembled with him about our plans for the night, Guinevere and Lancelot concealing their love from Arthur. His defensiveness about attending prom— "Spare me any more of your too-cool-for-school crap," he'd said when Chuck mentioned our Second City reservation—had prevented him from sniffing out the musky new aromas. A week before, when we'd all gone to see Buffalo Springfield at the Cellar, a converted warehouse in Arlington Heights, Chuck and I danced together, which we never did, but since Alex had brought Patti along, he'd assumed our togetherness was just old-friendly pre-graduation double-date symmetry.

But as soon as Chuck and I arrived at the Crawfords' after-party, Alex locked his arm around Patti's waist, mingling like someone playing a married man, and glanced at me again and again for a beat too long, stiffly smiling and silent. Sometime around three A.M., after I'd been reduced to drinking a Scotch and Mountain Dew and gone to the bathroom for the millionth time, I rejoined Chuck and Alex in the Crawfords' backyard. Patti was indoors, and the two boys had lit up a joint. They weren't saying anything, just smoking and staring at the moon and stars.

Finally, I spoke. "Want to go see *Blow-Up* tomorrow at the Wilmette? I mean today?"

"Who," the fully inhaled Alex croaked, then deliberately exhaled straight into my face, "are you asking? Both of us or just the boyfriend?"

"Don't be a jerk, Alex," I said.

"*Me?*"

"Really," Chuck said, "don't get all weird and uptight."

" 'Jerk'? 'Weird'? 'Uptight'? *I'm* not the one who's been sneaking around keeping this secret for months."

" 'Sneaking around'?" I said. " 'Months'? And there was no 'secret' to 'keep.' That's so unfair."

"Oh, really—'unfair'? How about betraying their supposed best friend? That's fair, I suppose."

" '*Betray*'?" Chuck said. "Oh, man, come *on*. Cool it."

This duel of aggrieved scare-quoting continued for another minute.

The back door opened, and over the sudden blast of James Brown's voice and horn section, we heard Patti shout, "*Alex!* Come in and play Twister! There's four mats! It's a *gas.*"

Alex didn't respond but waited until the laughter and party roar and "Papa's Got a Brand New Bag" were muffled again.

"And what's more," he told us, "you wait to go public—"

" 'Go *public*'?" Chuck said.

"—until *after* I've told Penn no and sent my deposit to Harvard. Thanks. Thank you both so much."

"You're actually claiming," I said, driving in for the cross-examination, "that you would've gone somewhere else to college, that you would've turned down Harvard so you wouldn't be with us, if you'd known a month ago that we, that things were changing, and we might, you know . . ."

"Start *fucking*?" I had never heard the word used literally, out loud, not even in a movie. "No, fine with me. Do your own thing. But I don't want to be *lied* to, especially not about this. It's so . . . *bourgeois*."

The sun was just rising when Chuck pulled up to my house. We made out for a while, and we would've kept going—*bliss was it in that dawn!*—if I hadn't needed to pee so badly.

In the delirium of that phase-changing night, I chalked up my odd spiral of unquenchable thirst and endless urination to enchiladas and Pabsts and having my period, to overexcitement and staying up late and Mountain Dew. But it continued the next day and the next and then the next, and on Tuesday a doctor in Evanston told my mother and me that I had juvenile diabetes. For mysterious reasons, my pancreas had stopped working. I would have to inject insulin every day for the rest of my life.

"You are a very lucky girl," the doctor told me, "because you live *now*, in the 1960s." Not only would I grow up and live "a relatively normal life," but I could use the new strips to test my own urine for sugar every day at home! I'd have disposable plastic syringes I'd use just once! No muss, no fuss!

On the other hand, the chances of my eyes and kidneys and circulatory system failing had skyrocketed in the previous week, and my life expectancy diminished by a decade or more.

I had to comfort my mom, who was crying before we reached the parking lot. I was stunned by the news of my condition. But I did not cry. Within a few days, I was making jokes about it. One night at dinner, my dad said he'd learned that some scientists believed that diabetes is caused by one's own immune system going haywire, attacking the pancreas and destroying its insulin-making capacity.

"What do you know," I said, "I was the victim of a military coup inside my own body by my treasonous white blood cells, who decided my pancreas was the enemy within. And it's May! My own *Seven Days in May!*"

Peter and my father laughed. My dad suggested I use the idea in my speech at commencement. Sabrina, obviously fed up with the new gobs of nonstop attention I was getting—Radcliffe, commencement speaker, and now a serious illness—excused herself to go watch *The Monkees.*

After my mom finished the dishes and was about to head off to St. Joseph's to continue her anti-diabetes novena, I asked her if she thought God was punishing me because I'd stopped believing in Him. She didn't smile and didn't answer.

Although the endocrinologist had been ridiculously upbeat about my half-full glass, I did feel lucky. One of my uncles, my father's older brother, had died from diabetes when he was four, in 1921, only months before scientists discovered and extracted insulin. And although Mom's Catholic faith seemed ridiculous, I immediately formed my own superstitious understanding of what had happened to me that spring. I decided that luck came in clusters, good and bad bunched together, and that luck also existed in some cosmic balance, like matter and antimatter. In under two months, Harvard University admitted me and my two best friends; I was named salutatorian of my graduating class; I landed a cool summer job in New York City; Scott Norquist asked me out; and my love for Chuck Levy was at long, long last requited; but my pancreas stopped working. I just hoped that the diabetes was a large enough piece of bad luck to pay for my bumper crop of good. You can take the girl out of the church, but apparently, you cannot take the church out of the girl.

Until I got my diagnosis, nothing really terrible had ever happened to *me.* The misfortune of diabetes made me a more admirable and authentic human being. It didn't make me want to surrender to a higher power. Instead, it reinforced my rationality and sense of self-reliance: something *I* did twice a day, every day, was the only thing keeping me alive.

It wasn't just that my hard luck balanced out the great gift of Chuck revealing his feelings and plighting his troth. I was now his tragic inamorata, a fierce and doomed (but not too doomed) Juliet to his fierce enraptured Romeo, the two of us lovers and comrades headed off to an ivy-covered bower far away.

By graduation, we'd apologized to Alex for keeping him in the dark, and he had evidently forgiven us. I did mention the diabetes from the podium at commencement, although I badly misjudged the effect. The title of the speech was "Amerika the Beautiful." I talked about how New Trier was named after Trier, a German city, and quoted JFK's *Ich bin ein Berliner* line. After a series of rhetorical questions about what it meant to be an American in 1967 ("Is it 'American' to make war on civilians abroad and benefit from racism at home?"), I asked, *"Bin ich ein Amerikaner?* Am I an American? Am I an American?" I thought the *Seven Days in May* line would make me seem like Mort Sahl, soften them up for my hectoring, but rather than laughs, the announcement of my illness provoked gasps and mass pity. At least I went over better than Jimmy Graham, who summarized *The Lord of the Rings* as a geopolitical parable, recasting the Dark Lord Sauron as both Hitler and LBJ, the orcs as Gestapo and CIA, Gandalf as Ho Chi Minh and FDR, and the hobbits variously as World War II veterans, the Vietcong, and the members of the Class of '67. "Go forth to college and beyond," he told us, "to unmake the Ring." Alex accused him of "completely ripping off my *Henry the Fifth* concept," but Dad said it didn't matter, because "the Graham boy was even more confusing and sentimental than Mr. Tolkien."

A couple of weeks later, Chuck took me to a club in Hyde Park to see Muddy Waters. I hadn't considered myself a blues fan, but I was really enjoying the music.

"This is going to sounded stupid and conceited," I said halfway through the set, returning from the bathroom, where I'd gone to inject a dose of insulin.

"No, it isn't," Chuck said. "What?"

"I feel like I finally understand this music," said the eighteen-year-old daughter of a Danish marketing consultant to the eighteen-

year-old son of a Jewish engineering professor. "I mean, I *get* the blues now."

He grinned and glanced down. Muddy Waters had just played "(I'm Your) Hoochie Coochie Man," so Chuck thought I felt newly bluesy because we'd started having sex.

That wasn't it, not mainly. "Because of the diabetes. Because now I really know I'm going to die. And probably why. And it's not as far away as I'd assumed." I shrugged.

Chuck put a hand on each of my shoulders and looked deep into my eyes. "The carp is God," he said.

I laughed hard, and teared up, and kissed him right there at our table in front of the world. Back in ninth grade, Alex and Chuck briefly convinced me that "Carpe diem" is a corruption of *"Carp est Deus"* and thus literally meant not "Seize the day" but "The carp is God." In the month since I'd gotten diabetes, my seize-the-day outlook had been shaped by the line of Dr. Johnson's that I'd just learned in English class—"When a man knows he is to be hanged in a fortnight, it concentrates his mind wonderfully"—and by the Schlitz beer slogan that ran on TV all the time: "You only go around once in life, so you've got to grab for all the gusto you can."

Knowing you're going to die and therefore grabbing for gusto can go two very different ways. I alternated between both. Life did seem precious, each bite of burger and each cigarette drag perfectly delicious, every touch of Chuck's an unparalleled pleasure, music more electric, movies more intense and profound. But time felt in short supply. Which amped up an eighteen-year-old's natural impatience and inclined me to take risks I wouldn't have dared take before. Carpe diem: life is beautiful. Carpe diem: fuck it, life is short.

"You really think it's safe?" Alex asked from the backseat of Chuck's mom's Impala.

"Safer than driving this car," Chuck said.

"Those clouds are so dark," Alex said.

"They're moving away, out over the lake. You can see up ahead, it's already stopped raining. And this was *your* idea in the first place."

"I don't know, Chuck. I don't want to die for a silly reason."

"We're not gonna die. Don't be a pussy."

It was a Saturday in late June. The next day I was headed for New York City and my summer job, and Alex would be leaving soon for Eastern Europe and his student cultural conferences. It had been raining all afternoon. We were driving up the Edens Expressway, on our way to the Palwaukee airport. Alex had never flown with Chuck.

The plane was small. "It's only got one engine!" Alex said. "What if it conks out?"

"Then I glide in."

The rain stopped, the clouds were blowing east, and we could see a widening bar of blue on the western horizon.

We each put on headsets and took off. The trick was to keep the low late-afternoon sun behind us and fly east, over the lake, toward the rain—but then to circle back before we reached the cloud bank.

I was the first to spot one. *"There!"*

"Where?" asked Alex, who disliked not being first to see or hear or know anything. *"Where?"*

"There, at four o'clock," Chuck said. "No, *down*."

Alex gasped. "Oh my *God*. I didn't know you could even see one from *above*. It's like being an angel. It's like a God's-eye view."

Alex and I stared out the right side of the plane at the stripe of red fuzzing into a stripe of orange fuzzing into yellow, green, blue, darker blue, and purple. We were dumbfounded by the rainbow, unaware of everything else.

Until Chuck banked sharply left.

Alex screamed. I wet my pants a little. Chuck grinned as he finished the turn and leveled off, heading back toward the afternoon sun.

We didn't see another rainbow during our next four passes. As Chuck prepared to turn away once again from the vast cliff of dark, dark gray, he said, "This time, before I bank, close your eyes."

"It's okay," I said, "I'm used to it now."

"No, close your eyes. It's an experiment."

We did. We felt the sharp left turn.

"Keep your eyes closed."

"What are we waiting for?" I asked.

Alex started humming "Somewhere over the Rainbow."

"Okay," Chuck instructed finally, "I'm done with the turn, but keep your eyes closed. What direction are we going now?"

"West," we both said.

"Open your eyes."

Alex screamed again. I grabbed my right armrest with both hands and held tight, as if to keep myself from falling. The plane was tilted left at a shocking angle, and in front of us, the cloud wall to the east looked darker and more filled with menace than ever.

"I lied. We've been banked thirty degrees this whole time, flying in a circle. And now your eyes are lying to you. You felt me going into it, and you can feel me coming out of it"—he started leveling off and straightening out, back toward the sun—"but you can't *feel* the angle when you're *in* the turn."

A few minutes later, when we turned east again, we were pointed directly into the center of a rainbow that stretched over our entire field of vision.

"*Whoa,*" Chuck said.

We could see the whole thing, the complete arc, the top and both ends—and there was a second rainbow encircling the first, but in a mirror image, with purple on the outside and red on the innermost arc. Against the nearly black clouds, the colors of the double rainbow were super-brilliant, like neon. It looked fake.

"Could we fly through it?" I asked.

"Let's fly through it!" Alex said.

"You can't. See, it just keeps moving away. You can never reach it. We'd get to the rain—rainbows are *made* of raindrops, right?—and then it'd just . . . disappear."

I thought of God, maker of heaven and earth, of all that is, seen and unseen. It had never occurred to me before that He's a trickster.

After we landed and Chuck parked the plane, I asked, "What would happen if we *had* just kept flying straight through? The rainbow would disappear, and then what?"

"We'd be inside the thundercloud. We might've gotten hit by lightning."

"Oh, Jesus," Alex said.

"You're safer getting hit by lightning up there than down here. The problem would be these big currents inside the thundercloud, these intense winds in there, updrafts and downdrafts. They can tear you apart."

I grinned and kept grinning. Which was weird. But we were safe and sound, sneakers squishing and squeaking on the wet tarmac, walking under a blue sky toward a red Chevy washed shiny clean by the rain. We were eighteen.

Bliss was it in that dawn to be alive.

My parents agreed to let me spend the rest of the summer in New York City because I was staying in a dorm room at Barnard with an older New Trier girl whose parents they knew. I'd gotten a volunteer job in a tiny new organization trying to drum up support inside the Democratic Party for dumping President Johnson and nominating an antiwar candidate in 1968. When I got to New York, I discovered it wasn't much of an organization at all, but a few devoted typists and collators and phone answerers devoted to one guy, a lawyer and politician who seldom came to the office. But the office had a Xerox copying machine, so the operation seemed sophisticated and legit.

I became best buddies with one of the other interns. Sarah Caputo had grown up the youngest of six kids in Camden, New Jersey, where her dad worked as a welder in a shipyard. She had (still has) a voice like Judy Holliday's, roomed with an aunt and uncle in Queens, and worked nights as a waitress. She was about to start at NYU on a full scholarship. Sarah was the first person I ever met who'd gotten 800 on both SATs, and who used the words "preppy" and "broad"—after we became friends, she told me that at first she'd taken me "for some rich preppy folksinger broad." Sarah was also the first person to whom I was completely honest about my years of tortured pining for Chuck Levy.

We met some of the SDS kids from Columbia, who had a summer project to enlist regular New Yorkers, nonstudents, preferably black, into the Movement. The Columbia kids argued constantly over the relative merits of antiwar education and antiwar protest and antiwar "resistance." Whenever they used the words "resistance" and "struggle," which they did a lot, their already serious voices got quieter, deeper, grave.

I was afraid they'd think I was a silly, ignorant midwestern girl if I asked, *What exactly do you mean by "resistance"?* Instead, I mentioned that my boyfriend's uncle had been in the armed Jewish resistance in Palestine in the 1940s.

Israel's Six-Day War had taken place a few weeks earlier. "'Jewish resistance in Palestine,'" repeated one of the SDS boys, chuckling. "I'd call that an oxymoron." And so I felt like a silly, ignorant midwestern girl. Sarah said they were all "businessmen's kids, doctors' and lawyers' kids who spend their time feeling guilty about being comfortable instead of just fucking *helping* people who need help." I loved Sarah. I still do.

I missed Chuck. But I also took pleasure in missing him, especially when he phoned me at the end of my first week in New York. No one had ever called me long-distance. In addition to working as a lifeguard at Gillson Park, he said he was helping out at his father's electronics firm.

"You're working for your dad's *company*? I thought you had that big fight about him being a war profiteer?"

"I know, but he's not. It's not. It's just research into some kind of Teletype system for computer scientists. That the government happens to be paying for. Just like the government has paid your dad to do research." I'd made Chuck nervous, gotten him off-track. "Anyhow, I'm also mowing lawns on weekends. Saving up money for a surprise for you."

"How will it be a surprise if you already told me you're giving it to me?"

"Hmm . . . riddle me that, Catwoman."

In fact, it was a complete surprise, a few weeks later, one that

made me yelp, when I found Chuck sitting on the steps of the dorm where I was staying. I didn't recognize him at first, from far away, because he hadn't cut his hair since May. He'd taken the bus all the way from Chicago. He was going to stay in New York for a week.

I cried. Chuck laughed and hugged me. I felt as happy as I'd ever felt in my life, and I said so. "I'm glad you didn't tell me you were coming. I know we're supposed to always tell each other the truth and hold back nothing. But I'm glad you held this back. Some secrets are best if they're kept secret."

He'd booked a room for the two of us at a cheap hotel in Times Square, not far from where I worked. At the Northwestern library, he'd researched New York restaurants and had a list of a dozen where we could have dinner for under three dollars apiece, although most nights we ate at a place in Chinatown called Hung Fat, where the only other white people were also in their teens and twenties.

Bliss was it in that dawn to be alive.

Sgt. Pepper's was playing over the PA system in the basement of the Cafe Wha? in Greenwich Village as we awaited the boozeless Friday-evening "teen" show, and when Chuck sang along with the chorus to "When I'm Sixty-four," I leaned over and kissed him. We wandered over to a psychedelic dance hall in the East Village, where we were surrounded by kids and even some adults with snakes and stars and moons and flowers and words painted on their faces and chests and arms. I'm not sure I'd even smelled marijuana in a public place before, but here the smoke was like a fog.

"Alex would like to see this," Chuck said. "He sent me a postcard from Belgrade. He shook hands with Tito."

"I got one from Budapest. He saw some gigantic opera that lasted all day long. Sounds like he's having a great time."

A girl Sabrina's age with a bloodred LUV painted on her forehead offered me a joint, which I passed to Chuck, which he passed to a boy wearing braids and blue-tinted glasses. As the girl and boy drifted away, I said, "It's like they're *performing,* like they're playing the parts of hippies."

"We're all playing roles, right? We're all characters in the show."

That struck me as wise.

As a band started playing in the main room, Chuck was reminded of something. "I bought tickets to a concert Saturday night. At some stadium. Where's Queens?"

"Across the river. Who?"

"Technically, the Monkees—I *know*, I know, but one of the bands opening for them is the one I mentioned a while ago, with the black guitarist and singer who's completely amazing? At this huge three-day concert in California, he lit his guitar on *fire*. We don't have to stay for the Monkees if we don't want to."

We almost left before the Monkees came on, at the end of "The Wind Cries Mary," when Chuck quietly asked the two junior high girls next to us to "pretty please shut the fuck up," and the father of one of them stood and threatened to punch him. The girls and hundreds like them kept chanting "We want the *Mon-kees*" and "*Da-vy, Da-vy, Da-vy*" all through Jimi Hendrix's performance. It was annoying at first, but after the mescaline Chuck had gotten from Flip Macallister kicked in and we were tripping for the first time in our lives, we considered it urgent, as I said to Chuck, to "turn off the Chatty Cathy robots."

Chuck was on his feet jiggling and jerking and bopping while Hendrix played, so I stood the whole time, too. As with jazz, I felt like I didn't quite get it—the feedback, the distortion, the *noise*, like some science-fictional Factory of the Future falling apart, exploding in slow motion—but I loved the rollicking hell of it anyhow. It sounded like revolution. "He's playing directly from *inside* his *brain*," Chuck shouted over "Purple Haze." I'd never seen anyone so entirely, recklessly, virtuosically committed to making a spectacle of himself as Hendrix. And when he spoke, I was shocked by his sweet, modest, mouthful-of-marbles voice. He was like a character from *Alice in Wonderland*, funny and serious at the same time, dangerous and adorable.

My dad had said to me over the last couple of years that teenagers in every era feel as though they're experiencing life in original, unprecedented ways, confusing the novelty of their individual ado-

lescent experience with something marvelous and historic. "Solipsism," he'd said. "Look it up." Now I had a counterargument: this *was* unlike anything anyone had ever heard or seen or maybe felt before.

Jimi spoke less and less as the set went on, and the spaces between songs were more and more filled with crowd chants of *"Monkees, Mon-kees, Mon-kees."* At the end of "Wild Thing"—which he'd fractured and stretched into several digressions, some of them unintelligible screeches, some of them recognizable pieces of song, including "Strangers in the Night," which made us laugh—Hendrix was steamed. He walked to the edge of the stage, put up his right hand, and gave us all the finger before disappearing into the darkness. It made me feel like crying.

The most psychedelic special effect of the night was unintentional and Monkees-driven—the thousands of flashbulbs strobing all over the stadium, like a swarm of electronic lightning bugs in a giant jar. *We're all playing roles, we're all characters in the show,* Chuck had said. *Fool yourself so it doesn't even feel like lying,* Alex had told me. When the Monkees finally appeared and ten thousand screamies yelled and jumped and—in the case of the little girl next to me—sobbed, I had a revelation: they weren't *like* actors playing roles, they *really were* performing parts they'd learned from watching Beatles fans on TV and in the movies, and each one had fooled herself into sincerely believing her own performance of unhinged euphoria. Whereas the Monkees, a self-aware simulacrum of the Beatles, were funny about it: onstage between songs, they snapped pictures of one another, performing parodies of the Beatles and their unhinged fans in *A Hard Day's Night*. My post-Jimi embarrassment and sorrow lifted. We still left halfway through their set, driven away by the banshee screams that greeted the first bars of "I'm a Believer."

Chuck seemed to be replaying Hendrix songs in his head as we walked out. His eyes were huge, and his breath sounded like a horse snorting.

Because of our mescaline plan, and my fear that I would be unable to distinguish between hallucinogenic and hypoglycemic ef-

fects, I'd brought along six Hershey bars to keep myself sugared up. I was eating the fourth as we walked past the West Side Tennis Club's mock-Tudor clubhouse.

I mainly pretended but almost believed we were in England. Specifically in the south, in Kent, near Sandwich.

"The Royal St. Marks!" I said, my mouth full of chocolate glop.

As Chuck grinned, his lips and teeth seemed to stretch halfway around his head. The Royal St. Marks is the country club where Bond beats Goldfinger in a round of golf. Then I couldn't remember for sure if the scene was in the movie or in the novel or both, which prompted me to gobble the rest of my Hershey bar.

On the subway back to Manhattan, we said nothing for a long time. The sounds of wheels on tracks and the metal-on-metal shrieks of the train's turns were music, a Hendrix encore. The ride seemed to take hours. A middle-aged couple sat down across from us, talking loudly in some Eastern European language. Chuck leaned over and whispered, "Soon we'll be in Belgrade, Tanya. Sorry I dosed you earlier."

I grinned, and nodded, and clasped his hand tighter inside both of mine. In *From Russia with Love,* the assassin Red Grant puts a drug in Tatiana Romanova's drink aboard the *Orient Express.* I felt comforted at that moment. It was as if we had played our children's games in order to learn a private language we could speak when we were no longer children but still together.

Bliss was it in that dawn to be alive.

The Eastern Europeans had been replaced by three young black men. I reminded myself that despite appearances, this was not a supernatural transformation, that I'd simply missed seeing the old folks get off and the young guys get on. One of them kept staring at us. Chuck, looking back and smiling, raised the first two fingers of his left hand in a V, which made the black kid look away.

As we understood it, a hundred hours earlier and ten miles west, crowds of black people had spontaneously formed into platoons of street-fighting guerrillas. There had been riots earlier that summer— in Houston after a white cop shot a black child, in Tampa after a

white cop shot a black teenager, in Buffalo, Hartford, Atlanta, even in some small town in Iowa—but these riots right across the Hudson River, provoked by the arrest and fatal beating of a black cab-driver by white cops, were huge and escalating.

And that mob of chittering, screeching girls in Forest Hills who wanted Jimi Hendrix yanked off and replaced by four white boys, they were the brainwashed flying monkeys of the same rotten system. *No wonder Negroes feel like killing white people,* I thought, and then I revised my thought, replacing "Negroes" with "black people."

"Brainwashed flying monkeys" was a phrase of Chuck's in one of the sixteen letters he sent me that summer, what he called in another of the letters "our last months apart forever."

After I introduced Chuck to Sarah that week in New York, she told me she understood why I was "gaga for the guy," but that he "gives off a vibe like he's keeping some big secret. Although maybe that's just being Jewish. Which is like being a better-behaved Italian."

When I returned home from New York in August, I was delighted to see Alex. He had fully come to terms with the three of us accommodating the Karen-and-Chuck romantic subunit. He'd also become more entertainingly fake-British—his favorite adverb was "frightfully," New York City sounded "brilliant" although my work in the Dump Johnson office was "bollocks," *Sgt. Pepper's* was "a complete load of shite." He couldn't stop talking about the charms of Eastern Europe, especially of his new thirty-four-year-old friend Darko, an up-and-coming leader of the Yugoslavian Communist Party. "He's progressive and completely charismatic, sort of like their John Lindsay," and he had played for a professional soccer team called Partizan—all of which Chuck and I had to admit sounded pretty cool. And Bondlike.

I didn't ask Violet what she thought of all the ghetto uprisings, because I knew from the last two summers that she was ashamed of them. (She'd also told me once that she hated the word "ghetto," that she'd "never even *heard* of it until around the World War II

time.") On the Friday morning before Labor Day weekend, as I helped her fold sheets, she used her inhaler twice. I asked if she was okay.

"Oh, it's this rotten *humidity.*"

"It was really humid in New York." And jam-packed with black people! "Did you know I lived in Harlem?" This was only a slight exaggeration.

"You did *not,* Kay-Ray!"

"The dorm was on 119th, and Harlem's main street is 125th."

"Did your parents know that?"

"Uh-huh."

She shook her head. "I'm glad *I* didn't know."

"How's the handicapping been going?"

She shook her head again. "I'm glad you weren't here to waste your money on me. I done no better than *show* in three weeks. Kay-Ray is my lucky charm." She grinned at me. "I got a real good one today, though."

I was now old enough to make bets myself. "I can go out to the track if you want. One last bet before I go to college!"

"No, you're busy, honey."

"I've got nothing to do but pack. And Chuck and I are going to a concert tonight at the Cellar"—Captain Beefheart and the Magic Band, more music I didn't really get—"which is right near the track, so we can make your bet on the way."

Violet wasn't resisting my offer. "She's a long shot, but you'll like her, Kay-Ray." When she told me the name of the horse, I blushed.

My mom and her purse were at the beauty parlor, so I swiped four dollars from Sabrina's stupid little safe—the combination was 6, 23, 12, 11, the numbers of Paul, John, and the two Piuses, the last four popes. Chuck and I drove out to the track and smoked a joint in the parking lot. The plan was to pop into the racetrack, place the bet on Violet's horse in the eighth, and go spend the rest of the afternoon hanging out in one of the big, wild parks just beyond Arlington Heights. But Chuck made us stay for an hour, betting our own money and losing two dollars every race, because he loved

watching the horses running on Arlington Park's enormous new closed-circuit color TV screen, the largest on earth. "It's like the gigantic telescreen in the Ministry of Truth," he said. *1984* was his favorite novel. "I wonder if they ever show real TV on it. Imagine watching the *news* on this, footage from Vietnam. Imagine watching *Johnson* giving a *speech* from the *Oval Office.*" I did imagine, and it gave me the creeps, as did the anxiety and hysteria radiating from the crowd during each race, so we left and drove out to the woods and listened to the birdsong.

The next morning my family left for Oconomowoc Lake for the Labor Day weekend, but I stayed home. Sometime that Saturday afternoon, just before Chuck was supposed to pick me up to go see *Bonnie and Clyde,* I remembered the bet for Violet and dug the newspaper out of the trash to check the results—and discovered that, holy moly, *yes,* Violet's horse had gone off at fourteen-to-one and *won.*

I got Violet's number off the yellowed note card thumbtacked to the kitchen bulletin board and, for the first time in my life, phoned her. I was thrilled for Violet—her winnings were as much as she earned in a week—but also pleased by the good omen for myself, by the improbable victory of a long-shot filly called Chuck's Sweetie.

"Hi, this is Karen Hollaender. May I speak to Violet, please?"

"Hello, Miss Hollaender, this is Reggie Woods, Violet's son."

"Hello!" I'd never met him. I'd never met any member of Violet's family. "I have some great news for your mother!"

There was a long pause, and I heard voices in the background before he spoke again.

I don't know if he realized I was crying as he explained to me what had happened, that she'd had a bad asthma attack around midnight and called three times for an ambulance that never came, that she phoned him and he finally found a taxi at two A.M. and took her to the hospital, that she'd had a heart attack in the emergency room. And died.

My cheeks, my chin, my neck, even the top of my blouse was wet. "I am so sorry about your mother."

"Her horse you bet at Arlington? She *knew* she won that, she was real excited yesterday afternoon, so happy about that, she called me and my brother, Randall, about that—and said she called you, too, but nobody was at home."

"I loved her. I really loved her."

"She loved you, too. She sure did."

There was no phone at the lake house, so I couldn't call my parents to tell them. When Chuck showed up, I sobbed again, this time noisily.

I had a horrible thought: maybe Violet's excitement over Chuck's Sweetie had triggered the asthma attack. Which would make me responsible for her death. I went to the bathroom to see if my distress might be partly hypoglycemic, and when some of my tears dripped into the Dixie cup of urine, I started crying again and had to start over and pee into a fresh cup. The strip turned a deep blue, which meant my blood sugar was low.

I took the orange juice from the icebox and guzzled it straight from the plastic pitcher.

"You know," Chuck said, "it sounds to me like she died because she was poor and black. If some white lady on Lake Shore Drive was having an attack, you can bet the ambulance would be there in five minutes."

My family and I were the only white people at Violet's funeral. I was shocked to learn that she was fifty-one, just a few years older than my parents. She had always seemed ancient. I handed Reggie the fifty-seven dollars she'd won. And I was appalled by the fact, which I realized as I shook hands with him and his brothers, that they were the first black men I'd ever touched.

The riots had continued the rest of the summer all over the country, a new one every few days, each one put down by National Guard troops, thousands of black people thrown in jail. I took no pleasure in reading about policemen killed and stores looted and buildings torched, I told myself, any more than officials in Washington took pleasure in the destruction of Vietnamese towns and the deaths of

Vietnamese women and children. What he'd learned from World War II, my dad always said, from Dresden and Hiroshima and even his own experiences in Denmark, is that history doesn't happen cleanly or easily. Pain and ugliness and horror and regret are always part of the price of freedom and justice, he told me, and once a war starts, "good guys do terrible things."

My last night before I left for college, I was watching the evening news with my family. During the commercial after a report about "'black power' and the militant young Negroes who espouse it," I said that I'd told Reggie Woods at the funeral that he ought to sue the city of Chicago for violating the Civil Rights Act by failing to send an ambulance for Violet.

My parents both nodded. My mother said that when I grew up, I could be the first woman on the Supreme Court.

"It's terrible what happened to Violet," Dad said. "But you know, these days, this summer, a Friday night, after midnight, Negro snipers shooting at white men in uniforms—I bet those ambulance attendants were *terrified* to go into Violet's neighborhood. I would be."

My mother tensed up, anticipating my outrage.

"My God," I said, "that is *grotesque*, Dad! You're *excusing* it? By blaming the victims? Now it's black people's fault that the system is screwing them over?"

"Honey," my mom said, "your *language*."

"Fuck my language."

Had the word "fuck" ever been uttered in our house before that evening in 1967? Sabrina shook her head and went upstairs, but Peter, on the sofa, put his arms around his knees, eyes wide open and hunkered down the way he did when a TV show engaged him, dying to see what would happen next.

My father, damn him, sagely smiled. "Our Radcliffe freshman has become a woman of the world."

"By the way? *We* probably contributed to Violet's death, too. Chuck says his aunt has asthma and can't be around Windex or Pledge or anything, and what did Violet do here all day long? Breathe in cleaning sprays."

The news came back on, and we sat in silence during a report about the intensified U.S. bombing campaign against Vietnam, and the Johnson administration's claim that it was all about "bringing the Communists to the peace table."

"War is peace, just like in 1984," I said. They showed a clip of an air force fighter-bomber being struck by a North Vietnamese SAM and disintegrating in midair, and I muttered, "Bull's-eye."

My mother gasped. "That's a terrible thing to say."

"It's a terrible war we're waging on a country that can't do us any harm."

"I agree, you know I completely agree, but there was a man in that plane who died. An American *person*."

"Who had probably killed a hundred Vietnamese *people* five minutes earlier. I hate to tell you, Mom, but the war's going to be stopped by them winning, not by you and me disapproving of it and wearing peace buttons. Not as long as these . . . fucking fascists are in charge."

I had at last made my father angry. "Young lady," he said, "do not use that word."

"Okay, is this better? This genocidal war will continue and expand as long as these fascists are in charge."

"*Goddammit,* Karen, no, I mean *that* word, 'fascist'—they're bloody-minded, Johnson and the rest, stupid, tragic fools, but this country is *not* fascist. And the war's a horror show, but it is not genocide. I lived through fascism. I saw genocide."

"Maybe that's why you can't see *this* evil, now, for what it is—"

"You simply have no idea—"

"—just because General Westmoreland doesn't wear a swastika—"

"—*no* idea at *all* what you're talking about."

"—and the victims are incinerated in their homes instead of a camp."

My mother left her empty rocking chair rocking as she got up and walked out of the room without a word. My father buried himself in the *Sun-Times.* Peter turned the TV to channel 7 so he could watch the premiere of a new series about General Custer. I petted Curiosity and enjoyed my adrenaline high until dinner.

21

Trying to hail a taxi as I rush down the street, anxious about being late for a cable news appearance, checking email and watching a video of myself on my phone as I walk, I bump into a man on the curb passing out leaflets, who says, "Hollaender?"

I look up: it's Chuck Levy, which doesn't startle me, although I find my nonchalance surprising.

His flyers are laminated, and they're covered with a single phrase, NO MORE LIES, printed hundreds of times. I don't like his soul patch, but otherwise he looks fantastic.

"My *God*," I say, "you haven't changed a *bit*."

He laughs and says, "You have no idea." He looks around to make sure no one's watching and lifts his leather jacket to show me a gun in a shoulder holster. "This has been a lifesaver. Thank you."

I'm trying to figure out if he's being sarcastic when a cab screeches to a stop right beside us, and I notice that it's gray, not yellow. In fact, nothing—the sky, the sunlight, the buildings, Chuck's face, my hands and blouse—is in color. Everything's in black and white. Only then do I notice that the sidewalk and street are flowing with raw sewage.

Alex jumps out of the taxi. "Black and *shite*, you mean," he says. Then he says, or sort of sings, "Ding dong, the bitch is dead, the bitch is dead!"

That's the last of the dream I remember when I open my eyes and see Clarence Darrow on my pillow, staring at me, his face inches from mine. "Hello, cat," I say softly.

Since I started writing this book, I've dreamed about Chuck a lot, maybe every other month, but I'm not sure I've ever in my life dreamed in black and white until just now. My daughter, Greta, once told me about a study in which they asked people how often they had black-and-white dreams, then compared the results to those from an identical study conducted in the 1940s. Seventy years ago, 71 percent of people dreamed in black and white, whereas nowadays only 18 percent do. The conclusion was not that the advent of Kodachrome and Technicolor and color TV had transformed the neurological essence of dreams. Instead, they think that people's morning-after memories of dreams were mistaken in the 1940s, or are mistaken today, or possibly mistaken in both eras—that dreams are dreams, unchanging, but the mediascape of the waking world makes us jump to easy conclusions about the nature of our remembered dream imagery. I wonder if they'll do the study again in another seventy years and find that people imagine they're dreaming in 3-D.

Living in Los Angeles means that I arise most mornings with a backlog of electronic messages from the East Coast. And today I'm waking up late, so there'll be even more. I have a text from Waverly: *call me, grams? love you!* I glance at the time, 9:19, and start to dial, but hang up when I realize Waverly will be in school, since the state of New York doesn't recognize the birthday of César Chávez as a holiday. Chávez was an admirable person, and my assistant's father worked for his United Farm Workers. But now that George Washington and Abraham Lincoln have to share a holiday, and the only other individuals the state of California celebrates with an annual twenty-four-hour vacation are Martin Luther King, Jr., and Jesus Christ, does Chávez really deserve to be fifth in line?

I probably shouldn't say these things. Writing this memoir has unbound me from various fetters and gags of discretion. Stewart says I'm turning into Bulworth, the crazily honest, suicidal U.S. senator Warren Beatty played when he was in his sixties.

For instance, this year I was appointed to a university committee looking at grade inflation, and at the first meeting I said the good news is that the trend is self-eliminating—since the average GPA rose from B-minus to A-minus during the last half century, in another fifteen years every kid will be getting straight A's. I've just okayed a joint law school–medical school course that will speculate about the possible psychiatric disorders of U.S. presidents as well as of sitting members of Congress and the Supreme Court. During a panel discussion about immigration that I was moderating, I mentioned that in the 1960s and '70s, César Chávez and his union members lined up at the U.S.-Mexican border to keep Mexicans from entering the country illegally, and that they also turned in undocumented-immigrant farmworkers to the feds. An audience member accused me of "smearing a hero with falsehoods."

If I were smart, I'd now be cultivating the left, preaching to the choir, gathering allies in anticipation of the shit storm my confessions are going to provoke. I know this book will be meth-laced catnip to some people on the right, told-you-so proof of the terrorist sympathies of the arrogant liberal elite who hate America. The fact that I have tenure at a public university and can't (easily) be tossed out will feed the rage. I can see my platoons of enemies now, furious and sputtering, sending all-capital-letter emails to the chancellor and governor, on a thousand blogs and radio and TV shows demanding my banishment and prosecution. They'll be convinced of their righteousness, and of the evil of the cabal that controls the Establishment, but thrilled to be scaring the hell out of it. In other words, they'll be a lot like I was at age eighteen. It's strange that so many people of my generation who didn't throw political tantrums in the late 1960s, when we were young and it was fashionable, are letting it all hang out now that they're old.

One of my new disposable cellphones rings. Stewart is calling.

"The last time we spoke, you said your Coast Guard pal served in Vietnam, right? Well, he didn't. Never got as far west as Hawaii. Never saw action. From sixty-five to sixty-seven, Petty Officer Third Class Bernard Freeman ran a fucking lighthouse on the coast of Northern California."

"*Really?* Wow. That makes me sad."

"That's unknown unknowns for you. You start turning over rocks, for better and for worse you almost always find secrets you weren't looking for."

I tell him I've received official responses to two more of my Freedom of Information requests, and then I start reading aloud from the FBI's letter. " 'We conducted a search of the indices to our Central Records System. We were'—"

Stewart chimes in and recites along with me from memory: " 'We were unable to identify responsive main file records. If you have additional information pertaining to the subject that you believe was of investigative interest to the Bureau, blah blah blah, you have the right to appeal any denials in this release to the DoJ Office of Information and Privacy, blah blah blah, please fuck off and let us go back to the important Records Management Division business of watching porn and playing fantasy baseball.' So feeb-y, right? 'Responsive main file records,' 'pertaining,' 'the subject *that*.' Such losers."

"I also got one from the CIA."

"No shit? Did they Glomarize you?"

"Uh-uh. But all they sent were three pages of notes about me being in Czechoslovakia in 1992."

Let me digress. I spent a couple of months in Prague helping the new government there draft a new constitution. It's the legal-career accomplishment of which I'm proudest. I got the gig through a colleague at Yale—and, as Alex has reminded me repeatedly ever since, through Alex. In 1991 he recommended me to his friend Václav Havel, the playwright and first president of post-Communist Czechoslovakia.

"You were children of sixty-eight together, Alex and you?" President Havel said when we first met in Prague.

"Something like that. Although it wasn't quite the same there as it was here in Europe."

"Not so different. In May that year I was in America, in New York. The difference between us is, I came back here and they put me in prison."

Havel's underling with whom I mainly dealt spoke little English, and I assumed we'd rely entirely on translators to communicate. But we discovered we'd both had parents who forced us to learn Esperanto as children, which enabled us to have sidebar conversations about other people in the room that none of them could understand. President Havel said we reminded him of characters in his play *The Memorandum,* in which the totalitarian government bureaucracy adopts an artificial language called Ptydepe. I told him that in the spring of 1968, Alex and I happened to be in New York City together, and he had wanted to see that play.

"Synchronicity!" President Havel said.

I describe to Stewart the record of my CIA surveillance from 1992. "It's got all the times I arrived and left the presidential palace, street addresses I visited, and this incredibly detailed report on a dinner conversation I had with a Czech newspaper reporter. It's spooky."

"That's why they call them spooks. And the Cold War had been over for thirty seconds—that poor GS-12 in Prague had to do *something* to earn his six grand that month. But nothing about 1968, huh?"

"Nope. So do you think Buzzy not serving in Vietnam means he definitely wasn't a defense intelligence agent in college?"

"Definitely? No. But army intel hiring some random Coastie would be weird. And I totally don't buy that a guy like that, after he becomes a big-time right-winger, never blabs about having done his undercover duty for God and country fighting subversives in the late sixties."

"So Alex was the snitch, working for the CIA."

"For starters."

"He was a spy for someone else, too?"

"Doubt it. But why did this whole thing get erased and deep-sixed as thoroughly as anything I've ever seen in thirty years in this racket? Like I've said from the start, there had to be multiple agencies fucking up multiply and simultaneously. Negative synergistic convergence. FUBAR panic times FUBAR panic equals FUBAR panic cubed."

"I have no idea what you just said."

"I think you must have had more than one federal asset embedded."

"Wow."

"It's insane, right? But back then, the government had at least a couple thousand fake radicals working undercover all over America—the fucking army alone had a thousand, probably more. And you *know* the interagency coordination must've been totally for shit. I'm inclined for obvious reasons to eliminate Charles Levy as a candidate, so if there was a second embed, it probably was your lighthouse keeper, Freeman."

"Wow. That's amazing." I think of how Alex and Buzzy have come to despise each other as adults. "So you think they didn't know about each other at the time?"

He starts to say something, stops, then speaks. "I said *probably* Freeman. The other possibility, my darling, is you."

"Ha ha."

"Did you cooperate with any government agency during the years 1967 and/or 1968, in a paid or unpaid role?"

"*What?*" My throat tightens.

"Yes or no."

"*No,*" I say. "But I thought you didn't want me to tell you anything more than I already have. To keep your investigation 'clean'?"

"That was then. I'm getting closer now. Different rules. I don't care what your answer is, okay? I won't think less of you personally either way. So: yes or no?"

"Yes. I had a federally guaranteed student loan, and a passport."

"Don't get cute. Did you have any ongoing relationship with a law enforcement or national security organization in 1967 and/or 1968?"

I take a deep breath. "No."

He says nothing for a few seconds. "Okay, good," he finally says. "My machine believes you're probably telling the truth about not being an agent. Maybe Freeman is your second man after all."

"On your *phone,* you've got a *lie* detector?"

"There's no such thing as a lie detector. But I gotta say, this fifth-gen DVSA algorithm, it's a Secret Service deal, is really a cut above. And your last gram is a nice, smooth, low hillock."

"What the fuck are you talking about now?"

"A voice-gram, a line generated by digital voice stress analysis software. What you would call a lie detector. In order to eliminate the possibility that you were what you would call an agent provocateur."

"You freak me out."

"I know. Sorry. You started this thing. By the way, I got the full OSS file on your old man. But hey, I've buried the lead! Yesterday I found out the leverage they used to reel in Alexander Macallister the Third. On the twelfth of August, 1967."

"'They' being the agency that I call the CIA, and 'reel in' meaning enlist as an informer."

"Yep," Stewart says. "Macallister was a regular Bond girl."

While he tells me about Alex, I feel as if my brain is firing on too many cylinders, or too few, and I find myself scrambling to keep up, coherence slipping even as I carefully take notes. Why is Stewart talking about the CIA's belief in 1963 that Castro had sent Oswald to kill JFK? I'm confused about whether I'm confused. I'm low. As I listen, I go to my desk drawer and pour three big sugar tablets directly from their plastic tube into my mouth.

"Honey, those were different eras," Stewart says. He has just finished telling me what he's learned about Alex, and started to tell me what he's learned about my father, and his little commentary seems to concern both pieces of information. "People in extreme circumstances make choices they don't expect to make. Especially when they're young and times are weird."

"Right."

"When you're young, you feel immortal, but that cuts two ways—it can make you brave, or it can make you terrified of fucking up that endless beautiful future spread out in front of you."

I prick a finger, take my blood—59; still low—and eat a fourth sugar tablet.

I keep forcing myself to pay attention and take notes, then test my blood again: 100. The perfect round number always pleases me, as if I've won a gold star. My brain chemistry is once again objectively normal.

Now Stewart's new facts begin snapping into place where they belong, mapped onto history and memory, contextualized, sense made, surprising and strange—and, in one respect, shocking—but no longer inexplicable and terrifying rogue objects shooting wildly through my mental galaxy.

"So," he says, "that's the briefing for today."

"Okay. Thanks."

"You're upset."

"I just found out my father, the brave young Resistance journalist, was actually a Nazi collaborator. Yeah. I'm upset. It's totally shocking and depressing."

"I didn't say 'collaborator.' He was publishing *anti*-Nazi satire in 1943, for Christ's sake. Collaborators didn't get put in internment camps, and he was definitely locked up in Frøslev for the last year of the war. He gave them some names of a few Communists. Period."

"Oh, he just turned in some of his friends to the Nazis. That's all?"

"Listen, this wasn't some little bullshit HUAC Hollywood blacklist thing—they were gonna ship him east, to Germany, to Poland, to one of the *real* fucking camps. Which they did to a thousand Danes like him."

"No wonder he never wanted to talk about the war."

"The Danes were very, very practical during the occupation. They got along, didn't go out of their way to piss off the Nazis, didn't push their luck too far. Which, by the way, is why they managed to save ninety-nine percent of their Jews."

Earlier in the conversation, when I was low, I hadn't thought to ask Stewart what my father did after the war to endear himself to American intelligence and get fast-tracked for emigration and U.S. citizenship. "And the OSS liked him so much *why*? Because he named more names for *them*?"

"Actually, it turns out he named exactly the *same* six names he'd given to the Nazis. Most of them still alive and on their way from the camps back home to Denmark. And he provided nifty psychological profiles for each one."

I suddenly remember Christmas 1992 with my parents in Wilmette, when Greta, at age seventeen, became the first of us to notice her grandfather's Alzheimer's symptoms. Or so we thought.

"What, you mean because of the vasectomy thing?" I asked her at the time. Dad had gotten it into his head at age seventy-one that he should get a vasectomy, what he called "the Steinach operation," which his father had undergone as an anti-aging measure in Copenhagen in the 1920s.

"No," Greta said, "much stranger and crazier." My father and she had gone for a walk around the village on Christmas Eve to look at the decorations, and he'd started weeping about what the Serbs were doing to the Bosnian Muslims in the former Yugoslavia, then wept about his own supposed war crimes. "Morfar thinks he was a Nazi during World War II."

On the phone now with Stewart, I take a deep breath. Tears are running down my cheeks. "No wonder he wanted to escape, to go to America. He wanted to get away from the people he'd betrayed."

"Could be. Also? He apparently fixed up his sister with the OSS station chief. I have a feeling that's what got him the free pass."

"Oh my God—that makes complete sense! My uncle Ralph!" My aunt Gaby was a Danish war bride who married Ralph, a U.S. Army major, in Copenhagen in 1946.

"That's one reason I pulled my little VSA stunt, by the way. Your uncle was OSS in forty-five *and* Strategic Services in forty-six, so I thought you might've been an Agency asset in sixty-eight. Seemed unlikely. But you never know. He went to Yale."

"Uncle Ralph was *not* in the CIA. He came home and ran his family's department store in Greensboro, North Carolina."

"Check."

After we hang up, I reread my three pages of legal-pad notes for a few minutes. I quickly Google some things. And I replay the events of 1968 through this new template. Now I understand why Alex wasn't worried about being drafted. I understand why he never wanted to talk afterward about what had happened.

I feel pulled along in the rapids of the fresh information flow. I've been handed a piece of evidence, an important piece, and I want to show it off right *now*, to demonstrate that I have the means and methods and willingness to disinter the truth. It used to work for the police when they were interrogating my Legal Aid clients, and it used to work for me sometimes in corporate depositions, rattling a witness to encourage him to settle, or even enough to make him blurt out some new bad fact.

I stare at the phone in my hand. The longer I wait, the wimpier I will become. I also want to take my mind off my dad. I wish I hadn't learned what I now know about my father. It makes me want to sob. I think of what Stewart told me when we first met, that the CIA and the rest of the intelligence community were "America's front-line Fausts," makers of the country's necessary deals with the devil, acquiring vast knowledge in exchange for eternal damnation. My brother will be undone when he finds out what Dad did.

I dial the home number first, but even there an assistant answers and tells me he'll "see if I can get him."

I listen to some nervous Philip Glassian music playing on his end, rising and falling cellos and saxophones. Perfect soundtrack.

"Have you rung me to curse some more? Or do I take this to mean your knickers are no longer in such a frightful twist?"

"Hello, Alex. Last time we talked," I say, all sweet and reasonable, "you just surprised me. By having recollections apparently so different than mine."

"You really did throw a bit of a wobbly, but no need to apologize. Memory plays tricks. Especially on people our age."

I almost lose it at "apologize." But I recover, force myself to smile so he can hear it. "You're many months older than I am, Alex."

"Ha! Remember that fight we had freshman year in Cambridge, about where we'd first seen that photo of Malcolm X holding the rifle, peeking out his window?"

"I haven't thought of that since then." But yes, I absolutely remember. Eating a very late dinner at Tommy's Lunch, the two of us debating with an SDS boy what "by any means necessary" meant, Alex insisting he'd seen the Malcolm picture in *Life,* whereas in fact I'd found it in one of Violet's copies of *Ebony.* This is good: proof, without any leading of the witness, that he suffers from no amnesia about conversations in early 1968 that involved guns and violence and radical politics. I make a note. "But Alex? I have a couple of things I need to tell you."

"Of course, darling. What?"

"When the book comes out, you can deny everything I say. You can accuse me of writing fiction and pretending it's nonfiction. You can say I'm insane. You can sue me if you want—"

"Here, steady on, you don't want a libel action on your hands."

"You can sue for libel, invasion of privacy, breach of confidence, whatever, take your pick. And you might even be able to get an injunction to prevent publication in the UK. But going behind my back to tell lies to my daughter, pretending you're concerned about my mental health, trying to convince her I have dementia? That is really low. And stupid, because she's not convinced. In any case, it's not going to stop me."

"This is why you rang?"

"No, why I called is to tell you that among the things I've discovered about you"—the tip-of-a-nonexistent-iceberg gambit—"is that you were a CIA informer."

I wait for a denial, harrumph, a *"What?",* some kind of response. Or the sound of a hang-up. Instead, I hear Alex walking. So I press on.

"Beginning in August 1967, on your way home from Belgrade. August twelfth, the day you arrived in Paris, after two CIA officers

approached you at your hotel. And took you to an apartment, a CIA safe house, and spent all night convincing you to cooperate with them, to feed the CIA and the U.S. government information about your new boyfriend Darko Vidovic and other Yugoslavian Communist Party and government leaders. And you agreed"—here I am going out on a limb, but Stewart said he was fairly certain—"because they threatened to tell your parents and Harvard and everyone you knew that you were homosexual. Then, sometime later, you also started working for Project RESISTANCE, which was part of the CIA's Special Operations Group. Which was run by a guy named Richard Ober, Harvard class of forty-three."

I speak slowly and calmly and come to full stops. I learned this in doing depositions if my facts were good. It ratchets up the deponent's sense of one's omniscience. I have no idea if Alex ever met Ober, and I got his name off Google ten minutes ago, after Stewart mentioned Alex's involvement in Project RESISTANCE, one of the CIA's secret domestic operations that spied on people like us starting in 1967.

"And then"—this next is total inference—"you made sure the CIA knew what we were up to. That's why you disappeared that whole morning in Washington, right? After the march on the Pentagon? To meet with your handlers 'in Virginia'? And that morning in New York, right after we called off the attack and you disappeared for two hours? You went to brief them. To snitch."

I feel a little bit like the self-satisfied Ian Fleming villain who, having captured Bond, shares way too much information about his scheme for world domination. My motivation isn't hubris or a weakness for clunky exposition. I want Alex to know the secret I know, and to imagine that I know others so that he might reveal more of the truth or, in any event, realize that resistance is futile. Okay; maybe some hubris.

"You are really being a bit of a berk, Hollander. You do know that I am *very* friendly with members of your Board of Regents. And the CEO of the company that owns your publisher now, Gottfried? Is a friend of mine. A close personal friend. He's sailed with me."

So he's not capitulating. He's implying that he can get me fired from UCLA and have this book canceled. I'm relieved, almost delighted. He's given up pretending that we didn't do what we did in 1968, and he's no longer claiming I've lost my mind. He's moved on from the denial stage to something between anger and bargaining.

"There are other publishers," I say, "whose owners don't give a shit about you. There's the Internet. I'm not a nobody. People will pay attention. So . . ." I hesitate and then go there: "Even if you threaten me, even if you were to have me killed, there's no stopping this. It's all written," I lie. "All done and safely stored in the clouds."

"It's 'the *cloud,*' singular, but Hollander, what fools we are, talking to each other this way! It's stupid. Don't be melodramatic! As though I'd *do* anything to you, for crying out loud. Or you to me."

"No, of course not," I say. Has he decided to relent, to let all the chips fall? Will he ask me to soften the edges, treat him nicely? And why do I have an inkling of déjà vu about this conversation? "Alex, the real reason I called is to ask if you wanted to, you know, fill in some of the blanks. Make it more truthful."

"Right-o. Good. Because I do think you're just a little mixed up about things."

Shit. "No, Alex, I'm really not."

"I'll say it one last time: you should leave this thing alone, stop trying to be a policewoman, the last hero standing, opening up a very cold case. Besides, there's no proof."

I really feel as if I've had this conversation before. "Have you been listening? I've got secret government documents." Not exactly; I've got notes of an oral summary of secret government documents pilfered by an anonymous source. "Your 201 file is very interesting." I haven't seen it; Stewart used the term. It's what the CIA calls its files on individuals.

"You're hell-bent on destroying the both of us, is that it, and Freeman as well? On sending your suicide package out into the world? This will now be the leads in our obituaries, Hollander. Is that really the legacy you want?"

"This isn't going to destroy anybody. It'll make you even more

interesting. And I haven't thought about my obituary," I lie, again, "but the only 'legacy' I care about is being a truth-teller."

"Ah, *truth-teller*," he repeats. "It's a far, far better thing you do than you've ever done?" Then he sighs and chuckles and sighs again. "I say legacy, you say *legacy*, you say truth-teller, I say *truth-teller*. Did our generation start that, inverted commas around everything—shorthand sarcasm in place of actual argument?"

Again he's softening, so I soften. "Another modern bad habit that people our age can claim credit for."

"I'm having a déjà vu," he says, "some night in Wilmette, late, we were outdoors, and I was pissed at you both, you and Chuck, and we just kept flinging each other's words back and forth at each other like turds."

"Senior year, prom night, the Crawfords' backyard."

"*Yes*. I felt so abandoned. I was so angry at you for being a couple—for keeping it *secret* from me. For not telling the truth. We'd always done everything together. I thought there was nobody I could trust more." After a long pause, he says, "You know, Hollander, what happened to Chuck was his own fault."

"Yeah. But it was a game of chicken that we all started playing together. We've all got dirty hands."

"If they make the movie, Malcolm McDowell can play me now. And I suppose Tommy Lee has to be old Buzzy." He means Tommy Lee Jones, the football player two years ahead of us at college on whom Alex had had a secret crush. I'd thought of Tommy Lee Jones as Stewart. "So long, Hollander."

I don't know exactly how I expected that conversation to go, but not like it did. While I was talking with Alex, Waverly texted me again—*PLEASE call*—so now I do.

"What is it, sweetie? Is everything okay?"

"Grams, you're going to hate me. I read your book. I'm so sorry. I feel horrible about it. I won't tell anybody anything, I swear. I'm not a snitch. Don't hate me."

Two weeks ago in Miami, she explains, in my hotel room, the night Hunter got hurt and Sophie got busted, she was using my

computer, and came across the manuscript, and just peeked at it, and was about to stop reading when she came to the first passage about herself, and then kept reading, and couldn't stop, and finally copied the whole thing onto her flash drive and finished reading it on the bus ride home.

"Oh, Christ. You didn't tell Hunter about it, did you? Or your parents? Or anybody else? Or print it out or email it?"

"*No.* I swear to God, Grams, *no.* I hammered the flash drive and threw the pieces in different sewers and wiped the data on Hunter's hard drive completely, better than the Pentagon recommends."

"*What?*"

"Oh, the Defense Department has this sanitization matrix they use on computers, but they say to overwrite your deleted data seven times, and I did it like *twenty-five* times. Don't worry. It's gone. I'm so sorry, Grams."

"I'm really glad you told me, Waverly."

I find myself relieved, glad, even, that someone apart from Stewart and my lawyer now *knows*—someone I love.

"It's cool that when you were, like, twelve years old," she says, "you guys *invented* LARPing, huh?"

"LARPing?"

"Live-action role-playing games. But Grams?" She's whispering. "What did you *do*? The big bad thing."

Right: she's only read up to 1967. I take a breath, intending to cut to the chase, then I stop. I could blurt out the salient facts in a few sentences, like the counts in an indictment. But why I'm writing a *book* is to lay out something approaching the whole truth, with the thousand relevant dots in place, ready to be connected—some of the lines drawn by me, the overdetermining author and apologist, some by you, my jury of dispassionate strangers—and turned into a picture with the queer complications and shadings that make it a life. I don't want to summarize my story in a tweet, not even to Waverly. Especially not to Waverly.

"How about this—how about I send you each chapter as I finish it? All the way to the end."

"Really? *Really?* Thanks, Grams, that would be amazing."

"And after you read each one, use your sanitization matrix to make it self-destruct in five seconds and then disavow all knowledge of my actions."

"What?"

"Nothing. Stupid joke. Until I finish, you are my one and only reader."

"That makes me feel like crying, Grams."

"*That* makes *me* feel like crying." Her mother once told me that women produce lots more of a certain hormone than men, and have tinier tear ducts, so we cry four times as often.

Waverly says the second surgery on Hunter's hand went well, but the Miami prosecutors will agree to drop Sophie's hoax-weapon-of-mass-destruction charge only if she pleads guilty to possession of a counterfeit driver's license. "Which is still a *felony*," Waverly says, "and she might have to go back down there and spend a month in jail this summer. They're being total fascists about it."

"That doesn't sound too fascist to me."

After I hang up, I pour myself a seltzer and, still in pajamas, walk out to my patio carrying the laptop and legal pad. I sniff the Chinese snowballs and look down past my unbelievably red bougainvillea over the big bowl of Los Angeles—millions of people within my purview but not a single human being visible, the kind of still, clear, warm L.A. day that seems perfectly sweet or foreboding, depending on my mood.

I sit on the less bird-poopy chaise, the cat curls up at my hip, and I begin transferring notes of my Alex conversation onto a computer file. Even more strongly than before, I have the sense that I've heard these transcribed words some other time. I think of the line from *The Matrix* that won me over to the movie—when the rebel Trinity explains to Neo, "A déjà vu is usually a glitch in the Matrix."

I start Googling some of the phrases in my notes. *Fools we are talking this way . . . as though I'd do anything to you . . . you're a little mixed up about things . . . you should leave this whole thing alone . . . no proof.*

The omniscient cloud reveals all. My cat stands up, alarmed, when I say "Oh my *God*."

Whole chunks of his conversation were from the Ferris-wheel scene in *The Third Man*, Orson Welles wheedling and warning Joseph Cotten. Graham Greene is the uncredited writer of a quarter of what Alex said to me on the phone a half hour ago.

"It's a far better thing that I do," the Harry Lime character mockingly says to his old pal, the writer Holly Martins, quoting Dickens. And then, "Don't try to be a policeman, old man." And on and on: "You know you ought to leave this thing alone . . . Don't be melodramatic . . . There's no proof against me, beside you . . . Oh, Holly, what fools we are, talking to each other this way. As though I would do anything to you—or you to me . . . You're just a little mixed up about things . . . Nobody left in Vienna I can really trust—and we have always done everything together." Even the farewell—Harry Lime's "So long, Holly" became Alex Macallister's "So long, Hollander."

When Google can't find the other line I'm sure I've heard before, I spring up, sending Clarence Darrow scurrying inside ahead of me as I run to the room where I keep the fiction, crouch down to pull an old book from the F shelf, flip pages, read, flip pages, read, flip another page, and find it. James Bond, on the golf course at the Royal St. Marks, having been accused by the cheating villain of cheating, says to Auric Goldfinger: "Here, steady on. You don't want a libel action on your hands."

Alex Macallister is a walking, talking real-time remix of fictional midcentury villains. Is he aware he does it? Does he do it all the time, with everyone, and from other movies and books? Is his entire life a nonstop work of performance art that only he fully appreciates? Or is it an unconscious tic, some kind of OCD cultural kleptomania? Either way, I think, it's stunning, and he's a fucking nut.

22

YES, I'D CHOSEN to attend a 331-year-old New England university, a place that fetishized its traditions and the idea of tradition, but in the fall of 1967 Radcliffe and Harvard Colleges struck me nonetheless as ludicrously old-fashioned.

I was ready to launch my modern, independent young adulthood. But I wasn't allowed to eat with Chuck and Alex and the other freshman boys in their dining hall, and the boys had to wear jackets and ties at every meal. When Chuck visited me at my dorm, he had to sign in with the desk attendant in the lobby, who rang a bell alerting me, whereupon I was supposed to step out into my hallway and yell "Man on" before he shambled up, and then I had to leave the door to my room open as long as he was there. Boys were invited to the dorm lounge en masse a couple of times the first semester for little parties called jolly-ups.

The first petition any Radcliffe student stuck in front of me was a protest against the threatened end of the Saturday-night girls-only milk-and-cookies parties. I declined to sign. (If that wasn't enough to earn her everlasting hatred, I subsequently overheard that same girl refer to fellatio as *fell-LOT-ee-o*. When Alex and I passed her in

the Yard one day and I told him about the mispronunciation, he walked back and said, "Excuse me? It's *fellatio*," then returned to me and whispered, *"The bitch is dead."*)

The college newspaper still called black people Negroes. We were supposed to consider it a great milestone that ours was the first Radcliffe class allowed to use Harvard's libraries.

All the vestigial quaintness served to fire up my conviction that Alex and Chuck and I were part of a vanguard of a new and improved modern species. As I look back on my freshman year from here in the future, it *all* seems quaint—not just the twee final days of nice-young-ladies-and-gentlemen New England, but our absolutely wide-eyed embrace of the liberated age unfolding and exploding.

I called my parents collect every Sunday after *The Smothers Brothers*. But the only conversation I specifically remember from September until just before Thanksgiving was the one in which my mother, extremely upset, told me about Sabrina's single great act of adolescent misbehavior. They'd come home early two nights earlier and caught her showing a pornographic double feature in the basement to two dozen fellow New Trier sophomores whom she'd charged $2.50 apiece. Sabrina had learned about renting movies and projection equipment when they'd organized the Esperanto Club screening, and apparently, getting prints of *Gentlemen Prefer Nature Girls* and *A Taste of Her Flesh* was no more difficult than booking William Shatner's *Incubus*. She was trying to earn enough money to fly to L.A. for the national Esperanto convention with her boyfriend, Jamie, whose family had moved to Ohio over the summer. I loved every aspect of the story except the lack of punishment. Because of her Esperanto excuse, and because my mother felt responsible for having shown Sabrina the movie-exhibitor ropes, they were going to let her go to L.A. and then spend Thanksgiving with Jamie and his family in Cincinnati on the way home.

"Is that what they do in Junior Achievement these days?" Chuck's roommate said when I told them the story. Buzzy Freeman was nice to me from the get-go—like him, I was a lapsed Catholic; also, I was

interested in Vietnam, I cursed, and I injected myself with drugs. He was premed. I liked him because he was so graceful and mature concerning Chuck and me, unembarrassed and embarrassing about popping out to the library whenever Chuck and I wanted to use their room to make out or have sex. Buzzy liked Chuck because they were both outdoorsy and athletic and *male*—the hunting and fishing, the leather jackets, the firecrackers, the Morse code, the radio-controlled airplanes. And Alex was fond of Buzzy because he was attractive, "a civilized *cowboy* or something," and recently had, like Alex, read Winston Churchill's *Memoirs of the Second World War.* Buzzy Freeman was almost twenty-one. He had short blond hair but a full beard, and he'd tacked a dirty, tattered red, yellow, and blue National Liberation Front flag to the wall over his bed. He was the coolest person my age I'd ever met. "Buzzy isn't circumcised," Chuck told me our first week in college.

He'd grown up in Las Vegas, where his father worked on the government's nuclear bomb tests. "You could feel it like an earthquake when they'd blow one at night," he told us the first time we all smoked grass together. "From our backyard, you could see the flash on the horizon. It was like a thunderstorm with lightning but all compressed and shot in slow motion." Mr. Freeman had become an alcoholic after the government rejected his plan to explode an atomic bomb on the moon to collect lunar samples, and he committed suicide the day President Kennedy signed the nuclear test ban treaty in 1963. Buzzy joined the Coast Guard in order to pay for college, and said he "was in country September sixty-five to November sixty-six, on a cutter out of Danang." Beyond the basic details of his tour—"Coastal Surveillance Force, Squadron One, cruising the seventeenth parallel"—he didn't much discuss his experiences in Vietnam. "Boarded junks, fired on sampans. Interdicted NVN supply lines to the VC. It was heavy. So I owe the people." I knew "VC" meant "Vietcong," and I found out later that "NVN" stood for "North Vietnamese Navy." And by "the people," we understood that he meant the beleaguered Vietnamese struggling for liberation from the vicious American Moloch and its puppet regime in Saigon.

Buzzy was our tragic antihero who had been to hell and back and done terrible things but seen the light, an apostate filled with remorse and seeking to make restitution for his imperialist crimes.

All of this we'd learned by our third week in Cambridge. Buzzy had gone to a crappy high school and was excited about being among fellow intellectuals at last. Late one September night in the Hayes-Bickford cafeteria, when the four of us were discussing Malcolm X, Buzzy ran back to his room and returned to lay a tattered, underlined copy of Frantz Fanon's *The Wretched of the Earth* on the table. Another night, all of us taking turns playing pinball at Tommy's Lunch, Buzzy said we *had* to read Antonio Gramsci's prison notebooks—that "Gramsci on the 'masks of consent' in liberal bourgeois society is *mind*-blowing." That's the way we talked in the fall and winter of 1967. It didn't sound stilted or ridiculous to us.

One Saturday afternoon in October, we lounged together in the sun on the grass by the river, eating potato chips. We teased one another—Chuck for his striped bell-bottoms, Alex for describing a passing rowboat as "that yellow punt," Buzzy for liking the Beach Boys, and me for calling the band we'd just seen perform in a Boston parking garage the Cream instead of Cream. We created an impromptu quiz show in which we had to recite passages from the left-wing philosopher Herbert Marcuse—mine was "people recognize themselves in their commodities, they find their soul in their automobile, hi-fi set, split-level home."

"Or in their *television* sets," Buzzy added with a smile, looking at Alex. Alex was probably the only kid in Harvard Yard who had a TV in his dorm room.

Hearing the thirty thousand fans across the Charles chanting and singing and cheering louder and louder as Harvard's football team beat Columbia, Alex said it reminded him of the Nuremberg rallies in *Triumph of the Will,* which he'd just watched in his freshman seminar.

"I think one reason Marcuse is so persuasive," Chuck said, "is because he saw Nazism firsthand."

"Did you know," Buzzy asked, "that he worked for U.S. intelli-

gence, not just during the war in Europe, total Oscar Sierra Sierra man, but also afterward, in the fifties, in Washington?"

"Wow," I said, "Herbert *Marcuse* was in the *OSS*? Which became the CIA, right? Did you guys know that?"

Alex and Chuck shook their heads, said nothing, and ate more chips.

"Also?" Buzzy continued. "William Sloane Coffin: CIA in the fifties, in West Germany, a genuine secret agent."

Coffin, Yale's chaplain, was a national antiwar leader.

"I knew that," Alex said.

"Not to be paranoid," Buzzy said, "but it makes you wonder. I mean, do people ever really, completely *quit* the CIA?"

I almost never skipped my classes, loved them more than I was comfortable admitting. In my freshman seminar, I discovered the stories of Jorge Luis Borges, which I told Chuck were "like jewels from another planet," and I got to meet Borges that fall—he was a visiting lecturer. "What is this ravishing *scent*?" he asked when he walked into the North House lounge to have tea with fifty Radcliffe girls. I blushed but said nothing; it was my patchouli. The physics course I took became especially interesting on weekends at night, when we got high and I'd tell Chuck and the other guys what I'd learned that week—about this new notion of "black holes" in space, about the "quantum weirdness" that makes certain impossible things happen, about Kurt Gödel's idea that time was an infinite closed loop like a Möbius strip.

Except for an introductory history course covering the last half millennium, none of my classes was remotely political. Which didn't stop me from inferring politics. When I read about the scientists who said "everything not forbidden is compulsory," I took it as a law of history as well as quantum physics. When I'd encountered that very line at age nine in *The Once and Future King*—young Arthur, transformed by Merlyn into an ant, sees it on a sign over an anthill—it confused and disturbed me. Now, at eighteen, hearing it from a Harvard professor, I understood it as a kind of coded command to take action, fulfill my destiny. "The Might is there in the

bad half of people," King Arthur had said to his comrades. "Why can't you harness Might so that it works for *Right*?"

I was stoic about my diabetes, never complained or whimpered. Buzzy joked about it, which I enjoyed, asking if I'd packed my "works" so I could "shoot up" when we all went out for a late-night snack, offering to "score some fresh insulin" for me when he was heading to the pharmacy. Because I was always urinating into cups to test my urine, and comparing the colors on each pee-dipped test strip to a little printed rainbow—dark blue meant low glucose, chartreuse was higher, bright orange was highest—and noting each result and everything I ate in a little notebook, calculating dosages, filling syringes from vials, Buzzy said I should apply for independent-study credit to satisfy my natural-science requirement. And when I started injecting myself semi-publicly, in dining halls and restaurants, my coolness quotient went up a notch.

I'm sure diabetes helped keep me chronically pissed off that first year, even though I considered my anger entirely a function of my political awakening and the escalation of the war. The mental effects of low blood sugar complemented the peculiarities of that era. Especially if you were new to coping with the disease and unaccustomed to finding yourself rereading a paragraph three times uncomprehendingly, or not contributing to a conversation for ten minutes, or feeling worried and suspicious without any good reason, or, when your blood sugar dropped very low, imagining your best friends were pestering and pitying and maybe somehow deceiving you. Even though scarfing down a Coke or a Snickers snapped you right back, hypoglycemia amplified the weirdness of late adolescence and of late 1967 as it turned into 1968.

Not that hypoglycemia was all bad. I discovered a sweet spot that the doctors never mention, somewhere south of normal and north of uncomfortable, where my energy was upped and my alertness tweaked, my focus sharpened, my ideas more original and interesting. And this wasn't the way other kids had epiphanies when they got high but which, in the cold light of day, didn't seem so brilliant. If I felt sluggish or uninspired, I'd sometimes deliberately overshoot

my insulin by a hundredth of a milliliter or two, and the next few hours of mild hypoglycemia actually turned B papers into A papers.

"Karen," Chuck whispered one night in his bedroom in Penny-packer Hall, his lovemaking breathlessness switching from desire to horror as his face hovered a few inches above my naked middle section, "what the fuck did you *do?"*

I sat up and looked down. High on my right thigh near the hip-bone was the darkest, largest bruise I'd ever had, deep purple and the size and shape of a coaster, made even more disgusting and lep-rous by the yellow-gray mercury-vapor streetlight gloam. I was frightened for a second, then understood the problem. I'd been in-jecting myself too often in that easily accessible bit of flesh. I had never felt so miserably naked. Chuck kissed the bruise and after-ward started treating me even more like a saint on her slow, heroic march to martyrdom. The next morning I began a new injection regimen: I made a sketch of my legs and midsection in my note-book, recorded each injection site with a dated dot, and never again stabbed the same spot twice in one week. Buzzy called me a "con-scientious injector."

One night in bed after we'd made love, as the parietal deadline approached, Chuck turned and asked in a low voice if I thought "monogamy is a pathological form of bourgeois individualism."

I should have laughed, but Chuck was taking two sociology courses, and "bourgeois" was a word we'd all started using with completely straight faces. At first I thought it meant he wanted to sleep with somebody else, the way he had brought up oral sex as a way for us to engage in the "polymorphous perversity" that Mar-cuse writes about.

"I don't think so," I said. "Why?"

"Alex was saying that today. He and Buzzy saw *Jules and Jim* in their freshman seminar, and he says that's why Jeanne Moreau kills herself and one of the guys in the end—that she was a victim of 'bourgeois individualism.' And Buzzy sort of agreed. Buzzy kind of has the hots for you, I think."

"Well, I don't have the hots for Buzzy." That wasn't entirely true.

"Having a relationship with more than one person at a time would be too complicated for me. Maybe after the revolution," I said with a smile but not entirely as a joke, "I'll feel differently."

"You're not ready to be Tatiana Romanova?"

"Huh?"

"Colonel Klebb telling Tatiana she has to sleep with Bond." He pursed his lips and did his terrible European accent: " 'Tanya, your *bow*-dee belongs to ze *state.* ' "

When I got out of bed, he sat up. "In sixth grade? At a sleepover at Alex's? The two of us sort of . . . fooled around. Sexually."

"Really?" Maybe this was Chuck's guilty secret that Sarah had intuited over the summer. "Who started it?"

"Who do you think? We did it a few more times over the next few months. But then Alex ejaculated—his first time ever, and I never had. It was completely shocking. To me, anyhow. After that, we never did it again. Fooled around with each other."

"Okay," I said. "I mean, kids experiment."

"Did you ever mess around with a girl like that?"

We were supposed to tell the truth always and hold back nothing. "Uh-huh, once. Mary Ann Stalnaker from St. Joseph's, that girl in my confirmation class."

"Really? In *eighth grade*?"

"Fuck you," I said, smiling.

"Do you think there's anything I could tell you about myself that would make you hate me?"

"I don't know—theoretically, I suppose, yeah. If you'd done something really terrible. But it'd have to be something a lot worse than jerking off Alex."

"Don't tell him I told you."

"Duh." It was almost eleven. I put on my sweater and shoes and kissed him good night.

We smoked dope most weekends, and Chuck grew a beard. Chuck and I took mescaline a second time, with Alex and his fifteen-year-old math-prodigy roommate. But we were definitely *not* hippies.

Although hippies were part of the Movement, and we felt more simpatico with them than the straight kids, they seemed childish, self-indulgent, soft. Buzzy was more charitable. When the mayor of Cambridge declared an official War on Hippies, busting a row of druggie crash pads just off campus, Buzzy said they were "the rodeo clowns of the revolution," diverting the authorities' attention, his implication being that we were the revolutionary cowboy stars, riding the broncos and roping the cattle. Hippies and their Halloween lifestyle, we told one another over numberless coffees and cigarettes, were so easily co-opted, turned into tools of repressive tolerance, zany decoration on the masks of consent.

"Look at *this*," I said to Chuck and Buzzy one night at Café Pamplona, shoving my *Boston Globe* toward them. Next to an article about a battle in South Vietnam, there was an ad for Filene's department store with the headline: TAKE A TRIP! BUY A PSYCHEDELIC DRESS!

The war was fantastically hideous, getting bigger and deadlier every day. My sense of grievance was obsessive, and it was no longer theoretical. Chuck's and Alex's student draft deferments would end when they graduated—or, according to a shocking new Selective Service rule, if they demonstrated against the war. The crackdown, we all agreed, was a glimpse of the true face of fascism behind the masks of consent, the beginning of the end of civil liberties in America.

The day Chuck sent in the form for his deferment, I asked if he was scared it could be revoked.

"I'm angry," he said, "but I'm not scared."

Later that fall a boy we knew, a sophomore, was reclassified from 2-S to 1-A as punishment for participating in antiwar protests. He faced immediate induction into the army.

"You may not be scared," I said to Chuck, "but I am. I don't want you to go to Vietnam."

"I won't. Don't worry. Everything will be okay."

He seemed so cocky. But I knew the difference between Chuck Levy bluster and Chuck Levy self-confidence, and this was clearly

the latter. His character was being tested, and it turned out he was brave, which made me swoon. More surprising was Alex's sangfroid.

"I'm covered," Alex said when I asked if he was worried about being reclassified 1-A. "I've got a Plan B." I assumed he meant escaping to Canada with the help of his relatives in Toronto.

That I wasn't subject to conscription made me feel like a girly bystander. The fact that Chuck and Alex seemed so resolute and unconcerned, devoted to the antiwar struggle and damn the consequences, made me redouble my own commitment. In our war against the war, I had to make myself hard and courageous, too.

The hippies were young adults behaving like naughty children, and the liberal students—working within the system, collecting petition signatures, conducting symposia, engaging in meaningful dialogue—were children playing at responsible adulthood, like me at fourteen and fifteen. I had moved on.

"Who's Walter Mitty?" Chuck whispered, sitting between Alex and me at the first meeting we attended of the Harvard-Radcliffe Students for a Democratic Society. "Some right-winger?"

"No," Alex told him, "a Danny Kaye character in an old movie."

"From a short story by James Thurber," I said, trumping Alex, even though I'd never read the story. "He's this normal wimpy guy who fantasizes he's a daredevil hero and outlaw."

The president of SDS was reading aloud from an official college report about the previous school year in which the university president, Nathan Pusey, referred to "our self-professed student revolutionaries" and "Walter Mittys of the left." A year earlier, when the secretary of defense, Robert McNamara, spoke at Harvard, SDS demonstrators threw themselves in front of McNamara's car and pounded on it, forcing him to get out, climb up on the hood for face-to-face hectoring by the mob, and finally, to run away through an underground tunnel. The SDS upperclassmen preened as they talked about the McNamara blockade, delighted at being (as one of them said that night) "bêtes noires here in the belly of the beast."

Because we'd already had our chapter in Winnetka, already

learned the New Left catechism, already experienced the first high of denouncing liberals and calling ourselves radicals, I was jaded about SDS. It was too much like Model UN. And in some ways even dopier, since in Model UN, we knew we were engaged in a role-playing exercise and not actually determining the fate of the world.

"Bêtes noires?" Alex said as the four of us walked through the Yard afterward. "Give me a break. They seem like wankers, a lot of them." I didn't know the word, but I knew what he meant, and I laughed.

Buzzy looked around to make sure no one was nearby. "Not to be paranoid," he said, "but I've got my doubts about that Li'l Abner in the cammies and the beard."

"The guy," Chuck asked, "who talked about 'mother country radicals' developing 'a guerrilla mentality'? Yeah, that was heavy."

"Exactly," Buzzy said, "he was like *too* heavy, you know? For a public meeting? I've got a feeling he might be some kind of undercover."

"You think they're really doing that?" I asked. "Planting agents posing as Harvard kids, pretending to be radicals?"

Buzzy stopped walking for a couple of seconds and looked at me with his mouth open. "Yes, Virginia, and there's no Santa Claus, either. SDS may be a bunch of fake rich-kid revolutionaries, but the cops and the FBI don't know that."

As we walked past the president's house, Buzzy shouted into the pine trees and dogwoods, "Up against the wall, Octopusey!"

"You're into *Bond*?" Alex asked.

"Used to be. The books, not the movies. I think I read every one when I was in Danang."

After we all stipulated that James Bond was an imperialist pawn, we had a spontaneous rapid-fire ten-minute colloquy outside Lamont Library—favorite and least favorite Fleming books and villains and girls and deaths, and Buzzy's suggestion that it might be possible now "to *actually* disrupt the Pentagon's missile tests using radio beams, like Doctor No."

That Bond conversation, our first extended one in years, was the moment the three of us became the four of us.

My journal entries petered out in the middle of October, then stopped. I no longer squirreled away every single stray memento. Partly, this was a self-conscious makeover, a decision to stop doing what I'd done as a child and *live life* instead of collecting its ephemera. Buzzy's paranoia also had an effect: it seemed unwise to keep a record of what I and everyone around me thought and said and did every day.

So this 1 percent of my life, the last quarter of 1967 and first third of 1968, is uniquely underdocumented. As a result, it seems less a series of minutes and hours and days that flowed like all the others before and since, as implacable as a river. Instead, it's more fantastic, like some story I once heard. I know I was not at all alone back then in experiencing life as simultaneously unreal and hyperreal. But even with the clarity of hindsight and the luxury of the long view, I can't get over the feeling that this chronicle of this particular period feels more like fiction than the nonfiction it is. That Robin Williams joke—"If you remember the sixties, you weren't there"—has some truth, and not even mainly because of the drugs. At some moment, Karen went through the glass and jumped down into the looking-glass room.

Harvard was constantly burning that year, and I don't mean metaphorically. Every month a fire broke out in some dorm or academic building.

One afternoon in Chuck and Buzzy's room, we made Magic Marker protest signs for our expedition to Washington. The Mobe—the National Mobilization Committee to End the War in Vietnam—had provided no signage guidelines. Alex insisted we be succinct, no more than five words per sign. We all agreed that peace symbols and MAKE LOVE NOT WAR were "hippie clichés." Chuck and I debated the comma between his HELL NO and I WON'T GO. For his sign, Buzzy decided on STOP THE WAR MACHINE rather than US OUT OF VIETNAM.

We arrived in Washington on a Friday night. It was my first visit, and when I got goose bumps looking out the bus window at the

Capitol dome, I told myself the feeling was not standard patriotic instinct but excitement that we were about to Confront the War Makers. We slept on the floor of a common room at an American University dorm, which Alex had persuaded Patti, his ex-girlfriend, to arrange.

We got to the Lincoln Memorial very early the next morning. Everyone was supposed to organize themselves into groups and gather around the appropriate two-foot letter near the reflecting pool—R for religious protesters, F for flower people, N for Negroes. We milled in the vast unlettered area designated for students.

The trees on the Mall were turning, the weather was sunny and cool, rock bands played, and my delight at being among so many people like me—a *hundred thousand kids* in jeans and long hair, high on their shared happy hatred for the war and the government and the status quo—was extreme, incredible, sublime. Most of the signs and chants were about peace *now,* peace *now,* peace *now.* Some people carried Vietcong flags and chanted "Ho, Ho, Ho Chi Minh, NLF is gonna win!" One kid was dressed like an old-time hangman in a hooded black robe, dragging an effigy of President Johnson in a noose. Another had a sign that said WHERE IS OSWALD WHEN WE NEED HIM?

Alex panned the crowd with his movie camera and then zoomed in on me. "Why're you grinning like an idiot?" he asked.

Bliss was it in that dawn to be alive.

I specifically recall the remarks by Benjamin Spock, the celebrity pediatrician whose dog-eared guide to childrearing had been a permanent fixture on my mother's bedside table. With the giant white marble Abraham Lincoln seated in the shadows behind him, Dr. Spock reminded us that the Vietcong and the North Vietnamese were not bogeymen—the real enemy, rather, "is Lyndon Johnson."

As the speeches ended, an older man's voice came over the loudspeakers, sounding like a high school principal on Bizarro World: "Those who wish to proceed closer, and perhaps more militantly, to the Pentagon, may do so." A large fraction of the crowd—the cool kids, the radicals, members of the resistance—oozed across the Po-

tomac for hours, puddling at the northern edge of the huge, low stone building.

To Chuck, it was as he'd imagined the fortress of Isengard in *The Lord of the Rings.* Alex said it looked like the set for Wagner's *Götter-dämmerung* that he'd seen in Budapest, "I mean *exactly,* with the looming wall and thrust stage"—the Pentagon's deep flight of steps—"and the hundred spear carriers in white helmets all lined up downstage." The spectacle of menace was perfect. It was a fantasy come to life. Helicopters hovered close enough for us to make out their insignia, their low-frequency high-decibel quarter-second thumps filling our bodies. Uniformed men with binoculars and rifles stood and crouched on top of the building, backlit by the setting sun, watching us watching them. The men on the steps in white helmets were U.S. marshals, each one holding a billy club in front of him. It was *The Pentagon.*

I remember hippies chanting "Ommmm," which embarrassed me.

I remember watching, amazed, as actual soldiers ran out of the building and down the steps and formed a line just behind the marshals, and saying how odd it was that they were holding rifles and wearing *neckties,* to which Buzzy replied, "MPs, out of Fort Bragg."

I remember people singing "America the Beautiful" and trying to figure out whether it was sincere or ironic—and then, when a couple of kids stepped right up to soldiers and stuck flowers, stems down, into their rifle muzzles, petals against bayonets, I understood it was a completely brilliant new kind of gesture that *combined* sincerity and irony.

I remember watching a girl right next to me open a zip-top Coke and guzzle it without stopping and then throw the empty can at the men with guns and clubs, and realizing that I needed a can of pop or something because I was low and had already shared my two candy bars with Buzzy and Chuck for lunch.

I remember the terrible sour smell that made me think I was at Centennial Pool the summer the chlorine machine went haywire,

and I remember Buzzy saying *tear gas* as people began shouting and pulling their shirts over their faces and trying to run.

I remember feeling angry and frightened when a second wave of MPs trotted down the steps, and one of them, a dozen feet away, stared at me as though he thought he could read my mind.

I remember being pushed forward, and seeing the back of Alex's head way over to my left, and wondering where Chuck and Buzzy were, and saying *Hey* when somebody shoved me again, and stumbling and falling to my knees, and grabbing somebody's arm with both hands to try to get up, and being struck and seeing stars and saying *Fuck*—and then (I think) hearing the marshal who'd clubbed me inhale before he whammed me again on the head.

The next thing I remember is lying on cement, just apart from the crowd, looking up at Alex with my head on his lap as he carefully dabbed at my face and neck with the sleeve of his beige Brooks Brothers windbreaker, which was not quite drenched but much more than spattered with my blood. I felt incredibly pissed off and incredibly lucky.

I licked my lips and touched my fingers to my mouth. "I had chocolate milk?"

"A nice woman gave me her Thermos of Bosco for you. You were acting a little out of it, so I figured you needed sugar."

"Thanks. Out of it how? Did I cry?"

"Uh-uh, you said, 'I'm gonna bash that bastard in the balls' like five times. It was funny."

My blood sugar must have dropped really low. "Sorry about your jacket."

"My property is your property. Plus, it's old." He was still dabbing my head. "This bump is *so* big. It's like there's half a golf ball stuck in there. The bleeding's stopped, though, mostly."

"Have you seen Chuck or Buzzy?"

"Present and accounted for," Buzzy said, and when I turned to see him standing behind Alex, my golf-ball bump hurt. "But our boy's in the brig. Right after you were wounded in action, the

same Wyatt Earp asshole who decked you hauled him off." Buzzy sounded very cheerful.

Alex explained, "When Chuck started yelling at the marshal who clubbed you, the guy arrested him."

"*Bravo Zulu,*" Buzzy shouted, which is what he said when he thought somebody had performed well. "Chuck was very alpha male," a phrase concerning wolves that Buzzy had just learned in his social relations class. "It's all good training."

After a first-aid stop at the American University clinic, we got back to the dorm. Surprisingly, thrillingly, Chuck was already there, freed, waiting for us. He had a black eye.

Before we left Washington on Sunday, Alex went off by himself to "visit some family friends in Virginia," and then we all met up with Sarah Caputo and her NYU friends at Union Station for the ride home.

When we told her about Chuck's arrest at the Pentagon, she wondered why he had gotten sprung so quickly.

Chuck shrugged. "Lucky, I guess."

"Really lucky," Sarah said. "Two people we know from NYU are still in jail, aren't getting out until tomorrow at the earliest."

On the train trip north, Chuck was reading a book of James Thurber's short stories, including "The Secret Life of Walter Mitty."

"This is funny," he said to me. "You'd like it."

"Okay."

"We're not Walter Mittys, like Pusey said, because we're not just fantasizing adventures. We're having them."

We stopped in New York to spend the night on Sarah's dorm-room floor at NYU. Alex wanted to go to a theater see a new musical he'd heard about, *Hair,* but Buzzy and Chuck and I didn't much like the sound of it. "If I want to feel like a far-out hippie," Buzzy said, "I'd rather spend my two and a half bucks on a hit of acid." Instead, at Sarah's urging, we went to see a different political play in the Village. *MacBird!,* as Alex said at intermission, was a "pastiche and a burlesque" of *Macbeth* and other Shakespeare plays—the Lyndon Johnson character, MacBird, murders the President Kennedy

character. Only because we'd smoked a joint before the play, I think, did we laugh, even at the sad and scary parts.

"Not to be paranoid," Buzzy said as we walked back to Sarah's dorm, "but I wouldn't bet that Johnson *wasn't* involved in Kennedy's assassination."

"I think that's bullshit," Sarah said. "I mean, the guy obviously doesn't even like being president! And covering up a conspiracy like that? I don't buy it." The era and our age notwithstanding, Sarah's reality-check instincts never wavered.

"In *Vietnam*," Buzzy said, "Johnson's *proven* he's a homicidal maniac, right? And J. Edgar Hoover. Who knows?" He'd read that right after JFK's assassination, Hoover buried evidence of Oswald's Communist connections so the FBI counterintelligence unit wouldn't be blamed for letting it happen. "Cover-ups are the Washington MO, man."

Buzzy and Sarah did not get along. She was annoyed by his high-falutin New Left bluster, and unlike we Wilmettians, she wasn't intimidated by his age or his military service. One of her older brothers and a lot of her high school friends were serving in Vietnam.

We were still a little high. Buzzy proceeded to describe, in the only vivid combat story I ever heard him tell, how he'd watched a napalm bombing run over a Vietnamese fishing village "way out in the boonies, this mud-mover, an A-6, thunders in at like a hundred feet, maybe less, dropped his canisters, and just fucking smoked the place."

"What *is* napalm?" Alex asked.

"Jellied gasoline and white phosphorus. Sticks to your skin and burns and burns at fifteen hundred degrees. It is literally hell."

I must have continued taking tests and writing papers that fall and winter—I have the report card showing two B-pluses, an A-minus, and an A—but in my memory, the next six months consist of trying to throw monkey wrenches into the war machine and discussing the nature of effective rather than merely symbolic resistance to the

ever more demonic national security state. Starting in October 1967, I was thinking about death, violent death, most of the time.

Our experience in Washington—facing down an armed battalion! beaten! wounded in action! arrested!—made the antiwar rally in Harvard Yard the day after we got back to Cambridge seem timid and useless, a few hundred kids and professors who wanted to demonstrate their *concern* for an afternoon, "everybody spouting this gentle frowning Quakery bullshit," as Buzzy said.

The SDS action the following day against the Dow Chemical recruiter was much more our bag. Although the chapter leaders had decided against staging a sit-in—"Told you they were wankers," Alex said—on Wednesday morning in the chemistry building, we four were among the mob who spontaneously turned it from a nice picket-line protest to an act of militant resistance. We decided then and there that tolerance had its limits, and we would suspend the bourgeois civil liberties of the manufacturer of napalm.

During the discussion, Buzzy took out his underlined paperback copy of Marcuse's "Repressive Tolerance" and read aloud, telling the hopped-up, wide-eyed multitude that we'd been brainwashed to "'protect false words and wrong deeds . . . Different opinions can no longer compete peacefully for persuasion on rational grounds.' People, it's time for the Great Refusal!" People applauded.

I agreed, and I got goose bumps when Chuck pointed out that Dow's product was technically called Napalm B, then asked, "If this were Munich in 1938, and the manufacturer of *Zyklon* B showed up, wouldn't *stopping* him be the right thing to do?"

By noon in the hallway outside the room where Dow's research director was supposed to be interviewing chemistry students for jobs, there were hundreds of us sitting knee to knee and standing arm in arm, physically preventing him from leaving and interviewees from entering.

More protesters continued to arrive. "'Bliss was it in that dawn to be alive,'" I said softly to Chuck, "'but to be young was very heaven.'"

"What?"

"Wordsworth. The poet? Writing about the French Revolution. He was our age when it happened."

Black-eyed Chuck kissed my bruised forehead quickly, almost furtively. Bliss was it, indeed. Very heaven.

"Exactly how do we think this show is going to end?" Alex asked quietly as the lunch hour passed.

"I don't know," I whispered back, "but that's what's so great about it—it's *real* instead of everyone politely following a script."

"Improvisation," Chuck murmured.

"Like *war*," Buzzy said in his big twangy voice.

Amazingly, several professors showed up to urge us on.

When the new dean of Harvard College appeared, the boys sat up a little straighter, opened their eyes wider, quieted down. I watched the muscles in Chuck's neck and jaw tighten. The dean seemed to recognize most of them, and they definitely knew him— the year before, he'd been the college admissions director, the very man who had turned each of these boys into a Harvard man. He said it was wrong to restrain the freedom of expression of people with whom we disagreed, that we were running the risk of being kicked out of school because the university could not countenance threats.

Buzzy piped up. "Is that a threat?"

Everybody laughed, the dean included. "Touché," he said.

Sometime that afternoon the mob somehow decided we would let the man from Dow go—*if* he would sign a pledge that he'd leave and never return. He refused. At sunset the group decided to let him go anyway.

That same week FBI agents appeared on campus, visiting the dorm rooms of boys who'd ceremonially turned in their draft cards at the Justice Department during the protests in Washington. The Johnson administration reaffirmed its determination to bomb and kill in Vietnam.

"Not to be paranoid," Buzzy said, "but the crackdown has started. The masks of consent are coming off, boys and girls."

So the four of us began our fall offensive.

Buzzy knew how to make M-80s—big firecrackers he called "small charges"—using purple swimming-pool cleaner and the aluminum powder from cracked-open Etch A Sketches. A friend in California sent him ten yards of green fuse. Twice we set them off just outside Shannon Hall, where ROTC had its headquarters, and once inside the building, right by the ROTC office. Each time we left Xeroxed photographs of napalmed and machine-gunned Vietnamese children with the Magic-Markered legend YOUR ENEMIES.

Chuck managed to acquire a palm-size canister of Mace. We took turns attending the classes of Harvard government professors who advised the Johnson administration on Vietnam—Samuel Huntington and Henry Kissinger are the two I remember—and with a couple of surreptitious squirts of pepper mist, people started coughing and the lecture halls cleared.

Quiet protest was ineffectual. Militance worked, the newspaper taught us daily. The secretary of defense had resigned, we read one morning. "Of course he's going to go run the World Bank," I said. "War by other means. Making sure the rich countries and the corporations keep the third-world countries poor and powerless."

"My parents' friends in Washington," Alex offered, "the ones I visited when we were down there? They say Johnson pushed McNamara out because he was going soft on the war."

"I thought they lived in Virginia," Buzzy said. "Your parents' friends."

"Right, they do. But they work, you know, for the government. In Washington."

I was scanning the newspaper. "'A twin-engine U.S. transport plane carrying twenty-six Americans and secret documents crashed in the enemy-held lowlands south of Saigon. There were no survivors, but the documents were recovered intact.'"

"Hooray," Chuck said. I wasn't sure whether he was being sardonic about the retrieval of the secret documents or expressing solidarity with the Vietcong.

"That's like the third plane crash over there in two months," I said.

Chuck looked sad and nodded, which made Buzzy shake his head and say, "Hamlet here can't quite decide which side are the good guys."

I smiled, and Chuck flipped Buzzy the bird.

Three Sundays in a row I'd told my mother I would not be home for Thanksgiving, and that she'd "just have to *deal*" with having only one of her three children at the table for "your Norman Rockwell picture." When the phone woke me sometime after midnight on the Monday before the holiday and it was my dad, my first thought was that she'd forced him to call to make one last try at persuading me.

That wasn't why he was calling, although I did end up flying home to Chicago that day. He was calling to tell me about Sabrina. She had been in Los Angeles for the Esperanto convention and flying to Cincinnati to spend the holiday with her friend Jamie.

"Honey," my dad said, "your sister died."

Their plane had been landing in a snowstorm that night, came in too low, and crashed a mile short of the runway.

After a pause, Dad added, "In an apple orchard in Kentucky." He spoke the words as if they were meaningful, like a line from a poem. After another pause, he said, "Jamie's alive."

"What?"

"He wasn't killed. There were survivors. Jamie broke his collarbone and an arm, but he's alive."

I cried for a while and didn't go back to sleep. It was weird being hugged by Chuck at seven-thirty A.M. in my nightgown in front of the lady at the desk downstairs. It was weird being stared at with such pity by girls I didn't know as Chuck lugged my little suitcase out to the taxi. It was weird to board a plane fourteen hours after my sister had died in a plane crash.

I hadn't been in a church since her confirmation, and it was only my fourth funeral. The first had been almost exactly ten years earlier, for my baby sister Helen, when I was too young to hold a candle during the Mass.

It was weird to attend Sabrina's funeral and burial on the day after Thanksgiving.

Sometime that weekend, between crying jags, my mom started suggesting she had been responsible—because *she* had pushed Sabrina into Esperanto in the first place, and *she* was the one who agreed to let her fly to Los Angeles and Cincinnati despite the dirty-movie stunt, so maybe God was punishing her, my mother, for failing to punish Sabrina.

My father stared at her, speechless, and then took both her hands in his and said, "Your God may be mysterious, Helen, I understand, but He *cannot* be so perverse and cruel as that." I'd never heard him say anything negative about religion in my mother's presence. And he wasn't through. "There are more than enough bad actions in each of our lives for which we *should* accept blame and guilt. But do not concoct reasons to hate yourself. It isn't your fault Sabrina is gone."

I felt no blame for Sabrina's death. But I did feel acute guilt, like a physical pain, about being a bad sister, starting the moment the priest stood by her coffin at St. Joseph's and said, "May Thy mercy unite her above to the choirs of angels." A month earlier I'd failed to wish her a happy sixteenth birthday, and I had been consistently bitchy to her for the last five years of her life. She had died, and *now* I loved her.

It was weird seeing the smoldering wreckage of TWA 128 on TV and reading in the *Sun-Times* about the crash, finding Sabrina H. Hollaender among the seven-point names of the VICTIMS and James O. Harwood on the list of ten SURVIVORS.

I read in the paper that their flight had been two hours late arriving in Cincinnati because the plane was a last-minute replacement—the one they'd originally boarded at LAX had a mechanical problem. I read that the crash was the second at the Cincinnati airport in two weeks, the fourth in two years, the third since 1961 of a plane making the very same approach to the very same runway during the month of November.

Why did Sabrina die and her boyfriend live? If the mechanics in

L.A. had managed to get the cabin door to shut tight on the original plane, would that flight have avoided the tree in Kentucky? Was the run of crashes at the Greater Cincinnati Airport a coincidence, random statistical noise, like flipping a coin and getting tails seven times in a row, or did it mean some technician or air traffic controller or aviation bureaucrat was to blame?

My mother eventually found consolation in retreating to her faith in God's plan, in all of its beautiful riddling black-box mumbo-jumbo. But to me, the deaths of both of my little sisters made "God's plan" seem like a sick joke. After Sabrina died, I started thinking hard—obsessing, really, for the rest of my life—about the unholy power of chance, good luck and bad luck, in governing human affairs. Luck became my subject, the animating mystery of my life.

23

*Y*OUR HONOR, *I intend this to be an explanation of why my client was led to do what he did, not an excuse for it.* When I was a Legal Aid defender, that was my customary preface before I asked a judge to cut my convicted client some slack—the "mitigation report" tally of extenuating factors that might, if you were lucky, get your unlucky robber or drug dealer or killer a lighter sentence. I don't like whiners or people who reflexively blame "society" for the bad things individuals choose to do. But. But. But.

Between 1964 and 1967, the war and the antiwar countercultural fantasia grew symbiotically, centrifugally, exponentially, like a cascading nuclear reaction. I was eighteen at the very moment when American teenagers were being conscripted to kill and die in a deranged war *and* being encouraged to believe they could see and feel more clearly and vitally than anyone else on earth the differences between smart and stupid, authentic and fake, free and oppressed, right and wrong.

I was a fissile creature by the end of 1967 and the beginning of 1968. In the space of a year, having redefined myself as a radical, I'd

started using mind-altering drugs, lost my virginity, come down with the incurable illness that occasionally addled and would some-day kill me, experienced true love, lost my closest (black) adult friend to casual (white) malfeasance, left home, been beaten by a deputy U.S. marshal on the steps of the Pentagon, gotten punished by my college for opposing the manufacture of napalm, and lost my sister in an airplane crash.

My impatient belief in my own higher sanity became so sure and fierce that it eventually moved into the suburbs of insanity. Sarah, who is the sanest person I know, always says about expensive heels that snap off the second time you wear them or people who use "literally" wrong or her husband spitting into the kitchen sink, "That makes me *so crazy.*" The Vietnam War literally made me crazy. But it didn't and doesn't make me not guilty.

Something is buzzing somewhere. I remember and run to the kitchen, yank open the drawer, rifle through the screwdrivers and pens, and grab the second disposable cellphone, the burner.

"Hi, fella," I say, since it can only be Stewart.

"Did you know your boyfriend's old man invented the Internet?"

"Professor Levy? I knew he was some kind of computer engi-neer."

"In 1968 his company got one of the early contracts from the Pentagon to help build ARPANET, which became the Internet."

"Okay. So?"

"Spent half the rest of his life working on MILNET, the Penta-gon's private Internet."

"And?"

"I don't know. It's a new fact. It's at least ironic, given what his son did. I thought you were a connoisseur of irony."

"That's why you called?"

"I called to tell you I'm still working it and may have a new way into the lockbox. *And* that I'm going to be out there next month, in the Mojave, and if you're not otherwise engaged, it'd be my privi-lege and pleasure to buy you dinner the evening of the nineteenth

at Osteria Mozza, let you drink most of a bottle of Selvarossa Riserva, drive you home along Mulholland, and then, with your kind permission, fuck you silly."

"Okay. Except that's a Monday and I kayak late Monday afternoons, and I'm not drinking half bottles of wine until the book's finished, and Mulholland Drive's totally out of the way."

"I'm just—"

"Also, that's my birthday."

"Don't you think I *know* that, you unromantic harpy?"

24

I STAYED AN EXTRA week in Wilmette after Sabrina's funeral. When I got back to school, Chuck seemed a little different, more anxious, weird. I chalked it up to the obvious—being eighteen, the academic squeeze of the end of our first semester, the world continuing to shatter—but then Chuck told me that he and Buzzy had dropped acid together while I was gone.

"It was really intense," Chuck said. "It got heavy."

I had to pry out the details of the heaviest heaviness. It wasn't Buzzy's rap about wishing he didn't have a foreskin, or Chuck's sudden terror that he'd been somehow responsible for Sabrina's plane crashing, or the two of them staring out their dorm room window at an unleashed collie on Harvard Street and making it dance, or the nearly endless pause between the sixth and seventh chimes of the church bell in the morning. About halfway through their trip, Chuck "suddenly grokked" that Buzzy was probing and testing him. The boys had rebonded over their tag-team psychic-puppeteering of the dog, but the trip had shaken him.

I mentioned it to Buzzy when I saw him the next day. He told a different version. During a conversation about the Pentagon pro-

test, he'd asked why the cops had let Chuck out so quickly, and Chuck moved very close to him, put his face right up to his, and whispered, "You aren't who you pretend you are, are you?" For the next hour or so, Chuck would rephrase and ask the question again—"Who are you *actually*?" and "If there's a God, lying isn't possible, you know?"

"At first," Buzzy said, "I thought maybe he was doing some kind of snitch jacket. Earlier he'd said he wanted to phone you, and I thought maybe he had, secretly, you know. And that you were listening in long-distance. I unplugged the phone from the wall."

"What's a snitch jacket?"

"An informer accuses someone else in the group who's not an informer of being an informer. To fuck everybody up."

"You are paranoid."

"Yeah, I guess he was just really, really high. That's Lima Sierra Delta for you."

And that was that. A couple of afternoons later, Chuck told me he was going to Kirkland House after dinner to hear a professor give a talk about politics. "He used to work for Johnson. You want to come with?"

"I thought we were out of Mace."

"Buzzy got another can from his buddy in Nevada," Chuck said, "but no, I don't mean to do an action, I actually want to go hear this guy talk—he was the War on Poverty guy, and my freshman seminar teacher says he's not a racist like everybody says . . ."

"Yeah, right, and Johnson has a heart of gold."

"This guy has been against the war. He's a pal of Bobby Kennedy's." Chuck liked Kennedy, and Alex adored him. My parents had trained me to disapprove of him because of his early red-baiting work in government, and he reminded me of all the cute, mean, well-to-do, self-satisfied Catholic boys I'd known growing up. But I agreed to go.

With their high ceilings and arched windows and fireplaces and nineteenth-century portraits and wood paneling, the fine old public rooms at Harvard had a powerful bipolar effect: the clubby gran-

deur simultaneously seduced and disgusted me. That's the speed-
ball feeling I remember on that dark, wet night in the Kirkland
House junior common room listening to Professor Daniel Patrick
Moynihan talk in his ridiculous and arrogant, charming and brilliant
fake-patrician way about America's nervous breakdown.

"The most compelling phenomenon in the United States today,"
he said to a hundred of us, "is the advent of a level of violence that
no one believes to be characteristic of our society. We are approaching a crisis." He said he thought that antiwar protests would make it
impossible for President Johnson to campaign effectively for reelection next year.

I raised my hand. "Why is that a *bad* thing?"

He started to smile but quickly pursed his lips, suppressing it, and
defaulted to some boilerplate about unfettered free speech being
the mother's milk of democracy, and said he hadn't lost his faith in
the wisdom of good, decent, ordinary Americans to put things
right.

"Hitler was *elected*," some kid said, "by good Germans."

Moynihan replied that he was about our age during World
War II, and he could assure us unequivocally that Lyndon Johnson
was no Adolf Hitler.

I looked at Chuck, expecting him to make his Nazi-death-camp
analogy that I'd heard so many times, and when he didn't, I spoke
up again to offer his two cents as mine. "Johnson may not be a
Nazi," I said, "but there are twenty-five thousand Vietnamese civilians dying every week as a result of his policies. Same as the exter-
mination rate at Auschwitz and Treblinka."

As Chuck walked me the mile back to Radcliffe and asked if I was
crying, I lied, saying it was raindrops on my cheeks. But then I said,
"We can't just go on like this, discussing and debating forever." Our
roles had reversed from when we were fourteen, when I was the
one bringing up moral uncertainty and unintended consequences.
"There has to be something we can *do*."

"The poll in the paper the other day said half of Americans think
the war's a mistake."

"A *mistake*," I said, "running a red light and rear-ending somebody is a *mistake*. Spilling coffee on your notes while you're studying is a *mistake*."

"Harvard stopped buying grapes." The boycott of nonunion California grapes had been the great progressive victory of the fall semester.

"Whoop-de-do."

"It took Castro and Che six years to win their revolution."

Six years ago we were twelve. Six years was forever.

"Of course they let us 'dissent,'" I said, "because it makes everybody feel better and does nothing to stop the war." President Johnson had just announced his intention to continue full speed ahead with the bombing in Vietnam. "In fact? That's like a definition of ineffective resistance—it's permitted by the authorities."

"The Dow sit-in was a start," Chuck said.

As punishment for imprisoning the Dow recruiter for seven hours, 245 students were either "admonished" or, like the four of us, put on probation. Chuck's parents had been surprisingly mellow about it, which I figured was because Chuck had agreed to return to Wilmette in February for his little brother's bar mitzvah. Alex's father was livid, and Buzzy said his mother either threw away the dean's letter unopened or was too drunk to understand what it meant. My parents, naturally, were a little proud, especially since in her form letter to them, my Radcliffe dean apologized for "the sternness of tone" and referred to "your daughter's moral objections to various features of our society." Not one kid had been kicked out of school.

"I'll bet Dow won't be back on campus," Chuck said.

"Well, *exactly*. Exactly! Physical action *works*! Liberals freak out and give in."

He was shaking his head. "White people are not going to rise up and revolt like the black people in the ghettos. They just aren't. They're too comfortable. We're too comfortable. We're pussies."

Chuck's ambivalence and hesitance had started to annoy me. "Something's got to be done, something more than 'protest' and

symbolic bullshit. Like Buzzy says, the only moral choice is to act, as individuals, to stop the evil. Like my dad when the Nazis occupied Denmark. Like your uncle in Israel." Mrs. Levy's brother had been an anti-British guerrilla in Palestine in the 1940s.

Just ahead in Harvard Square, we saw some Christmas carolers and then recognized them—four SDS kids. We heard the end of "O Come All Ye Mindless" and the first verse of their "Jingle Bells" spoof:

> *Preppie boys, corporate joys, Harvard all the way,*
> *Oh what fun it is to have your mind reduced to clay!*

I didn't even smile. A week earlier, as my dad drove me to O'Hare for the flight back to Boston, he'd said he was my age when World War II started, but that during the five years the Nazis occupied Denmark, even in the internment camp, he'd never lost his sense of humor. He said he worried that, during the last year, I had. "Sorry, Dad," I replied humorlessly, "but I don't find pointless wholesale slaughter very amusing. Maybe I will when I'm older."

The four of us had stopped going to rock concerts and Hollywood movies. The weekend before Christmas, we went to see *The Survivors,* a documentary filmed in North Vietnamese hospitals about the women and children maimed and burned and widowed and orphaned by American bombing. I was crying by the end, and I was the one who suggested we stay and watch it a second time.

Over Christmas break, Alex went skiing in Switzerland with his parents and made a side trip to visit his friend Darko in Belgrade. Buzzy drove his old wagon home to Las Vegas, so Chuck and I got a ride with him as far as Chicago. I was surprised by how sad I felt when he dropped us off in Wilmette—sad about being home, where Sabrina's death cast a pall, but also about saying goodbye to Buzzy for two weeks.

My parents were hopeful about Senator Eugene McCarthy, who'd announced he was running as a peace candidate for the nomination against Johnson. Mom had even memorized lines from the

poem McCarthy had written and recited at the press conference launching his candidacy—"I'm an existential runner / Indifferent to space / I'm running here in place."

I snorted. I told my parents they were naive.

"*We're* naive?" my father said, snorting back at me. He was losing patience. "You are the utopian, my daughter."

"Uh-*uh*." I wasn't. I was extreme in my loathing of the current government, besotted by my notions of the possibility of right action. But I thought people who believed America was ripe for socialist transformation were like religious freaks—wankers, delusional.

"You're not going to get a revolution, Karen," my father said. "And if by some chance you do, you are not going to like it."

I agreed with him, which I didn't say. "Actually," I said, stealing a quote from a book I'd read by a former national president of SDS, "the fundamental revolutionary motive? Is *not* to construct some kind of paradise. It's to destroy an inferno."

Two nights before Christmas, my parents and Peter and I were watching the news. The TV, now color, had finally been allowed into the living room. Eleven-year-old Peter sat as close as he possibly could to the semicircular pile of beribboned boxes under the tree, so close that his face was bathed in red and yellow from the hot Christmas lights. My mother always started her shopping early, so there were several gifts for Sabrina that would go to Catholic Charities after the holiday.

The top story was from South Vietnam. The correspondent said that "as 1967 ends, the U.S. has dropped almost a million tons of bombs on North Vietnam—more than in the entire Pacific theater during World War II, seventy pounds of explosives for every man, woman, and child in the country. Yet they struggle on."

President Johnson was paying a holiday visit to the U.S. Air Force and Navy base at Cam Ranh Bay.

"All the challenges have been met," the president said.

"I so despise him," I said. His Southern-hick accent made even easier to hate. During my entire childhood, whenever I'd watched the news and seen a squinty middle-aged white man talk-

ing in a Southern accent, he had been some loathsome enemy of decency and freedom.

"The enemy is not beaten," the president said, "but he knows that he has met his master in the field."

"He is such a lying, evil pig," I said.

The correspondent came on and said that Johnson was "recommitting himself more strongly than ever to his war policies." Then came a shot of Air Force One taking off for Rome.

"Maybe he'll crash," Peter said.

Even I was shocked. No one said a thing.

Peter realized his faux pas and said, "I'm sorry."

The president, according to the TV newsman, was heading to the Vatican . . .

"Maybe he wants to get a pep talk from Cardinal Spellman," I said.

. . . where he would meet with Pope Paul VI to discuss the war.

"Good," my mother said, "*good*. Karen, did you see the latest thing Pope Paul said about Vietnam?"

"That it's 'Christ's war for civilization against the Vietcong and the people of North Vietnam'?" I was quoting Cardinal Spellman's remarks from when he visited the U.S. troops.

"That America," my mother said hopefully, "had 'tragically aggravated' the 'atrocious severities' of the war. The pope!"

"Oh, great—that ought to take care of it, then. I guess tomorrow Johnson will agree to peace talks and the war will be over by New Year's. Let's celebrate."

My mother sighed.

"See, Dad? I haven't lost my sense of humor."

At Harvard and Radcliffe, January consisted of a month of unsupervised self-obsessed hunkering, a two-week reading period and then a two-week exam period, a whole month without any classes or supervision or organized diversions. In other words, January 1968 was perfectly constructed to let us slide off the deep end.

Buzzy had returned from Christmas vacation with a white con-

tainer the size of a peanut butter jar, still in its Smith, Kline & French Laboratories seals, that contained a thousand little white tablets, each a ten-milligram dose of amphetamine—"*pharmaceutical* bennies," he said proudly as he shook his plastic container. He planned to sell a hundred for a dollar apiece to cover his costs, but the rest were for us. Alex and Chuck and I had never tried speed. I knew about bennies from *On the Road* and from *Moonraker*—" 'Benzedrine,' said James Bond. 'It's what I shall need if I'm going to keep my wits about me tonight. It's apt to make one a bit over-confident, but that'll help too.'" Alex mentioned that during the war in the Pacific, his dad's B-29 bomber crew called themselves "the Benzedrine-29 boys." Chuck said his mom, a devotee of pep pills, was annoyed when she'd had to start getting a prescription for them. In other words, bennies seemed modern and benign as well as cool.

We slept when we slept and awoke when we awoke, leaving our dorms only to go to one another's rooms or out to eat. We occasionally watched TV on Alex's set, but we exclusively smoked cigarettes, not pot, and the only movie we went to see all month was *Inside North Vietnam*, a documentary about the dauntless peasants pushing their wheelbarrows and riding their bikes to rebuild the dams and schools that U.S. bombs had wrecked. We studied some, but mainly, we read the harrowing news out of Vietnam and Washington and talked and talked and talked, wallowing in our anxiety and horror, stewing in our own bitter juices, feeling more and more as if America had gone mad and time was running out.

It was a wide-awake month of deepening nonstop doom and gloom but also of four-way thrills and chills. Every couple of days, almost always between midnight and dawn, we would achieve some breakthrough moment of insight and confidence and solidarity, followed by a celebratory snack of coffee and cold pie at the Hayes-Bickford, sharing the all-night fluorescence and Formica with taxi drivers and glowing, twitching hippies.

I stopped writing to Sarah after she told me I sounded "Chicken Little–ish" and that I should "go to New Hampshire and work for

McCarthy instead of just bumming yourself out deeper and deeper with those bullshitting *boys*."

The boys' and my unspoken project that month was to temper and fortify ourselves, to leave childhood behind and turn ourselves into consequential radicals clear-eyed enough to help stop the war and somehow reduce the misery in the world. Unlike the SDS Walter Mittys, we never called one another brothers and sisters and mother-country radicals, or talked about creating liberated zones and a culture of total resistance, offing the pigs, smashing the state. "Sloganeering BS" was our phrase for all that. Which isn't to say we were embracing nonviolence. "Bring the war home" was a New Left slogan we didn't ridicule. Buzzy had said that was what we were doing with the homemade M-80s we planted at the ROTC building.

Late one night I said it seemed as if we had "reached this critical turning point in American history for better *and* for worse."

Everyone nodded.

"At some moment," Buzzy said, "armed chaos becomes preferable to fascist order. Political consciousness comes from action, from struggle—not just the other way around."

Everyone nodded.

Buzzy turned to Chuck. "What's that line of your uncle's, the Israeli, the thing on his tombstone?"

" 'Making a more beautiful world can be an ugly business.' "

Everyone nodded.

The next morning I phoned Chuck to tell him I hadn't slept but that I had a good head of steam going on my Borges paper.

"I'm in a nightmare," he said. His voice was small and squeaky.

"What do you mean? I'm sorry I called so early."

"I feel like I'm trapped in a nightmare I can't wake up from. Like life is nothing but crisis, some kind of unending surreal lie."

"You mean the war? And everything?"

"Everything. When I woke up just now, I thought I was in a nightmare. Literally. I feel . . . I feel like . . . I don't know."

"What?" He didn't answer. "You sound like you're feeling how I

feel when I'm really low and need sugar. Maybe you should go eat breakfast."

"It's like I'm, like, holding myself hostage. Like I'm torturing myself to make myself talk. It's horrible."

"I'm sorry," I said. I didn't ask what he meant, because I assumed he didn't mean anything much except that he was a sleepless, speedy, freaked-out kid, like the rest of us. "I'm going to write until I finish, and then I'll come down and we can get a late lunch?"

It was already dark when I got to Chuck's room. Buzzy answered the door, and I was startled. He'd shaved off his beard. He looked like a *man*.

"Karen?" Buzzy said quietly. "Not to be paranoid, but we should all probably stop having important conversations on the phone."

When Chuck came out of the bathroom, I could see he'd been crying.

I hugged him. "I'm okay," he offered. "I'm exhausted, but I'm going to be okay. I'm going to stop taking the speed."

Buzzy rolled his eyes and his entire head.

"Do you want me to stay?" I asked Chuck.

He nodded. Buzzy popped out to give the two of us privacy, as always, and we lay in Chuck's bed, but we didn't do anything, and he fell asleep.

We and the upperclassmen who lived in our dorms, the proctors, were pretty much ignoring parietals by then. Chuck and I were mainly violating the letter rather than the spirit of the rules, because we were having sex as often as, say, married people do.

I watched him sleep, and I wondered if my secret four-year-long adoration had made my *idea* of Chuck Levy too wonderful for the actual Chuck Levy to sustain. Although he was still sweet, his sweetness now seemed a little soft. We were all upset and angry all the time, but he was morose. Maybe the reality of being with him could never measure up to the fantasy, the bedoozled virgin's hopeful *fiction* of someday becoming his girlfriend. "America was more amazing from across the ocean, before I'd ever been here," my dad once told me. I wondered if maybe the half-life of my love for Chuck

wasn't a lifetime, like uranium-232's, but closer to californium-248, 333 days.

When Buzzy returned an hour later, Chuck mumbled that he was down for the count, so Buzzy and I went out, got a pizza to go, and headed over to Alex's.

Alex's math-prodigy roommate had decided to drop out when he was home for Christmas, and the hockey-player roommate stayed mostly at his girlfriend's Boston apartment, so Alex's empty suite became our cigarette-stocked, TV-equipped January clubhouse, the way his parents' basement had been in Wilmette. Spending so much time in that neutral zone, instead of in my room at Radcliffe or in Chuck and Buzzy's across the Yard, also enabled the flowering of my infatuation with Buzzy Freeman.

Even though we had all become deadly serious, I appreciated Buzzy's humor even as I argued that jokes and entertainment amounted to self-indulgent folly. He was both the adult and the mischievous child among us. He insisted on watching the Super Bowl and the premiere of *Laugh-In*, which he said would "keep us in sync with real Americans." He accused us of "refusing to laugh" at his new record by a comedy group called the Firesign Theatre, which Alex derided as "countercultural pastiche" and "hippie burlesque." Back in the 1920s, I said, the fun and games of the Dadaists and Berlin cabarets had done nothing to stop the rise of fascism. "And maybe they greased the skids for the Nazis," I said, "since the people who should've risen up to stop them looked at everything as a big joke."

"Can't we have a little fun *and* resist?" Buzzy replied.

By the middle of January, the jar of Benzedrine was a third empty. I discovered a side benefit—when a hit of speed didn't have any effect on me, it meant my blood sugar was high and I needed to inject insulin. "I'm telling you, man," Buzzy said, "it's an all-round revolutionary wonder drug, gives you fucking superpowers. We *are* the Justice League of America!" He rechristened each of us—Chuck was Aquaman, Alex was Batman, I was Wonder Woman, and Buzzy made himself the Flash.

"Karen is *Catwoman*," Chuck said without smiling, as if making an important factual correction.

"Somebody's grumpy and needs his go pills," Buzzy said.

"Sorry. I don't want to become an addict," Chuck said.

"Oh, you're fine with smoking two packs of butts a day," Buzzy said, "but a tablet that makes you smarter and better and doesn't kill you is a terrible thing?"

"Hollaender injects insulin twice a day to make her brain operate better," Alex pointed out.

I never liked two or three against one, even when I was in the majority. "That's not the same," I said. "I'm not addicted, it's a rational choice I make every day to stay alive."

"And taking bennies," Alex said, "is a rational choice we're making every day to *feel* alive."

Buzzy left the room without a word and returned a half hour later from the library with a photocopy of a medical journal article. "'Subjectively,'" he read, "'Benzedrine produces increased confidence, initiative and ease in making decisions,' etcetera, etcetera, 'thinking processes appear to be speeded up *without* impairing attention, concentration, or judgment.'"

"Yeah, '*subjectively*,'" Chuck said.

"What else *is* there but subjectively?" Alex asked.

"'And,'" Buzzy continued quoting, "'intelligence scores are improved.' Is that objective enough for you, man? 'Among mildly obsessional personalities there were some who responded extraordinarily well, especially hesitant individuals who show a tendency to obsessional doubt and difficulty in making up their minds.'" He paused and theatrically popped his eyes at Chuck. "See? It cures Hamlet syndrome! And here you go, from *doctors*: '*Addiction* will be *rare*.'"

Alex turned on the news. Our acute sense of crisis was not just a function of being young and alarmed and cooped up in a room for a month in the middle of a gray winter with an endless supply of Benzedrine. The day before, the North Koreans had captured a U.S.

Navy spy ship, the *Pueblo*—and if they didn't return the ship and its crew immediately, the Democratic chairman of the House Armed Services Committee was saying on TV, President Johnson should fire a nuclear missile at them, see to it that "one of their cities would disappear from the face of the earth."

"Stupid squid spooks," Buzzy said, referring to the captured navy men, and moved to sit right in front of the television so he could turn the dial back and forth among NBC, CBS, and ABC.

"This guy I met who works for the government," Alex said, "told me that LBJ has three TVs in the Oval Office so he can watch the three news shows all at once. Also? A button on his desk he presses just to have a servant bring him a Fresca."

"That's gross," I said.

"Yeah," Alex said, "but cool, too. I'd like to have three TVs, all lined up."

Buzzy turned to Alex. "What guy you met who works for the government?"

"In Europe over Christmas, in Zurich, an American official. An embassy official."

"An embassy official? Bern is the capital of Switzerland. That's where they have embassies. Not Zurich."

"I don't know, a consulate official, State Department or something. I didn't ask for his ID."

I'd started to suspect Alex had a secret romantic life, and I was unhappy that Buzzy had caught him in some kind of fib about his unspoken homosexuality.

The second story on the news was the nightly war report, about a huge new battle at Khe Sanh in South Vietnam, where the North Vietnamese Army was laying siege to a U.S. Marine base.

"This is big," Buzzy said. "This is hellacious." We watched footage of jungle exploding beneath American planes "like three hundred meters from the fucking perimeter . . . Fox Fours *and* Thuds *and* Big Ugly Fuckers"—the nicknames he used for F-4 Phantoms and F-105 Thunderchiefs and B-52s.

Watching and listening, I felt panic. Twenty thousand Americans had died in the war so far. The deaths had doubled between 1966 and 1967, but now the number was doubling every *month*.

The next story was about a Strategic Air Command B-52 that had crashed and burned on an ice bank off Greenland. Its four hydrogen bombs had gone missing.

"Holy shit," Chuck said, lighting a new cigarette off the one he was smoking.

At a press conference, the president assured a reporter that the missing bombs were nothing to worry about.

The wave of horror was unlike any I'd ever felt, panic on behalf of the whole world but with the additional voltage of personal threat. "The idea that *that* monster," I said, "has a button he can push to destroy the world right next to the button he can push to get a fucking Fresca is—I mean, that is *insane*. Beyond his being a murdering redneck fascist prick, that is just *terrifying*." I pointed at the TV. "The fate of mankind is in *his* hands, *his* insane senile brain. That is just *wrong*."

"There's not really one nuclear button like that," my boyfriend said. "And people don't get senile at fifty-nine."

"Oh, Jesus Christ, Chuck, you're not my fucking professor grading my paper!" I had never blown up at him. In front of other people, we'd never even bickered.

"It's not like I'm defending—"

"I'm tired of you correcting me, always trying to calm me down, 'Things really aren't *that* bad, honey.' Were you *watching*? Things *are* that bad. How could they be worse?"

No one made a peep. I wasn't going to let my anger turn to tears, and I wasn't through. "At the Dow thing that morning, *you* were the one who said this is a do-or-die moment like Germany in the thirties. *You're* the one who says your relatives were liquidated because they refused to believe the Nazis were evil until it was too late. So either that's all bullshit, and we should all go dress up nice and knock on doors and give out McCarthy buttons—or else it's real."

I lit a cigarette, and Alex bummed one of mine.

"Want a Coke?" Buzzy asked me after a little while. That was code for *Do you think your blood sugar's low?* If it had been, I almost certainly would have snapped at Buzzy and denied it—and when I went to the bathroom, the test strip came out a perfect blue. My panic and anger were real.

On TV, Huntley or Brinkley was saying that Dr. Spock and William Sloane Coffin, the Yale chaplain, "have been indicted by a grand jury in Boston on federal conspiracy charges for advising young men to dodge the draft. If convicted, the activists face prison terms of five years."

Buzzy was nodding. "Not to be paranoid, folks, but that grand jury is right across the river. The shit is officially hitting the fan."

Chuck stood up. "I've got a sociology exam at nine tomorrow," he announced, and left. I stayed.

At lunch the next day Chuck told me that he'd ended his speed hiatus; he'd taken three bennies that morning and filled two blue books with exam answers "about the pseudo-objectivity of sociologists who are puppets of the reactionary power elite." He also said he was sorry about giving in so often to his niggling, paralyzing, wishy-washy liberalism, and that he had also started writing me a long letter "explaining everything." I accepted his apology and told him he didn't need to write a letter. He had snapped out of his funk, and my anger was once again homed in on people I'd never met. Benzedrine *was* an all-around wonder drug.

The feeling of Armageddon in progress, however, did not abate. In Khe Sanh, the swarms of American planes continued their devastation around the clock, day after day, dropping thousands of tons of bombs on a few square miles of Vietnam, the most concentrated continuous bombardment in human history. Respectable people in the newspapers and on TV were saying that Vietnam might be about to trigger World War III.

We decided to mark the end of exam period by tripping—Alex for the second time, me for the third, Chuck for the fourth, Buzzy for "I don't know, the fifteenth, maybe." The drug we took the after-

noon of Groundhog Day 1968 wasn't mescaline or acid but something called DOM that Buzzy had gotten in the mail from his Benzedrine supplier in California, "Dimethoxy-something, totally new, just invented. Chemically related to speed, so you know— never mix, never worry!"

As soon as we each swallowed a pill, Buzzy grinned and wouldn't stop.

"What?" I asked.

He handed me the envelope that the pills had come in, pointing to the postmark. "Walnut Grove, California," he said. "About twenty-five clicks east of Oakland. Big corporate research lab." He was still grinning.

We waited for the punch line.

"The following psychedelic experience is brought to you by the Dow Chemical Company."

He also told us the drug's hippie street name was STP, for Serenity, Tranquillity, and Peace. We made fun of that, but for the first couple of hours, I did feel pretty tranquil. Instead of the extradimensional pixies-and-elves strangeness I'd felt with mescaline, reality was not so much distorted or fractured as enhanced and intensified. When we listened to "Manic Depression" and "Purple Haze" on the stereo, I didn't wonder if Jimi Hendrix was a time traveler, and Alex's Oriental rug did not look like a field of writhing neon worms, and this time, when I looked out across the Yard at the statue of John Harvard, he didn't lift his head and look straight up at me. The reds and purples on the carpet were *incredibly* red and purple, rich and subtle, at least as startling as when I got eyeglasses in fourth grade and saw leaves clearly for the first time. And through the midwinter dusk from fifty yards away, the golden patches of depatinated bronze on John Harvard's forehead and left shoe gleamed like the special effects on Glinda in *The Wizard of Oz*.

The mood of the room instantly turned inside out when Alex switched on the TV. We'd heard about the big military offensive launched by the Vietcong two days earlier at the beginning of the Vietnamese New Year, Tet. It was epic. A hundred South Vietnam-

ese cities and towns had been attacked by eighty thousand guerril-las.

We were warned by Huntley or Brinkley that we were about to see a disturbing scene filmed by an NBC cameraman on a street in Saigon. All right; okay; fine. I had been a collector of disturbing news stories since I was eight. For two years I had gorged on the ghastliest reports and pictures from Vietnam.

A skinny man in shirtsleeves, the chief of the South Vietnamese national police, sauntered calmly across the TV in front of a hand-cuffed Vietcong wearing a plaid shirt, took a snub-nose revolver from a holster, raised it a few inches from the man's right temple, and fired, executing him with a single shot. I heard the bang. I saw the blood gushing from the dead man's head onto the pavement.

I was not prepared for what I'd seen. For an instant I wondered if I was hallucinating, but the looks on the boys' faces told me we had all watched the same thing. Chuck threw up in Alex's wastebasket.

President Johnson was on the screen from Washington. He said the Vietcong's Tet offensive was already "a complete failure."

"That is one gung ho madman motherfucker," Buzzy said.

"Such a bloody *liar*," Alex said.

"The enemy will fail again and again," the president said, because "we Americans will never yield."

"I think he's literally psychopathic," Buzzy said. "I mean it. *MacBird!* was no joke. He's the most dangerous man on earth right now."

When I was a girl in Sunday school, and as I studied the cate-chism, the notion that I'd always found most alluring and most frus-tratingly unimaginable was when Christians, saints in the making, had epiphanies and revelations, when they didn't just *believe* the truth but all of a sudden *experienced* it on a gut level, independent of reason. No brilliant light from heaven shined round about me, but now, for the first time, I didn't merely have a strong opinion. I sud-denly understood all that is, seen and unseen. I knew.

"He's a fiend," I said. "He's a demon."

Chuck stared at the TV, shaking his head until Alex turned it off.

For hours we talked about the nature of evil in the world, about whether Vice President Humphrey was saner than President Johnson, about Faust and Gandhi, about the various Germans who tried and failed to murder Hitler, about the morality of killing to save lives and whether the phrase "military-industrial complex" was (in Buzzy's phrase) "a brilliant psyop trick by Ike" to make us believe that blows against it were impossible, whether history was shaped by individuals or by impersonal forces, how extreme and unprecedented the present moment was, how Kennedy's assassination had altered the course of history because he might've pulled out of Vietnam already, and how *that* suggested the war lovers inside the government had a motive to kill him and replace him with Johnson, about the impossible odds against Gene McCarthy winning the nomination and the presidency and ending the pointless massacre in Vietnam. It didn't feel like one more endless dorm-room bull session. It felt like four hardheaded friends finally, unflinchingly coming to grips in an orderly way with the whole ugly truth and our own destinies.

As we sat and sprawled in our circle, I kept thinking all night of my first long-ago moment of political understanding, half a lifetime earlier, reading at age nine about young Arthur learning from Merlyn that the only just reason for war is to stop a much worse war, to use Might for Right. We were turning into knights of our own Round Table. Instead of referring to the children's book I'd loved, I quoted the Malcolm X speech I'd written about for my summer school class at Northwestern.

"And I don't think it applies only to the evil inflicted on black people. It's about stopping the war, too. 'Don't ever think,'" I recited more or less verbatim, "'that they're going to stop it just because they're convinced it's immoral. We need action that we're justified in initiating by any means necessary.'"

As it started getting light outside, we were no longer high, exactly, but still talking up a storm, continuing as a group to shave away and erase the grays until nothing remained but unbelievably

clear and sharp blacks and whites, looping back every few minutes to the subject of Lyndon Johnson.

"So we could zap him," Buzzy said. "We could actually *do* it. *We* could actually do it."

"What do you mean?" I asked.

"Zap him, cockadau him, terminate with extreme prejudice."

Holy shit. Buzzy wasn't smiling.

"The CIA," he said, "gets rid of guys all the time, right? Like Che. Even presidents—Trujillo in the Dominican Republic, Lumumba in the Congo. And in Nam, Diem . . . plus, it's what Special Forces guys do every day when they go in and ding some particular Chuck."

Chuck snapped to attention. *"What?"*

Buzzy was cool as ever. "I never told you that? Chuck, Charlie, Vietcong. I called them 'Chucks.' Better than 'gooks,' right?"

I suppose we'd been heading here for hours, or for weeks or maybe months. But at that moment the irresistible logic loomed suddenly and shockingly.

"We're four people," Buzzy continued. "Correct size for a special-ops direct-action team. Short-duration strike, precise use of force to achieve a specific objective."

"You're not serious, right," Alex said, "about, I mean, you know . . ." We were alone in his dorm room, but his voice shrank to a whisper. *"Assassinating Johnson?"*

Buzzy turned to Alex. *"You* were the one who said democracy *started* twenty-five hundred years ago with the assassination of a tyrant in Athens, and what a hero Brutus is for killing Julius Caesar. *You're* the one who said the murder of one good person to prevent the death of a thousand or a million innocent people is 'morally right, obviously.' What, so now everything you and he and she have been saying for the last twelve hours is all hypothetical college-kid jerk-off fairy-tale bullshit?"

"No," Alex said, "no, I, I just . . . I don't know. I get it, I wouldn't be unhappy if it happened. And Humphrey might end the war if he were president. But . . ."

"Nixon sure as shit won't if he's in there a year from now," I said.

"A year less of war," Buzzy said. "Tens of thousands of lives saved, maybe more. Who can argue with that? Maybe we prevent World War III. Let history be our judge."

I waited for one of us to say *What the fuck? This is insane!* None of us did.

"I mean," I said, "he has lived his life. He's almost *sixty.*"

"But is it possible?" Alex asked. *"Us?"*

"Don't reject it out of hand," Buzzy said. "Don't assume you're powerless. That's what they count on."

For a minute or more, none of us said a thing. Buzzy looked at each of us. I listened to the wind against the windows and my heart beating. I looked at Chuck, who stared at his hands.

Finally, Alex said, "This is very heavy."

Then Chuck inhaled deeply and loudly, and on the exhale, he shot to his feet like a missile launching, startling everyone. "It's not impossible," he said. "It's not."

I thought of something. "It'd be the tenth mission."

"The what?" Buzzy asked.

"It's like we were training for this," I said to Chuck and Alex. I don't know exactly how the variables interacted at that moment— remembering my clubbing at the Pentagon, ten weeks spent imagining and reimagining the violent particulars of my sister's pointless death, seeing the casual point-blank murder on the evening news twelve hours earlier, the final molecules of 2,5-Dimethoxy-4-methylamphetamine ricocheting around my possibly glucose-deprived brain, the magical-thinking apocalyptic spirit of the age— but at dawn on the third of February in 1968, I believed in what Buzzy had proposed and what I was saying. "It's like our destiny."

"What the hell are you talking about, 'training'?" Buzzy demanded. Apparently, none of us had ever told him about our nine junior-high-school-kid jerk-off fairy-tale espionage missions.

"James Bond," Alex said. "These things we did when we were young. These games, these 'missions.'"

25

WHEN WAVERLY CALLS, what surprises me most about her reaction to the previous chapter is that she doesn't seem a bit freaked out that her grandmother conspired to assassinate the president of the United States forty-six years ago. But then I realize that if my mother's darling mother had told me when I was seventeen that she'd plotted to kill Warren Harding in 1920, when she was seventeen, I might have laughed, and it wouldn't have made me love my grandma Scattergood any less.

"I was confused," Waverly says. "I thought 'LBJ' was a typo or something. I knew LeBron James wasn't alive then, but . . . How come everybody called presidents by their initials back then?"

"I don't know." Nor did I know until a few minutes ago that the star player on one of the teams headed for the NBA finals next month is known as LBJ.

"Also? Nobody called weed 'weed' back then? When did that start? And why?"

"No idea."

"I can't wait to read more to find out what happens."

"We don't get away with it."

"That's funny, Grams."

I'm glad she knows who was and wasn't assassinated in the 1960s. Briefly, last summer, I'd thought about writing this story as a counterfactual fiction, a novel in which some college students succeed in assassinating Lyndon Johnson in 1968, which triggers a full-scale American police-state crackdown for a decade, like in Chile and Argentina, with hundreds or thousands of American citizens secretly tortured and murdered by the government. When I pitched that novel, my editor encouragingly said, "I get it, Frederick Forsyth meets Philip Roth, *Day of the Jackal* crossed with *American Pastoral* and *The Plot Against America,* plus Philip K. Dick." Then I saw the 3-D JFK documentary last fall and decided not to be a wuss, to tell the nonfictional truth instead.

"I have a question," Waverly says. "Did Grandpa know? What you'd done?"

"Nope, he didn't, uh-uh."

"Weird. And he never . . . suspected?"

"I don't think so."

When I married Jack Wu in the summer of 1974 and decided not to tell him about the plot, I told myself I was doing him a favor, that it would be too burdensome, and that my secretiveness wasn't a negative leading indicator for the marriage. It was the moment when I understood I wasn't ever going to tell anyone.

He made it easy by being incurious about my past, indifferent to politics, and opposed to real-life drama. Jack was very even. When we were dating he never complained that I spent too much time working on the *Law Journal* and studying. He was not fazed by my diabetes or by the fact that I'd never heard of most of his favorite composers; wasn't obsessed with Nixon and Watergate; didn't mind when my mother asked him if he had "any theory about why Orientals are *so* intelligent and musical." I wasn't head over heels for Jack. But I'd decided I didn't want to be head over heels about anything ever again. And I convinced myself that was a long-term plus for the marriage, because in year five or year twenty, I wouldn't suffer the disappointments of hot young love gone tepid.

I can pinpoint the moment when I knew my marriage had gotten bad. One night, just before my forty-first birthday, I turned over in bed and found Jack staring at me—and I embraced him not because I felt any rush of desire but to avoid looking into his eyes. The next morning I woke up from a sex dream and realized it had been better than any actual lovemaking in ages, and then, reading the paper, I came across the first story about mad cow disease and the fears that it might destroy British agriculture. "It's Blofeld's plot *exactly!*" I shouted with a big smile to Jack at breakfast. He looked at me as if I'd gone mad. He said he had no idea who Blofeld was. "In *On Her Majesty's Secret Service?*" I explained. Had I never mentioned Blofeld? We'd been married sixteen years. Jack started taking antidepressants around the same time Seth did. I knew they could diminish the libido. But it was Greta who told me, right after I demolished his BlackBerry and left our marriage, that they also biochemically reduce one's ability to feel love.

That I never told my husband what I'd done when I was eighteen obviously baffles and upsets Waverly more than the thing I never told him about.

"So Grandpa's gone, but why," she asks, "are you writing about all this *now?* Won't it cause a lot of trouble for you and your friends?"

I sigh. "The short answer is that I need to get the truth down before I go. No more secrets and lies." Part of the longer answer is that in the several decades since I decided I ought to kill the president, I have strenuously avoided making any grand, self-destructive, compulsive gestures in my life. Writing this memoir is my grand, self-destructive, compulsive last hurrah.

"You're not sick or anything? I mean, 'before you go' in like twenty years, right?"

"Sure hope so."

Speaking of LeBron James, she tells me, Sophie "copped a disorderly conduct plea" in Florida and just finished serving her one-week sentence in the Miami-Dade Women's Detention Center, an experience for which she's receiving independent-study credit from their high school. "She's like this celebrity now," Waverly tells me.

"It's sick." I know "sick" isn't exactly a pejorative. The night of Sophie's release from jail, paparazzi photographed her standing next
to LeBron James at Mark Zuckerberg's thirtieth-birthday party at a
South Beach nightclub called Snatch.

"So you," I ask Waverly, "are not freaked out by what I did?"

"You didn't *do* it."

"Wait and see what we did. What happened."

"When I got back from Miami, Dad gave me a book on cults."

"He thinks you're in a cult?"

"He thinks Hunter's brainwashed me. You know, Hunter's always
talked about how insane the Vietnam time was, but I never understood what he meant until now, from reading your book." She
pauses. "I'm not saying *you* were insane."

"Oh, I pretty much was."

"Right," Waverly says. "Temporarily. Right?"

"Yup," I confirm, and we say goodbye.

My temporary insanity aside, I think it should be noted for the
record that the slaughter in Vietnam was staggeringly and unnecessarily huge. More than a million soldiers and another million or
maybe two million civilians died.

We know now, however, that a considerable fraction of those civilians were killed by the North Vietnamese and Vietcong. We
know now that the Tet offensive really was, as Lyndon Johnson said,
"a complete failure" militarily for the Communist side.

And we know now that the prisoner we watched being executed
on TV had previously killed one of his executioner's men and the
man's wife and children. We also know now that the general, the
cold-blooded killer who so shocked my conscience that evening,
had been considered a humanitarian figure in South Vietnam.

We also now know, by the way, the truer stories behind some of
those ghetto riots in the summer of 1967. The taxi driver in Newark
was roughed up by the police, but he didn't die. The kid shot by the
Tampa police had robbed a store. The kid in Houston was shot not
by the police but by another kid. I am not saying that racism in
America in 1967 wasn't savage and deep-seated, only that some of

the spontaneous violent uprisings against it were ignited by plausible fictions.

And as disinclined as I am to feed my son-in-law's hysteria concerning my granddaughter, in 1968 my friends and I did constitute a little cult. Which is why I've been allergic ever since to groups of people with single-minded visionary passion and without any doubt that they possess the one truth—why, ever since, I've seen cults everywhere I look, not just literal cults, like Scientology, but the astoundingly successful ones around Warren Buffett and Oprah Winfrey, Linus Torvalds and Steve Jobs, Ronald Reagan and Barack Obama.

Ours was a cult based on our narcissistic love of our beautiful young American selves and hatred of the horrible American pod people callously killing millions. As with the Muslim cult of hate embodied for a while by Osama bin Laden, and as with the worst and nuttiest of the new American haters, ours was a nihilism that fancied itself utopian. On the spectrum of self-righteous madness, we were somewhere between the lunatic Islamists and the lunatic American right-wingers.

I call Greta. She asks if I'm relieved to be finished with the school year. Commencement was two days ago. I'm touched that she keeps track of my academic calendar.

"It feels excellent. I can lock myself in my bunker and finish the book by Labor Day. Which is why I'm calling."

I tell her I need a primer from her on the neuroscience of hate, which is, along with love, the focus of her work.

"You really want *my help?*" she asks.

The surprise in her voice makes me feel like crying.

Over the winter I asked her about the neuroscience of free will, but I didn't tell her it was research. She'd told me the evidence mainly indicates that free will is an illusion, an instant revisionist trick our minds do to fool us into thinking we *decide* what to do and *then* do it—whereas it's more like the reverse of that, our unconscious lizard brain initiating every action on its own, and only then our conscious brain rubber-stamping those actions as "choices." Or

occasionally vetoing them. I find that somewhat comforting, as I contemplate what I did back in 1968, but also disturbing as a user's manual for human consciousness.

"Yes, sweetie, I do want your help."

She tells me about the "neural correlates of hate" that she and her fellow researchers have started pinpointing, no longer solely by taking fMRI pictures of blood flow but by injecting photosensitive proteins and then shining blue light on the exposed brain to see how it responds. And, in her newly funded project with neuroscientists in Shanghai, by implanting electrodes directly into the brains of people who are consumed with hate.

"How can you do that?" I ask.

"Technically, you mean?"

"No . . . ethically."

"They're volunteers."

I don't raise the question of what "volunteering" might mean in China. "Cutting to the chase, the bottom line is? Give me 'Neuroscience for Dummies.' "

"I *hate* it when you do that." We both laugh. "Correlating isn't the same as causing, of course, but hate seems to burn mainly in the right side of the front of your brain. One's brain. That's where hateful feelings are either denatured or amplified."

"Each of us is wired to either hate more or hate less?"

"Basically, probably, yeah. Certain families and certain cultures *intentionally* build up the—so to speak—hate muscles in the brains of children. Hurting them, insulting them, steeling them, maybe indoctrinating them with false beliefs."

"Your grandmother indoctrinated me with plenty of false beliefs about the Father, Son, and Holy Ghost—"

"No, no, I mean false beliefs about the people you're supposed to hate."

"Ah."

"By the way? One thing that *really* interests me? A couple of the neural correlates for hate are also significant neural correlates for

love. Makes sense, right? The happy or angry tunnel vision that won't switch off."

Like in Karen Hollaender, ages seventeen and eighteen. "Right."

"As with most brain states, there's a useful mode and a pathological mode—schizophrenia bad, creativity good. A guy I know in San Diego is doing interesting work on athletes, how the best ones develop tunnel vision, psychologically as well as literally, in terms of visual perception. Swimmers, especially."

"Swimmers, huh?" Such as a boy who swam the 400-yard freestyle at the 1966 Illinois state championship in under four minutes? "That's interesting."

As we chat about Waverly, Jungo gets on an extension, tells me he's trying to "really Six Sigma her college admissions process," and reads aloud from his Excel spreadsheet of "places we're planning on applying to," so that I can give him the names of all the professors and deans and trustees I know at each institution. I'm so relieved that Stanford is not on the list. Alex is on Stanford's board.

"Thanks, Mom," Jungo says, "I'll shoot you a follow-up email with action steps," and when he hangs up, I ask Greta if she's talked to Alex Macallister again.

"Uh-uh, why?"

No reason in particular except that he's the only person alive for whom I feel actual hatred. "Oh, I had a conversation with him after you and I talked in New York, and . . . I just thought he might have been in touch with you again."

I rarely feel anger, let alone hate. I sometimes feel frustrated and disgusted and despairing, but it almost never blossoms into true hate, not even for the ideologues on TV and radio and their overexcited cult followings of ignorami. I never hated Jack. Not only did I not hate my acquaintance who slept with Jack at the start of the last decade of our marriage, but it was my lack of anger when I discovered her betrayal that made me realize I didn't want to be married to Jack much longer. I did hate the psychiatrist who told my son Seth at fourteen that his Asperger's is "in all likelihood due in some

measure" to my "mothering style." I hated a man who called me a "self-satisfied corporate pawn" and "chilly crypto-conservative" in his review of my first book, and until he went to prison for securities fraud, I hated the asshole at my law firm who said with a smile at a partners' meeting in 1989 that "as a smarter-than-average gal," I was "living proof affirmative action can sometimes work." Mostly, I hate feeling or seeing hate.

In 1967 and 1968, however, I truly and viscerally hated every American official responsible for the war in Vietnam, in particular Lyndon Johnson. I had merely a simmering antipathy for people like those I would become, the self-satisfied corporate pawns and crypto-conservatives who refused to admit how wrong and untenable the system is, grown-ups who let a nice paycheck and a dry martini and a good book in a comfortable chair prevent them from challenging the racist, warmongering, imperialist status quo.

At age sixty-four—and tomorrow, sixty-*five*—I still disapprove of imperialism when it humiliates and immiserates and brutalizes people. But visiting which cities makes me happiest? Charleston, Cuzco, Cartagena, Cape Town, and Hanoi, the glorious antique urban residue of European colonialism. I am a postcolonial colonialist, just as I am an irreligious lover of religious art—Michelangelo, Mozart, cathedrals, "Amazing Grace." I still disapprove of unnecessary wars, but does even the leftiest lefty today refuse to use GPS because it's an app invented and operated by the Pentagon?

After the waiter takes our order and we clink our glasses of red wine, Stewart says, "I'm afraid, my dear, you've proved a theory of mine about you."

My throat tightens. Tonight is supposed to be pure fun. Until now, neither of us has mentioned 1968. I fake-smile. "I thought you and your gizmo decided I was telling the truth."

"Whoa! The lady protests too much. I'm talking about you and menus—your dinner."

"What? I like mozzarella, I like spicy pasta, I like crab. And since you love garlic, I figured you'd forgive the pesto breath."

"You always order the items on the menu that have the most words. Every time."

I smile authentically and shake my head. I ordered two dishes—bufala mozzarella with pesto, salsa romesco, tapenade, and caperberry relish to start; for my main course, squid-ink chitarra freddi with Dungeness crab, sea urchin, and jalapeño. "You know me better than I know myself."

"This is the business I have chosen."

"Speaking of which, what brings you to the Mojave this time?"

"Not much, quick look-see at the new FEMA concentration camp and mind-control facility we're building out there. Usual bullshit."

"Ha ha. Do you not want to tell me?"

He lowers his voice but raises the pitch. "I was out at Edwards looking at this *unbelievable* new UAS."

"Ah, a new UAS."

"Yeah, the thing can cruise *stratospherically* for almost a *week*. It's got imaging resolution of half an inch at twelve kilometers. I could make out each of your buttons from fucking forty thousand feet. And get your heat signature."

"What's a UAS?" I finally ask.

"Oh, right—unmanned aircraft system. Unmanned aerial vehicles."

"A drone, a Predator."

"You are such a civilian, and so 2011. A Predator stays up for a day, day and a half. It flies low, lower than a passenger plane, and it's noisy as a garbage truck, so the bad guys hear you coming. This thing is *quiet*."

"What a nice birthday party—learning about a new, improved way for my country to kill people."

"*Bad* people."

"I'm sure."

"And a lot fucking fewer not-so-bad people. With this, we might be able to reduce the NCCCR, no bullshit, from ten down to like one or two."

I give him a look.

"Noncombatant collateral casualty ratio. The friends and family we unavoidably whack when we take out a bona fide target with a Hellfire." He smiles. "You know what else? No, I shouldn't tell you this. You're going to think I'm a totally cold, callous motherfucker."

"That horse left the barn fifteen years ago. Go ahead."

"This thing is hydrogen-powered, the engines on the new drone. Totally *green*."

Nineteen sixty-eight hasn't come up by the time the waiter takes away our plates, commencing the interval of quiet pre-coffee glow.

Then Stewart says, "So: eighteen United States Code *1751*."

I sigh. He knows.

"A wet job," he says. "*The* wet job."

"Yup."

"I mean, *that* shocked *me*. You fucking *inhaled*, baby. Capital crime."

I nod. *Whoever kills any individual who is the President of the United States,* according to 18 U.S. Code 1751, the relevant statute, shall be punished by death. "Except," I say, "it didn't happen in the end. The capital crime."

"Conspiracy to commit still gets you life, even if nobody dies."

I nod again. "I know the U.S. Code." *If two or more persons conspire to kill . . . and one or more of such persons do any act to effect the object of the conspiracy, each shall be punished by imprisonment for any term of years or for life.*

"You know what else?" he says. "The great irony? Well, a great irony among several great ironies. It was *Johnson* who muscled his new director of Central Intelligence in sixty-seven to collect intel on campus un-Americans like you. The smart people at Langley hated it. If not for Johnson, your boy Macallister the Third wouldn't have become such a friend of the Agency."

"And the CIA wouldn't have known a thing about what we were doing. So the president's illegal domestic spying saved him. And maybe me."

"Something like that. The piece of the story I still don't have nailed is the other asset in your group. Which I still think there must

have been, and which has to be what saved you. It's *killing* me. Like when you can't get a final, big thirteen-letter phrase in a crossword puzzle. I can't pry shit out of INSCOM."

"That reminds me."

"You forgot to tell me you were a Defense Intelligence Agency asset after all? Signed up by your uncle Ralph?" He isn't obviously joking.

"*No.* I got a Freedom of Information letter back from them a week or so ago—'in the interest of national security, involvement by the U.S. Army Intelligence and Security Command in the activities which are the subject matter of your request can neither be confirmed nor denied.' They Glomarized me."

"There you fucking go." He seems both happy and unhappy, intrigued and disappointed. "The puzzle's done."

After he pays the check in cash and then shows off by having a conversation in perfect Spanish with one of the parking valets, we get in his car and he opens a manila envelope with both hands and holds it in front of me. Inside is a fat number 10 envelope, which I take out. "Happy birthday," he says.

As we drive, I barely look up, marvel at no L.A.-by-night panoramas, do nothing but skim a sheaf of xeroxed CIA documents originally typewritten and sent via special pouch and specially numbered blind memoranda, many of them circulated directly to the director of Central Intelligence. Stewart tells me I "lucked out." Richard Helms, the CIA director back then, tape-recorded conversations in his office, and before leaving the job in 1973, he didn't manage to destroy all seven years' worth of transcripts. "Somebody made a few temporary stayback burn copies that didn't turn out to be temporary." Thus, what I'm holding is the unredacted lowdown on Alex Macallister, junior spook.

"Wow," I say. " 'EYES ONLY safekeeping.' 'Destroy the one burn copy and the ribbon copy.' 'Destroy all notes and other source materials.' It's so . . . spy-novelish. OCI is what—Office of Central Intelligence?"

"Current Intelligence."

As we make the right off Sunset up into the hills on Beverly Glen, I make a plosive sound. "Why do they *write* like this?"

"Don't get me started. It's one of the worst parts of the job."

" 'Beginning 1967 Americans with existing extremist credentials'— 'extremist *credentials*,' that's hilarious—'have been assessed, recruited, tested, and dispatched for assignments. Agents who have an American "Movement" background are useful as agents to obtain biographic and personality data, to discern possible susceptibilities, and to develop operationally exploitable relationships with recruitment targets of the above programs.' "

"That's Updike," he says, "compared to the shit I see."

"What, are they paid by the syllable? I thought CIA were supposed to be the intellectual ones."

I read on silently, except when I need Stewart's help deciphering. "RYBAT?"

"Highly sensitive information."

"Coo-bark?" I ask, mispronouncing KUBARK.

"It's K-U-bark. Headquarters, Langley. K-U is the prefix for the Agency."

"So K-U-DOVE is . . ."

"Clandestine Services."

We turn off Mulholland down Skyline Drive. "What's A-M mean?"

"Cuba."

"And A-M-THUG?"

"Castro."

"Huh. Some code. Whoa—my *name*. Spelled right! Why does it have an asterisk penciled in?"

"Unclear. Your old man's connections, your uncle Ralph, some stray clerk sometime making a stray mark for whatever reason. I don't know. You're completely ruining the view with the light on, by the way. Those pages are not going to disintegrate. You can read them all later."

I ignore him and continue reading. "I know O-D means 'other

departments of the government,'" I say as we turn down Benedict Canyon, "but what's O-D-FOAM?"

"Secret Service."

At my house, I take off my shoes but spend another half hour on the bed reading the trove. After his initial recruitment by the CIA in the summer of 1967 to spy on his Yugoslavian Communist friend, Alex started reporting on us and members of Harvard SDS as part of Project RESISTANCE. He contributed to a secret report called "Restless Youth," produced by the CIA's Office of Current Intelligence on student radicals and commissioned personally by LBJ. Alex informed his CIA handler in the spring of 1968 of a potential threat against the president in Washington, D.C., and CIA in turn informed the Secret Service—which was, according to a memo, already aware of the assassination plot against Johnson. Alex continued feeding information to the CIA about Cambridge radicals until 1971, when we graduated. He even had a CIA code name, WHEEL-14.

That must be why his movie company is called Wheel Life Pictures. I always assumed it was just a lame pun that some boyfriend of Alex's made up.

After examining the mysterious chronic dampness in the corner of my bedroom, Stewart says I need to get the roof repaired. He's taken off his pants and turned on the TV. He's on the bed, watching the new live-action HBO show about cats and dogs and horses and rats who talk and curse and dream and have sex and occasionally kill one another.

"Is that supposed to be a comedy?" he asks as he flips to the news channels.

"I don't know, but one last question. What is CHAOS?"

"From the ancient Greek, abyss, a state of extreme confusion, formlessness."

"Seriously."

"In the summer of sixty-eight the Agency put all the domestic anti-radical crap under one roof. That's what they called it."

"Unbelievable! Did they name it after the evil spy organization on *Get Smart*?"

"Beats me. Maybe."

I put down the papers. "This is just stupendous." Life imitates entertainment. Alex Macallister, my James Bond playmate, worked on Project RESISTANCE, became a CHAOS agent, had a code name containing a number. "*Thank* you." I lean over and kiss Stewart.

"If reading old files counts as foreplay, you're sicker than I am."

As I brush my teeth, I realize I didn't understand something Stewart said at dinner.

"Honey?" I say as I walk barefoot and half-naked back into the bedroom. "One more thing, absolutely the last—"

"*Shhh,*" he says, pointing at the TV.

There's an old silent clip of Buzzy in black tie talking to George W. Bush. "The influential Washington insider and FOX News commentator," the anchor says, "was found dead early this morning, killed by a hand grenade, in his luxurious northwest Washington home."

"Oh my God."

"Although it was initially reported as an execution-style terrorist killing, ATF and FBI sources now tell FOX News they believe Bernard Freeman's death to be a suicide."

"Oh, Christ, oh, fuck, fuck, *fuck*. He killed himself because of me, because I'm outing us."

Stewart takes me in his arms. He does not refute my theory. I'm shivering, not because I'm cold.

"How close are you to done?" he asks. "With the book?"

"Why? Fairly close, I guess."

"In case Freeman left a note. Telling all. Burning you before you can burn him. Check your voice mail, see if anybody's called. I should probably clear the fuck out of here before the camera crews or the feebs show up."

26

ON THE FIRST Saturday in February 1968, I didn't wake up until after the sun had gone down, so my father's favorite cliché, the cold light of day, could not literally apply. But I was pleased and surprised to discover that I remembered everything we'd discussed and debated and decided to do. I was clear and calm, as if I'd been initiated into a secret club of heroic problem-solvers, had at last made a real moral choice, the only moral choice—to *act,* to eliminate the bloody tyrant. The night had had its dreamlike qualities, but it was a dream unlike any I'd ever had, because it made perfect sense while it was occurring and still made perfect sense afterward.

I phoned Chuck, and he phoned Alex, and we all agreed to meet at Tommy's Lunch—nominally for dinner, since none of us had eaten a real meal in twenty-four hours, but implicitly and actually to reaffirm our decision in the cold light of day, to make sure none of us was chickening out.

Each of us was tentative at first, and we addressed the matter at hand by indirection, in a kind of ad hoc code. By the time our sandwiches were ready, however, Buzzy was referring to the plan as

"Lima Bravo Juliet"—LBJ—and it was clear we were all in. Alex was grinning and wide-eyed, as if he'd been cast in a movie. Chuck seemed reborn, loose and determined; a weight had been lifted. Buzzy said it was important that we act and speak in public as we had all year, keep the same hours, go to classes as usual, everything outwardly unchanged.

"So: D-day?" he asked. "We need a couple of months."

"April Fool's?" I proposed.

They all gave me sharp, shocked looks.

"I'm not saying it's a prank! I just mean the first of the month."

"Right," Alex said, "that is during spring break."

"Okay," Buzzy said, "we'll aim for one April."

As we walked out into the frigid darkness of Mount Auburn Street, Alex declaimed loudly, "Into the breach, we band of brothers, we happy few."

"Brothers and sister," Buzzy said.

I wondered if I would lose my nerve.

However, as we focused on our secret plan to improve the world instantly, the world obliged by becoming more atrocious. Consider the following Thursday, the eighth of February. On that single day, police shot and killed three students, two of them in the back, and wounded dozens of others during a protest at a black college in South Carolina; George Wallace, the segregationist former governor of Alabama, announced his third-party candidacy for president and said *he'd* make Washington safe "if it took thirty thousand troops with two-foot bayonets"; and we read an Associated Press dispatch in *The Harvard Crimson* about the spasm of bombs and artillery shells that had wiped out Bến Tre, South Vietnam, and a U.S. Army officer's explanation that "it became necessary to destroy the town to save it." The following week, more than three thousand Americans were killed and wounded in Vietnam, the most ever and twice the rate of the previous month. The tipping point that had sickened and frightened me in January was tipping all the way.

The newspaper was full of stories suggesting that Johnson might be about to turn Vietnam into a nuclear war. The Pentagon admit-

ted that H-bomb experts from MIT and Columbia had gone to Saigon to assess "the effectiveness of new weapons." Early one morning
Buzzy called me to read aloud from an article in the *Times* about the
chairman of the joint chiefs testifying to a Senate committee. "They
ask him if they're planning to use nukes anywhere in 'Nam, and the
fucker answers, 'I do not *think* that nuclear weapons will be required
to defend Khe Sanh.' He doesn't 'think' so, not in Khe Sanh, anyhow. What about anywhere *else* in Vietnam, General Wheeler?"

How could we shrink from the obvious conclusion? It was clear
to us that by eliminating one person, the right person, we might
save the lives of many thousands of people. We really might prevent
World War III.

The radical wankers around us that winter and spring seemed
more impotent and vain than ever, talking and talking and talking
some more, which only fueled our conviction that we were serious
and they were whiny children. They insisted that the university hire
more Marxist faculty members. When another Dow Chemical job
recruiter came to campus and said that he supported the manufacture of napalm and was "proud to work for Dow," SDS did nothing.
For a week, I shook my head or rolled my eyes every time I passed
a kid wearing a black armband, one of the hundreds of students
who were supposedly "fasting" to protest the war—and who then
demanded rebates of fifteen dollars apiece for the week of cafeteria
meals they'd skipped in protest.

True, public opinion seemed to be shifting a little. Walter
Cronkite came back from a tour of Vietnam and, shockingly, ex-
pressed his opinion on the evening news—"with each escalation,"
he said, "the world comes closer to the brink of cosmic disaster."
Two weeks later, Eugene McCarthy, the peace candidate, ran a close
second to Johnson in the New Hampshire primary.

We four, however, had our own take on these supposedly hopeful
signs. "Armbands and peace rallies aren't what's doing this," Buzzy
said. "*Resistance* is. Those never-say-die Charlies in Saigon and Khe
Sanh are. Fighting fire with fire is."

"By the way?" Alex said. "In New Hampshire? Gene McCarthy

lost, and LBJ *won.* My dad says Adlai Stevenson told him that McCarthy is never going to be nominated, let alone elected president."

We were not unlike the clipboard-clasping eager beavers all around us campaigning for McCarthy, my roommate and Sarah Caputo organizing car pools up to New Hampshire and out to Wisconsin. Like them, we were smart and hopeful and indefatigable, well organized and goal-oriented, with time on our hands. Which was why we thought we had a special destiny. Instead of harnessing our youthful energy to stuff envelopes and phone strangers and knock on doors and drive voters to polling places in order to rid the world of Lyndon Johnson and end the war, *our* little Children's Crusade was efficient and didn't require convincing thirty million Americans to vote for some goofy Minnesota poet. Unlike the fires set and store windows smashed and random cops shot by poor black people, the act of violence we envisioned was rationally, carefully, coolly premeditated and planned. We weren't wild-eyed romantics or dead-enders, I thought. We would be effective. We were *pragmatic.*

What I think each of us felt, although none of us said so, was that we were invincible. We'd gotten away with every Bond mission unscathed, and with driving drunk and missing curfews and calling ourselves radicals and taking drugs and having sex and cursing our parents. We'd been admitted to *Harvard.* We'd gotten away with planting the M-8os in the ROTC building and holding the Dow recruiter hostage, and Chuck had even gotten away with fighting the U.S. marshal at the Pentagon. What hadn't we gotten away with? Luck had always been on our side. Now we were daring it to abandon us.

Through February and March, we all kept eating tablets of speed from Buzzy's plastic jar as if they were Four A Day Supervitamins.

After a couple of discussions, we decided on the basic logistics for Operation Lima Bravo Juliet.

Buzzy's military jargon made it seem less outlandish, almost sensible. "It's a fairly standard paramilitary op," he said.

He and Chuck both had experience with rifles. "Oswald would've

gotten away with it if he hadn't also shot the Dallas cop," Chuck said. "That was his big mistake."

"*His* mistake," I said, "was his connection to the CIA—even if he wasn't an agent, like that district attorney in New Orleans says, they knew who he was. They would've taken him out. And maybe did."

"I don't believe he was CIA," Alex said. "He was a loser."

Buzzy argued that in the post-Oswald age, snipers are exactly what the Secret Service was guarding against—they now drove enclosed presidential limousines with bulletproof glass and armor plating, and had big security perimeters for outdoor appearances.

Chuck told us about some Levy family heroes, Czech friends of friends of his dad's, who returned from London to Prague during World War II to use a machine gun and a bomb to kill the number-two SS guy who had helped plan the final solution.

"They got away with it?" Alex asked.

He nodded.

"Really," Buzzy asked, "they escaped Nazi-occupied Czechoslovakia?"

"No. But they killed a dozen more Nazis in a shoot-out. And committed suicide before they could be captured." Chuck also said his uncle had known one of the two guys in his Zionist guerrilla group, kids our age, who assassinated Britain's Middle East minister in Cairo in the 1940s, with pistols, point-blank.

After a pause, he said to Buzzy, "You had pistol training in the Coast Guard, right? We could do it with pistols."

We could.

"Yeah, well," Buzzy said, "a sidearm would be iffy with the Secret Service right there to jump you. If you didn't care about dying, the way to do it'd be with a frag in your pocket, a grenade, sidle up to him, 'Hello, great to meet you, Mr. President,' *kaboom*. But I'm headed for medical school—poor people to treat, promises to keep, miles to go, etcetera."

I was grateful that a suicide mission was off the table, and I could tell Alex was, too. Buzzy, sensing the mood in the room, flipped into teasing mode.

"I'm wondering, Mr. Bond," he said to Chuck, "would you use your .25 Beretta or your 7.65-millimeter Walther PPK?"

Now I felt sorry for Chuck, so I told one of my dad's few World War II tales, about an acrobat and juggler with the Copenhagen circus who formed a troupe to provide entertainment at some Nazi officers' celebration, and then, during the finale, threw grenades into the audience.

"Because my father loved the circus and could juggle, when I was little, I wondered if that story was about *him*."

"Nah," Buzzy said, "that had to be a one-way mission." He turned back to Chuck. He wasn't ready to let him off the hook. "You're a pilot. We could rent a plane, and you could crash it into Air Force One."

"Like they tried with de Gaulle, right," Chuck said to me, "in Algeria? You told me about it that day at the library in Evanston."

"*No,*" I said, vetoing the plan, not denying my perfect memory of that day. "Besides, how many people fly with the president? Dozens of innocent people would die."

"That's relative," Buzzy said. "How 'innocent' the henchmen are."

We accommodated ourselves to the unfortunate fact that if we weren't going to shoot Johnson, people near him would probably die as well. But we would endeavor to limit what Buzzy called "the collateral damage," a phrase new to the rest of us.

"A couple of times with de Gaulle," Chuck asked me, "didn't they plant bombs in the street where his car was traveling?"

"Explosives," Buzzy said. "That's where I was headed, too."

I had an idea. I had the perfect idea. "Your *model* airplane, Chuck! You put some kind of bomb inside it and then fly it into him by remote control from far away. That might work, wouldn't it?"

On Washington's Birthday, Buzzy and Chuck returned from a weekend in Wilmette—Chuck's brother Michael's bar mitzvah was the pretext—with Chuck's seven-foot-long silver World War II bomber in the back of Buzzy's station wagon.

The following Saturday we all drove up to New Hampshire, ostensibly to ski but actually to practice flying "the Dauntless," as Chuck called his model plane. Alex had wanted to bring his movie camera and film us, but Buzzy said, "Yeah, why don't we just invite the fucking FBI to watch, too?"

Chuck hadn't flown it in three years, not since he'd started flying for real, and he worried that his new pilot instincts would trip him up. "Because you're not inside of it," he said, "flying the model, it's like you have to switch back and forth between first person and third person all the time."

He'd also never flown it with such a heavy payload. It was packed with ten pounds of Play-Doh—or, as Buzzy said, "five kilos of simulated plastique." It also had a hundred feet of fishing line tied to its nose, with a Ping-Pong ball on the other end.

As soon as it took off, though, Chuck looked to us like a virtuoso as he gently tugged and nudged his two control sticks but kept his eyes on the plane.

Alex complained he was cold, I lit a cigarette, Chuck said something about the rudder and new servos, Buzzy asked about the range of the radio signal and the plane's speed.

"Three hundred, four hundred yards," Chuck said, "and maybe thirty-five knots. Forty miles an hour."

"I know what a knot is, man. In W-W-Two the Dauntless really *was* a dive-bomber, right?"

"Yup."

Buzzy drove his car to the far side of the field, about a hundred yards from us, then walked to a hedgerow a hundred yards from the car and us. He had one of the two-pound walkie-talkies and the field glasses we'd bought at an army-surplus store; I had the other walkie-talkie; and Alex had his fancy graduation-gift binoculars. Buzzy had made us all study a glossary of military talk and insisted, for clarity's sake, that we speak its language on the mission.

"Kilo Hotel, this is Bravo Foxtrot, fack, over."

Karen Hollaender was Kilo Hotel, and Buzzy Freeman was Bravo Foxtrot. "Fack" meant "FAC"—forward air controller.

I answered. "Readable loud and clear, over."

"Kilo Hotel, this is Bravo Foxtrot, fack, over?"

"Push the *button* to talk, Hollaender!" Alex shouted.

"Shit. Bravo Foxtrot, this is Kilo Hotel, you are loud and clear, over."

"Dauntless spotted at a hundred and fifty meters altitude, one hundred meters southwest of me."

"Roger."

A couple of minutes later, Chuck had the plane flying in tight circles high above the car.

"Kilo Hotel, this is Bravo Foxtrot: engage."

"Okay," Chuck said to me, "tell him I'm diving."

"WILCO, Bravo Foxtrot, proceeding with post hole, over."

"Roger, Kilo Hotel."

The plane started spiraling down, directly toward Buzzy's old green station wagon. Its lawn-mower buzz got much louder.

"*Whoa,*" Alex said.

The dangling Ping-Pong ball touched the car, and Buzzy's voice shouted over my radio: "Target *marked,* over!"

The plane came out of its dive. "Roger, affirmative!" I said.

Chuck circled the Dauntless back up into the sky. Buzzy moved the car to a different corner of the field, and we did it again, and again, and again, for hours.

On the last go, the plane came down below the far treetops, and the moment after Alex shouted "*Chuck!*" and Chuck shouted "*Shit!*" at the same time, it pulled out of its dive and zoomed just barely over the trees.

"Delta Hotel," Buzzy shouted, "over!"

"What? I mean, say again?"

"Direct hit! Bravo fucking Zulu, team! Reset to home plate! It's Miller time, over."

After Chuck brought in the plane for its final landing, he turned to me and said, "I guess we're gonna do this." I nodded. But we were playing with a model airplane. It still seemed like a game to me.

"Even if it doesn't, you know, *work*," Alex said, "it'll seriously be bringing the war home. It'll make the news. It'll be cool."

On the ride back to Cambridge, we talked about the possibility of things going awry, how we might escape, how much money we'd need to fly abroad. Chuck joked about "Alex's pal Fidel fixing us up in Havana," but Alex had done research on possible exile locales and decided that Addis Ababa, Ethiopia, was the place to go, if necessary. "It's this really sophisticated city, I mean really *happening*, with cool galleries and clubs, plus perfect weather, and really beautiful people, Christian, not Mohammedan, and," he said, turning to Chuck, "they've even got a lot of Jews." Alex already had a passport, and Buzzy and Chuck and I would all get them. Buzzy said that he'd lost his in the 'Nam.

It still felt a bit like a game when the boys began their daily exercise regimens at the Harvard gym, as it did when we discovered, in a *Washington Star* from the Harvard Square newsstand, that the president's travel and appearance schedules were published every week in advance.

Buzzy and Chuck drove up to a gun store in New Hampshire and used fake IDs with aliases James Bond had used—Peter Franks from *Diamonds Are Forever* and Hilary Bray from *On Her Majesty's Secret Service*—to buy two pistols. The guns, a .32-caliber automatic and a 9mm Luger, looked a lot like the toys we'd used as props on Bond missions.

It was only when Buzzy showed me the two boxes of ammunition they'd also bought in Portsmouth—"a hundred rounds," he said—that our scheme no longer seemed like a game. The plan didn't envision shooting anyone, but Buzzy had insisted on getting "sidearms as a contingency," in case things went bad. "You know the Boy Scout motto," he said. No, we didn't. "'Be *prepared*.' And by the way, not to be paranoid, but here," he said, handing Alex and me each a box of bullets to keep in our dorm rooms. He wanted us "to have some skin in the game"—to be materially, unequivocally bound up in the conspiracy.

Buzzy conscripted all of us as his lab assistants when he mixed the sulfuric acid, hydrogen peroxide, and acetone in their dorm room. Our Benzedrine supply came in handy that week.

We were very, very careful. We had to keep the beaker of acetone peroxide below 50 degrees as the mixture formed crystals, so we took turns, in four-hour shifts from eight A.M. one Saturday until eight A.M. Sunday, replenishing the ice in the ice bath. The second phase of lab work was much simpler, making what Chuck called "the AP putty"—acetone peroxide powder mixed with acetone and smokeless gunpowder (also bought in New Hampshire)—but it required a few days and a dozen sealed jars. Buzzy mixed up the ignition powder that would go in the nose of the Dauntless to ensure that the ten pounds of plastic explosive and buckshot in the fuselage would explode when it dive-bombed and crashed into the president.

Because we discovered that the president's actual appearances didn't always conform to the published schedule, we decided, in Buzzy's phrase, to "stay nimble and opportunistic" and wait for the right moment.

Back in December, before we'd ever thought of Operation Lima Bravo Juliet, Chuck and Buzzy and I had gone down to New York, at Sarah's invitation, to participate in a huge protest outside the army induction center. The day afterward, as it turned out, President Johnson made a surprise appearance at Cardinal Spellman's funeral at St. Patrick's Cathedral, so we were there on Fifth Avenue, carrying signs—mine was VIETNAMESE DON'T DIE PEACEFULLY, Chuck's was HELL NO, Buzzy's was NAPALM: JOHNSON'S BABY POWDER, Sarah's was simply STOP—and chanting "LBJ, LBJ, how many kids did you kill today?" We watched Johnson arrive and leave Manhattan in a helicopter that landed in and took off from Central Park.

When Cardinal Spellman's replacement was announced in early March, I had a brainstorm—I figured Johnson would return to St. Patrick's for the ordination of the new Catholic archbishop as a cardinal, scheduled for the fourth of April, right in the middle of spring break. If Johnson once again took a helicopter in and out of the big

wide-open field in the park, we would have two ideal opportunities to send in our radio-controlled scale-model dive-bomber.

One Friday in the middle of March, Alex flew home for the weekend; Chuck was writing two papers due the following Monday. Buzzy and I had just stayed up for twenty-four hours, making the acetone peroxide, and decided we needed a break. We went into Boston to see Country Joe and the Fish at the Psychedelic Supermarket. It was the first time I'd smoked grass since the fall. At some moment between "Superbird" (*It's a bird, it's a plane / It's a man insane / It's my president, LBJ*) and the "I Feel Like I'm Fixin' to Die Rag" (*Well there ain't no time to wonder why / Whoopee we're all gonna die*), I knew how the night was going to end. A couple of hours later, on my bed in North House, I threw off the shackles of bourgeois individualism and the folly of bourgeois monogamy. I had a box of 9-millimeter rounds at the bottom of my jewelry box, and I'd just helped manufacture ten pounds of plastic explosive intended to kill the president of the United States. In another few weeks I might be in prison or dead. I wasn't sure whether I'd fallen out of love with Chuck Levy, but it seemed stupid at that point to deny my desire for Buzzy Freeman.

The next morning I woke up feeling as if I'd made a quantum leap deeper into adulthood: I was only eighteen, but I was having an *affair,* which made me both happy and sad, as I imagined it was supposed to do. It had also been the most satisfying sexual experience in my nineteen months as a nonvirgin, which accrued to both the happy and sad sides of the ledger as well.

I'd fallen for Buzzy for reasons people are ordinarily smitten. But as I admitted to myself a long time afterward, it was also because, after he brought up the idea of assassinating Johnson and the rest of us went along, he became our alpha male. Being the only female in our pack, I was alpha by default.

I resisted my childish impulse to go to Saint Paul Church to make confession—would even some Harvard Square priest consider "relations" with my boyfriend's roommate any more sinful than "rela-

tions" with my boyfriend?—and stayed in my room studying for the French lit midterm, rereading the passages in Sartre's *Dirty Hands* that I'd underlined. A year ago, the world depicted in the play had seemed as fantastic as Arthur and Merlyn and Guinevere and Lancelot—Communist cells in a fascist country, guns, assassinations, life-and-death deception, lovers' betrayals. Now I was living it. I was Jessica, the cold young wife of the confused young would-be assassin Hugo in the play, treating their assassination plot as a game and cheating on him with their charming, more experienced older comrade.

"It is the *good* children who make the best revolutionaries," Jessica declares. "They say nothing, they don't hide under the table, they eat only one candy at a time—but later on, they make society pay dearly for it."

"An assassin," Hugo observes, "is never *entirely* assassin. They play a *role*, you understand."

My phone rang sometime after lunch. It was Alex, excited, calling to tell me he'd just seen a special report on TV—Bobby Kennedy had announced that he was running against Johnson for the nomination. When the four of us met up after dinner for ice cream at Brigham's, I was glad we had an urgent new discussion topic that might prevent Buzzy's and my sexual electricity and lies and guilt from coalescing into some unmistakable, undeniable telltale form, like a freakish thundercloud issuing lightning bolts. We decided over hot fudge sundaes that the news of the day had not changed our plans. Lima Bravo Juliet was still a go—now more than ever, since removing Johnson from the equation would immeasurably improve Kennedy's chances of becoming president and ending the war.

I didn't know if Buzzy and I would continue our affair. "You know," he had said before he left my room, "*Jules and Jim* doesn't have a happy ending." But later that week, as I walked out of an afternoon class, there was Buzzy, who admitted when I asked that he hadn't just happened to be passing by, which made me melt. I suggested we go to a movie, any new movie at all. In the theater, I came

closer than I ever have in my life to having sex in front of other people. It was also the first time I laughed in the middle of making out—when, up on the screen, Charlton Heston shouted, "Take your stinking paws off me, you damn dirty *ape!*"—and the first time I'd really laughed in months.

After the movie Buzzy went to the gym and I went to Chuck and Buzzy's dorm room. Chuck seemed even more grim and keyed up than usual. I saw a patch of white dust on the bedside table. Lately, he'd taken to crushing and snorting Benzedrine. He was rereading the title story in *For Your Eyes Only,* one of his Bond books that he'd brought back from Wilmette a month earlier, and before I sat down, he picked up the book to read aloud a passage where Bond is about to assassinate a Nazi war criminal in America with a sniper rifle. "'Tension was building up in him. In his imagination he could already hear the deep bark of the Savage.' The gun store in Portsmouth had a Savage for sale," Chuck told me without looking up, "just like this one in the book."

I hadn't sat down, and he continued reading. "'He could see the black bullet lazily, like a slow flying bee, homing down into the valley towards a square of pink skin. There was a light smack as it hit. The skin dented, broke and then closed up again leaving a small hole with bruised edges. The bullet ploughed on—'"

"Stop," I told him.

He paused for barely a second. "'The bullet ploughed on, unhurriedly, toward the pulsing heart—the tissues, the blood-vessels, parting obediently to let it through. Who was this man he was going to do this to? What had he ever done to Bond?'"

He closed the book and looked at me. I didn't know what he expected me to say. I wasn't in the mood to discuss morality again or to do another "gut check" of our commitment to going through with the attack. "I'm going to the library to work on my folklore paper," I told him. In honor of April Fool's Day, the teacher had assigned us to write five pages on a trickster figure. I'd chosen Loki, who killed a Norse god with a magic arrow, thus provoking Götterdämmerung, in which the world is destroyed and reborn.

During March, Buzzy and I had two more full-on trysts—a word
I'd only just learned, along with "assignation." I didn't think I loved
him, and not just because in 1968 "love" had come to seem school-
girlish, old-fashioned, irrelevant. The disconnection of sex from the
pretense of love made it seem more adult—hot and crazy instead of
warm and cozy.

We'd all worn gloves and used rubbing alcohol to wipe our fingerprints from every inch of the Dauntless, inside and out, as well as
the radio control unit. We'd very carefully wrapped the ten pounds
of AP putty in several old sweatshirts and sweaters and inside a
backpack.

On Saturday, the thirtieth of March, the first day of spring break,
we all headed south.

Buzzy said that OP-SEC—operational security—required us to
travel in pairs, in order to be less conspicuous. Chuck and Buzzy left
for Washington in the Plymouth wagon with the plane and the
bomb and one of the guns. Alex and I were more familiar with New
York City, so the two of us took the train there. The plan was for
each pair to spend the weekend lurping—"LRRP" stood for "long-
range reconnaissance patrol." In D.C., Chuck and Buzzy would get
a firsthand fix on the security around the president. In Manhattan,
Alex and I would familiarize ourselves with Central Park, pace off
distances, check out getaway routes, test the range of the walkie-
talkies in midtown. On Monday the first of April, Chuck and Buzzy
would drive up to New York, and we'd rendezvous for the possible
operation on Thursday the fourth. If the opportunity didn't present
itself—if Johnson didn't come to New York for Cardinal Cooke's
ordination at St. Patrick's, if he didn't take his helicopter in and out
of Central Park this time, if something didn't seem right—it would
be a rehearsal, and we'd pack up, rethink, and wait for our next
chance.

"Don't I know you?" the clerk said to me with a smile as we checked
in to the hotel. "Weren't you here last year?"

I was shocked that he remembered me from when Chuck and I had stayed there seven months earlier, and shocked that a Times Square hotel clerk would be so indiscreet. And terrified that we'd already made the amateur-outlaw mistake that would get us busted. I forced a cheerful smile—

"Wow, good memory! Yeah."

—but on Sunday morning Alex and I moved to a different Times Square hotel and called the Washington YMCA to leave a message for Chuck and Buzzy about our new location.

We went to St. Patrick's—not for Mass but to time the walk from the cathedral to the right spot in the park (nineteen minutes). Then we timed the walk around the perimeter of the Sheep Meadow (twenty-two minutes).

As we'd reckoned from the map we studied in Cambridge, the Sheep Meadow was just big enough: with Chuck and me in the trees at the western edge, the Dauntless would be within transmission range no matter where the president's helicopter landed. The walkie-talkies worked perfectly. I would operate one of them alongside Chuck and his transmitter; Buzzy would have the other walkie-talkie as the spotter—the forward air controller—on the eastern edge; and Alex would be in Buzzy's car on Central Park West as our driver.

We examined the parking spots and signs on Central Park West. We took a taxi from West Sixty-sixth down to the brand-new Penn Station to time the getaway—seven minutes, but the traffic would be much thicker on a weekday. Particularly if a guided missile had just struck the president of the United States in Central Park.

"You know," Alex whispered as we took the subway the rest of the way downtown, "it's amazing that I can, you know, be carrying *this*"—he patted his peacoat—"and no one has any idea. Not who we really are, not what we're really doing." In his right pocket were the unfired .32-caliber pistol and a box of fifty bullets.

Walking through the neighborhood around City Hall, we saw no one but a pair of cops. At the Manhattan School of Firearms, Alex told the guy in charge, unnecessarily, that he dreamed of becoming

a pentathlete, that he'd mastered fencing and equestrian jumping but needed to learn to shoot.

We each fired eight rounds. Neither of us had ever fired a gun, and we were surprised by how slight the recoil was. It turned out I was a much better shot than Alex. I got three bull's-eyes.

While Alex went to the matinee of *Hair,* I returned to our hotel room and read the papers. In the *Daily News,* a columnist had written that he had it "on *excellent* authority that LBJ *will* be at St. Pat's Thursday for Cooke's installation as archbishop."

It was happening, like in a script. And I would play my part.

Because it was Sunday, I phoned the parents, as usual. I worried that they'd be able to tell from the honks and sirens that I was in a Times Square hotel rather than a Radcliffe dorm. But no. My mother asked how Chuck and I were spending spring break, and I said he'd gone down to Washington. She'd been scandalized to read, she told me, that during President Johnson's visit to the Vatican, Pope Paul had given him a gift of a Renaissance painting and the president had given the Holy Father a little plastic LBJ bust in return. "He's a jerk," I said.

Right after I hung up, the front desk phoned to tell us a long-distance call had come in while I was on the phone—a "Mr. Leiter" from Washington, D.C. I waited in the lobby for Alex, and when he appeared, we went out to a phone booth on Eighth Avenue to dial the number of the phone booth in Washington.

Alex talked first, telling them that our recon had been successful and that they wouldn't have liked *Hair.* He handed the phone to me.

"Driving down here for ten hours made me really anxious," Buzzy said.

It had made me really anxious, too. I worried that with the two of them alone so long, he might wind up telling Chuck that we'd had sex. Also, they were carrying ten pounds of plastic explosive in the backseat.

"Even with the ordnance wrapped up," Buzzy said, "if we got in a wreck, it'd be all over."

Then Chuck got on. He sounded strangely calm. That made me

anxious. Was he overcompensating, dealing with his discovery of my infidelity by acting nonchalant? He said that morning they'd walked to a Catholic church where they'd watched the president and Lady Bird and their daughter Luci and Luci's husband go to Mass. "Some woman told us Luci converted to Catholicism when she was our age. I didn't know that."

"Me, neither. Weird."

"The son-in-law, the marine, shipped out for Vietnam last night, the woman said."

I didn't like this fact. I wanted it to make me feel that Johnson was an unfeeling ogre, sacrificing even his own daughter's new husband, but it threatened to make me feel sorry for him, as if he were some king in an ancient Greek tragedy.

After scoping out the first family at church, Chuck and Buzzy had walked two miles to the White House, arriving around noon, as the president and his family returned from church.

"I was standing near a Secret Service guy," Chuck told me, "and heard a voice come over his walkie-talkie: 'Volunteer, Victoria and Venus in stagecoach on Pennsylvania crossing Fourteenth, over.' Buzzy says those must be their code names—Johnson is 'Volunteer,' and they call his limousine 'stagecoach.' A second later, there was the motorcade right *there*, zooming past us."

"Motorcade" startled me. All of us had learned the word at the same moment, four and a half years earlier, in the news reports from Dallas.

"And in the car following his limousine, I saw a guy in the back-seat facing backward, holding a rifle. It was all real . . ."

"What? Real what?"

"I mean it just made everything seem really *real*, you know? I love you, Karen."

Before I could answer, I heard Buzzy say something in the background.

"Buzzy says let's meet tomorrow in New York at six instead of five at—"

I heard Buzzy say something else, more emphatically.

"*Okay*—we'll *rendezvous*," Chuck repeated, "at *eighteen hundred hours*. In front of the hotel."

Alex and I bought Orange Juliuses and coffee and went back up to our room. We were going to watch *The Smothers Brothers*, then head downtown and meet Sarah in the Village for a late pizza.

But the TV show was being preempted for a speech by the president from the Oval Office.

There he was, *live*.

"Tonight I want to speak to you of peace in Vietnam and Southeast Asia," he began, and then a few minutes in, he got to his big announcement: "unilaterally, and at once," he was ordering an end to the bombing and shelling of North Vietnam, "in the hope that this action will lead to early talks."

"Wow," Alex said. "He's really going for peace talks."

But then Johnson dialed back his peace initiative—fighting would continue all over the South, and bombing and shelling would continue in the North near the DMZ. By the way, he was going to send over an additional thirteen thousand U.S. troops.

"Yeah," I said. "Sure sounds like peace to me. This is such utter bullshit."

"I would ask all Americans, whatever their personal interests or concern, to guard against divisiveness and all its ugly consequences."

"'Ugly consequences,'" I said to the TV. "He is such a hypocritical fucker. Isn't he?"

Alex nodded, but he hadn't said much.

Johnson changed the subject to economics, and I would've changed the channel if he hadn't been on every channel. We sucked on our giant drinks as we watched. I found a piece of eggshell in mine and spit it out. Near the end of the speech, the president returned to the subject of Vietnam.

"I do not believe," he said, "that I should devote an hour or a day of my time to any personal partisan causes or to any duties other than the awesome duties of this office . . ."

I shook my head. "Yeah, it's a really awesome duty to have to kill hundreds of people every hour of every—"

"Shhh!"

"Accordingly, I shall not seek, and I will not accept, the nomination of my party for another term as your president."

Alex stood up. "Wow, wow, wow," he said. "Jesus."

"Thank you for listening. Good night, and God bless all of you."

Neither of us spoke for a long time. Finally, Alex said, "Well . . . that's it."

"What do you mean?"

I knew what he meant.

He was suddenly full of energy, bouncing around the room. He turned off the TV and opened a new pack of cigarettes and turned on the radio—a Bob Dylan song was playing, the *fun* Dylan, "Rainy Day Women," and Alex sang along.

We didn't have much of a discussion. We sat and listened to Dylan, and then the Monkees ("Daydream Believer") and Otis Redding ("Sittin' on the Dock of the Bay") and the Beatles ("Hello Goodbye"), drinking coffee and chain-smoking, thinking and staring.

It took me a half hour to admit to myself that the game was over.

We were not going through with Operation Lima Bravo Juliet.

We were not going to assassinate a president who was now making the first serious effort since the war had begun to end it, and who would be out of office in months, possibly replaced by a president who would withdraw from Vietnam immediately.

We were not insane.

I thought of Tiger Tanaka, the Japanese intelligence director in *You Only Live Twice,* who trained as a kamikaze pilot but survived because World War II ended days before he could go on his mission.

When the Beatles finished their song about lovers fallen out of sync—"You say yes, I say no / You say stop and I say go, go, go"— I was no longer thinking mainly about the war, or presidential politics, or all the careful plans and dangerous preparations we'd made. I was thinking that if I hadn't stepped up to the edge of this abyss, hadn't given myself over to the glamour of heroic gloom, I wouldn't have cheated on Chuck. As I sat on the floor in a Times Square hotel

room, like the one where Chuck and I had spent an ecstatically perfect week a half year earlier, I felt myself turning back into an ordinary girl, a college freshman in her bell-bottomed blue jeans and purple polo-neck ribbed cotton jersey sweater. I was Alice abruptly shoved back through the looking-glass to the ordinary world, Dorothy returned at supersonic speed from Oz to Kansas. The net result of my strange adventure was a frivolous act of betrayal of my first love.

We called the pay phone at the YMCA in Washington, but there was no answer. Surely they'd call us.

"I don't mean to sound silly," Alex offered, "but it's the thought that counts. We were *ready* to do it."

We had been. Hadn't we? Until only a couple of hours before? Now it seemed no different than the nine Bond missions that had preceded it, a piece of improvised fiction, an elaborate make-believe stunt, kids playing grown-ups, the scariest game of chicken ever. At the terrifying last second before the runaway car sped over the cliff, we were jumping out.

It was a nice night, clear and around sixty, and when we got off the subway and walked through Washington Square and the NYU campus, it was like stepping into a giant party. Kids and adults were blasting rock and roll and Mozart from their rooms and apartments, opening windows, spilling outside, playing conga drums, sharing their joy and incredulity with friends and strangers, hugging, drinking, cheering, chanting "Peace *now*," singing "We *have* overcome."

I couldn't resist. I was happy, too. And relieved, so relieved that we didn't have to go through with the murder—*murders*, no doubt— that we'd spent the two months between Groundhog Day and April Fool's preparing to commit.

"We *did* it, Karen," Sarah said when I got to her dorm, where three dozen excited students were milling in the lobby, chattering up a storm, drinking beer. "The fucking system *works*." PEACE was spelled out in empty bottles on the floor, and somebody had tacked up posters of Gene McCarthy and Bobby Kennedy on the walls. She said, "It's like a *miracle*, right?"

As Alex and I were returning to Times Square that night, we saw

a dozen elephants walking down the street, and behind them a gorilla and chimpanzees and tigers in cages. The Ringling Bros. and Barnum & Bailey Circus had just arrived on the train from Washington, D.C., and was marching toward Madison Square Garden. When we got back to the hotel, there was no message from the boys in D.C. They were probably out celebrating.

The next morning when I woke up, Alex wasn't in our room. I took my paperback of *Cat's Cradle* and walked out to read on a bench in the middle of Broadway. It started drizzling, but I kept reading. After a while, Alex appeared.

"Crikey, Hollaender, you're piss-wet!"

"Where'd *you* go?"

"Oh, I, you know, woke up early and popped out, ran errands. Did Chuck and Buzzy call?"

I shook my head.

"They might've rung while you were out here," he said. "They'll ring."

We had breakfast at Howard Johnson's. Alex was delighted that we'd aborted the mission, said he'd "realized it would probably be terrible for the Movement if we'd gone through with it, given this new situation." He was reanimated, his old self, commenting sotto voce on our fellow diners ("Check out the *enormous* bum on the pigtailed chick") and suggesting that we stay in New York for a few days anyway, all four of us, and have a real spring break.

"We've got the rooms booked. And at the theater where I saw *Hair*? There's a new play Darko told me about that spoofs Esperanto, by this Czech playwright, Havel. And through WMAQ, my dad could get us tickets to Johnny Carson, to be in the studio audience. Maybe I could also do my interview at Warhol's." He had applied to be a summer intern at the Factory, Andy Warhol's studio. "And there's a big Dada and surrealism show I *really* want to see at the Modern."

He was kind of manic. I was not yet prepared to have fun. "Yeah, you mentioned the art show. You said you thought we could fit it in before Lima Bravo Juliet."

"Come *on*—what happened last night threw a giant spanner into the works, but it's not like it's a *bummer,* you know? It's a *happy* ending! All's well that ends well! And at the Whitney, there's a show by this guy who makes these absolutely plain metal boxes, like dresser drawers—like, if *that's* art? *I* could be an artist."

"I think I just want to go back to Cambridge."

"Hollaender, you don't need to be all . . . stroppy."

I hadn't noticed until then that for the last couple of months, Alex had stopped trying to sound like a British person—no "pop out," no "ring us," no "enormous bum," no "rooms booked," no "stroppy." He had been Gravely Serious Alex. Now he was Blithe Cosmopolitan Alex again. He had stepped back into character. Or stepped out of his temporary character.

"Sorry," I said. "What errands did you do this morning?"

"What?" He dug into his pack for a cigarette.

"Why did you go out?"

"Oh, right, I had to make a phone call."

"From a pay phone?"

"I didn't want to wake you."

"Who?"

"What?"

"A phone call to who?"

"Oh—my fine-arts section leader. He's in Paris for spring break, so I had to ring before it got too late there. To, you know, discuss a paper I'm writing. That I plan to write."

"Fine Arts 13 has papers?"

"No, but that's why I needed to talk to him. It'd be, you know, for extra credit."

"On what? The paper."

"Aren't you a nosy parker? It's about Duchamp."

I didn't know who Duchamp was. But as when Buzzy had interrogated Alex during reading period about his "family friend" in Switzerland, I was sure I'd caught him in another lie, that he was covering up some secret New York sexual assignation. Who was I to press that point? After breakfast, Alex said he was going to the Mu-

seum of Modern Art to see the Dada show and that he'd meet me at noon in Central Park across from Rumpelmayer's, a restaurant he'd loved on family visits when he was little—his treat.

When I got back to the hotel, there was a phone message with no name, just a number with a 202 area code and the notation *ASAP*. I didn't bother walking out to a pay phone. Security was no longer an issue. The plot was finished.

The man who answered identified himself as a Penn Central Railroad assistant manager. He put Buzzy on.

"Chuck's gone loco. After the thing last night on TV, he's more gung ho than ever, the war's not over, I'm a hypocrite and a pussy if I'm going to back out now. We have this knock-down, drag-out, huge fight, and he walks off, just splits. He shows up back at the Y around three this morning, wakes me up, and—I assume you guys agree, right, we're *done*, the whole . . . the thing is moot, right, because—"

"*Yes.*"

"Good. Good. Because I fibbed and told him I'd talked to both of you last night and that the three of us completely agree. And he just . . . freaks out. He starts yelling and punching me, and then some YMCA guy shows up, and Chuck insists on getting his own room. And then this morning he's gone. Disappeared." Buzzy's voice became a muffled whisper: "He left a note: 'The worse the better' and 'Tell Jessica that Hugo still loves her.' I get the first"—it was a Bolshevik saying from before the Russian Revolution—"but who are Jessica and Hugo?"

"Nobody. Fictional characters. I'll tell you later."

"He took everything."

"Your car?"

"Everything. You know? *Everything.*" He paused to make sure I understood his meaning.

I felt as if I were floating, literally, physically, sickeningly, like on a roller coaster plummeting downhill.

"All I had is the twenty bucks in my billfold, which is barely enough to get me back to Cambridge. Which is why this very nice

gentleman is letting me use the phone in his office. The fucking pay phones here—oh, sorry, sir—the phones at the station don't accept incoming long-distance, and the Boston train leaves in, crap, six minutes."

"Jesus," I asked, "where *is* he? What's—what's he going to do?"

"Can't really talk now."

"I'm coming down there. Alex and I will catch the next train."

"That's stupid, Karen. That makes no sense. In fact, you know, it's probably . . . you know . . ."

"Dangerous?"

"Exactly."

"Did you try looking for him?"

"Look *where?* He could be anywhere. Doing . . . *whatever.* D.C. is bigger than Boston, and I don't know my way around."

Oh, *Christ.* "Buzzy, did you tell him? About us?"

"I'm afraid so. Yeah. This morning. Although he was kind of grokking it on his own, too. I'll explain. Gotta go."

Oh, God, oh fuck, oh fuck, oh shit.

I smoked a cigarette.

Jesus Christ.

I'd never felt more fond of Buzzy, and I realized, as I rushed out of the hotel and headed for the museum to find Alex, one of the reasons why: during our phone conversation, he had not once used any of his ridiculous military slang, no "Lima Bravo Juliet," no "AWOL," no "ABORT," no "zero-700 hours." He wasn't playing a role. He was being a normal person.

I was panicky, and being in New York amped up the panic. After two years of self-indoctrination and three months in our Harvard Yard militant hothouse, the four of us had made a mad leap of faith hand in hand—but at the last second, one of us couldn't manage the midair twist and leap back.

Alex and Buzzy and I had let rationality reassert itself, but Chuck—earnest Chuck, realistic Chuck, irresolute Chuck, cuckolded Chuck, three-against-one Chuck, Chuck now all alone—was going for broke.

I thought of the times I'd called him a wishy-washy liberal, the times I didn't rise up in defense when Buzzy and Alex called him Hamlet. He was going to prove *he* was the stalwart one, tougher than a Vietnam vet, the true hero among us all. Hamlet? Hamlet finally *acts* by embarking on a righteous killing spree.

In twenty-four hours, I had gone from feverish tunnel-vision commitment to miraculous release from the delirium at the eleventh hour to . . . chaos, life out of control, my fortunes tied to a betrayed and berserk runaway boy.

He was alone in Washington, D.C., wandering with a pistol, fifty rounds of ammunition, ten pounds of explosive putty, a couple of hundred dollars, a hundred Benzedrine tablets, and a 1956 Plymouth station wagon. And the giant radio-controlled model airplane he'd built by hand with his dad when he was eleven years old.

I was terrified of what he might do and terrified of what might happen to me. He was on his own, but we would be liable. For two months I had swatted away the obvious, bothersome possibility that my life was about to be ruined because of the choice I'd made, but on the afternoon of April 1, I couldn't stop thinking that my life was about to be ruined despite the sensible new choice I'd made the night before. My ruination, if it came, would be the result of another irrevocable choice—the emotional decision I'd made after making the rational decision to kill Lyndon Johnson and before the rational decision that assassinating him no longer made sense. I was paying the price for deciding I might as well fuck Buzzy Freeman.

I ran most of the way to the museum. I waited almost an hour, until twelve-thirty, but Alex never came out, so I headed up Sixth Avenue toward Central Park to our appointed meeting place.

He said the line at the Dada show had been too long, so he "went for a stroll, window-shopping, people-watching."

I practically shouted the news—that Chuck was determined to go through with it, had taken the pistol and speed and money and car and bomb and set out on his own, and Buzzy had no idea where he was. Alex said I sounded hysterical and suggested I was hypoglycemic or going through Benzedrine withdrawal. I was hysterical.

"Okay, *yes*," Alex said, "this thing has gone *completely* pear-shaped. But he'll spend a day or two sulking alone and figure out what makes sense and get a grip. Flying the Dauntless by himself and then getting away? I don't think so. I mean, Karen, come on, Chuck isn't a *nutter*."

"He's got the explosive. He's got the gun. It sounds like he may not be thinking about getting away. Remember, at the beginning, he was the one who said, 'We could do it close up.' "

"Yeah, but we were brainstorming. He didn't want to go kamikaze. Remember? We quoted Churchill, and he agreed."

The Churchill quote had come up when we were hatching the plan—Buzzy had said " 'Although always prepared for martyrdom,' " and Alex finished the sentence with him: " 'I prefer that it should be postponed.' "

"That was two months ago," I said. "A lot's happened since then. Once we made the putty and bought the pistols—"

"*They* bought the pistols."

"—I think Chuck sort of started, you know, tripping on violence."

"Ours is now *gone,* by the way, the pistol," Alex said, "along with the bullets. Down a sewer."

"He used to play with the Luger sometimes, he'd look at himself in the mirror holding it. And one night a month ago, he asked if I'd ever believed in an afterlife, and when I said yeah, until I was eleven I thought I was going to heaven, he told me he'd never believed any of it—that Jews don't. I said, 'Another reason to like Jewish people. They're rational.' He said his dad says that's why Jews are so neurotic, because they know *this, life,* is it. 'No do-overs.' But Chuck said now he realized the flip side of that—he said, 'I don't have to worry about dying because I don't have to worry about going to hell.' "

"He'll ring. We can talk him off the ledge. Take a deep breath. Sit down."

I took a breath, and then another, and we sat on a bench. "Buzzy told him we slept together. Buzzy and I. We did. We are. We have been."

"*What?* Oh my *God,* Hollaender! I *knew* it. I mean, I didn't actu-

ally know it, but I'm not surprised." With the slightest smile, he leaned back and looked me over and shook his head, not so much in disapproval, I thought, but interestedly, maybe enviously. "Very déjà vu, Hollaender."

I had no idea what he meant.

"'Oh, my *goodness,*'" he cooed in a high-pitched voice meant to be mine, "'what can you *possibly* be talking about?' *Last* spring, when you and Chuck started your shagging and kept it secret from me. Now I get why he's so freaked out. He feels betrayed. By you two."

I wanted to curse Alex, slap him. But he was right. So I resorted to the tactic we, especially he, used when we were little—*I know you are, but what am I?* "Keeping secrets from your best friends, huh? Secret sex, huh? Like you and your secret rendezvous, your 'friend' in Yugoslavia and your 'friend' in Switzerland and calling your teacher and 'window-shopping' this morning. Give me a break."

"No—you don't have any idea what you're talking about. *No* idea."

I already regretted my bitch gambit. Alex's private life was none of my business. And arguing about sex and lies was a stupid digression. We had to figure out some way to stop Chuck from killing people and destroying himself and wrecking our lives.

"I'm sorry," I said. "Maybe I should drink a pop."

He bought me a Coke from a hot-dog cart, and after a few minutes I felt better, my anger gone, my panic and regret still intense but proportionate, no longer spiraling down into some hypoglycemic pit. I cried, and Alex got me a napkin so I could blow my nose.

We talked about going to the authorities, turning Chuck in, but apart from the ethics of squealing, the chances of that ending badly seemed high. Besides, then we would be implicated.

Alex said Chuck was not the sort to try to kill us—which hadn't even occurred to me—because if he did make some final grand gesture, he would want us to feel one-upped and admiring and guilty, to understand that he was nobler and braver than any of us, a bold maker of history.

Surely he would call or just drive back to Cambridge alone, and when he heard our voices and felt my love, we could, Alex said and I hopefully half-believed, reel him back in. Except, I didn't say, I wasn't sure I still loved him, and maybe he would hear and see and feel *that,* and then what?

"Come on," he said, "it's just *Chuck.*"

We walked down Sixth Avenue, and Alex said he was going to the Dada show now, but I begged off. As I zigzagged west and south into Times Square toward our hotel, I wasn't certain I was going to stop at a pay phone until I did.

As I dialed Washington directory assistance, and then after I asked for the number and waited for the operator to come back, I kept my index finger—"your trigger finger," Buzzy had called it a month ago—on the phone lever, ready to end the call.

As I was dialing the eleven digits and even after I deposited my quarters, I thought I might hang up and keep walking. I thought so even after the switchboard operator answered and started putting me through.

But when the second voice came on the line—"Good afternoon, United States Secret Service, Special Agent Hardison, how can I help you?"—I did not hang up.

27

I KNOW I'VE REACHED the practical end of my working day because I'm checking email every ten minutes, and I just spent an hour Googling the assassination of Reinhard Heydrich by the heroic Levy family friends of friends. The assassination so upset Hitler, I learned, that the Nazis immediately murdered a thousand Czech civilians in retribution, and named the extermination-camp phase of the final solution in his honor, "Aktion Reinhardt." Which makes me think of all the conversations Chuck and I had about unintended consequences.

I check my email again and see a new one, from the FBI. Did I give them my email address when I submitted my Freedom of Information request?

It's from the Anti-Terrorist and Monetary Crimes Division, J. Edgar Hoover Building, 935 Pennsylvania Avenue, Washington, D.C.

Oh, Jesus.

You have just 72 hours to prove to us you are not a terrorist. Failure to comply with our instruction, you will be arrested and detained until this matter is settled.

Fortunately, the second paragraph informs me that *the sum of $10.5 million United States dollars were transferred to the Bank of America here in the United States, bearing your name as the beneficiary, from the Central Bank of Nigeria.*

Ah, Nigeria.

We did not believe this at first until we saw the transfer. Note that we have done a proper investigation on this transaction and from our investigation, this funds truly belongs to you and it is not a scam, but we have instructed the Bank of America not to release the $10.5 million to you until you prove the legitimacy of the funds you are about to receive.

We have your full contact address, which makes it easier for us to arrest you when ever we want to. As a matter of fact, you will be charged for money laundering as well as terrorism if you fail to prove to us that you are not a terrorist or a money launderer by obtaining the above mentioned certificate from the funds originated country, and if you are found guilty as charged, you will go to jail. Therefore you have been advised to get back to us immediately you receive this email or you will be arrested by the FBI. YOU HAVE BEEN WARNED.

Appealing to fear as well as greed seems like a brilliant scam-email innovation. However, you'd think that among the eight million people in Lagos, they could find an editor who might nudge the language of their fiction closer to plausibility. Good concept, but execution is everything.

Waverly calls. She's finished reading the previous chapter. "Were you really willing to go to jail or die?"

"It's hard to know for sure. It's hard to remember exactly what you were thinking so many years ago, at that age, in those strange times. But yeah, I think I thought I was willing."

"Did you *want* to die? Was it like a suicidal feeling?"

"No." I think for a second. "Although the line between a willingness to sacrifice yourself and a desire to do so can get pretty thin."

"But you really would've gone through with it if he hadn't stepped down, the president?"

"Again, I can't be absolutely sure. I think yes. Although since the CIA apparently knew what we were up to, thanks to Alex, I'm sure they would've come in or told the Secret Service to pick us up."

"Sophie thinks somebody in Miami snitched on her, told the cops about her fake dynamite. She thinks maybe it was that Dartmouth kid she hooked up with."

Sitting alone on my patio this Friday of Memorial Day weekend, relishing the L.A. weather, reading the new paperback of Daniel Moynihan's correspondence, I marvel at how wise and grown up Moynihan was, how he managed to take the long view in the late 1960s when almost nobody else did, to see each frantic flibbertigibbet twist and turn as a curious moment in the continuum of history. And I think of that rainy night in the fall of 1967 when a high-strung Radcliffe freshman made the forty-year-old professor smile, almost, in the Kirkland House junior common room by suggesting that Lyndon Johnson shouldn't be allowed to campaign for reelection. "In a sense," I read now in Moynihan's memo to President-elect Richard Nixon from a year later, Johnson "was the first American President to be toppled by a mob. No matter that it was a mob of college professors, millionaires, flower children, and Radcliffe girls." I don't smile, but I sigh and sip my seltzer. I sigh a lot these days.

Buzzy did not leave a suicide note because, as *The Washington Post* definitively reported today, he had staged his death to look like an assassination by an al Qaeda killer. When he was in Chicago giving a speech in April—six weeks after I told him about this book—he had paid a Yemeni taxi driver twenty dollars to write SERVING JUSTICE TO THE ZIONIST REGIME AND HER WASHINGTON MASTERS in Arabic on the back of a menu from a D.C. hookah bar. The evening of his death, with Mrs. Freeman in Maryland on a Presbyterian overnight retreat, he used a brand-new Home Depot crowbar to jimmy open the locked front door of his house, went on his regular evening jog through the park, stopped at a reservoir and tossed in the crowbar, returned home, stuck the fake jihadist message with a letter opener to the wood paneling in his den, sat down in his desk chair, tied his hands and ankles with Home Depot bungee cord, and

pulled the pin from a Swiss-made hand grenade. The authorities believe he acquired the grenade during a visit to El Paso. "Although Freeman had grown increasingly alarmed about what he termed 'the free world's delegitimization and betrayal of Israel,'" according to the article, "family members and colleagues said he was proud of the book he had recently completed, and that they know of no illness or other motive for suicide."

His death saddens me—the fact of it, the blame I bear for it, his deception, the failure of his deception. And I feel horrible that I feel fortunate that he left no suicide note. His deceit has made my life more convenient. He hasn't broken the embargo on my book before it's finished.

The *Post*'s headline calls the suicide a "mystery," as do two people quoted in the article, a former senior administration official friendly with Freeman and Buzzy's head of PR. "'God only knows why he took his life,' said the spokesperson for Freeman's Civilization Group, 'and that mystery will be an unknowable mystery forever. But the legacy of Buzzy's heroic lifetime of work on behalf of freedom and justice remain unambiguous and untarnished for all time.'"

There's a wishful null set for you: *legacy . . . unambiguous and untarnished for all time.*

I know why he killed himself. He didn't want to be around when the world learns that, as a young man, he instigated a conspiracy to assassinate the president of the United States.

There are nevertheless at least two small unknowable mysteries. Buzzy's faux-martyrdom was driven by vanity and politics and maybe kindness toward his family, yet I wonder if he also thought that by making it look like murder instead of suicide, he was doing me one last favor, trying to prevent me from feeling responsible for his death. I also wonder if he instructed his Arab scrivener to write "her" instead of "its" as a bit of faked illiteracy, to make it seem more authentic.

"You got to hand it to him. Going to all the trouble of acquiring a late-model HG 85 from a Mexican narco instead of just picking

up some army-surplus Vietnam-era piece of shit at a gun show in Virginia. For an amateur, that's an admirable commitment to tradecraft."

"Hello, Stewart."

He has called my third disposable cellphone for the first time. I'd found it hard to throw the perfectly good ones in the trash, although that's what you're supposed to do with burners. I play by the rules. I assume correctly that Stewart is praising Buzzy's choice of hand grenade.

"If the broad at Dalecarlia Reservoir," he continues, "hadn't seen him toss the crowbar, I think he would've gotten away with it, gone down as the first victim of homeland terrorism in 2014. And don't you love *why* she called the cops?"

"Stewart, I am really not into joking around about Buzzy Freeman's suicide."

"I know, I know, but seriously—because she saw him praying and he had a beard, she thought he was an Islamic terrorist tossing poison into D.C.'s water supply? I mean, whoa, you really can't make that shit up. Oh, and speaking of calling a suicide a homicide, another thing? That nobody's mentioned?"

"Stop. Come on. Please."

"Remember right after 9/11, when FOX News and the White House tried to get everyone to call suicide bombers '*homicide* bombers'? You know whose bright idea and personal mission that was? Your boy Buzzy."

I didn't know that. "This is why you called?"

"Uh-uh. His archival life has suddenly become more, as they say, transparent. Spectacular death tends to do that to privacy scruples. I can now tell you with almost a hundred percent confidence that during the 1960s, except for his sweet two years of service in the U.S. Coast Guard getting high and tending the lighthouse in Mendocino, Bernard L. Freeman had no direct contact whatsoever with any government agency concerning your un-American activities. He wasn't one of your snitches."

"Okay. Good."

"Unlike you."

Stewart knows I called the Secret Service. "How long have you *known*? About me?"

"Known for sure? Mmm, let's see, about . . . four, five seconds now. When you and I first discussed this, you said you'd FOIAd Homeland Security, which I figured had to mean Secret Squirrel. And I told you early on that somebody dropped the dime on Levy to Secret Squirrel headquarters in 1968. Then after I voice-stressed you in April, I had a fairly good idea that somebody was you."

"But you told me your machine said I was telling the truth. You lied?"

He chuckles. "I didn't lie. About your lie to me. I was economical with the truth. There wasn't any stress showing when you said you had no 'ongoing relationship' with any agency. *Before* that, though, when I asked if you'd 'cooperated' with any agency? Your voice-gram was like a fucking postcard from Yosemite, this nice big El Capitan. I busted you accidentally. You'd be surprised how often the game gets played that way. Part of the fun of it, really."

"Ah, the ninja jester."

Not long after we first met, when Stewart told me about a shocking, funny secret deal he'd brokered years before to get *Sesame Street* on TV in the Persian Gulf by arranging for the sale of advanced weapons to Arab governments, I told him I'd never imagined the same person could be a ninja and a jester. He'd said, "Well, they were both medieval and both employees of the regime—and besides, what about the Joker in *Batman*?"

He asks me about Greta and Waverly, and I tell him I'm sorry to hear his father died.

"Hey, I'll be in L.A. again, next month, on my way out to Seoul. Want to hook up?"

"Sure. But people our age should not say 'hook up.' What're you doing here this time—more super-duper unmanned aerial vehicles?"

He laughs. "I'm not your age. Yeah, an unmanned aircraft system incorporating surf and turf. Big system-integration show. The navy's got this new electric gun up the coast, fires these giant rounds

with no propellant or powder at Mach fucking ten. From Malibu they could push a button and destroy your house twenty seconds later."

"Nice to know."

"Don't be so un-American. The idea's for the UAV flying out over the desert, eight miles high, picking targets for the electric gun, and *simultaneously* finding buried bombs, IEDs, that this new gadget, this all-terrain robot laser, can go fry. Multitasking—same platform protecting the good guys at the same time it's dealing with the bad guys."

I don't mention to Stewart that our 1968 plan to deal with our bad guy involved a small UAV that we'd turned into an improvised explosive device. I don't tell him that we mixed up a big batch of acetone peroxide in a dorm room—the same explosive, I recently learned, used by the failed al Qaeda shoe bomber in 2001 and the failed al Qaeda underwear bomber in 2009, and in the successful bombings of the London Underground in 2005 and the Boca Raton yacht in 2013.

Stewart is joshing when he calls me "un-American." *Anti*-American, maybe, from age sixteen to age nineteen. But *un*-American? Operation Lima Bravo Juliet was a hell-bent, self-dramatizing, wildly optimistic improvised do-it-yourself scheme to improve the sinful world, not entirely unlike the English Puritans' plan to create utopias in the American wild, not unlike the American patriots' attacks on the British before the Revolution, not at all unlike the abolitionist John Brown's attempts to organize a violent slave uprising before the Civil War or the bombings of abortion clinics and murders of abortionists. For those first three months of 1968, we embodied that part of the American character that has troubled and scared me ever since. On the other hand, as it turned out, three out of the four of us never entirely lost our minds or abandoned common sense. When the facts changed and it seemed crazy to carry on, we stood down. Except for Chuck Levy, we were flexible and pragmatic, the way Americans pride themselves on being. For better or worse, in 1968 I think we were *very* American. Terribly American.

28

LEX AND I did wind up staying in New York for two more days, sleeping on Sarah's floor at NYU. She asked why I seemed so freaked out. I told her it was because I'd slept with Buzzy, and Chuck had found out and disappeared.

None of us heard from Chuck on Monday or Tuesday. On Wednesday, when North Vietnam responded positively to Johnson's Sunday peace initiative and agreed to begin negotiating, we thought: *That's good, that might help make Chuck come to his senses, understand we've made the right choice.* But Chuck didn't call.

When I got back to Cambridge, Buzzy told me he hadn't intended to tell Chuck about us. But as the first round of their argument about aborting the mission got angrier and louder Sunday night, Buzzy said, and Chuck insisted *he* knew that *I* wouldn't want to back down, "it just kind of came out. In the heat of the moment. I also sort of thought, to tell you the truth, that it'd be a slap in his face in a good way, to bring him back down to terra firma—you know, chicks, guys, instinct, real life."

After breakfast on Thursday, I was nervous, because that afternoon was Archbishop Cooke's installation. Johnson did go to New

York City, did fly his helicopter into midtown Manhattan. That night on TV at Alex's, the three of us watched Air Force One landing at JFK, the president waving and walking across the Sheep Meadow, antiwar protesters outside St. Patrick's on Fifth Avenue. As it turned out, Johnson had walked out of and back into his helicopter four different times during the afternoon.

None of us said what each of us was thinking, that we'd have had four separate opportunities to dive-bomb him by remote control in the middle of Central Park. There was nothing on the news about a radio-controlled model airplane, or an explosion, or shots fired, or a would-be assassin taken into custody.

After a commercial, Walter Cronkite came back on and announced that just minutes earlier there *had* been a shot fired, *had* been an assassination—not in New York City but in Memphis, and not President Johnson but Martin Luther King, Jr.

"Oh, *shit*," Alex said.

The world was flying to pieces. Monsters had been unleashed. I might have cried no matter what, but my crying was for myself as much as for Dr. King, because I felt partly responsible for his death. I had been infected by the assassination pathogen. I had bought into the insanity. When Walter Cronkite said "police have issued an all-points bulletin for a well-dressed young white man seen running from the scene," I shrieked.

"It's *not Chuck*," Alex said. "He loves King."

"It was obviously a *rifle*," Buzzy said.

"I know, I know," I sobbed.

Black Americans started rioting everywhere, in a hundred different places, and kept rioting all weekend long. The National Guard was called out in two dozen cities. Buzzy kept buying the Washington newspapers, so we read detailed coverage of the thirteen thousand troops deployed in Washington, D.C., marines with machine guns on the steps of the Capitol and army infantrymen guarding the White House. Still nothing about a radio-controlled airplane buzzing the president, or an explosion, or shots fired, or a suspicious young white man taken into custody by the Secret Service.

I was fortunate that I hadn't gone down to Washington to look for Buzzy. I felt lucky, and I felt bad about feeling lucky.

We didn't hear from Chuck that weekend. Monday, April 8, was his nineteenth birthday.

The three of us anguished about our rogue member, but I alone secretly anguished about my secret call to the Secret Service. I felt like a poseur in class, pretending to make pertinent comments about Colette and explain the similarities among the trickster figures in Native American and Caribbean myths. I imagined the worst. I had occasional hopeful thoughts, too, ranging from the banal to the extravagant. Wouldn't he come back to campus for finals in May? Or maybe he wasn't waiting for his moment to strike but had decided to take off, assume a new identity, go to Addis Ababa by himself. He had his new passport and a lot of cash. If he'd flown overseas on April 1, the day he disappeared, the Secret Service wouldn't have had time to put his name on any list.

On Tuesday I went to the memorial service for Dr. King at the church in Harvard Yard. Again my crying was partly selfish, because it started when Chuck's freshman seminar teacher rose to deliver one of the eulogies. With his beard and long hair, twenty-nine-year-old Professor Peretz looked like Chuck would look in ten years— that's the thought that made me choke up, and then his words made me start weeping. "It is now five minutes before midnight," he said. "Not earlier. Five minutes before midnight."

On Sunday, April 14, I phoned my parents. My mother had spent every weekend all winter ringing doorbells in Wisconsin for Gene McCarthy, so she was ecstatic that he'd won the primary by a landslide, and even happier when I neglected to pooh-pooh his victory.

"I'm so pleased you called us on *Easter,* Karen."

"Good." *It's Sunday, Mother. I call every Sunday.* "I'm glad."

"Are you feeling all right, honey? You sound out of sorts. How's Chuck?"

"The same." We talked for another few minutes, and almost as soon as I hung up, the phone rang.

I was going to kill the president, and I cheated on my boyfriend with one of our best friends, and Chuck has gone into hiding with the arsenal we assembled, so yes, Mother, I guess I am feeling a little out of sorts. "What is it?"

"He called." It was Alex. "I just got off with him. He's still in Washington. So that's good."

I didn't stop to ask why that was good. I wondered if Chuck had tried calling me and gotten a busy signal. "How does he sound?"

"Not *quite* as mad as a box of frogs."

"Did you get his address? Or a phone number?"

"He refused. 'Operational security,' he said."

"Oh, Jesus."

"When I asked if he'd heard Johnson's speech to Congress"—the president had convened a joint session to propose "constructive action instead of destructive action in this hour of national need"—"Chuck just laughed. He's staying in some rooming house in the ghetto down there, and he was thrilled to be in the middle of the riots last week. He was thrilled that some guy he met where he's staying, some random Negro, told him that Stokely Carmichael was talking to a crowd in the street right near where they were. Chuck went out and heard him say, Stokely Carmichael, 'It's time to end this nonviolence bullshit.' He talked about sneaking out after curfew with the Luger, like he was playing some kind of game. And he kept saying, 'Alex, *this* is the revolution . . . This *is* the revolution.' He asked if I'd heard about Rudi Dutschke." A few days earlier in West Berlin, our number one favorite New Left leader had been shot in the face by a young neo-Nazi. "He said, 'It's sad, but man, the worse the better.' He's almost out of money, though, so that's good, too. And he said to tell you not to worry the Cubs have lost two of their first four games. Which seemed sort of . . . sane-ish."

"Does he have the plane and the putty?"

"He didn't say. I didn't ask. I assume so."

"Did he mention me and Buzzy?"

"He said, 'I guess I had it coming.'"

"What does that mean?"

"He said, 'We're all human.' He said, 'Along the way, we've all been sneaky and disloyal in our own ways.'"

"What does *that* mean?" I thought of my one-minute conversation two weeks earlier with Special Agent Hardison. I'd never told Alex or Buzzy or anyone else about the call.

"Who bloody knows? But I think there's a real chance it may work out okay. Johnson's going to Hawaii tonight, so that's another fairly brilliant piece of luck. I think I've made a good start, you know, to bring Chuck in from the cold."

"What, he's calling it quits and coming back to Cambridge?"

"It's delicate, Hollaender. It may not be that simple. He and I are going to talk again tomorrow night."

Maybe because I'd heard a lot of Scripture at the service for Dr. King, or maybe because it was Easter, I spent the rest of the night thinking about Genesis 22, one of the stories in the Bible that I'd always found horrible and unfathomable. That's the one where God, (apparently) in order to test Abraham's unquestioning faith, commands him to murder and burn his young son Isaac in "a holocaust," but then (apparently) sends an angel at the last instant to stop the sacrifice. Was I Abraham or God? Was Chuck Isaac or Abraham? Was the angel Alex or me? In any case, the story in the Bible ended happily.

29

FORTY-SIX SPRINGS AGO, after we ended the plot, I decided my tragic flaw was an overactive imagination, my love of stories, that I would never again assume the guise of some fictional character—no more young King Arthur or Alice, no more *Howl* beatnik, no more Bond girl, no more New Left mother-country guerrilla. As things turned out, I've had to play a different fictional character for forty-six years, a version of Karen Hollander who did not conspire to assassinate the president.

I admire my eighteen-going-on-nineteen-year-old self for having the acuity and will to see clearly what I'd been doing my whole life—imagining myself as a fictional character—and then decide to quit doing it. It wasn't until many years later that I came to understand it wasn't only Alex and Chuck and I who had quasi-fictionalized ourselves; that we'd been afflicted by a pandemic perceptual glitch.

In the 1960s, metaphors started to seem more real to more people than ever before. Sure, we all lived in the ordinary world, writing checks, shampooing our hair, stopping at red lights. And we continued to understand that novels and movies and comic books and dreams were unreal. But with the '60s, I think, came a new hybrid

consciousness, an in-between realm where the metaphorical and the fantastical mingled with the literal and the everyday.

I don't think it was *caused* by the sudden wholesale use of marijuana and LSD, although those drugs certainly intensified the sensation of not-quite-real-but-not-quite-fictional life. The three times I took psychedelics, I never thought the strangers I encountered were *literally* lizards or mutant angels or extraterrestrials, and when I was stoned, I didn't *literally* think the TV had turned into one of Big Brother's telescreens from 1984. But some of those strangers seemed very, *very* lizardy, and the government seemed powerful and malevolent in a way it never had previously.

To millions of other people as well, starting in the late '60s and early '70s, notions that for years had been safely metaphorical—such as the miraculous stories in the Bible—turned literal. Because so many people of so many different types experienced the same glitch at the same time, it seemed like a new feature of consciousness rather than a bug.

This glitch spread beyond hippies and radicals and Jesus freaks, and it was never entirely repaired. Twenty-first-century people fictionalize themselves like mad.

When I was little, the women who dyed their hair were outré; now we all do. Cosmetic surgery is all about self-fictionalizing. Young people these days routinely talk about themselves secondhand, as if they're describing characters in a novel or a movie; instead of Waverly's friend Sophie complaining, for instance, *I hated what that boy did,* she said, "I was like, '*Hello,* just shoot me, please.'"

People have online avatars and pseudonyms, and turn themselves into fictional online farmers or killers who form guilds and cults to embark on missions and quests to raise immortal cherry trees or destroy vampires and elves, and spend billions of real dollars buying entirely fictional digital merchandise. I just discovered that in the 3-D virtual world Second Life, there's an "FBI Careers Island" where "Bureau job-seekers and their influencers" interact with "in-world mentors." In the real world, adults compete to become fictional "mayors" of actual restaurants and shops, and roam city streets in

superhero costumes to fight crime, and insist that counterfactual fictions (the U.S. government arranged the 9/11 attacks, the president is a foreigner) are true, and dress up in eighteenth-century drag to call moderate politicians fascists, socialists, traitors, Antichrists. Real life has become a massive multiplayer role-playing game. This week I watched a ten-minute video of a big battle last month in Pakistan, filmed from a high-rise in Islamabad. The video had been "tilt-shifted" with a computer effect to make everything look miniature—the tanks firing and buildings exploding and soldiers and jihadists dying all looked like little toys.

The most serious argument I ever had with my granddaughter concerned the "truth about 9/11" nonsense, which she discovered on the tenth anniversary, in 2011, when she was fourteen. Having finally convinced Waverly that such a conspiracy and cover-up were impossible, I worry that, as she reads my story—a conspiracy, a cover-up that lasted for decades—she will be nudged away from the reality-based community.

Waverly told me last week that she'd done some research into SDS and its positions during the years I was a member, when I was in high school. "It doesn't sound 'radical' at *all*," she said. She has a point. The 1967 SDS national convention passed a resolution in favor of reproductive rights and suggesting that husbands and wives share housework equally. And one of my projects the summer I worked for JOIN in Chicago involved buying hamburger meat in supermarkets in working-class and well-to-do neighborhoods, frying it, measuring the fat that cooked off, and presenting to the city council our findings that poor people paid more for fattier meat.

Imagine if a random New Left kid could be fetched from 1968 to the twenty-first century. Wouldn't she look around and think the revolution had succeeded? The draft ended, the Vietcong won. Communist China isn't just in the UN but on its way to becoming the most powerful nation on earth. Socialists run Venezuela and Nicaragua as well as Cuba. Since Vietnam, the biggest U.S. wars have been tiny by comparison. Apartheid ended in South Africa, and

a billion fewer Asians are poor. All sensible people take ecology seriously. Feminism triumphed—most new doctors and lawyers are
women, and so is a majority of the American workforce. Abortion
is mainly legal and marijuana practically so. On television, people
curse and have sex, and there's a twenty-four-hour leftist news channel. Respectable grown-ups wear blue jeans and sneakers and listen
to rock music and get high. A black man who did drugs and admired
Malcolm X was elected president. And Henry Kissinger and other
old conservatives formed an organization promoting total nuclear
disarmament.

Our young time traveler would find that the utopian New Left
notion of "post-scarcity," the idea that humankind can produce
more than enough stuff to satisfy everyone on earth, has been
achieved in one realm: information and entertainment. To our 1968
kid, that aspect of the present day—cheap instant access from anywhere on earth to billions of books and journals and magazines and
maps and pictures and charts and pamphlets and catalogs, as well as
every movie and show and song—would seem like some stoner's
sci-fi fantasy come true.

But I wonder what she would make of the fact that the Rolling
Stones and Bob Dylan and Cream are playing gigs as seventy-year-
olds. I'm not sure she'd be pleased to find that the chant she shouted
at Vietnam demonstrations—"Hey, hey, LBJ"—has been continually
repeated ever since by crowds outside police stations and embassies
and corporate headquarters and the White House: "Thatcher, Reagan, CIA," "Hey, Clinton," "Hey, Bush," "Hey, Obama, what do you
say, how many kids did you kill today?" I think it might seem annoying and freaky, like an album that kept skipping for fifty years and
nobody lifted the needle to move it past the scratch.

After a while visiting our era, in fact, she might become dispirited
by all the familiar political tropes, what Waverly calls the "cover versions of the sixties." The rest of the world is still complaining about
the wealth and power and obliviousness of America, as they began
doing in the '60s. American leaders still warn that negotiating with
foreign dictators is like the British appeasing Hitler, the way the sec-

retary of state warned in 1966 against making peace overtures in Vietnam. Hip white kids are still romanticizing ghetto violence, un-smiling costumed Panthers then and unsmiling costumed rappers now. Armageddon and apocalypse were right around the corner in the late '60s, and they're right around the corner now. Now as then, true believers loathe the moderates in their midst. She would defi-nitely understand why, since her era, we've coined the phrase "been there, done that."

30

URING THE DAY after Alex talked to Chuck on the phone, I convinced myself that this adventure would finally, yes, have a happy ending. Chuck was just freaked out. He wasn't crazy. Alex was right. Someday we'd all laugh about it. That's what adults always said about the fucked-up things that happened to them when they were young.

When I called Alex that Monday afternoon, he hadn't yet heard from Chuck, but he told me not to worry. But then when I called after dinner, he sounded weird, reticent. The chipper hopefulness was all gone.

"Chuck called, didn't he? He's going to try to go through with it, isn't he?"

"No."

"What did he say?"

"I didn't talk to him."

"When are you supposed to talk to him?"

Alex didn't say anything.

"Alex?"

"There was no specific time."

"Maybe we should both hang out in your room, so when he does call, I'll be there. I mean, if he wants to talk to me. If it seems like that would help."

"No, I don't think so."

As I left my Folklore and Mythology class the next morning, where the professor talked about the mythic Norse super-warriors known as *berserkers*, I stood in the big arched front doorway of Sever Hall slipping on the knit gloves Sabrina had given me two Christmases before. I looked up and saw Buzzy and Alex standing at the foot of the steps, a few feet away. They were both looking at me. Buzzy was holding a *Washington Post* with both hands.

The article was tiny, a couple of inches at the bottom of a page deep in the paper. The only newsworthiness was flagged in the headline, 3 WHITES FATALLY SHOT IN SOUTHEAST D.C.—Caucasians had killed other Caucasians in a black neighborhood.

Three men were shot and killed yesterday after a brief gun battle on the third floor of a rooming house in the Anacostia section of Southeast Washington. All of the men were white. According to DC police, the first shots were fired by one of those killed, Charles A. Levy, 19, of Wilmette, Ill., who had been renting a room there for two weeks. The identities of the two other victims, one of whom died later of his wounds at Walter Reed Army Medical Center, could not be immediately confirmed. Both were said to be Virginia residents. The surviving gunman is in federal custody.

A DC police detective said that the shootings "appeared to be the result of a drug deal gone bad," adding that a large empty amphetamine canister was found at the scene.

Mildred Thigpen, a resident of the rooming house, located on Good Hope Road near 17th Street, said she heard shots, "but we hear guns all the time anyhow." Miss Thigpen also said that following the shooting, "there were about ten plainclothes all up in here everywhere right away. I never seen nothing like that. Because of the rioting, I guess. And because they were white men who done the shooting."

DC police say that no other suspects are being sought.

My face was wet. Buzzy had his arm around me. We were still standing in front of Sever. Kids walked past us, going to the library, going to class, laughing, looking at the budding trees. I felt sick. I thought I might pass out.

"That's it?" I asked.

That was it.

"Who were the other men?"

Alex shrugged and shook his head. "Feds," Buzzy said. "Had to be."

We all went to Buzzy and Chuck's dorm room. I sobbed until my eyes were almost swollen shut. I had been in love with Chuck Levy for a third of my life. I'd never felt such agony.

But it was hard to separate my grief and guilt from my fear. Whoever killed him had known who Chuck was. He had been shot twenty-four hours earlier, plenty of time for the authorities to search every scrap in his room and to know who his friends were. I was surprised we hadn't already been busted, and I figured that soon we'd be questioned and arrested by the Secret Service or the FBI, charged with conspiracy to murder the president, possession of explosives, God knows what else.

I could tell Buzzy was scared, too. " 'No other suspects are being sought' is obviously bullshit. Not to be paranoid, okay," he said, before sputtering and speculating at high speed about whether the new Supreme Court ruling on confessions meant that if we immediately blabbed as they were arresting us, before they warned us we didn't have to talk, maybe our convictions would be overturned . . . and then about a theory he'd studied last semester, "the prisoner's dilemma," where three criminals are arrested and interrogated separately, and how each of them has the choice of ratting out the others, which, if they all do, achieves almost nothing; or keeping quiet, which works out okay if none of them snitch; or, if two keep quiet but the other one rats out those two . . .

"Actually," Alex said, "I think this is it. I think we might be okay. I mean, yes, absolutely, if they question us, none of us knows anything about, you know, the plan. In fact, I think *this* should be the

last time the three of us talk about it even to each other. But it's not like Chuck kept a diary or anything. Right? 'No notes,' that's what you kept saying, Buzzy, 'no notes, nothing written down, optimize OP-SEC.' Right?"

"I've already combed this room three times in the last two weeks," Buzzy said. "But who knows what he might've been writing at the end down there by himself."

I remembered Chuck telling me in January that he was writing me a letter to "explain everything." I'd never gotten any letter. He probably had it on him. It would give the government everything they needed to put us away. But I didn't want to add to the bonfire of fear unnecessarily. I didn't mention it.

"And for all we know," Buzzy said, "they forced him to squeal before they offed him."

"That doesn't seem likely," Alex said. "That doesn't happen in real life."

I wanted Alex to be right. I wanted the nightmare to be finished.

"Alex, when we talked about Chuck last night," I said, "you had a bad feeling already."

"I just had a hunch. After I had some time to think about how he'd sounded on the phone, 'this is the revolution.' I mean, I *know* Chuck better than I know anybody. He and I were best friends before you guys were even friends." Then he added, "If you'd talked to him, you would've gotten the same weird vibe."

Alex's clarity and calm impressed me.

We talked for another couple of hours, grieving, regretting, going through the possible explanations of how and why Chuck had been killed. Maybe somebody saw him carrying the gun and reported him. Maybe he told one of his new black friends about his plans to kill the president. Maybe he was selling the remaining speed. Maybe this, maybe that, maybe maybe maybe.

I knew Buzzy had calmed down when he started using military slang again—he said the gun battle on Good Hope Road sure sounded to him "like a fucking Alpha Bravo," meaning an ambush.

My attention wandered, and after a while I couldn't avoid staring

at each of Chuck's possessions scattered around their living room—the fishing gear in the corner that he'd unaccountably insisted on bringing to college, his leather jacket hanging on a hook, the Thurber paperback and Bond novels in the bookcase—each object now radiating tragic Chuckishness.

I thought of the end of *From Russia with Love,* where Bond is killed by Rosa Klebb's *fugu*-poisoned knitting needle—and how he appeared again, miraculously alive in M's office, at the beginning of *Doctor No.*

But I knew Chuck was really dead. It wasn't a Bond story we'd been acting out, I thought as I smoked and stared and cried, but *Rebel Without a Cause*—spoiled surly teenagers doing our own Chickie Run, drag-racing stolen cars toward a cliff, then all stupidly shocked when one of us, the unlucky one, catches the sleeve of his leather jacket on the car door as he's about to leap out.

Except I knew that Chuck didn't die accidentally. I had encouraged him for a year to take a harder line against the war and the government, to be more radical. I had slept with Buzzy Freeman, and not just once. I had given the Secret Service his name. I had gotten him killed.

I remembered when Chuck finally made me read Thurber's "The Secret Life of Walter Mitty," and the funny final scene, when Walter, waiting for his annoying wife, lights a cigarette and imagines he's facing a firing squad, "erect and motionless, proud and disdainful, Walter Mitty the Undefeated, inscrutable to the last."

The boys seemed talked out. "Chuck was committed," Alex said. "He *believed.*"

"He's a believer, all right," Buzzy said. After guys died in Vietnam, he explained, their buddies called them believers.

Around dinnertime I walked back to North House alone and cried until I fell asleep.

3 1

M Y FOURTH AND last burner rings for the first time.
"Hey," Stewart says, "you know about religion, right?"

"I know what a Catholic girl learned in catechism around 1960."
I wonder if he's going to ask me about confession and absolution
and reconciliation. "You're not having some crisis of faith, are you?"

"Perpetually. But I've been thinking about omniscience. Really
religious people all think God knows everything about everything
and everybody, right? A guy from the G-I-P, Saudi intelligence, just
gave me his card with this quote from the Koran on the back—it
says, 'Whatever deed ye may be doing, we are witnesses thereof.
Nor is hidden from thy Lord the weight of an atom. And the least
and greatest of these things are recorded in a clear record.' That's
pretty much the Christian idea, too, yeah?"

"Pretty much."

"Right. So *God* didn't create *man* in *His* own image, it's the other
way around—man created God as a *goal* for himself, the ideal version of himself, and then spent the next five thousand years trying
to become that. Inventing stuff—even new species in the lab, right?
Like God did. And setting up systems of justice—all that used to be

God's business. And for the last couple hundred years, working hard on omniscience. Novels: omniscient narrator—you even told me you felt like God when you wrote your novel. Physics: the Big Bang, *check,* the weight of atoms, *check,* that lab where they've cooked up RNA out of chemicals, *check.* And surveillance—whatever NSA and NRO and all the NSAs and NROs on earth aren't listening to and looking at with satellites and wires, a billion people have signed up to show on Facebook. We dreamed up an omniscient God, and here we are, almost there."

"Wow. I had no idea there was a theologian in there struggling to get out."

"So I dug up an awesome ELSURS log from 1968, the fifteenth of April."

"I don't—"

"Electronic surveillance, ELSURS. They had bugs in Charles Levy's room in Anacostia when the thing went down. I think you can finish your crossword now. By the way? Levy never fired his weapon in the O.K. Corral that day. Another piece of excellent luck for you at the time.

"So I think *Levy,* Levy *had* to be run somehow by somebody federal, or else the black-boxing wouldn't have gone down the way it did afterward. There'd have been no cover-up, and you'd be a convicted felon. I think Defense Intelligence. Nobody else apart from the Agency and the feebs was infiltrating radicals in 1967 and 1968 at scale. And why else would the army Glomarize you now?"

Stewart says that in the next couple of days he'll have a chance to scan the 1968 surveillance log and email it to me, but that we'll both have to use "sanitized machines." I tell him I'm leaving for Chicago this afternoon.

"There are Internet cafés in Chicago," he says. "But you aren't going all the way out there to try to get to the bottom of your little red squad episode, are you? I told you, the feebs weren't involved in your sixty-eight business at all. There's thoroughness and then there's fucking insanity, Karen."

I'd told Stewart the last time we spoke that I'd received a second

Freedom of Information reply from the FBI. They were mistaken before, the letter said, due to my "surname misspelling." I am mentioned once in a half-century-old file, a report by the special agent in charge of the Chicago field office based on a phone call he received from a Lieutenant Murray of the Subversive Activities Unit of the Intelligence Division of the Chicago Police Department in the late summer of 1963. It described an incident "at a night club on No. Michigan Avenue involving one person (female), Karen Hollaender, who claimed to be a Soviet national and daughter of a senior Communist official, and two others, Alec McCallister (male) and Emilio Largo (male)."

"Don't worry," I tell Stewart, "I'm not insane. I'm going out to visit somebody I used to know. An old lady."

On the flight from L.A. to Chicago, Faye Dunaway is sitting across the aisle from me, alone. She looks good for a woman of seventy-three, in the terrifying cosmetic-surgical mutant sense of "good." The last time I saw her in a new movie was fifteen years ago, the remake of *The Thomas Crown Affair*, in which Pierce Brosnan, the James Bond of the time, played the title role. We're sitting in business class, but she's brought her own food in Tupperware containers.

Even with my detour to drive past our old house on Schiller Avenue, I make it from O'Hare to the town of Glenview in under an hour. I stop at the guard booth and tell the young woman no, I am *not* here as a prospective resident, and the reason I don't know my plate number (do they train these people to be patronizing?) is because it's a rental car. Before arriving, I wasn't sure whether the facility is geared toward independent living, supportive housing, supportive living, residential care, assisted living, or senior living, but a large gilded wooden sign tells me it's the Continuum Care Dwelling Complex, which I guess means all of the above. (I can't keep track of the distinctions. Last year my son-in-law was raving about the "super, super" old people's home where his eighty-six-year-old mother lives, and Greta told me later that Jungo took my

nomenclature confusion as a bad sign, a function of either denial or early dementia.) This place is like a tasteful resort where, at a certain moment around 1978, all the vacationers mysteriously decided to stay forever and grow old together.

For July in Illinois, the heat's not bad. We meet outside in a little garden. She's holding a manila envelope.

"*Hello*—it's Karen Hollander. It's so great to see you after all these years."

As we hug, I worry I'll pinch off the plastic tube trailing from her nose to the oxygen cart near her feet.

"I can't believe it," she says. "It's like time traveling, isn't it? You look exactly the same, Karen."

Mrs. Levy does not. "You're kind."

"And even more glamorous than you do on TV. I see you all the time! They say I'm bragging when I say 'I *know* her, I *know* her,' that I was practically your mother-in-law once upon a time."

So far, so good. She seems mentally with it.

"Except your hair," she says. "Weren't you a brunette? Didn't you have long brown hair parted in the middle?"

Totally mentally with it. "Uh-huh. And ridiculous pink lipstick, and way too much mascara and black eyeliner."

"Your skin is so *beautiful*. You're so lucky."

When we go to sit down on a bench to talk, I offer to drag her oxygen for her, but she says, "You don't need to, he follows me wherever I go." Sure enough, the tank is mounted on a little robot that also carries her pills and hairbrush and magazines and automatically trails after her and stops when she stops.

She says she stayed in their old house in Wilmette for nine years after Professor Levy died, but last spring, when she turned ninety and Chuck's radiologist brother semiretired to San Diego, she decided to move out here. I tell her it's been three years since my mother passed away, a phrase I never use. I tell her I sometimes see Alex Macallister in Los Angeles, and that Bernard Freeman, whom she met exactly twice in 1968 but whose career she has followed ever since, had recently passed away. I tell her President Obama's "pro-

Arab sentiments" were not the reason I declined to be nominated by him to the Supreme Court two years ago.

She abruptly hands me her big unsealed envelope. "Here's the book and Charles's letter, just like I found it. I didn't read the letter. Didn't even open it."

Inside, I see my mother's pink hardcover copy of *From Russia with Love,* the first Bond novel I read. Like my childhood house, which seemed so big when I was growing up, the book seems so small. The bikinied woman in the drawing on the cover used to be skinny, but now her hips are substantial, way too big for a model's. The last time I looked at the back-cover photo of Ian Fleming, touching the barrel of a pistol to his chin and lips with his finger on the trigger, he was an old man, but now he's only forty-nine. The summer after sixth grade, I lent the book to Alex, who lent it to Chuck that fall. Was he planning to return it to me?

Tucked inside is a sealed envelope stamped with an uncanceled five-cent Henry David Thoreau and two half-cent Benjamin Franklins. It seems impossible that I lived in a time when the post office issued half-cent stamps.

"I did take out the little program from Michael's bar mitzvah to send to him. It was stuck in there with the letter."

Michael Levy is Chuck's younger brother. Chuck must have finished the letter when he and Buzzy drove to Wilmette to bring the radio-controlled airplane back to Cambridge. On the envelope is my name, but no address. Mrs. Levy found it when she was cleaning out her house and packing up her things. She sent me a postcard at UCLA asking if I wanted the letter, and I wrote back, saying— lying—that I happened to be coming out to Chicago anyway and would pick it up from her personally.

"Thank you," I say. "I'll read it later."

"You know, I know why Charles really died. That it wasn't a drug thing. That he didn't shoot anyone. Bennett told me all about it later." Bennett was Professor Levy. "I was so relieved. So *proud.* But also so frustrated all those years that I could never tell anybody." She glances down at her robot pal. It has a built-in camera, a cyclops eye.

"*National security,*" she whispers. She takes my hand. "I always assumed you knew the truth, too. So now it's our secret."

I nod. *Proud?* What in God's name is her version of the truth?

"Afterward, Bennett always said he felt a little like he was Abraham and Charles was Isaac, but that no angel arrived in time to prevent Isaac's death."

"Why did Professor Levy feel responsible? For what happened to Chuck?"

"Why? Because Bennett was the one who helped him get recruited!"

"Aha. I didn't realize."

"Uh-huh. From the time he was little, Charles always had an interest in the military."

"I remember." He wanted to be an air force pilot the summer after eighth grade, when he was a boy. And he died when he was an only slightly older boy.

"Through Bennett's contacts in the Defense Department, when they were first inventing the Internet, well, they needed some bright young people, the Defense Department did, to keep an eye on subversives during all the terrible Vietnam *mishegoss.*"

"But he—he, Chuck, wasn't in the army."

"No, no." Again she glances down at her robot. "An auxiliary special-agent kind of thing, on the QT. And you remember, it was right after the Six-Day War, and the campus radicals were in *love* with the PLO, and, well, he always wanted to be some kind of hero, Charles did."

"Yes, he did. He really did."

She says that if we were doing our "James Bond, whatever they were, scavenger hunts" today—

"You knew about our Bond missions?"

"Why would Charles keep them secret? Of course we knew! Anyhow, these days you'd want to do them over in Skokie. Karen, you would not *believe!* Skokie might as well be Peking or Bangkok or Tokyo! And these days you kids wouldn't even need to go into the city to have your . . . whatever, the jazz." She glances at her

robot. "I mean, *Evanston,* Karen, from McCormick Boulevard al-most all the way to Northwestern—Bronzetown! Totally black now."

We talk awhile longer. She would go on for hours if I let her. "Well, it's been wonderful to see you, Mrs. Levy." I lift the envelope. "And thank you *so* much for this."

"Before you go, Karen? And don't take this the wrong way, please, but I've always wondered. If you and Charles had married, would you have raised my grandchildren as Jews?"

I smile and shrug and kiss her, and before midnight, I'm back home here in Los Angeles, at my desk on Wonderland Park, where I am, as the sales manager of the Glenview old people's home in-formed me on my way out this afternoon, aging in place.

Other than that, Chuck wrote near the end of his long letter to me dated February 18, 1968, *and I know that's a huge and unforgivable one, I've only been anything other than completely truthful two times in all the years we've known each other. I _did_ go to see* Thunderball *(with Wendy), and the summer before last, after you told us about your professor at North-western, I asked my dad to check him out, because I was jealous. But that's it. I love you, Karen. I will never love anyone more.*

Other than that—other than the fact that he spied on me for army intelligence for several months.

So my discovery phase is finished. Now I know what happened with a high degree of confidence, as Stewart would say.

I'm tempted to turn this into a PowerPoint presentation.

After the CIA threatened Alex with exposure of his homosexual-ity in August 1967, he agreed to spy on his Yugoslav lover. Sometime that fall, maybe in October when we went to Washington, he agreed to spy on radicals at Harvard as part of the CIA's Project RESIS-TANCE.

He told the CIA about our plan. And the CIA secretly taped those debriefings. "WHEEL-14," says one of the CIA documents, using Alex's code name, "had provided information in April 1968 regard-ing a domestic plot to assassinate POTUS. Surveillances included

technical coverage of debriefings of him by SOG representatives in New York and Boston."

Chuck, it turns out, became a government informer some months before Alex. He'd felt terrible after he called his father a war criminal and modern-day Judenrat for designing a computer communications network for the Pentagon, and in the spring of 1967, when Professor Levy introduced him to a young colonel in the Army Intelligence Command for the continental U.S., CONUS, Chuck agreed to pass along information as one of hundreds or thousands of agents and informants engaged by the army in their domestic intelligence-gathering operations. Which is why he didn't think he had to worry about the draft and why, after he was arrested at the Pentagon protest in October 1967, he was sprung immediately.

But over that fall and winter, according to his letter to me, Chuck decided he'd made an awful mistake, that he couldn't have it both ways, that he was on the wrong side of history, the rest of us were absolutely right, the war was irredeemably evil and we had to do something to try to stop it. In January 1968 he started giving *disin*formation to his army handler from Fort Devens. He was fully committed to Operation Lima Bravo Juliet and had not, as of February 18, 1968, told army intelligence or anyone else about it.

After Johnson announced he wasn't running for reelection and the rest of us decided to call off the mission, why did Chuck persist? What was he thinking? About this I can only speculate. He'd switched from would-be air force officer to earnest young antigovernment radical to government informer and back to committed comrade. He had signed up to be a double agent for army intelligence but then became such a radical true believer that he became a *triple* agent—on our side but pretending to be on the army's side and pretending to the army that he was still only pretending to be on our side. And in the end, by himself, on nobody's side. Maybe the toggle on his moral bearings short-circuited and burned out, and he was unable to flip the switch again. Maybe it would have happened even if he'd never learned that I cheated on him with Buzzy. Maybe he got too invested in becoming an action hero. Maybe the acid trip

with Buzzy over Thanksgiving had frazzled crucial bits of his brain. Gobbling a hundred Benzedrine tablets during the last two weeks of his life certainly didn't help. ("Side effects," I know now, "may include aggression, grandiosity, excessive feelings of power and invincibility, and paranoia, and with chronic and/or high dosages, amphetamine psychosis can occur.")

The last time Stewart and I spoke, he said that "Macallister definitely was the one who really gave up Charles Levy. Gave him up in the process of trying to save his ass, actually. Sort of beautiful and tragic." When Alex and Chuck had their phone conversation on Easter 1968, Alex confessed that he, Alex, had been working with the government—"we've all been sneaky and disloyal in our own ways," Chuck said to him in response, alluding to but not revealing the fact that he, Chuck, had been a federal informant as well. Anyhow, Alex thought Chuck could somehow be cajoled, maybe recruited, at least neutralized—brought in from the cold—by an experienced intelligence professional. He set up a meeting between Chuck and a CIA officer the following day at Chuck's boardinghouse in Washington. Meanwhile, Chuck arranged his own meeting with army CONUS intelligence agents at the same time and place—and for some reason, he didn't tell either his CIA contact or his army handlers that the other would be there as well.

What precisely was Chuck's plan on that day in 1968, the fifteenth of April? Did he want to prove to each set of spooks that he was connected, a real player? Did he think he was somehow protecting himself from each by having the other present? Did he lie to the army about who the CIA man was? Did he have some James Bond–ish denouement negotiation in mind? Or was he just goofing with them all? Did he *intend* to go out in a glorious, murderous, murky blaze? Had he gone completely nuts? The possibilities are not mutually exclusive.

According to Stewart's electronic surveillance log, the CIA man, during the fifteen minutes after he arrived to meet with Chuck, chatted good-naturedly about swimming and Alex and Harvard, took an offered cigarette, and suggested twice that Chuck "put the gun away." Chuck asked the guy which languages he knew and if he

had been posted overseas, what subjects the CIA preferred its officers to study in college, and whether or not he thought JFK had been killed by a government conspiracy.

The CIA man's last line in the ELSURS log is "You expecting somebody, Chuck?", to which Chuck's answer is "Maybe (unintelligible)."

Then comes "Unidentified Male 1: 'Don't, asshole—'" and the notation "Shouts (unintelligible), multiple rounds fired, 11 seconds," and finally, "Unidentified Male 2: 'I'm hit, f***, I'm hit.'" The transcript ends at "1418 hours."

Stewart says the two unidentified males were army intelligence agents, probably CONUS undercovers in costume—long hair, mustaches, hippie clothes. The CIA man, thinking he was being ambushed by radicals, drew his weapon and fired at the armed intruders, hitting one of them, who died later. Both CONUS men fired back, killing both the CIA officer and Chuck, who was holding a loaded .9mm Luger that had never been fired.

The CIA and army intelligence immediately took over jurisdiction from the D.C. police. The case never became a criminal case, never officially passed through the local prosecutorial system at all, which was undoubtedly easier to accomplish in Washington than it would have been anywhere else, since the U.S. attorney for the District of Columbia—that is, a federal government official—also acts as the local district attorney.

One CIA memo I got from Stewart refers to "information classified pursuant to an Executive Order in the interest of the national defense involving intelligence sources or methods." Another refers to "the likelihood that public exposure" of "the Agency's interest in the problem of student dissidence would result in considerable notoriety," and that "the incident carries the highest embarrassment potential for the Agency, activities and relationships which in certain contexts could be construed as delicate or inappropriate and would have serious domestic implications." A third CIA memo notes that "ODFOAM, which was informed of the case two weeks prior to the incident, has declined to take responsibility for it, on the grounds that POTUS was in Hawaii on 15 April and the incident

concerns CIA and ODIBEX internal security." POTUS is the president, and in CIA jargon, ODFOAM is the Secret Service and ODIBEX is the army. "CIA Office of Security is severely inhibited in the actions it can take against any of the suspects, Agency employees or proprietaries for fear of compromising other operations."

In other words, it was a Keystone Kops tragedy in which confused agents from competing intelligence agencies accidentally killed each other. So the CIA and army intelligence decided to engage in cover-ups. Both agencies' domestic spying operations were secret and probably illegal. If they'd been revealed at the time, with a nineteen-year-old Harvard boy dead in the bargain, a catastrophic political crisis might have resulted.

What was more, prosecuting Buzzy and me would have been difficult, given that Alex and Chuck were, legally speaking, federal agents operating improperly—Alex's evidence against us might have been inadmissible, in the criminal bar's term of art, as "fruit of the poisonous tree."

Did the army lie to Professor Levy about the circumstances of his son's service and death, or did he fabricate his own story to make his wife feel better? I don't know.

I encouraged Chuck's radicalism and our plot. I cheated on him. Mea culpa. But not mea maxima culpa. For forty-six years, I've believed it was my long-distance call from the Times Square pay phone to the Secret Service that got Chuck killed two weeks later. That was the straightest, simplest explanation. Now I know it wasn't so, that the mysteries of why Chuck died and why Alex and Buzzy and I were allowed to walk away are much, much more complicated. Occam's Razor is a good rule, but there are exceptions to the rule.

There are things I'll never be certain about. Alex and Chuck each believed that spying for the government was their ace in the hole, giving them immunity from the draft and maybe protection from prosecution. Neither knew the other was a spy, at least until the very end. So: did the sangfroid and commitment to the cause that each of them showed that winter and spring increase both their mutual admiration and their feelings of guilt about being snitches?

Did the secret-agent provocateurs unintentionally provoke each other?

As I began writing this morning, I thought the puzzle was finished, the soluble mysteries solved.

Buzzy had been a true believer and, like me, at the final crossroads, took the right fork while Chuck zigged and zagged and took the left.

Alex, clever, hard-hearted Alex, had been a snitch all along, telling the CIA what we had planned, waiting for the last moment to call in the feds and shut down the plot.

Looking over one of the old typewritten pages from the CIA yet again, I focus on a stray fact I didn't really notice the first twenty times I read it.

I actually think: *Aha.*

"Sorry. Mr. Macallister is in South Africa, on safari. He can only be reached in an emergency. Would you care to leave a message?"

"I'd like to set up a meeting if I can."

"Will he know what this is in reference to?"

"Uh-huh. We're friends. When does he return home from *safari*?"

Why am I wasting energy on *attitude* with an assistant?

"I'm afraid he's going straight from Jo-berg to Rio for the World Cup, so . . . Ah, you're in luck—he has an opening on Monday afternoon, August fourth."

"Perfect," I say, not wishing this imperious boy in Santa Monica to think I'm even a bit put out by having to wait almost a month for an appointment with Alex the great and powerful.

You're in luck, the scheduler at Wheel Life Pictures said. I feel sometimes as if half my life consists of people telling me how lucky I am. Sometimes the congratulations concern actual good fortune. But sometimes when I feel lucky—becoming a grandmother at forty-seven, ending my marriage at fifty-eight—no one else sees it that way. And often the luck is the glass-half-full kind—lucky that I got diabetes when treatment was improving, lucky that my dad died seven years after getting Alzheimer's rather than twenty. People of my generation

constantly talk, with smiles more self-congratulatory than abashed, about how lucky they were to escape death during their daredevil youths, stories that tend to involve drunken swimming off rocky shores at night and driving cars without seat belts while drug-addled. *The shit we got away with as kids!* We are the Smuggest Generation.

I am lucky. But people haven't known the half of it.

I was lucky I didn't blow myself up as we mixed our batches of acetone peroxide. I was lucky that Lyndon Johnson made his political-surrender speech four days before we planned to kill him. I was lucky, as it turned out, that two of my coconspirators had been independently in league with the government, which forced the government to let me go free.

Because my father had survived a Nazi camp and breezed into America, I grew up thinking that luck ran in our family. Now I know that my father wasn't just lucky, that he supplied information about his friends to the Nazis while he was imprisoned and then to the Americans after liberation. He possessed knowledge that he traded to improve his own chances for survival and contentment. He snitched. I told myself in 1968 that my call to the Secret Service was intended to save Chuck from his own haywire behavior, but it was also—maybe mainly—about self-preservation and self-advancement. I snitched. You can decide how far the apple fell from the tree.

I've been lucky for decades that the government files on our case were never accidentally or deliberately pried open, that I was never blackmailed, that no personal or professional or political enemy of mine ever used my brief but inexcusable criminal past to besmirch and destroy me. Again, however, it wasn't just luck. I've been careful, too, mostly.

An hour ago, the Ink Spots came up on my iPod shuffle. *I don't want to set the world on fire / I just want to start a flame in your heart . . . I've lost all ambition for worldly acclaim / I just want to be the one you love.* It's too pat, right? But it's true. As a young girl, I had large ambition for worldly acclaim *and* to be the one he loved. As an older girl, for a time, I wanted to set the world on fire more or less literally. And then as a young woman, I reverted overnight, trying for the rest

of my life to set the world on fire in a strictly figurative sense, to work hard, become successful, and leave both radicalism and true love—every form of wild romance—to others.

When I first moved to L.A., I was fixed up with an older guy who ran some kind of left-wing storefront operation. On our first and last date, before he used the phrase "back in the day" five different times and before we got into a shouting argument about charter schools (I'm pro) and Hezbollah (anti), he said he remembered seeing me at SDS events in Cambridge in 1967. He'd "developed a thing" for me, but then I "just, like, disappeared," and he assumed I'd "gone underground." When I said I was sorry I didn't remember him, he told me that in 1970 he'd been indicted for attempted murder after "somebody fired a rifle into the Cambridge police station." He smiled as he said it. I remembered reading about the incident at the time. The charges were dropped, he told me. "The shit we got away with back in the day, huh? We were so lucky."

Until the last year, I'd never read any of the memoirs published by the old '60s radicals. They were people who'd genuinely believed they were making a revolution, who had set off bombs in government buildings for years and really did go underground for a decade. Now I've read every one, and I find them unsatisfactory.

They are too fondly sentimental about their crazed young selves, coy and opaque about exactly what they did and disingenuous about their motives. They don't quite regard their crimes as real crimes, and definitely not their madness as madness. For them, "Mistakes were made" has no ironic stink. They mainly blame the Man for their mistakes and still think of themselves as noble veterans of a great and ongoing crusade for justice. They give sincerity a bad name. I'm not saying every '60s radical was obliged to undergo a political apostasy, or that their careers in education and prison reform and all the rest have been unworthy. The balance in their memoirs between candid explanation and self-justifying rationalization, however, is tipped way, way too far toward the latter. They remind me very much of members of the Bush administration talking about the wars they waged and bungled.

32

As I awoke the morning after we found out Chuck had been killed, and every morning for days, I had a quick flicker of hope that it had all been a dream, like at the end of *Through the Looking-Glass*. I experienced that same hopeful instant the morning the three of us took a taxi to the airport to fly to Chicago for Chuck's funeral, and the morning we went to sit shiva and I told Mrs. Levy that Chuck was not a drug dealer or a drug addict and I didn't know whom he'd gotten involved with in Washington on spring break.

After those half-awake instants of magical thinking stopped, I woke up every day wondering only if that would be the day the men in suits knocked on my door in North House or stopped me in the Yard as I walked to class and informed me, as they snapped on the handcuffs, that I had the right to remain silent.

But a week after and then two weeks and three weeks after Chuck died, nobody questioned us. Alex and Buzzy and I avoided discussing what we had done and what had happened, both as a matter of operational security—who knew, Buzzy said, how or when they might be eavesdropping?—and for me, to avoid jinxing this uncanny

limbo condition. The flipped coin had landed on its edge, and I didn't dare move or breathe. Life during the months leading up to April had been one kind of implausible dream state, and life afterward was another kind.

I would cry, then feel like crying until I cried again.

The world at large, meanwhile, was boiling over, which made my frozen cowering anxiety feel all the weirder. What I considered to be Chuck's last words—*This is the revolution*—seemed like a prophecy coming true. It was as if the signal had gone off, and millions of angry, energized young would-be agents of history were running wild. While I skulked off carefully and silently in the opposite direction.

The newspaper front page might as well have been spinning toward me each morning, like in an old movie.

At the end of April 1968, as SDS embarked on its nationwide antiwar campaign, Ten Days to Shake the Empire, Columbia students occupied buildings and took a dean hostage. After a thousand cops busted them, Columbia was shut down for the rest of the semester, and two hundred thousand New York college and high school kids stopped going to classes in protest, chanting "No class today, no ruling class tomorrow." The student marches in Paris in early May became riots and repeated themselves, more spectacularly and with more people, in Paris and other cities around France, day after day, until the whole country went out on strike. The revolt spread to West Germany and Italy, even to Prague and Zagreb.

The afternoon I arrived home in Wilmette for the summer, my mother said, "It looks like President Johnson *heard* you."

What? I was speechless.

"He wants to lower the voting age to eighteen—he's sending Congress the constitutional amendment this week." I watched her face drop as her very hopefulness made her sad for a few seconds— she was thinking of Sabrina, who would have been old enough to vote in 1970. But my mother refused to give in to the blues. "He also said he wanted to end the draft. Thank God, for your little brother."

"They're not drafting twelve-year-olds yet, Mom."

"And for Alex. And all the boys." I saw her fighting sadness again as she thought of Chuck.

After dinner, Alex called and asked if I'd seen on the news that Andy Warhol was going to pull through. We'd read in the paper that morning at Logan Airport that an actress from one of his movies had shot him. I'd noticed but didn't mention that she had used a .32-caliber automatic, the same as the pistol we'd taken to New York. Alex wondered how long he should wait to phone the Warhol people and ask whether his internship was still on.

I stayed up late that night with my parents and Peter, watching the election returns from California. For my mother, an unhappy outcome was impossible. She loved Senator McCarthy, but Bobby Kennedy was every bit as liberal, and a Catholic, and quoted Aeschylus and Shakespeare, and had won two out of the last three primaries, so when he came on TV around two in the morning to give his victory speech, she said to my little brother, "Peter, I think you're watching the next president of the United States."

A few minutes later, Kennedy was shot dead.

When Peter quietly asked, "Why do they only kill the good guys?," I was surprised when I realized it wasn't a rhetorical question.

I think my family was surprised by how hard and long I cried.

Buzzy had gotten a form letter from the D.C. police telling him his car had been found abandoned. And empty. Overcoming his paranoia that it might be some kind of trap, he went down to Washington, paid the parking tickets, and drove west, arriving without warning in Wilmette on the last day of June, on his way home to Las Vegas.

As soon as he arrived, I knew my attraction to him had fizzled, that my lust had depended on our affair being illicit. My parents and brother had gone to Wisconsin for the Fourth of July long weekend,

so on his final night in Wilmette, Buzzy and I drove out way into the sticks to watch a fireworks show. We smoked a joint in his car beforehand.

After the last explosions, as we stood up and turned to leave the Downers Grove park, three DuPage County sheriff's deputies were standing directly behind us. Two of them had their hands on their holstered pistols. The other one asked to see our identification.

It's over, I thought. Obviously, they'd been waiting for us; obviously, we'd been followed all the way from Wilmette; obviously, the local cops had been sent to pick us up and then hand us off to the federal authorities. Maybe they'd busted Alex and he'd squealed. *It's all over now. I'm through.* My astronaut's tether cut, I was spinning out into the infinite blackness of space, done, lost, gone.

Buzzy said, "Officer, we left our IDs, um—"

Maybe they hadn't followed us. Maybe they didn't know about the car.

"We lost our wallets," I said, "we lost all our stuff yesterday. At Centennial Beach."

In fact, our IDs were in Buzzy's car a couple of blocks away. But so was the roach of the joint we'd smoked an hour earlier. I didn't want to be busted for drugs as well.

We told them who we were. I hadn't known until that moment that Buzzy's name was Bernard.

"How'd you get to Downers Grove?" the lead cop asked. "Driving without a license?"

"We hitchhiked," I said.

"Where you from?"

"Wilmette," I said.

"From Las Vegas, sir, I am," Buzzy added.

"You in school?"

We nodded.

"Where at?"

"We go to college in Boston," I said. "We're on summer vacation, though."

"I know how college works, miss. Which college?"

At this point I was sure he knew the answer. He was toying with us, seeing if we would lie or tell the truth.

After the obligatory pause, Buzzy said, "Harvard, sir."

It was their response to this answer that gave me the first itsy bit of hope that maybe I was not about to spend the rest of my life in prison. Their surprised and amused disdain, I thought, their smiles and nods and the cop who possibly muttered *"Shit"* or maybe just spat, seemed like reactions to fresh information, not simply confirmation of a fact they already knew. But maybe I was being wishful.

"Are either of you in possession of illegal drugs?" the lead cop asked.

"No, sir," we both said.

"We'll see if you're telling me the truth about that. You're under arrest . . ."

The flicker of hope winked out. The other two cops were unhooking handcuffs from their belts.

". . . for disorderly conduct. I don't know how they do things out in Las Vegas or in Wilmette or up at Harvard, but in DuPage County, we require people to carry some kind of proof of who they claim they are."

Hope bloomed! And beautifully, breathtakingly exploded, like fireworks, like the Big Bang itself. *Disorderly conduct?* Lots of people I knew had been arrested for disorderly conduct. Sarah had been arrested for disorderly conduct in New Hampshire for handing out McCarthy leaflets too close to a polling place.

By the time we'd made our phone calls (my uncle's cabin had no phone, and Alex didn't answer), it was clear that the DuPage County sheriff's deputies thought we were a couple of random hippies, not dangerous radical assassins. I was so relieved I cheerfully answered all of the cops' other questions—whether we'd ever been arrested before, why we'd come all the way out to Downers Grove to see fireworks, and more. And then when I was taken out of the group jail cell in the morning to sit down with an assistant district attorney, I had a gambit in mind. An unbelievably cocky gambit.

He was friendly, a year out of Northwestern Law School, he told

me. ("A few of my friends go to Northwestern," I said.) He said he'd hitchhiked last summer to California for a big rock music festival. (I told him I saw Jimi Hendrix perform last summer, too.) He said his law school roommate's little brother was a junior at Harvard. ("I don't know him personally, but I recognize the name," I lied.) I'm sure I'd flirted before, but never consciously, and never with specific ulterior motives.

"So, Mr. Widdicombe—"

"Didn't I tell you to call me Will?"

I giggled. "Well, before you go to all this trouble and fill out all those forms, I've got a question."

"Yes, ma'am."

"It's probably stupid."

"I doubt it. What?"

"None of the officers, when we were being arrested, or after we got here to the station and they questioned us, nobody ever gave us our warnings—you know, from that Supreme Court case, what was it, *Miranda versus Arizona*? Didn't they decide that police officers have to tell people that they have the right to remain silent and talk to a lawyer and all that stuff? They never did that." I smiled in a friendly way.

He grimaced and rolled his eyes and shook his head and left the little office for ten minutes. When he returned, he told me the disorderly conduct charges were being dropped.

When Buzzy called me "Bonnie"—as in Bonnie and Clyde, as if we were Movement fugitives gone underground—I wanted him to go. I had no interest in taking the outlaw mise-en-scène to the next chapter. The next morning, after he left for Vegas, I drove alone to a Catholic church where none of the priests would know me. Thus on the first Saturday in July 1968, I wound up sitting in a confessional at Saint Mary Catholic Church in Evanston.

I confessed to what I considered my two mortal sins—plotting a murder that I decided not to carry out, and anonymously giving the name of one of my fellow plotters in order to stop him from committing murder, thereby inadvertently causing his death and the deaths of two other men.

I'd decided beforehand that if the priest insisted I turn myself in to the police before giving me penance and absolution, I would refuse the deal. He didn't. I told him I didn't believe in hell, which might have helped make my case that I was confessing because I was heartily sorry for what I'd done and not just to escape (in the Catholic sense) eternal damnation. He told me he believed I was showing "perfect sorrow" for my sins, which is the Catholic term for a sincere confession. When I promised "to avoid the near occasion of sin" in the future, I meant it, as far as these kinds of sins were concerned. And in the name of the Father, and of the Son, and of the Holy Ghost, a man with a kind, high-pitched voice whose face I never saw absolved me of my sins.

I felt a little better. And although I didn't and still don't believe in God in any sense reconcilable with his church's, on that afternoon I scrupulously committed to performing every bit of the elaborate penance he prescribed.

The following week my boss from the SDS community organizing office in Uptown called to ask if I wanted to work on the new project he'd set up over in Gary. I declined and spent the rest of the summer typing and filing and greeting clients at my uncle's law firm, still wondering each morning if government men might show up that day to take me away.

Alex's Warhol internship had been canceled, but we saw each other only a couple of times that summer in Wilmette. Taking his lead, we never once discussed Operation Lima Bravo Juliet, and we rarely talked about Chuck.

"Chuck would've loved that," he said the night we went to see *The Thomas Crown Affair*.

"Uh-huh."

I forced myself not to cry. The movie is set in Boston and stars Steve McQueen as a sportsman who wears a leather jacket and flies gliders and robs banks for fun. He has an affair with Vicki, Faye Dunaway's character who tries to turn him in—but at the end, as the police dragnet falls, he escapes, coolly, with a smile.

"Although I liked her better in *Bonnie and Clyde*," Alex said. "She's better as a crook than a cop."

I was not Bonnie Parker or Vicki Anderson, and I was not Tatiana Romanova or Gala Brand or Honey Rider or Viv Michel or Vesper Lynd. I was not a fictional character. My life was not fiction, or a simulation, or a game.

In August, an SDS girl I knew from Radcliffe phoned and asked if she and two friends could "crash" at my house in Wilmette. I said no, sorry. With the Democratic National Convention as a pretext, thousands of kids were coming to occupy Chicago, to protest the war, the government, capitalism, the American way of life.

On the second day of the convention, I was surprised when Alex told me he was driving into Chicago to attend the protests with Patti, his ex. "I need to shoot everything and everybody," by which he meant he wanted to make films of the protests. "It's important. Like the guy said on TV today, 'the whole world is watching.'"

He could see I was shocked that he was going to put himself in the middle of such a spectacle.

"Hollaender, we can't just hunker down for eternity. Life goes on."

I didn't reply, but I disagreed. I tried not to overdramatize our situation, and I found that my fear of getting busted was very slowly diminishing—its half-life would be years, I knew, not months—but I still felt like a fugitive. Waiting for the secret to be discovered and my life to be wrecked, I decided, would be like living with a chronic disease—like my diabetes, which I knew I would have forever, until, probably, someday, it destroyed me.

According to the news, President Johnson was staying away from Chicago, watching the convention—and the mobs and screaming and beatings—at home on TV. I did the same thing. My mom and dad were surprised.

I felt silly going to the college bursar's office on my first day back in Cambridge to change the spelling of my last name from Hollænder to Hollander, but I needed to codify my rebirth.

I felt nauseated and dizzy a lot that fall. The University Health Service doctors could find no medical reason. They encouraged me to quit cigarettes. They asked if I wanted to see a psychiatrist. I

didn't. How could I honestly talk to some shrink about my secret torment? As my father had said when we'd discussed the Catholic sniper in Texas two summers before, psychiatrists don't observe any priestly Seal of Confession.

To freshmen, I'd been that pitiful girl whose sister died in that plane crash, and to sophomores, I was that pitiful girl whose boyfriend died doing that drug deal in Washington.

As hard as I tried to resist overindulging in metaphors and taking my life cues from fiction, the universe didn't cooperate.

In my class on the nineteenth-century European novel, the first book we read was *Madame Bovary*, and I considered it a personal rebuke. I had been Emma Bovary—a spoiled, dreamy, overimaginative, adulterous young thrill seeker who refashioned her life in imitation of the romantic stories and heroines she adored. Once again, I was overidentifying with a fictional character, this time a character whose tragic flaw was overidentifying with tragic fictional characters. I was glad when she killed herself, because I despised her, and because it meant I wasn't as crazy as she was.

I was desperate for normalcy, but when my new girlfriends smiled and joked and bummed cigarettes and talked about boys and classes and the Beatles' *White Album*, I felt like an impostor.

Over the summer, Alex had said we needed to "avoid going all Edgar Allan Poe." I'd figured he meant "The Tell-Tale Heart," but I'd never read the story until one afternoon in October, standing alone in the dim, musty, silent stacks of Widener Library, hearing my breath and feeling my heart beat. The narrator is a murderer. "You should have seen how wisely I proceeded—with what caution—with what foresight, with what dissimulation!" He's hidden his victim beneath the floorboards, and when police come to question him, he hallucinates the sound of the beating heart of the dead man, imagining that the police must hear it, too. "The sound increased—and what could I do? . . . steadily increased . . . steadily increased . . . arose over all and continually increased. It grew louder—louder—louder! And still the men chatted pleasantly, and smiled . . . louder! louder! louder! LOUDER!"

I put the book back on the shelf and raced out. *I am not a character in fiction,* I told myself. *This is not a story by Poe or Sartre or Flaubert or Ian Fleming or anybody else. This is real life.*

I remembered the retroactive precognition epiphany I'd shared with Chuck and Alex on that druggy dawn when we first talked about assassinating Johnson: *It's what we were training for all along with the James Bond missions.* But now I realized that our Bond games had been a different kind of training, not for killing villains but for keeping secrets and leading a double life.

I threw up as soon as I got outside, on the library steps.

I mostly succeeded for the rest of college in leading a life that looked normal—in fact, abnormal in those years only for being completely apolitical.

I wasn't interested in taking the new courses—"Imperialism and the University," "Radicalism in America"—that Buzzy and other undergraduates helped teach. A thousand kids signed up for these "cooperative explorations," and until the college put its foot down, grades were to be assigned randomly.

I wasn't among the hundred students who staged a sit-in at the faculty meeting about ending course credit for ROTC, or the hundred who barged into the design school's course on preventing urban violence, forcing the cancellation of the class.

Nor did I join up with the hundred SDS kids who took over the main university administration building for most of a day and a night in the spring. I ran into Alex the next afternoon as I was going to the library, and he couldn't wait to tell me that he'd filmed the bust from outside University Hall at four that morning, including a cop billy-clubbing a kid in a wheelchair.

"It was amazing," he said, "it was almost like a scene from *If . . .*"

If . . . was Alex's new favorite movie, and not just because everyone told him he looked like its twenty-four-year-old English star, Malcolm McDowell. It was about a teenager leading an armed uprising at his English boarding school in which the insurrectionists fire on other students and parents and faculty. I didn't want to see it.

When my roommates went to the mass meeting at the stadium

after the University Hall takeover and bust, and voted with the majority of the thousands of students to strike, I stayed in our room studying. When I went to dinner that night, I stopped to read one of the silkscreened posters that had been plastered all over campus encouraging students to strike and giving thirteen reasons to do so, printed entirely in capital letters. I thought two of the reasons—STRIKE BECAUSE THERE'S NO POETRY IN YOUR LECTURES and STRIKE BECAUSE CLASSES ARE A BORE—were factually untrue. And although two others—SEIZE CONTROL OF YOUR LIFE and BECOME MORE HUMAN—were precisely what I was now trying to do, I didn't think skipping classes was the best means to that end. The next day was the first anniversary of Chuck's death.

Coats and ties were no longer required in dining halls, more lectures were disrupted, people screamed at college officials, bomb scares were called in, classes stopped meeting, final exams were canceled once again.

In the fall, I did not go with the super-radical new SDS faction calling itself Weathermen to vandalize, twice, the Center for International Affairs. One afternoon in the spring, on my way to a lecture on luck and morality by a visiting British philosopher, I happened to run into a huge mob of kids, hundreds, marching from the Yard to the ROTC building. They were chanting, "Burn it down, burn it down." As I kept walking in the opposite direction, I passed some stragglers, hippies, who had their own chant: "Dare to struggle, dare to win, Charlie Manson, live like him!" They were smirking as they said it, but still.

I continued to feel like Wile E. Coyote in a Road Runner cartoon, suspended in midair just past the edge of the cliff, waiting to fall. My heart beat faster every time I picked up the phone and heard an unfamiliar voice, or found a letter from an unfamiliar address in my mailbox. When I got a call from the dean's office in the spring asking me to come in for a chat "as soon as possible," I warned Buzzy and Alex. But the dean just wanted to gauge my feelings about moving into one of the coeducationalizing Harvard dorms the next fall. "You seem able to stand on your own two feet around boys," she said.

During junior year, I'd begun to accept the idea that maybe, somehow, we really had gotten away with it. But at the end of a nervous week in March, I was reading yet another newspaper story about the three SDSers who'd accidentally killed themselves making bombs in a New York town house. The *Times* said that one of them had bragged of sloughing off "bourgeois hang-ups like privacy and monogamy" and recently told a college buddy that "for security reasons," they were dividing into cells of four people. "I know now I'm not afraid to die," he'd said to his friend two weeks before he blew himself up. The article had a photo. I recognized him. He was one of those *resistance* and *struggle* Columbia boys I'd met with Sarah in New York in the summer of 1967, and I remembered him writing down my name and Radcliffe dorm. In the spring of 1970, I found myself hoping that his little address book from three years before had been destroyed in the town house explosion.

In May, the night I arrived home in Wilmette, as my family sat down to dinner, Dad very ceremoniously told me that he wanted to apologize.

He had been fifteen minutes late picking me up at O'Hare that afternoon.

"Oh, come on, don't worry about it. I'm twenty-one! And I didn't think you'd *forgotten* about me."

"No, I'm apologizing for what I said when we were sitting at this table three years ago, the night before you left for college. Talking about the war, you said the Johnson administration was 'fascist,' and I got very angry with you."

I remembered, and so did my fourteen-year-old brother. "It was '*fucking* fascists.' "

"*Peter,*" my mother said.

Dad sighed and shook his head. "So many more people have died since then, tens of thousands of American kids. For no good reason."

My eyes were filling with tears.

"And My Lai," Dad said. The world had just learned of the massacre by an army company of several hundred unarmed South Viet-

namese civilians, mostly women and children, and its cover-up by the U.S. government. "And now these kids in Ohio." Three weeks earlier, Ohio National Guardsmen had shot thirteen students at Kent State University during an antiwar protest, killing four of them. "I've realized you weren't so wrong after all, Karen. And I'm sorry."

"*No,* Daddy," I said, my voice quaking, "*I'm* sorry. *I'm* sorry."

I started sobbing, and as I rushed away from the table, I heard Peter ask, "What's Nuthatch sorry about?"

That summer, my last at home, I worked for Alex's father's law firm in Chicago, doing more or less the same stuff I'd done at my uncle's in Evanston, though the cases were more interesting, and my title was one they'd made up for college-educated girls who didn't want to be called secretaries. I was a paralegal. "You've heard of paramilitary forces in the war?" the office manager asked me on my first day. "It's like that, but for attorneys."

The last time I spoke to Buzzy Freeman for the next quarter century was at a party during senior year. He was imitating what he called George McGovern's "faggy preacher" voice and regretting his "piss-poor timing"—because Harvard and Radcliffe had fully merged and the number of black and Asian students was ballooning he'd be "missing out on so many fantastic new fucking opportunities."

Alex and I got together for drinks right before commencement at a preppy bar called the Casablanca. He had majored in Visual and Environmental Studies, but he'd always been "fairly clever at maths," as he once said to me. After they installed a computer console in each dorm connected to what Alex called "the SDS mainframe"—I'd thought he was joking, but it stood for Scientific Data Systems—he had also become a computer whiz. After graduation, he was heading out to San Francisco for a job writing computer programs for the movies and television.

"You're not worried about getting drafted?" I asked. Most boys I knew were going to grad school in order to keep their student deferments.

He'd had three gin and tonics. "Not remotely. The war's ending. And I'm covered."

"What about your terrible number?" In the draft lottery, his birthday had gotten him 43 out of 366. Boys as low as 195 had been drafted.

"What can I say, darling? I know people. I'm covered." I assumed he meant that some of his father's well-connected Washington friends had pulled strings.

Another drink later, I asked about his senior thesis, a half-hour-long film I hadn't seen. All I knew was the title, *The Fourth Man,* and assumed it was some kind of homage to *The Third Man.* Alex told me it was "actually more like *Citizen Kane*" and consisted of fictional monologues by him, in old-age makeup and wig, reminiscing in 2021 about his life back in the 1960s, intercut with the documentary footage he had shot of protests and demonstrations in Cambridge and Washington and New York and Chicago during the last four years.

I was not entirely surprised that he'd done something so close to the bone. Liquored up, I welcomed the chance to talk about Operation Lima Bravo Juliet. "I'd love to see it. When he was young, did your fictional old guy plant any bombs or try to kill anybody or anything?"

Alex's smile became forced and fixed. He was a good actor but not a flawless one.

"Or was your character," I asked, "just an SDS wanker? Or what?"

"You are a sly bitch, Hollander." He took a long drink. "In New Haven next fall, you should get to know my friend Ed, who's going to the drama school."

"You don't need to change the subject. We can talk. Finally."

His smile crumpled. "I . . . I, oh, Hollander. I loved Chuck so much. So much. I mean *loved* him." He took a deep breath. "I'm homosexual."

Maybe he was trying to change the subject again, but at least he was being honest. Now, I thought, I understood his lack of draft

anxiety: being homosexual disqualified you. "That's not exactly a shocking revelation, Alex."

"Really? Did Chuck know, too, do you think?"

I shrugged and wiggled my head back and forth. "Probably?"

Alex said he'd realized he was "gay"—I'd read the word but never heard it spoken—the summer after eighth grade, the night he'd gotten an erection watching Chuck bowl.

"All he does, the character in my film, is go to the Pentagon protest and burn his draft card. He just . . . he feels like, at seventy-whatever, almost like an *actor* who had this one amazing, starring role when he was young—that being young *was* that starring role, and nothing in his life nearly as amazing happened afterward. His final soliloquy is about whether it would've been better to die young so he wouldn't have had to deal with the anticlimax of being old." He was crying. "God, I am a silly sod, aren't I?"

"I don't think it'd be better to have died."

"I got him killed."

"No, Alex, we all did what we did. It was an insane time. Buzzy and I are as responsible as you. More."

"Nope." He was shaking his head emphatically. "It was my fault. In the end. It was me." He took a deep breath. "Although maybe he wanted to die. Maybe he did."

As we finished our last drinks, I asked if he'd told his parents he was gay.

"Are you *kidding* me? And don't tell yours, either, Hollander, I'm serious. I mean, I'm not embarrassed, but some people prefer to be kept in the dark. People *say* they want to know the truth. But really? They want certain secrets to stay secret. Trust me."

33

WAVERLY JUST TEXTED, asking if she can call me.

The last time we talked, she asked if I was suicidal in early 1968, and I've been thinking about that a lot. No. I did not want to die.

However. On the other hand. That said. To be sure. But. Our scheme, given the risks—in particular, the explosive we manufactured and the high probability of arrest and long prison sentences—shows a disregard for our lives as well as for life. It was an embrace of doom, of suicide figuratively if not literally. I'd been brought up to revere saints who welcomed death, including a few who killed themselves for God's sake. As a twelve-year-old reader of Beat poems, I understood that modern saints flirted with self-destruction, and as a sixteen-year-old English student, I learned that the great Romantics died young. Maybe Che Guevara didn't want to die, but it was his death, before he turned forty, that transformed him into a revolutionary saint.

When I was eighteen, accepting the possibility of self-destruction was a measure of my seriousness. And then, given a last chance to step back and climb down, I did so promptly and unequivocally. Af-

terward, ever since, I've felt like one of those people who leap from a bridge but miraculously survive, who say they realized in midair, as soon as they jumped, that they had made a terrible mistake.

Women tend to be much less successful at suicide than men. This has always made sense to me. For us, it's the thought that counts. We want people to recognize that things are awful and ought to be fixed. Whereas men just up and fix things by definitively checking out, boom, making damn sure they won't have to think or talk about the problems anymore, ever.

Chuck more or less committed suicide, I think. After twisting himself into a man of action, ready to risk death for a cause he considered noble, he had too much momentum and could see no other satisfactory conclusion to the story we had all written for ourselves.

And Buzzy didn't take pills or lock himself in his garage with the engine running. There was no possibility of being saved. Sitting alone and holding a grenade to your chest is not a way to get people to start paying attention to you.

The last time Alex and I spoke, he called this book my "suicide package." I didn't recognize the phrase and took it as a piece of Alex hyperbole. But the other day, I was reading about the FBI's electronic surveillance of Martin Luther King, Jr., in the '60s and how they mailed him a tape of secret recordings they'd made of him telling filthy jokes and having sex. "You are done," they wrote in an anonymous cover letter. "There is but one way out for you. You better take it before your filthy, abnormal fraudulent self is bared to the nation." Among themselves, the FBI agents called it a "suicide package."

Chuck and Buzzy both died on romantic, ill-advised missions to remake the world, each of them dead set on looking like a martyred hero. At my moment of truth in the pathologically romantic spring of 1968, I decided I was not a romantic, and Chuck's death cleansed my system of romanticism. At nineteen, I retraced my steps to make myself over into the person I'd started to become at thirteen, the sensible girl who wouldn't go through with confirmation, who considered St. Gertrude's return to Catholic dogma a sad failure of

imagination, who refused to embrace the unreasonable and pretend to believe the unbelievable.

For good Catholics, as for all true romantics, the whole point is accepting truths beyond the power of human reason, agreeing that certain mysteries must by definition remain mysterious. The closest I can come is my love for my children and my grandchild, which has an absolute unquestioning ferocity that feels irrational. Although some mysteries are probably insoluble, I take it as the human project to keep trying to solve all the ones we can. To me, ignorance isn't sacred. A mystery is something to be figured out. Which is another reason why I'm writing this book.

Waverly phones. "So I guess Dad was sort of right about you."

"*What* do you *mean?*"

"He always said you had some mysterious 'unresolved inner turmoil' that made you and him unable to 'bond.' Then after you left Grandpa Jack, he decided your unresolved turmoil is being a secret lesbian. He said that during the last big fight Mom and him had."

"Mom and he. I'm sorry they're fighting, but I'm not gay," I say as I hear the buzzing and head for the kitchen, "and honey, I do want to hear all about how your Virtually Homeless thing is going—"

"Virtual Home."

"—but I've got another call I need to take. Talk later. I love you." I put down one phone and pick up another. "Hi."

"Have you told anyone I've helped you?"

"Only my granddaughter."

"*Fuck*. Karen."

"Waverly doesn't even know your name. She's read my manuscript, but I call you Stewart, Stewart Jones, and don't say where you work or have worked. Why?"

"Weird conversation I had the other day with a gal I've known a long time, senior person at NGA. Maybe nothing. So you're finished? With the book?"

"Just about. I've got a couple of loose ends I want to ask Alex about face-to-face, but he's not in this hemisphere until next month.

But wait—NGA?" Sometimes I think Stewart makes up fictional government agencies just to fool with me. Such as the National Media Exploitation Center, which he mentioned a few months back; it turned out to be real. "What's the NGA?"

"National Geospatial-Intelligence Agency."

Sounds fictional. "Really?"

"You haven't said anything to him, have you, Macallister the Third, that would compromise me? I didn't trust him the second I laid eyes on him."

What? "You *know* Alex?"

"Early ninety-nine, the night the Senate acquitted Fat Boy, you and I were at that Moroccan joint in Georgetown, and we ran into him. He was in D.C. for some Gore fund-raiser, the three of us had a drink, you pretended we weren't fucking."

Now I remember. I'd thought Alex was attracted to Stewart that night after Stewart said he had never been married. "All I've told him is that I've got documents proving he was CIA. Not how I got them."

He doesn't say anything.

"Are we still seeing each other," I ask, "the week after next?"

"Uh-uh. Unfortunately. I'm going to be out of the country. That's why I'm calling."

"Aw, that's a drag. Where are you going?"

"Going to be in theater for a bit."

That presumably means Pakistan or Afghanistan. "Oh, Christ. Be careful."

"Listen, when you talk to Macallister the Third, don't refer to me even obliquely, okay?"

"Of course. Absolutely." He doesn't respond. I remember now that I also told Sarah Caputo that Stewart has been helping me. "Don't be angry."

"Don't worry about it."

"I've been wondering—why would the CIA keep using Alex after what happened? You said he kept doing stuff for them the rest of college."

"Two reasons, seems like. Keeping an eye on you and Freeman to

make sure you weren't involved in any more un-American criminal shit. And lucky timing. In the summer of sixty-eight, the White House tasked the director—"

"Of the CIA?"

"Yeah—with finding out if Communist governments were directing you antiwar freaks and the Weathermen. And with your boy's help, they realized uh-uh, not."

"So why didn't Alex keep working for the CIA after we graduated?"

"Because why would they trust some guy long-term who pulled the shit he did with you? And because when you graduated college, the sensible people in Langley decided spying on American citizens in America was a bad idea and eighty-sixed Operation CHAOS. And because you don't get to live in Bel-Air and have a Gulfstream as a fucking GS-18. By the way? I hate the name Stewart. And I don't love Mr. Jones, either—people will think of me as the asshole square from that Dylan song."

34

For hours or sometimes even days at a stretch during the last forty years, I've managed to forget about my nutty period and its terrible consequences, to go about my business—getting kids to school, meeting with clients, teaching, writing, going on vacations, buying shoes, all of it—as if my life were as normal as it seemed. Then I would remember. Whatever the reminder, I would recall that I was engaged in a lifelong cover-up, an elaborate fiction, and that the Karen Hollander known to my family and friends and the world was partly, slightly, deeply false.

In the mid-'70s, I started taking some risks again. Nineteen sixty-eight seemed far away. As a candidate for a judicial clerkship, I submitted my name and personal details to an officer of the U.S. government. I pretended to my friends and family that I was concerned only about my disorderly conduct arrest in Downers Grove. Law school was always stressful, so Jack apparently didn't notice my extreme anxiety that spring.

Nothing happened. No terrifying calls or letters, no unusual requests for further information, no visit from federal agents. It turned out they did no background check at all, and I got the clerk-

ship. Which encouraged me to go through with my pregnancy and with marrying Jack. Normal life was inviting me to step on in.

My year in our Hyde Park apartment, clerking for the 7th Circuit, was splendidly normal, because my mother and dad, with Peter off at college, were eager to come down to the city to babysit for Greta whenever we asked.

Jack did notice my months-long spike of stress when I applied for a Supreme Court clerkship with Justice William Brennan, but he attributed it to the high stakes and the presumed sexism—only about a dozen women had ever clerked for the Court. I figured they—the *Supreme Court*—would do background checks. Once again, nothing, no call from a special agent, no mysterious request to withdraw my application, no blackball cast. I got the job. I think two things about me—my Roman Catholic upbringing and my baby, born the year after he'd signed on with qualms to *Roe* v. *Wade*—gave me an edge with Justice Brennan, who was the only Catholic on the Court.

Sarah was single and living in D.C. when Jack and I were there, so we lucked out again on babysitting. Jack was also an astoundingly good father, especially for 1976, getting up in the middle of the night, letting me sleep late every Saturday *and* Sunday morning, changing diapers, bathing Greta, mixing up homemade baby foods.

I remember one Saturday night on Dupont Circle, sitting on the living room floor surrounded by stacks of briefs and books, drafting an opinion on illegally obtained evidence in a criminal case—I'd offered to recuse myself due to the 1968 disorderly conduct arrest—and looking up at Jack in the kitchen, holding Greta in his arms as he boiled her pacifiers. I was fine with picking the binky up from the floor, wiping it off and sticking it back in her mouth. Not Jack.

He looked over. "Are you *crying*?"

"You're an excellent dad." *If I ever go to prison,* I was thinking, *Greta will be okay.*

I came to regard my diabetes as punishment for what I did at eighteen and nineteen, a soft life sentence—which is crazy, since I got it when I was seventeen. I've had only one terrible diabetes inci-

dent, the result of my rigorous commitment to normality, blood-sugar-wise. As I've explained, avoiding high blood sugars—what wrecks your blood vessels, your eyes, your kidneys—has its price, increasing the risk that your level drops too low, making you "spaz out" (as Greta used to say) and become confused, scared, scary, even unconscious. In 1987, when Jack was in Europe at a music festival and I was alone in Brooklyn Heights with the kids, who were twelve and three, in the middle of the night I had flailing convulsions and went into a coma. Greta awoke—I have no memory of any of this—after I knocked over and smashed the nightstand lamp, and called 911.

When I regained consciousness in the hospital hours later, in the middle of that familiar movie-scene netherworld of ultra-bright lights and medical equipment, physicians leaning in and gingerly asking if I knew the date and where I was, my first cogent thought was the fear that I'd talked about what I'd done in 1968.

Later on, I asked both the emergency room doctor and the surgeon who'd wired my separated left shoulder back together if I'd said "anything strange." The ER guy smiled and said yeah, but that was standard, and I shouldn't worry about it.

"What did I say?"

"Are you a big James Bond fan?"

"When I was a girl."

"You were shouting, 'I don't *have* a license to kill, I don't *have* a license to kill.' You made everybody in the ER crack up."

Is it meaningful that I've been "so completely *out*" about the diabetes, as Waverly says, testing my blood and injecting in public, never treating it as an embarrassing secret? Is it my compensation for the giant secret I've chosen to keep all this time? Confessing everything but the one great sin? Maybe. (Maybe that's also why, at law school, I told Hillary Rodham when we met that I recognized her from eight years earlier—that I was the snotty fifteen-year-old who had, with two snotty fifteen-year-old boys, heckled her and her fellow Goldwater canvassers on that fall afternoon in Kenilworth.)

Being female has made it easier to keep my secret. People, even people you're married to, chalk up moody or anxious days to hor-

monal tides. No one noticed that every April fifteenth (the day
Chuck died), I got very blue. My highly emotional reactions to certain news events have probably made people think I'm more femi-
nine than I am. Like when I was a 1L and Arthur Bremer shot George
Wallace. And every second month during the late '70s, when Red
Brigade or Red Army Faction squads—people who considered 1968
a fantastic beginning rather than a horrifying end—shot or kidnapped or murdered another European politician or businessman,
or got killed or arrested or committed suicide in prison.

I got upset my second year in law school, for instance, when Lyndon Johnson died, almost five years to the day after we decided to
kill him. And I got upset in 1977, when Jack and I went to see *Black
Sunday* in midtown Manhattan. All I'd known beforehand was that
it was a thriller set at a Super Bowl. When I started crying halfway
through, Jack asked if I was low and offered to get me a Coke. I was
upset because it's about a deranged former air force pilot who plots
with terrorists to kill thousands of people from the Goodyear blimp.
"It's just a stupid *movie*," Jack said.

We'd moved to New York right after the Bicentennial. Jack had
gotten a Guggenheim Fellowship, and I started my job at the Legal
Aid Society. My parents were pleased, but everyone else I knew was
surprised, completely baffled, since by then I wasn't at all a bleeding-
heart lefty. "Teddy Roosevelt liked Legal Aid," I said with a smile,
"because it kept the poor people from becoming revolutionaries."
To a lot of my classmates and fellow clerks, it looked like the worst
of all possible worlds—the low salary of public service, depressing
clients and unimportant cases, and not a rung on any ladder to
worldly acclaim in the judiciary or academia. I shrugged. "I'll do it
for a few years."

I was going to do it for exactly five years, because the priest on
the other side of the confession box at the church in Evanston had
assigned a penance of five years "serving the indigent and afflicted."
I didn't believe, as he told me, that on Judgment Day I'd go to heaven
if I had helped the poor and the imprisoned (or to hell, according to
Matthew 25, if I failed to do so). But I did accept Father Whomever's

absolution on that summer day in 1968, so now I had to do as he'd instructed.

Thus I spent three years in the Bronx and two in Manhattan representing unlucky nincompoops and psychopaths, many more of the former than the latter—hookers and three-card-monte dealers and car-antenna breakers, muggers and looters and men who'd beaten or stabbed or shot and sometimes killed their wives or girlfriends or perfect strangers. As a Legal Aid criminal lawyer—"lawrys," our clients tended to call us—I was mainly a negotiator, persuading people more or less like me to let a client out on a thousand dollars bail instead of fifteen hundred or to knock an E felony down to an A misdemeanor, then persuading people almost nothing like me to agree to the plea bargains I'd negotiated on their behalves.

At the beginning of the Legal Aid job, the details of my clients' alleged crimes—the handguns found hidden in ovens, the accomplices who ran amok, the fingerprint evidence, and their (indifference to) operational security in general—reminded me of 1968. I decided that was part of my penance, being forced to remember that there but for the grace of God go I. Over time, however, all those thousands of cases, the weapon serial numbers and gram amounts of heroin and wound dimensions and complicated alibis and lies, served to do something like the opposite, overwhelming and obscuring the memories of my own brief life in crime.

Once I became a corporate lawyer, wearing fancy clothes, meeting zillionaires, traveling first class, I experienced a James Bond moment every month or so—benign and imaginary, brief, silent, impromptu one-woman replays of our childhood games. The fictional template always lurked. Maybe, I think now, it was a way of not thinking about Operation Lima Bravo Juliet.

I'd feel Bond-girlish when I drove a European car with a stick shift on a European road, and when I ordered a martini at a revolving restaurant in Tokyo or Cape Town or overlooking Iguazu Falls in Brazil. It happened almost every time I passed through a big new

airport, especially in China or the Middle East. If I'm alone in a high-rise hotel room at night in my underwear—dressing for dinner, putting on perfume, half-listening to CNN International—for a few seconds, I become Vesper Lynd or Tatiana Romanova or Gala Brand.

Even though my adolescent immersion in the Bond books has made me freakishly alert to this subtext in glossy, sexy, chilly modern life, I know I'm not alone. The world must be crawling with make-believe secret agents. Every day and night in every city on earth, aging children of both sexes fleetingly and half-consciously enact some version of the fantasy, dazzled by the cosmopolitan sheen, reassured by the platinum and black credit cards and exotically stamped passports and electronic devices in their attachés, hoping to feel tough and adventurous instead of brittle and existentially marooned.

When I was born, before Bond girls (and *Playboy* and the Pill, all invented simultaneously), an unmarried woman who indulged in guiltless sex was pathological, debased, wretched; afterward, she was a standard-issue modern female. The world's obsession with "brands" is now so unremarkable that it no longer seems like an obsession, but a half century ago, James Bond's fetishes for obscure brand-name merchandise—Tattinger champagne, Charvet shirts, Beretta pistols, Aston Martins, all of it—were peculiar. After Alex came out in the late 1970s, he told me that Bond's extreme and snobbish brand loyalty had been one of the traits that made 007 seem, to a twelve-year-old gay boy in Illinois in the early '60s, "quasi-queer."

Have you ever looked at the names of makeup? Chanel has lipstick colors called Intrigue, Secret, Captive, Incognito, Clandestine, and Fatale. Rupert Murdoch and Silvio Berlusconi and Dick Cheney and Steve Ballmer and Vladimir Putin and Kim Jong-un are all Bond villains. Richard Branson and Tom Ford and Tom Cruise and Donald Trump and Julian Assange (such an Ian Fleming *name*) are Bond villains under the impression that they're actually Bonds. Valerie Plame Wilson and Carla Bruni-Sarkozy and Madonna and Anna Wintour are (well, *were,* in their twenties and thirties) Bond girls.

The annual conclaves of the World's Most Important People in chic, picturesque mountain resorts—Davos, Sun Valley, Aspen—are preposterously Bondlike. Globalization itself is a James Bond phenomenon. From the last Ian Fleming novel I read, *You Only Live Twice,* I still remember the speech by Tiger Tanaka, the head of Japan's spy service. "For the time being," he told Bond, "we are being subjected to what I can best describe as the 'Scuola di Coca-Cola.' Baseball, amusement arcades, hot dogs, hideously large bosoms, neon lighting—these are part of our payment for defeat in battle."

When the call came from the Department of Justice in the spring of 1997, at first I thought it was about an antitrust case that my firm was litigating. The DoJ guy—sounding terribly serious, according to my assistant—said no, "it concerns a private matter," which he wouldn't divulge to her. Maybe because the anniversary of Operation Lima Bravo Juliet was upon me, I thought, in a way I hadn't for twenty years, *This is it, the jig is finally up.* I thought: *Won't Jack be surprised?* I thought: *I've lucked out—I'm forty-seven years old, I've got money saved, Greta is about to graduate college, Seth is in high school.* I felt relief mixed with the terror. Before I returned the call, I made sure my best friend in the firm's criminal defense practice was in town.

Reality did not outrun apprehension. When the call turned out to be about a possible job, I was shocked. A different kind of relief swept over me, and a different kind of terror. Having spent a half hour adjusting to the prospect of being outed, I thought: *What have I got to lose?* And given that a former antiwar activist was president, and bombers and ex-cons who still called themselves radicals were welcomed into the Establishment—the City Club of Chicago had just named Bill Ayers its citizen of the year—what was stopping someone with no criminal record whom a newspaper columnist had once called "practically a conservative"?

A couple of weeks later, I heard from Alex for the first time in years. He'd gotten a phone call from an FBI special agent who was

interested in my background and character. Alex made him prove who he was by sending an email from his @fbi.gov domain.

"It's a government job," I told Alex. "A big government job."

"Brilliant! Judge Hollander?"

"Nope. I'm not supposed to tell you. Did you talk to the FBI guy?"

"Absobloodylutely! Gave him the finest arse-licking he's ever had. He asked, 'What kind of person is she?' and I said, 'She's a Taurus.'"

"You didn't."

"I did, and he laughed. I flirted with a G-man! I said, 'She's a totally *great* person.' I said that in the forty years I've known you, I've never met a smarter, better, tougher, more honest American. He asked if you're a drunk or a druggy or a racist or a spendthrift, and I said no, you quit smoking, you married an Asian, and you're cheap. He asked if I, quote, 'have any reason to believe Ms. Hollander is disloyal to the United States government.' I said, 'Agent Reiss, she's as all-American and patriotic as New Yorkers *get*.' I said, 'She voted for Rudolph Giuliani for mayor—*twice*.' And then he asked if there's anything in your, quote, 'past or background that could be used to pressure or compromise' you. It was like an actor reading lines from a script!"

"And you said . . ."

"I said, 'I can't *imagine*.'"

A few weeks later, amazingly, they offered me the job, and amazingly, I accepted. Later, I learned from a guy in the White House that I'd "shown up on the radar" because of my work on the Czech constitution. I was hired, he said, because I was "a woman with liberal cred from Legal Aid and intellectual cred from teaching at Yale, but with the hardball big-money corporate-litigator experience and no big liberal political record to upset the Republicans" during Clinton's second term. "We didn't want a lefty."

And so in the summer of 1997, I started living alone in an apartment in Washington five nights a week. I wouldn't have accepted the position if any of my responsibilities had been on the right-hand side of the Justice Department org chart—that is, if I'd been asked

to oversee the FBI, the Drug Enforcement Administration, the U.S. marshals, the U.S. attorneys, and the federal prisons. I had almost nothing to do with enforcing laws against criminals. The prosecutions of the 1993 World Trade Center truck bombers and Timothy McVeigh and Ted Kaczynski were entirely outside my bailiwick.

My Washington service, naturally, was thick with Bond moments. One morning I rode in a government Town Car past the exit for CIA headquarters to the (Bondish) Dulles Airport, flew into the (super-Bondish) TWA terminal at JFK, and then from New York on to China. Two days later, I fired an AK-47 at a Chinese government shooting range; put my bare feet into a pedicurist's glass tank to let hundreds of teeny carp nibble the dead skin off my toes; and, in a hotel shop, saw a brand of condoms called Jissbon. When I asked if Jissbon was derived from "jizz," a word my translator didn't know, she said no, it's short for *Jieshi Bang,* the Chinese transliteration of James Bond.

During my single personal moment with President Clinton, at the 1997 White House Christmas party, I told him we'd briefly met once before, at Yale, when he was twenty-six and I was twenty-three, the day our constitutional law professor posed the hypothetical about FBI infiltrators of radical groups and I hyperventilated. A year later, as Clinton was lying about his adultery in the Oval Office and losing his fight against impeachment, I met Stewart and embarked on my only extramarital affair (if we exclude from our definition of "affair" making out one time in a Manhattan law firm conference room at three A.M. in 1989). I was forty-nine and Stewart was forty-three, but that flattering fact was incidental to the deeper satisfactions that I'd denied myself for so long.

"Wow," Sarah said to me a few months after I met Stewart, "government work agrees with you!"

I'd lost fourteen pounds and changed my hair color, neither of which Jack seemed to notice. I was smiling more. People actually said I looked "radiant." I knew I was living a cliché, but I didn't mind. And I was living a lie, but at that I'd had thirty years' practice. My risk-management skills were good. I'd been successfully

background-checked by the FBI. I was working for the Department of Justice. Having an affair didn't seem as scary to me as it might to other married women. It ended—went "on hiatus," as Stewart said at the time—in 2001, when I returned to private practice and teaching and he was about to be posted overseas.

So, Chuck Levy: pilot, would-be air force aviator, intelligence operative, and freedom fighter. Buzzy Freeman: military veteran, cowboy revolutionary, and patriotic warrior. Both of them boy-men who kept secrets and believed in political ends that justified lethal means. Ditto "Stewart Jones," a foulmouthed combat veteran and cowboy intelligence operative, a professional secret-keeper and occasional overseer of government killing. I believe in the rule of three, so I can't deny the obvious. I fall for men utterly unlike the one I married. Men somewhat more like my father, it turns out. Men, yes, ridiculously, from James Bond's universe.

I absolutely never imagined I was in the running to be a Supreme Court justice. When the seat opened up and my name began appearing on journalists' lists of possible candidates, I figured it was bullshit, the result of my quasi-celebrity—the books and my appearances as a constitutional expert on cable news and PBS and NPR. I was about to give the commencement address at Harvard. Compared to federal judges of whom nobody had ever heard, I had a name that was more fun for media people to bandy.

Another female law school dean who had never been a judge? *Another* woman with Type 1 diabetes? *Another* 1970s alumnus of Yale Law School? *Another* New Yorker? The *seventh* Roman Catholic out of nine justices? *No way,* I thought, even as I enjoyed the attention.

My constitutional views have been described as "quirky" and "unorthodox"—for instance, I'm a non-Republican who really believes states' rights can't be wished away—and the novel I published features a heroic gay prosecutor, lots of salty language, and a main character who wonders why people who live on the Great Plains aren't constantly tempted to commit suicide. In my one appearance on *Oprah,* a booking I got only because I agreed to talk about

diabetes, I told her that when my blood sugar is very high, I feel like "a certain kind of American—dull-witted, heavy, sated but not really satisfied, faintly depressed. Greasy-brained." That caused a small uproar. I have a prescription for medical marijuana, and for years I smuggled Nicorettes into the U.S. and donated my used, HIV-free insulin syringes to an unauthorized New York needle exchange program for junkies. *No way could I get confirmed,* I thought.

None of that stopped me from gaming the fantasy. I run one of America's top five public-university law schools, I taught constitutional law at Yale, I very successfully practiced law in the real world. I helped draft a national constitution. For twenty-one years I was a member of the bar of the U.S. Supreme Court, where I argued nine cases at the advocate's podium. And I served as the associate attorney general of the United States. Given that I'd be replacing a woman, I would be the new third female justice, not a fourth. My lack of judicial experience meant I had no trail of decisions that could be held against me. A few years ago I wrote that overturning *Roe* v. *Wade* would be a disaster, but that the decision was poorly argued and had a whiffy constitutional basis. This is the big reason people on the left mistrust me, along with my twenty years of representing corporate clients, and why right-wingers loathe me less than they do other liberals.

It was all a game, a fictional exercise. No one from the White House had called to tell me I was under consideration or to suss out my interest in being appointed.

Naturally, I heard from Alex Macallister right away.

"It's a figment of the media's imagination," I told him. "The FBI hasn't called you to check on me this time, have they?"

"No. But it's an honor just to be nominated. That's true, you know."

"This is not the Oscars, Alex. I haven't been nominated. I'm not going to be nominated."

Then the White House did call. I had just arrived in Cambridge to give my Harvard speech the following day. I was on the administration's list for real. "It's not a long list," the fellow from the White House told me.

I didn't immediately say no.

For forty-four years, I had gotten away with it. I had made it under the radar three times, twice as a clerk in the 1970s and then as associate attorney general in the 1990s. A seat on the *Supreme Court.* Jesus God.

I could not push my luck once again, not this far. Could I? I had never actually lied about my past, never denied what I'd done, because all the forms I'd signed over the years inquired only about charges, indictments, and convictions. They didn't ask, and I didn't tell. But with the vetting to which I'd be subjected as a Supreme Court nominee, by the FBI and the White House lawyers and the press, the truth would surely come out. Wouldn't it? After fantastically, paranoically embellishing Obama's glancing association with one Weather Underground geezer during the 2008 election, in 2012 the Republicans would try to use me to destroy his presidency once and for all. And if I were nominated and confirmed? I didn't want to spend the rest of my life worrying and lying more than ever, did I? No. I did not.

I called back the nice man in Washington the next morning and told him thanks very much, I was honored beyond words, but no thanks. Then I gave my speech, in which I told the new graduates that we are all to some extent fictional characters of our own devising, and I quoted the narrator of Kurt Vonnegut's *Mother Night,* a fictional memoir by a former OSS double agent who pretended to be a Nazi during the war. "This is the only story of mine whose moral I know," the character says at the beginning of the novel. "We are what we pretend to be, so we must be careful about what we pretend to be." I choked up a little, which mystified and intrigued the audience. When I said later in the speech that "honesty in the defense of liberty is no vice" and that I'd just decided against spending the last chapters of my own story as a candidate for the Supreme Court, they all thought they understood why I'd gotten emotional earlier. Thanks to the Twitterers in the audience, my news was all over the Internet and on TV within the hour.

35

WHEEL LIFE PICTURES is in a building in Santa Monica that's old for L.A., which is to say a building built around the time I was born. Originally a small factory, it has been renovated, adaptively reused—also like me, although much more stylishly. I'd be surprised if any of the dozen people Alex employs here are more than half my age.

I've been standing and staring out the twenty-foot-high gridded glass window toward the Santa Monica airport for five minutes when I feel his hands gripping my shoulders.

"Ms. *Hollander*," he says in a soft growl.

I spin around and we kiss. When we were eighteen, he was slightly taller than I was, but now we're the same height. He's astonishingly fit. His hair is shortish but thick and luxurious, so white that I wonder if he bleaches it.

He tells me one of the reasons he bought the building is that he can leave his office and be aboard his Gulfstream 650 ten minutes later. "I can actually walk to the plane."

"Really? It's only a ten-minute walk?"

"That sounds about right. I said I *can,* not I *do.* It's a two-minute drive."

An assistant brings me a perfect cappuccino with a decoration on the foam that I guess is a wheel. I pass on the offer of "a few foie gras nibbles" left over from a lunch meeting. Selling foie gras has been prohibited in California for the last two years, but possession remains legal. The assistant closes the door to Alex's private office.

Rio was "fantastic, of course," watching England beat Germany in the World Cup final was "too perfect," seeing white lions in the African bush was "beyond."

"And this black panther we saw rip apart an impala? In Ethiopia? My God, *the* sexiest creature *ever.* Although did you know 'black panther' is redundant? All African panthers are black. Funny."

"You finally made it to Ethiopia. I remember your plan to live in exile in Addis Ababa."

This is my attempt to bring up 1968 gently, but he ignores it and proceeds to tell me that he's heading to outer space.

"How very Bond-villain of you," I say. "Someone I know went last year, on one of the first regular flights." After my colleague's wife died unexpectedly, he decided he could afford to drop two hundred thousand dollars of their retirement savings on a one-day adventure into space. "You take off from New Mexico, right?"

Alex frowns. "That's *Virgin Galactic,*" he says, as if I'd asked whether the Chevy out in the parking lot was his, or whether his round indigo eyeglasses were from LensCrafters. "It's cute. But it's just a few hours, up and down. Suborbital. They only go up sixty miles, the same as from here to . . . Laguna Beach. And they sell it like some theme-park ride—'Virgin Galactic Mission Control,' 'book with your local accredited space agent.' Please."

"So what are *you* doing?"

He smiles. "Lunar expedition." In eighteen months, two years at most, he will spend a week flying to the moon and back, orbiting a few times but not, alas, touching down. He's accompanying a forty-three-year-old South African entrepreneur (electric cars, solar power, spacecraft) named Elon Musk. "We'll be the first private space *explorers.*"

Alex explains all this with a straight face, but I will Google this Mr. Musk after I leave here to make sure he isn't a fictional character, maybe a Viennese coconspirator of Harry Lime's from *The Third Man* or a villain from one of the dozens of James Bond novels published since Ian Fleming died.

"Remember watching the pictures from the first Apollo mission that orbited the moon," he says, "those mind-blowing images of the lunar surface and the earth? Didn't we watch together, you and I, on the telly in my suite in Adams House?"

"I was never in your suite in Adams House, Alex."

"No! That's *impossible.*"

"We didn't hang out much after freshman year. And also? We wouldn't have been on campus, because that first lunar mission, *Apollo 8*, was at Christmas."

"Bang on! Nothing can stop Hollander the human search engine!"

"It's the book. I've spent a lot of time researching, getting all the dates straight. *Apollo 8* was Christmas—1968."

"Poor Buzzy, eh?"

My second attempt at a soft segue has worked. "It was *awful. So* sad. And so unnecessary."

"How much did he know about this book of yours?"

"He knew about it. I met with him earlier this year."

"Did you?"

"You know what? Buzzy never served in Vietnam. I found out that was total bullshit, complete fiction."

"Is that right? How interesting. He knew you knew that? He knew you were going to write that?"

I shake my head. "So: Alex."

"Yes, counselor?"

"In April sixty-eight, when . . . at the end, when you had your last phone call with Chuck, you told him you were CIA."

"I told him I knew people in CIA."

Thank God: he is no longer refusing to talk. "Did he tell you he was an agent, too, an informant for military intelligence, for the army?"

From his expression, the momentary but unmistakable look of surprise, I can tell he's impressed by what I know. He shakes his head. "I didn't find that out until afterward. Not from him. And I've never known that it was the army. They didn't tell me which agency. Interesting."

"At the end, you were trying to get him to work with the CIA, like you. Right? You were trying to bring him in from the cold, to save him."

Are his eyes moistening?

"I was. I really was, Hollander."

"I know that, Alex. That's one of the reasons I wanted to talk to you in person." All of the possible phrases seem thin: *I understand, I forgive you, no hard feelings.* "Both of us were trying to save Chuck."

He smiles. "This is like the end of *Gaslight,* when Ingrid Bergman has Charles Boyer tied up in the chair and toys with him, letting him think *maybe* she's going to let him go."

"I am publishing the book."

"So how were *you* trying to 'save' Chuck, Hollander?"

"Right after the rest of us decided not to go through with it and he kept going, I phoned the Secret Service from New York and gave them his name. Which is why, for the last forty-six years, I thought I'd gotten him killed."

Alex smiles. "Interesting. *So* interesting. All of us were compromised."

"Except Buzzy."

"*Buzzy.* He was a *clown.*" Alex stretches, clasps his hands behind his head, swivels around to look out his giant window, then turns back. "You know, I've decided I can deal with people knowing I stopped an assassination. Having worked with CIA has lost its old stigma. In fact? It may be the opposite now." He looks at his watch. "I *love* seeing you. And we absolutely *will* have dinner soon. But . . . are we about through with this, Hollander?"

We are not through. "The thing I don't entirely understand about you and our plot, Alex, is your state of mind. Your precise intentions at various moments. You were a CIA asset between August twelfth,

1967, and February second, 1968, and you were still a CIA asset after
March thirty-first, 1968, when we called it quits, and until we graduated in June 1971. But exactly what were you thinking during those
two months from February third, after we decided to kill Johnson,
until March thirty-first?" I'm being disingenuous, as all litigators
sometimes must be.

"I don't know what you mean," he says. "I don't have the calendar committed to memory like you, darling. A touch *Rain Man*–y,
no?"

"From the morning we decided to kill the president until the
night we decided not to, were you with us, or half with us, or what?
You turned on a dime and voted to cancel the plot as soon as Johnson said he wasn't running for reelection—"

"Doesn't that answer your question? As soon as I thought I had
an opportunity to persuade the rest of you to call it quits, I went for
it. I was the *opposite* of an agent provocateur! I was the agent *apai-
sant!*" I assume he's been dying to use this phrase for years.

"But Buzzy and I immediately backed out and called it quits, too,
Alex. You didn't need to do any persuading." I pause. "You didn't tell
the CIA about our plan until *after* we canceled the operation."

"I think you're mistaken on your chronology," he says, but he
seems nervous.

This is the sort of Perry Mason cross-examination check and . . .
mate moment that I had exactly twice in my thirty years of practicing law, once at trial with a mildly retarded accomplice to a homicide in the Bronx and once when I was deposing a very clever and
crooked chief financial officer.

"No, I'm really not mistaken," I tell him.

"It's 'he says, she says.'"

"No, I'm afraid it's he says, secret CIA internal memo says. According to a memo from 1971, WHEEL-14—you—provided information in April 1968 concerning a plot to assassinate President
Johnson. *April* 1968. In other words, two months after we hatched
the plot. And *after* we abandoned it. In other words, all the time
when push was really coming to shove, and we were making the

plastic explosive and buying the guns and testing the airplane and all the rest of it, you neglected to tell the CIA and snitch on your comrades. You were *with* us. You were as committed or crazy as we were. You were *in*."

He closes his eyes and breathes deeply.

"Don't pretend you betrayed us, Alex. You didn't."

He finally opens his eyes. "I'm bipolar," he says.

"So I read. So we've discussed."

"Everything *I* did in 1968? An eight-week-long manic episode, I now know."

As he describes the symptoms of mania—taking on risky and highly goal-directed new projects, having unrealistic self-confidence, behaving impulsively, making inappropriate plans for foreign travel, jumping from one idea to another, speaking rapidly, grandiosity—it does sound like a perfect description of his behavior in February and March 1968. It also sounds like a perfect description of Chuck's and Buzzy's and my behavior. I've never understood as well as I do right now why Americans have plunged so heedlessly and gratefully into this diagnostic age. Diagnosis is tidy and scientific. Diagnosis is easy shorthand explanation, the way text messages and tweets replace ambiguous conversation and complicated argument. Diagnosis replaces moral analysis and personal responsibility and censure. Bipolar disorder: two words, six syllables, end of story.

And now Alex is a victim whose certified illness I exploited then and am exploiting again.

"After the last time we spoke," he says, "I thought about pulling a Buzzy. How would you feel then, Ms. Truth-teller?"

I say nothing but keep looking straight at him.

"I even have a suicide *plan*," Alex says. "I meet with you here, today, then do it right afterward by overdosing on insulin, injecting a hundred units, they'll think you came in here and did a von Bülow on me, the way he did in his wife."

"He had a motive. I don't." And Sunny von Bülow lived on for a quarter century after the insulin overdose.

"But *how perfect*, assisted suicide that looks like murder—it's like

the end of *The Third Man,* when Harry Lime gives Holly Martins the okay to shoot and kill him in the sewer."

He's grinning. I don't say anything.

"You are so easy to freak out, Hollander. I'm *not* going to do myself in. I don't want to miss all the fun when your book comes out. And I was afraid I'd make a bollocks of it and spend the rest of my life as a pickled cucumber, like poor Sunny von Bülow. But the insulin-overdose idea? My new writer on the Afghanistan picture, the *Third Man* remake, *loves* the idea. So much more *intimate* than a gun."

Alex's last words to me are "We don't validate."

I have no ticket; his building has a free parking lot; he's joking.

I drive a few blocks from Wheel Life Pictures and park at the curb, so I can write down everything Alex has just said while it's fresh. A teenager in an old Camaro slows as he drives past with his windows open, super-loud hip-hop blasting the whole block, and stops next to me at the light. I think I just heard the singer rap "James Bond coupe," but I assume I've misheard until he gets to the chorus, which consists of the line "Aston Martin music" repeated a half dozen times. A Santa Monica police officer appears—a young woman in shorts on a bicycle; oh, Santa Monica, you are cute—and as the teenager checks her out, she stops and turns to him and leans down to make direct eye contact and taps her extended right index finger to her lips. The mimed *shhhh* actually makes the boy turn down his music fifty decibels before the light changes and he turns left on Pico toward the ocean.

I am inordinately cheered by watching this encounter.

On the drive home, I learn from *All Things Considered* that the complete disappearance this summer of the Arctic ice cap has a silver lining—big ships will be able to steam straight over the North Pole, circumnavigating the globe in half the usual time. And that a Russian multibillionaire's childless young widow has had all the egg cells removed from her ovaries, fertilized in vitro, and dispatched around the planet to impregnate thousands of surrogate mothers whom she's paying a hundred thousand dollars apiece to bear and

raise her thousands of children. And that the president of Brazil, who was a Marxist guerrilla as a girl in the late 1960s, has developed a special friendship with Vladimir Putin, the former KGB man. I'll say it for the last time: we live in a James Bond world.

Back on Wonderland Park Avenue, I call Stewart to tell him about my meeting with Alex and get a this-number-is-not-in-service message on all his burners. Then I text his regular cellphone. No reply. I send a carefully innocuous email to each of his personal accounts, and they all bounce back, undeliverable.

I'm accustomed to his occasional ghostliness—we didn't communicate at all for almost six months in 2001 and 2002—but he was supposed to return a week ago from Kabul or Islamabad or wherever the hell he went. "Don't worry like a wife," he said to me early in our relationship, fifteen years ago, after he'd flown off to East Africa and gone radio-silent for three weeks, "or I'll start treating you like one, which you won't like." But I'm worried.

I call the only other person on earth who knows what I'm up to. She's at a café in Bedford-Stuyvesant, Brooklyn, "eating an eggplant panino"—panini in Bed-Stuy? New York *has* changed since I've been gone—before returning to a shelter to finish digitizing a homeless family's documents, including the children's report cards. She tells me that the oldest kid in the family, an eight-year-old boy, missed three months of second grade last year. "He's totally a G-and-T kid. It's really depressing."

"Oh, God, that is depressing. Child Protective Services can't do something?"

"What do you mean? The mom's doing the best she can. She has a part-time job. She was taking a night course at CCNY until they got kicked out of their apartment. She's incredibly inspirational."

"But . . . an eight-year-old drinking gin and tonics?"

"G and T is *gifted and talented,* Grams, he scored ninety-seven percent on the official test. He's like a genius. I'm going to give him my iPad. You know what I've realized? What people like them really need? Are lawyers who can deal with all the stupid bureaucratic

bullshit they face. Did you know Legal Aid has to turn down like nine out of ten poor people who haven't been arrested or anything but just come to them for normal legal help dealing with their lives? It's so fucked up."

"It is." At the end of my Legal Aid service, I published an article about how the social welfare state had further embittered the poor and uneducated by creating an excessively legalistic system they aren't equipped to navigate. I compared it to the Bridge of Death scene in *Monty Python and the Holy Grail,* where one knight is allowed to cross by naming his favorite color but another is asked the air-speed velocity of an unladen swallow. I was accused of being a racist, a socialist, and anti-union. "It's very fucked up."

"Should I go to law school?"

"Maybe so, honey. I think you'd be a great lawyer. But you don't have to make any irrevocable choices now. You're not even eighteen."

She tells me that even though she believes in her Virtual Home project, which is about to expand to three other cities, she has "decided to go offline, personally." Her revelation came, she says, when she called Virtual Home's Web hosting service about a problem and "got totally freaked out by this IVRed computer I was talking to."

"IVR?"

"Interactive voice response. I got angry, and the computer *knew* I was a *woman* and knew I was *angry.* It told me to 'please calm down, ma'am.' Fuck that. Fuck texting every five seconds and Foursquare and Facebook and the rest of it. It's DIY fascism, you know? Totalitarianism lite. Big Brother as a group hug. Fuck the fucking Singularity."

The thing about young people who glimpse malign truths? They're hyperbolic and annoying, but they're not necessarily wrong on some of the essentials. Although my parents' generation may have paid too much attention to our generation's shocked and breathless truth-telling in the 1960s, nowadays I think a lot of us probably err too much in the other direction, shrugging in our Snuggies and pouring another drink.

"So Mom pulled the trigger," Waverly says. "Dad's moving out after Labor Day. It's really happening."

"I know. How do you feel?"

"Okay. At first he just kept saying 'I guess it is what it is,' but now he cries almost every day. Feeling sorry for him is better than thinking he's a dick."

"And how's your mom dealing with it, do you think?"

"Sad because she's not that sad about it."

Like mother, like daughter; like grandma, like grandkid.

As our conversation drifts into the backwaters of small talk—the rap song I heard this morning "is really old, like from eighth grade"; Sophie sold her fake dynamite on eBay for $2,245 and donated the money to Anonymous—I wonder why Waverly hasn't said anything about the most recent pages I've sent her. Neediness never ends.

"So," she says suddenly, "is Stewart hot? He sounds like he'd be hot."

"For an old guy. To me, he is. His name's not really Stewart, you know."

"Duh. Did you feel guilty about cheating on Grandpa? That's the most shocking thing to me in the whole book. So far."

"I did. But your grandfather wasn't faithful, either. There was a woman in New York and another in Helsinki. Maybe more." I'm pathetic.

"Do you like this Stewart guy more than you liked Grandpa?"

"Your grandfather was a good man."

"It seems from the book like you married him because he was boring. And not white."

"He was very nice. And very creative. And a *great* father." And entirely self-contained. And really boring.

"If you hadn't done what you did when you were young, the assassination thing? Do you think you would have lived your life differently?"

"Yes."

"How? Exactly?"

"I'm not sure. I would've had more fun. Taken different kinds of risks."

"Fun is overrated."

"That's funny. But I'm not sure it's true."

"You're the one who said it to me. When I was ten and made you take me to Disneyland. I wrote it down."

"Maybe just Disneyland is overrated."

"I should get going. Love you, Grams."

"I love you, too, Wavy."

When Christianity was new, confession of sin took place very differently. You didn't slip into a private booth and secretly confess your wrongdoings to some discreet divine bureaucrat, privately recite the prescribed words and go home cleansed. Nowhere does the Bible mention any such one-on-one confession. Nor did you confess habitually, not for serious transgressions, sinning and confessing, sinning and confessing, sinning again and sincerely confessing again— *for these and all the sins of my past I am truly sorry*—before being wiped free of sin and absolved yet again. You confessed publicly. You were absolved only *after* performing your penance. And you were permitted to do it once a lifetime.

Doing away with the public confession of sins and mandating private confession at least annually—"Rinse, repeat, rinse, repeat," as Stewart says—enabled Christianity to scale up. So did the Protestants' subsequent abandonment of confession altogether. Back when public, one-time-only confession was the rule, Christianity was a cult of a few million, 1 or 2 percent of all the people on earth. Today there are two billion of us.

Us? I'm afraid so. Fifty-two years after refusing confirmation, I'm still a Catholic, the way I'm still a midwesterner thirty-nine years after moving away for good—nonpracticing, diasporic, heretical, but never entirely former. It's like how I'll always be a person who was eighteen in 1968.

Although I dread the loss of heaven and the pains of hell only

metaphorically, I do detest and am heartily sorry for what I did, and having firmly resolved to do penance and amend my life, I confess my sins. Mea culpa. Amen.

Something like our modern legal system might have developed without a thousand years of religious practice beforehand, just as something like *Homo sapiens* might have evolved without a million years of intermediate species, without the *Homo erectus* and *Homo heidelbergensis* and etcetera. But that's not the way it happened. Christian confession and penitence in the first millennium were beta versions of the second millennium's legal trials and statutory penalties. Hell and purgatory were replaced by capital punishment and prison and probation, and the Bible by constitutions and statute books.

When I learned in law school that James Madison was the founder who insisted that criminal confessions must be voluntary—who wrote the Fifth Amendment to the Constitution, with its unambiguous rule that "No person . . . shall be compelled in any criminal case to be a witness against himself"—I smiled. *Like James in the Bible,* I thought, Saint James, the apostle who encourages *voluntary* public confession: *So confess your sins to one another.*

The Fifth Amendment has gotten a bad rap—the weasel amendment, the one that allows crooks to get away with their crimes by "taking the Fifth." However, I've always considered the clause prohibiting coerced self-incrimination one of the great underrated American achievements because it takes free will seriously, even to the point of letting scoundrels and liars go free. You may confess your crimes, or you may keep them secret; it's all up to you.

I didn't have to write this book. Nothing and no one forced me to confess. I did so, as the relevant Supreme Court decision says, "knowingly, voluntarily and intelligently." There were no threats or improper inducements. My secret might have remained my secret forever. Although I will never entirely forgive myself for what I did in 1968 and what resulted, I have sincerely confessed and thereby gotten, in the Roman Catholic term of art, satisfaction.

I may now be loathed and castigated, maybe deservedly, but I

don't believe that I can be prosecuted successfully. I violated Title 18 U.S. Code 1751, conspiracy to assassinate the president. Given that two of my three coconspirators were government agents, I could mount a defense of entrapment, but it would be weak, since obviously I didn't require much inducement by Alex or Chuck to engage in our criminal conduct. People died—Chuck, the CIA agent, and the army intelligence agent—but my accomplice didn't fire his weapon and killed no one. None of those three deaths was a capital crime, I had withdrawn from the conspiracy and notified the authorities two weeks earlier, and in any event the shoot-out was not an outgrowth of the conspiracy. I was never arrested or charged or indicted, so under the law, I was never a fugitive. In other words, as soon as we abandoned our conspiracy, the five-year federal statute of limitations began running, and therefore, since the spring of 1973, I have been free of legal liability for those crimes. And I am not waiving those applicable statutes of limitation now.

However, because America can put you to death for treason, treason is a capital crime, which means there's no statute of limitations. No American has been convicted of treason in my lifetime. But could I be prosecuted today for treason under 18 U.S. Code 2381? Were we levying war against the United States and giving aid and comfort to its enemies in 1968? Arguably. But because various federal government agencies have known what we did since 1968, that forty-six-year pre-indictment delay would get a federal prosecutor laughed out of court. In any event, I would be saved by Article 3 of the U.S. Constitution, which says that "No Person shall be convicted of Treason unless on the Testimony of two Witnesses to the same overt Act, or on Confession in open Court." Alex is the only living witness to my (and his) overt acts. And I don't intend to confess to treason in open court.

It has been a week since I met with Alex, and classes start next week. I plan to send this manuscript to my editor (and my lawyer) on Friday. It feels like the calm before the storm. Which would be enjoyable, I think, if I'd heard from Stewart.

I've sent more emails. I've left voice mails on his home number, which may not even be his number anymore; the outgoing message is computer-generated. I can't very well call the National Counterterrorism Center or the National Security Council or CIA and ask where the hell Stewart Jones is. I've never met any of his friends, and I don't know his mother's new last name. Several times a day I comb through Google News, searching for stories of Americans arrested or kidnapped or killed in Pakistan or Afghanistan or Iraq or Yemen or Iran. "In theater" is all I knew of his whereabouts in July. There are a lot of theaters these days.

I go out for a hike and walk three miles, sweating like a pig. I see a dead coyote.

Back home, I print out a fresh manuscript and start reading it again.

I can't concentrate.

I am worrying like a wife.

I make a tuna salad. It's only half past one. I can't have a drink.

There are twenty-four area codes in L.A., of which I'm familiar with maybe five, so I'm used to seeing entirely unfamiliar caller IDs. Area code 562? Long Beach? Maybe the roofer?

"Hello?"

"Hi. The eagle has landed. I'm here."

"Oh, *God,* I am so happy to hear your voice! I thought you were dead." Saying it makes my throat tighten and tears seep. "Why the *fuck* haven't you called? I don't care if I'm acting like a wife. What do you mean, you're here?"

"On the 405, about to get on the 710. Heading in your direction. To your house, if you're not otherwise engaged."

I haven't showered in two days. I have a kayak rented nonrefundably in Marina del Rey at four. I'm not getting my hair color touched up until the day after tomorrow. Shit. "Sure, yes, of course, come over. But why no word, nothing, for a month? I was terrified."

"Out of range for a while, then I didn't want to call or text or email. I'll tell you when I get there."

"Is everything okay?"

"I'm alive. My dick works. So, yeah. I'll be there in forty-five min-utes or so."

He rings my doorbell forty-seven minutes later. He's wearing a baseball hat that says General Atomics. I've never seen him so tan. "The Middle East is a sunny place," he explains as he steps inside to hug me. "You've got blood on your face."

Every hundredth time I test my blood, some of it sprays out a foot from my pricked finger in a super-thin mist. I've ruined a cou-ple of blouses this way. Stewart licks his thumb and wipes the spat-ter off my temple.

The day he returned to Washington two weeks ago, he explains, he was "called over to McLean" and dismissed from government service for "suspected security breaches, unauthorized distribution of classified material, blah blah blah"—that is, for acting as my back-channel researcher.

Another bad boy's life wrecked by Karen Hollander.

Until the dust settled—a signed agreement not to prosecute him, his pension secured—he thought it was unwise to be in touch with me in ways "vulnerable to comment."

"Comment by whom?"

"COM-MINT, C-O-M-I-N-T, communications intelligence." He means electronic eavesdropping.

He insists he's fine, he was planning to get out before he turned sixty anyway, what's a year give or take, it's all good. "Kind of a nice, friendly fuck-you adios, good for my buckaroo rep. And now they're all going to be eager to read your book. I think you'll sell a thousand copies in the 22102 zip code alone."

"How did they find out?"

"I got blown." It takes me a second to realize he isn't talking about a woman who performed oral sex on him. "By Alex Macal-lister the Third." Or a man.

"That evil scumbag motherfucker."

"Keep it up, I love that."

"How did he even know who you were? I swear to God I didn't tell him."

"He's a smart guy. That night we had the drink with him in Georgetown in ninety-nine, he made me give him a card. So now or back then, he put two and two together. Turns out he's in the spook auxiliary, keeps in touch with a couple of the old fucks he knew from when you were kids."

"I'm sorry."

"No, no, no, I told him who I was. And I did what I did for you. Fuck it. It was fun."

He grins and shrugs like a boy who's been grounded for getting drunk and staying out all night. When I hug him, I wipe my tears on his shirt. It has a slight foreign tang, lye soap and diesel and spicy tobacco.

"So . . . why are you in L.A.?"

"I've got nowhere else to go. School doesn't start for a week, right? Maybe I'll move here. Although I always thought Molokai. When your book comes out and they fire you, you can come hang out in Hawaii with me."

"Okay. You want to practice some Hawaiian living right now? If you're not too pooped."

"Does that mean fuck?"

"That means going out in a sea kayak at the UCLA Marina Aquatic Center in an hour and a half."

As we wriggle into our plastic boat and begin paddling, I smile—at the improbability of Stewart appearing here and participating in an actual outdoor leisure activity with me, at the cliché of rowing into the Pacific sunset. All Clichés Are True, as my friend Lizzie says, and their being clichés doesn't necessarily make them bad in real life.

"We look like a fucking Viagra commercial," he says. "California is *so* . . . lifestyle-y."

I tell him that for nine months I haven't felt like a fraud. He replies that he hasn't killed anyone for almost nine months but then says he's joking—that he has actually, personally killed someone only once, in Belgrade twenty-one years ago. "I'm surprised you

never asked until now," he says. And then: "Or maybe I'm not surprised."

I talk through the book in detail for the first time. He tells me I'm
"the ultimate poster child for my generation—you have everything
you could possibly want, sky's the limit, then you decide you've got
to burn down the joint, you do all this lunatic shit, then you suddenly change your mind and decide, 'Nah, America's not so bad
after all—waiter, I'll have another chardonnay,' tuck in to this sweet
life, and get away with it all scot-fucking-free."

"That's one way of looking at it."

"Although, actually? I'm busting your balls. Keeping big secrets is
a fucking soul suck. You've paid. Not retail, maybe, but I know
you've paid."

"It's after five. We should probably head in."

I'm in the back of the kayak, so he lifts his paddle from the water
and lets me turn us around, then starts paddling again.

"'So we beat on,'" he says, "'boats against the current, borne
back ceaselessly into the past.'"

I'm unspeakably happy that my friend the rough, tough former
secret agent has quoted the last line of *The Great Gatsby*. I stare at the
sweat dripping down the short hairs on the back of his brown neck.

"Would you be angry," I ask, "if I told you I loved you?"

"Not *angry*." Then: "Thanks." And then: "Don't make any rash
decisions."

We paddle in silence for a few minutes. Then he says that since
he's out of the game, I can use his real name in my book if I want. I
tell him I'll think about it. "I wouldn't want to make any rash decisions."

ACKNOWLEDGMENTS

FOR FIFTEEN YEARS, my friend and agent, Suzanne Gluck, has been an indispensable enabler. And Random House—especially and most recently in the persons of Gina Centrello, Kendra Harpster, and my impeccable editor, Jennifer Hershey, as well as Avideh Bashirrad, Karen Fink, Deborah Foley, Erika Greber, Susan Kamil, Sally Marvin, Steve Messina, Sarah Murphy, Tom Perry, and Emily Beth Thomas—the perfect publishers.

One large germ for this story came out of a discussion many years ago at *Spy* magazine that was consummated in Bruce Handy's brilliant article "James Bond Mania." So thank you, *Spy* comrades.

As I wrote the book, there were things I needed to learn about music, young women in the 1960s, Chicago in the 1960s, ultimate regret, Supreme Court clerkships, Danish, German, Harvard in the 1960s and early '70s, Los Angeles, flying small airplanes, the intelligence community, and the law, and I'm grateful to David Andersen, Kristi Andersen, Tom Dyja, Tad Friend, Jeffrey Leeds, Pejk Malinovski, Guy Martin, Frank Rich, John Rood, Colin Summers, Evan Thomas, and the very generous Bruce Birenboim, respectively, for filling in my blanks. Thanks also to Larry O'Donnell for his large and unwitting assistance; to Lauren Cerand for excellent advice; and to Bonnie Siegler for a brilliant cover.

Finally, I'm grateful to all the women I've known—in particular, the three I know and love the best, Anne Kreamer and Lucy and Kate Andersen, for their specific suggestions and corrections, and for splendidly teaching me day in and day out how the other half thinks.

TRUE BELIEVERS

Kurt Andersen

A Reader's Guide

A Conversation with Kurt Andersen and Anna Quindlen

Anna Quindlen is a novelist and journalist whose work has appeared on fiction, nonfiction, and self-help bestseller lists. Her book *A Short Guide to a Happy Life* has sold more than a million copies. While a columnist at *The New York Times* she won the Pulitzer Prize and published two collections, *Living Out Loud* and *Thinking Out Loud*. Her *Newsweek* columns were collected in *Loud and Clear*. She is the author of six novels: *Object Lessons, One True Thing, Black and Blue, Blessings, Rise and Shine,* and *Every Last One*. Her memoir *Lots of Candles, Plenty of Cake* was published by Random House in 2012.

Anna Quindlen: So I want to start with the obvious question about the genesis of this novel. Its protagonist, Karen Hollander, is female . . . which, as I'm sure you know, is considered a kind of feat in our business, since you're a male author. But it's even more important here because Karen's telling the story in a really immediate and intimate first-person voice. You not only had to imagine a woman; you had to *be* her. Did you have any hesitation about taking that on?

Kurt Andersen: Tremendous hesitation. Of course, you and I write all sorts of people deeply unlike us in many ways, but gender is the aspect most commented upon. It's done, but it's daunting. It gave me pause. I didn't begin by saying, "I want to write a first-person novel narrated by a woman." But the story came to be one that I thought would be best focused on a woman for lots of reasons.

When I decided that the story would jump back and forth between the present and the past, it occurred to me that women's lives have changed much more dramatically and interestingly in the last forty-five

years than men's. The fact that as a girl she would not be subject to the military draft was an important motivation in leading Karen to feel as if she needed to be more radical, harder, in 1968.

So I decided the main character should be a woman. I also decided the story had to be told in the first person, in order to convey viscerally Karen's dread and the sense of her having kept this secret for so many years. And to allow her to be sort of a detective investigating herself.

AQ: There's always a moment, particularly when I'm writing in the first person, when I think, "I've got it." A moment when suddenly it seems as though the dominoes have begun to fall. Can you remember the moment when you thought, "I've got Karen"?

KA: I'd never written a first-person novel, so I played around with voices a lot more before I really started writing the book. I spent weeks trying out voices. With Karen, there was an initial click where I thought, "Yes, I think this is right." And then, some thousands of words in, I felt as though I was *fluent* in her voice.

AQ: Did you get any outside help with the girl details? There's one discussion of female hair removal in this book that I swore reflected your wife, the writer Anne Kreamer.

KA: Well, I mean, she certainly laughed at and liked that scene. I got tons of help and advice, once I had finished a draft, from Anne and my two young-adult daughters. Very pointed advice from the women in my household. And my agent, my editors—everybody who read the book until it was published were women. All of whom here and there said, "No, no, no, don't have her say that or have to do *that*."

AQ: Karen is kind of a complete star. She's worked for the Clinton administration. She's been short-listed for the Supreme Court. She's a public intellectual. And she's preparing this memoir, which is going to spill the beans about a monumental event in her past. Several times in

the book, she repeats these sentences: "I'm reliable. Trust me." How come each time she says that it makes me feel as though what you're really saying is that no one is reliable, trust no one? Am I just paranoid, or is that part of what you're trying to do with this book?

KA: You're not paranoid. When I first wrote her saying that, it just came out of what I thought her character would say, her voice, as she introduced herself. It wasn't intended initially as ironic—that nobody is reliable—but became that as I realized that (a) nobody's memory is reliable and (b) there are always gaps of information, there are known unknowns and unknown unknowns, as Donald Rumsfeld told us.

So as careful and scrupulous as this lawyer has been, she realizes that there's no such thing as totally reliable narrators—or people. She understands that "the whole truth and nothing but the truth" has never been produced in a court of law. There's no such thing.

AQ: Ultimately, this novel seems to be about the reliability of memory and experience. Throughout the novel, many characters suggest that Karen may be mistaken about the facts of her own life. It seems to me that you're asking whether we can really ever understand ourselves even in the rearview mirror, or whether we can possibly only understand ourselves at a point like this one in Karen's life, when she is in her sixties and at some level is done reinventing herself.

KA: At least done consciously and extravagantly reinventing herself.

I think you're exactly right, although, again, I didn't start out with the *idea* "I want to write a novel that examines memory." It became something I was doing as I was doing it.

I made her daughter a neurobiologist so I could explicitly touch on the nature of memory as it's often understood today, as a kind of unconscious fictionalizing process—that the moment we experience something is the last moment that our perception of it is accurate, that a day later, a month later, and, God knows, thirty or forty years later, we have as our memory some highly edited, multiply revised fictional version of an event.

AQ: And not only of events but of ourselves. I recently read a piece that said we've always assumed that the person that you are at twenty-five is the same basic person that you're going to be at sixty-five. But in fact, this study showed, that's not true. We change a great deal during the course of our lifetime.

I think that development is so vividly illustrated in this book, with the difference between the person Karen is in high school and college and the person she is at sixty-four. She almost looks back on the events of her past as if they happened to someone else.

KA: Any adult looking back on her adolescence is probably going to have that experience. Because Karen's adolescence coincided precisely with the late 1960s and their various crazinesses, it's even more so—she looks back at what feels like an almost *fictional* version of herself because she was so different, the time was so different.

AQ: I was really taken by the way you compare and contrast in her mind the world of the 1960s with the present. At one point, her granddaughter, Waverly—who is a fantastic character—says everything's *stuck* about her own time, today, as though it's in stasis. Meanwhile, Karen is thinking about how completely the world in which she lived changed between 1962 and 1969.

Do you get a sense that we're in kind of a stuck cycle? And if so, why?

KA: I do think in many ways we are stuck. The way people dress or even the way cars look—in the last twenty years I think we've changed less than in any twenty-year period in the past century. And yet these twenty years have been this time of unbelievable transformation in technology and global geopolitics.

Maybe at this time of scary flux we're clinging to everything we can, all of us, and can't quite let go of the shore to go forward.

AQ: You have this great line: a kid who's a friend of Waverly says that all political action now feels like a tribute band, that it's just covering

the sixties, that all political action feels like it's a rip-off of what happened forty or fifty years ago.

KA: At least a replay or a revise. And there is also this sense of frustration with a lot of young people: "All right already, you baby boomers, get off the stage, stop dominating everything." I've had this conversation with my children, nephews, people in their twenties, and they're asking, "When do we get *ours*? When do we get to reinvent what life and values and dreams are? The way people your age did."

AQ: Well, for any baby boomer—guilty as charged—there are some irresistible moments in this book. I have not thought of *Kukla, Fran and Ollie* for so long. You're a journalist as well as a novelist, and there's clearly a lot of research in *True Believers*. How did you assemble the details of Karen's past—the music, the movies, the TV shows?

KA: Karen is somewhat older than I am, but I had older brothers and sisters. I was around. And once you really plunge fictionally into a time and a place, you realize, speaking of memory, that there're all these stray things in your head—whether it's *Kukla, Fran and Ollie* or a Ronnie Spector song—that you don't have access to until you're trying to conjure this fictional moment. So partly it was just wallowing in my own childhood memories that were in cold storage.

I did research too, wandered through the 1960s, histories, artifacts, coming across unfamiliar things that seemed telling or interesting or illuminating.

I spent a lot of time listening to music I hadn't heard in a long time and watched a lot of videos on the Internet, since you can now see clips of every show and film from one's youth. It's an amazing luxury and tool when you're trying to evoke a period.

AQ: How much of that inclination to ground a novel in the facts of history—you did it with your novel *Heyday* as well, although that was set in the nineteenth century—arises from your journalistic background?

The thing that I miss the most when I'm writing a novel is having a notebook next to me. I always love that soft bed of facts from which to do the hard work.

KA: When I was a journalist—because I wasn't ever a very serious shoe-leather journalist—most of my notes were *thoughts about* what I was seeing. Even then, in those first fifteen or twenty years of my professional life, I was already doing more of a fiction-writing kind of note-taking than straight journalistic note-taking.

There's a blurry line between the two crafts. But for sure, when I was figuring out my first novel, which took place in the technology and TV and financial worlds, I spent days with a friend running a show in L.A. and with a friend working at Microsoft and with a trader friend on Wall Street. Once you write about a world you know *nothing* about firsthand, though, and people from that world go, "Wow, you really nailed *that*," you realize, okay, fine, I can make it up.

AQ: Readers always love to know about the logistics of authors' work lives. You write essays and you host a fantastic show on public radio called *Studio 360*. Could you talk through your writing schedule and how you manage to compartmentalize around those things?

KA: First of all, it looks like I'm doing more than I am. When I'm working on a book, I get started as early in the morning as I can. That's when my brain is optimized for writing. And then I usually have lunch with my wife, who also works at home, and a few days a week go in and work on the radio show.

So alone in a room for four hours in the morning, making stuff up, and then, some afternoons, talking to writers and filmmakers and musicians for *Studio 360* and having a bit of a watercooler life. It's a perfect balance for me between solitude and collaboration.

AQ: I like how you describe it as "alone in a room . . . making stuff up." That's the tattoo all authors should get—ALONE IN A ROOM MAKING STUFF UP.

Anyone who's read this book will understand why I'm asking you this question: did you reread all of the works of Ian Fleming before you started or while you were working on it?

KA: I had never read an Ian Fleming novel until I decided to write this book.

My father, unlike most men, was a great fiction reader—mostly mysteries, thrillers, spy novels—a voracious reader. He had plenty of the James Bond books, but I never read one . . . probably because my father read them.

So after I decided that Karen and her friends as kids would become obsessed with Fleming's Bond novels, I read about half of them. It was good I read them all at once, because I came to them the same way my characters do when they're thirteen. I had that real-time experience of *inhaling* the books. They were better than I expected them to be.

AQ: There's also insider-iness in your novel in terms of the undercover aspects of how our government works. How much help did you get on that from people who work in Washington?

KA: Some. I talked to a journalist I know who has written a lot about the CIA. I talked with somebody who has worked at the CIA on a couple of things. And I have a very good friend who worked in Washington on whom one of the characters is significantly based.

AQ: Does he know that the character is based on him?

KA: He does indeed. He couldn't be happier.

AQ: Then it's got to be Stuart.

KA: Correct—Karen's boyfriend. As you know, writers steal things from people's lives all the time. Basically, in each novel I write, there's one character I ripped off pretty wholesale from an actual person I know.

AQ: I think that's true of many of us. I could probably say the same thing about almost every novel I've written—there's one person that I can point to and say, *aha*.

One of the really interesting aspects of Karen's character is that she's a diabetic, which is something you almost never encounter in fiction.

KA: Yes. She got what used to be called juvenile diabetes, Type 1 diabetes, when she was seventeen, eighteen years old. And I was diagnosed with Type 1 diabetes when I was thirty-two. No research was required.

AQ: I wondered if you were trying to make a point about how much of our human character is chemical. Another of the characters in the novel is bipolar, and another one has Asperger's. Karen's daughter is a neurobiologist. There's a sense in which the book says, "Okay, some of this is in our stars, and some of it is in our bodies."

KA: What you've just eloquently said is something that was never an intention. In fact, I wasn't entirely aware of it before now—but yes. And Type 1 diabetes was something I'd never seen in fiction, and I thought that would be an interesting character wrinkle for Karen in particular.

AQ: From time to time she behaves in a way that her friends see as crazy or aberrational. And their first thought is not "Karen's acting crazy," it's "Karen's blood sugar is low." Someone is always handing her a Coke.

KA: And even though she's annoyed at the dismissal, she's a glass-half-full girl: unlike most people who aren't always certain what's causing anxiety, confusion, she sees an upside to her ability, by pricking her finger and testing her blood, to get an instant confirmation or refutation of that—"Am I really upset or do I just need a Coke?"

AQ: Later, one of Waverly's friends turns out to be a Type 1 diabetic and is fascinated by Karen's openness about it. It's as though, at his age, having any kind of infirmity is a character defect.

KA: There is this cliché about young people today being so public about everything, no detail too personal to put out on Facebook. And yet here is this very modern kid who is both nervous and admiring of Karen—which suggests that there are maybe a few bits of wisdom that the younger generation can glean from the older.

AQ: There's also a lot about technology in this novel, a sense that it's becalmed us, made us bystanders instead of activists. Was that intentional on your part?

KA: Again, I didn't *begin* with that idea. But as I was writing a novel half set in the present day, the constant presence of devices and connectivity obviously began to define some of the characters.

And yes, the becalming—there is a kind of pacifier aspect. I can stare at my device and go into a little fugue state. We have all the *information* in the world but no more deep *knowledge* than we ever did.

AQ: You said you didn't start out with the intent of discussing technology. We travel a long way from when we begin to when we end. What was your initial intent?

KA: I was trying to depict an ambitious, smart kid in the 1960s whose adolescence overlapped exactly with that insanely rapid turn from the peaceful early sixties to the wild late sixties. And what that felt like, how we went from Frankie Valli to Jimi Hendrix in five minutes.

The other germ was that these kids are just obsessed as twelve-year-olds with James Bond, and then they're going to be playing the parts of heroic revolutionary activists six years later. So it was about self-fictionalizing—as all young people do when they're trying on different characters and figuring out who they are.

AQ: But it's also about the characters we *become*. You can't help but notice that Karen and her friends Chuck and Alex spend a lot of time when they're kids pretending they're somebody else, almost getting arrested because they use false names. In their sixties, along with their former friend Buzzy, they've actually *become* someone else.

KA: At a certain point those masks we put on become our faces. And one of the pleasures of writing and reading is to make ourselves aware of that. To remind ourselves that we become these people who might appall, amuse, or baffle our younger selves.

AQ: This novel is Karen's memoir. When her book is published, how is it received?

KA: With great controversy. I think there are people who are absolutely going to hate her, and those who will feel as though she's been a brave truth-teller.

People sometimes ask me, "Did you base her on anybody?" I say nobody in particular. But I think her life is sort of like Hillary Clinton's would have been if she'd never married Bill. Imagine that, if a person of her stature came out with a truly frank and intimate autobiography that admitted this crazy thing she got involved with and kept secret for forty years. It would create a ruckus. And it will in this fictional universe too.

Questions and Topics for Discussion

1. One of the epigraphs of *True Believers* contains the following lines from Wordsworth: "Bliss was it in that dawn to be alive / But to be young was very heaven." These lines encapsulate the sentiments of empowerment and enthusiasm driving idealistic supporters at the dawn of the French Revolution. How does Karen's own Vietnam-era experience—one distinguished by a widespread dissatisfaction and social unrest among youth—mirror the emotions fueling these words?

2. The blurring of fiction and reality is a major theme throughout the novel, in terms of both how the characters define themselves and how they interpret the world around them. Karen makes an interesting point that the emergence of modern entertainment and its obsession with turning events of the recent past into salable media commodities created a phenomenon in which "the people who lived through the events were tricked into believing they had *experienced* the fictions and docudramas." In what ways has this manipulation and glamorization of the facts influenced the characters and period that Kurt Andersen explores? How does this continue to be an issue today?

3. Alex, Chuck, and Karen's infatuation with the works of Ian Fleming leads them to believe that the extreme and outrageous happenings in the world of government and at large mean that life is imitating—and even anticipating—art. Do you think this makes it easier for them to justify their own extreme behaviors, perhaps by creating a dissociation between the severity of their actions and a world they begin to see as phantasmagorical?

4. Waverly says of her involvement as a twenty-first-century Occupy activist that "most protests seem like cover versions of old songs. Like we're all in a sixties tribute band." Does this seem accurate? In what ways have the circumstances and impetus for change either altered or remained the same from half a century ago to the present day?

5. How does Karen's view of her father change after she learns that he cooperated with the Nazis by providing the names of several Communists to avoid being sent to an internment camp? Do you think she should have more empathy for his predicament given her own late-1960s experiences? Based on the observation "People in extreme circumstances make choices they don't expect to make," what does the novel seem to be implying about the accountability of those forced to act in impossible situations? How have Karen and her father similarly managed to cope and assimilate back into normal life in the aftermath of experiencing guilt and blame?

6. After the conversation Karen has with Alex in which he speaks almost entirely in borrowed phrases from *The Third Man*, she comes to see him as a "walking, talking real-time remix of fictional mid-century villains." She asks, "Is his entire life a nonstop work of performance art that only he fully appreciates?" Later, she observes the tendency of twenty-first-century dwellers likewise to adopt personas and pseudonyms through alternate realities and cosmetic surgery, or to refer to themselves in the third person. Do you think that, unlike Alex and unlike Waverly's friend Sophie, Karen has succeeded, as she claims, in abandoning her inner Bond girl and living entirely as herself? Is it possible to assume an identity that is completely independent of preexisting stories and metaphors and fictional characters?

7. After abandoning the Roman Catholic religion of her childhood, Karen instead places her faith in the "unholy power of chance, good luck and bad luck, in governing human affairs. Luck became my subject, the animating mystery of my life," she says. Does this make her more prone to engage in risky behavior? What do you make of

her need to confess and spend years of her life—both personal and professional—repenting for her perceived sins?

8. Looking back on the tragedies of the 1960s—the slaughter in Vietnam, the televised killings, the civil rights battles being fought at home—Karen admits that there were certain misrepresentations and misinterpretations of facts that fueled the fire of American upheaval, which is why she has been "allergic ever since to groups of people with single-minded visionary passion and without any doubt that they possess the one truth." How does this type of tunnel vision—the blind and unshakable devotion to a single cause with imperfect or incomplete knowledge—seem to manifest itself throughout the novel, as well as in the present day, and what are the consequences?

9. Examining the spirit behind Operation Lima Bravo Juliet, Karen says, "For those first three months of 1968, we embodied that part of the American character that has troubled and scared me ever since," that is, the America that promotes visionary risk-taking, dogged determination, and fearlessness in the name of freedom and justice. "For better or worse, in 1968 I think we were *very* American. Terribly American," she says. Do you agree that the motivation driving Lima Bravo Juliet epitomizes a version of what it means to be American? In what ways is that mindset dangerous and in what ways is it inevitable or necessary?

10. Andersen has said he chose to tell the story from a woman's point of view because the changes in women's lives during the last half century have been consequential and dramatic. How did making *True Believers* one woman's story as opposed to a man's shape it?

11. After Chuck's death, Karen refers to the Bible story in which God orders Abraham to murder his son Isaac in a test of faith, but ultimately sends an angel to prevent the sacrifice from taking place. She questions whether, in the madness leading up to Operation LBJ, she acted as Abraham or God, and whether Chuck fulfilled the role of Isaac or Abraham. What do you think?

12. In writing *True Believers*, Andersen says he opted for a first-person account because he "wanted the characters to walk away from their conspiracy scot-free and keep the secret for decades. In order to convey the unnerving impact of living such a lie, I decided that one of the co-conspirators had to tell the tale." Did you find Karen to be a credible narrator? How was your reading affected by the idea of her writing a work of nonfiction, and how did this contribute to the sense of anxiety and inexorability that Andersen was driving toward?

13. Based on Karen's recounting of her teenage years in the late 1960s and her granddaughter's experience of being a teenager today, in which era is it easier or harder to be young? Forty or fifty years from now, how will today's teenagers have been shaped by their youth?

14. After reading the novel, how would you characterize a "true believer"?

BOOKS BY
KURT ANDERSEN

TURN OF THE CENTURY

Big and exciting, *Turn of the Century* is a good old-fashioned novel about the day after tomorrow—an uproarious, exquisite observation of our world as the twentieth century morphs into the twenty-first, propelled by the supercharged global businesses and new technologies that make everyone's lives spin a little faster.

HEYDAY

Heyday is a brilliantly imagined, wildly entertaining tale of America's boisterous coming-of-age in the 1800s—a sweeping panorama of madcap rebellion and overnight fortunes, palaces and brothels, murder and revenge—as well as the story of a handful of unforgettable characters discovering the nature of freedom, loyalty, friendship, and true love.

RESET

In this smart and refreshingly hopeful book, Andersen—a brilliant analyst and synthesizer of historical and cultural trends, as well as a bestselling novelist and host of public radio's *Studio 360*—explains how the Great Recession and its uncertain aftermath give us surprising opportunities to get ourselves and our nation back on track.

TRUE BELIEVERS

Kurt Andersen's most powerful and moving novel yet. Dazzling in its wit and effervescent insight, this kaleidoscopic tour de force of cultural observation and seductive storytelling alternates suspensefully between the present and the 1960s—and indelibly captures the enduring impact of that time on the ways we live now.

THE RANDOM HOUSE PUBLISHING GROUP

www.AtRandom.com

PHOTO: THOMAS HART SHELBY

KURT ANDERSEN is the author of the novels *Heyday* and *Turn of the Century,* among other books. He also writes for television, film, and the stage, contributes to *Vanity Fair,* and hosts the public radio program *Studio 360.* He has previously been a columnist for *New York, The New Yorker,* and *Time,* editor in chief of *New York,* and co-founder of *Spy.* He lives in Brooklyn.